Andi Osho is an accomplished actor, writer and film-maker. She has appeared in *Line of Duty, I May Destroy You, Good Omens, Sex Education, Breeders, The Sandman,* and *Blue Lights*. Her film credits include DC Comics' *Shazam* and *Lights Out*.

Andi has written for Sky, BBC TV, BBC Radio and several UK newspapers and publications. She also wrote and starred in Sky Arts short, *Twin Thing,* and wrote and produced award-winning films *Brit.I.am, The Grid* and *Amber.*

As a comedian she's featured on TV comedy shows such as *Live at the Apollo, Mock the Week, Never Mind the Buzzcocks, Room 101, Stand Up for the Week* and *The Late, Late Show.*

Her debut novel *Asking For A Friend* was longlisted for the Comedy Women In Print Prize 2021. *Tough Crowd* is her second novel.

Also by Andi Osho:

Asking for a Friend

Praise for Andi Osho's debut novel *Asking For a Friend:*

'Wise, witty and warm. Everything Andi
Osho touches turns to gold'
Richard Osman, author of *The Bullet that Missed*

'Witty, pacy and joyful, *Asking For a Friend* is
a truly uplifting celebration of friendship'
Beth O'Leary, author of *The Wake-Up Call*

'A sparky, spunky, sassy romcom'
Red

'A mistressclass in combining humour and lovely
characters, all wrapped up with a cracking story'
Jo Brand

'As soon as I started reading I couldn't put it down. The
humour and attention to detail slides off the page. This is
both realistic and inspirational. Andi Osho is a genius'
Jocelyn Jee Esien

'An impressive debut about the strong relationships
between friends. Osho's wit and charm give
the story a lively warmth and character'
Woman & Home

'A massively entertaining tale of wingwomen recharging
each other's love lives. Funny, spiky and fab!'
Beth Morrey, author of *Em & Me*

'As hilarious as Andi's stand-up while feeling
like a lively night out with brilliant friends'
Sara Pascoe

'An ultimately feel-good story about female friendships,
full of heart and humour. So relatable, I loved it!'
Angela Griffin

‘Fabulously fun. I found myself laughing out
loud at so many hilarious lines along the way.
An utter joy to read from start to finish!’
Helly Acton, author of *Begin Again*

‘A delightful read, a paean to female friendship
– genuinely funny and full of heart’
Roisin Conaty

‘I LOVED it. Funny, sparky and written with so much heart’
Daisy Buchanan, author of *Limelight*

‘A loving tribute to female friendship bursting
with funny lines and loveable characters’
Lucy Porter

‘A hilarious, laugh-a-minute, laugh-out-loud, relentless romp
through dating, women and friendship. Brilliantly vivid and
relatable characters. Brilliantly written, fun and joyous!’
Shazia Mirza

‘This brilliant warm book had me laughing
from the first page. I couldn’t put it down’
Lucy Vine, author of *Seven Exes*

‘A fresh, funny, relatable page-turner from the ever
brilliant Andi Osho – for anyone who’s ever navigated
the dating world and needed the sisterhood’
Deborah Frances-White, author of *The Guilty Feminist*

‘A debut novel that I’ll return to again and again.
An absolute triumph and I loved every word’
Susan Calman

‘From the first page, you can guarantee laughter. This
book is hilarious, warm and an absolute page-turner’
Angie Le Mar

Tough Crowd

ANDI OSHO

ONE PLACE. MANY STORIES

This novel is entirely a work of fiction. The names, characters and incidents portrayed in it are the work of the author's imagination. Any resemblance to actual persons, living or dead, events or localities is entirely coincidental.

HQ
An imprint of HarperCollins*Publishers* Ltd
1 London Bridge Street
London SE1 9GF

www.harpercollins.co.uk

HarperCollins*Publishers*
Macken House, 39/40 Mayor Street Upper,
Dublin 1, D01 C9W8, Ireland

This edition 2023

1
First published in Great Britain by
HQ, an imprint of HarperCollins*Publishers* Ltd 2023

Andi Osho asserts the moral right to be
identified as the author of this work.
A catalogue record for this book is
available from the British Library.

ISBN: 9780008430986

This book is produced from independently certified FSC™ paper
to ensure responsible forest management.

For more information visit: www.harpercollins.co.uk/green

This book is set in 11,2/15.5 pt. Bembo by Type-it AS, Norway

Printed and Bound in the UK using 100% Renewable Electricity at
CPI Group (UK) Ltd, Croydon, CR0 4YY

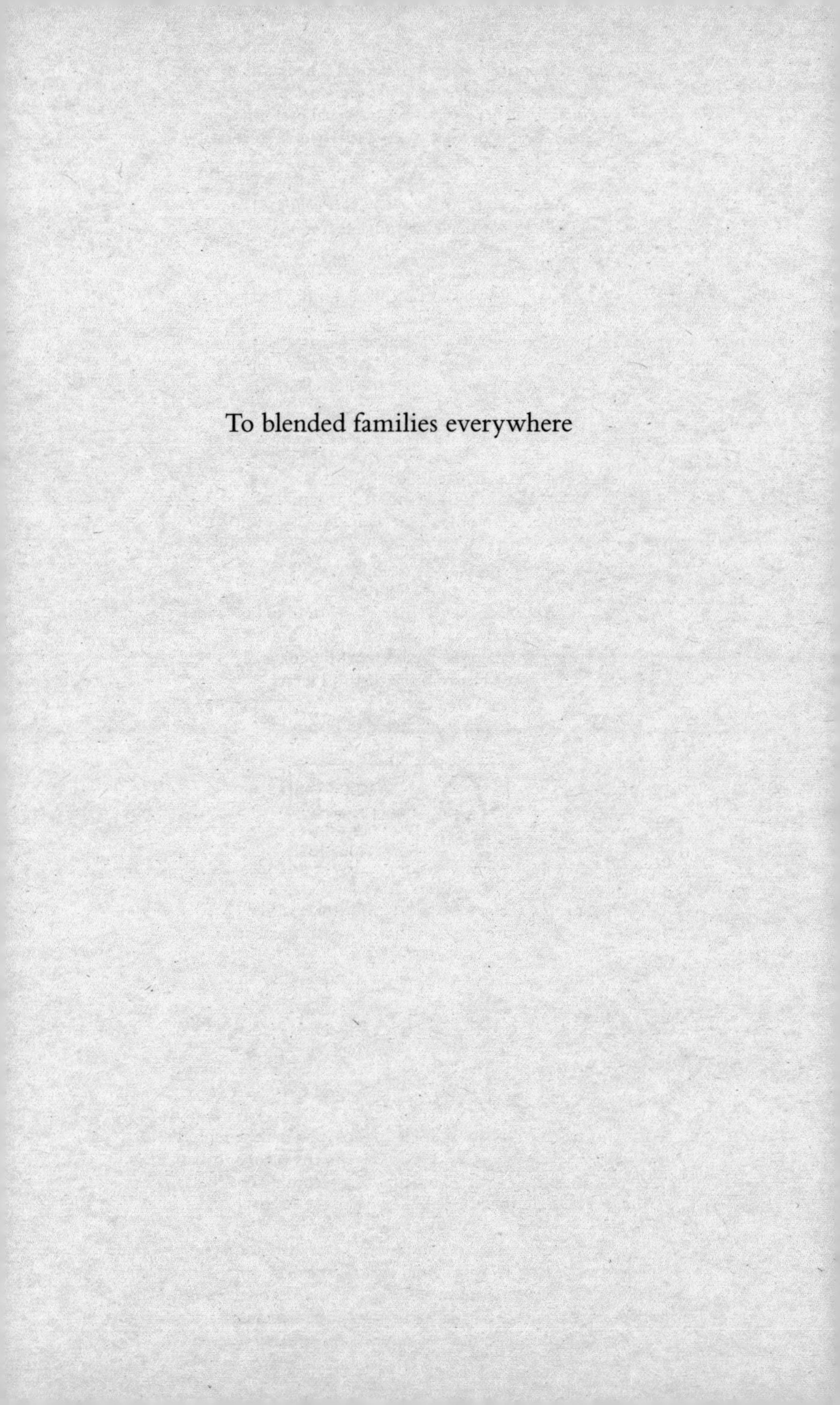

To blended families everywhere

Chapter 1

'Guys, you ever get tired of being told you're too much? I swear, it should be my middle name, Abi "too much" Akingbade. But look at me. I'm eleven stone and five foot four. I'm not too much. I'm compact!'

Pause for a laugh. The crowd's a bit uptight tonight but it comes – eventually. Then I always find the skinniest guy in the audience and give him a wink, a little topper that supplies another ripple. I look down from the stage at my mark.

'Honestly, babe, with these thighs, I would break your back.'

A double-pronged win. I make a fat joke before they can, plus I enjoy watching my target squirm. His pal gives him a 'you're-in' nudge. Trust me, mate, you're not.

'Thing is, I want a man that can handle all of me, and I'm not just talking about my magnificent rack.'

That doesn't get its usual cheer though two women applaud like they've just seen a marvellous rally at Wimbledon. What is *up* with this crowd? I push on.

'No, guys, I'm not just talking about my incredible, curvalicious bod. FYI, you English girls should be grateful God gave me this Nigerian behind. If you had it, you'd topple over. And you definitely couldn't

handle my Nigerian parents. My mum is so strict, if she met royalty, she'd get them to bow to her!'

A tittering but nothing substantial. Jeez, they're making me work tonight. Well, they won't be able to resist my best Nigerian accent. Guaranteed crowd pleaser.

'My mum would be like, "Get down, Your Highness! A crown and sceptre does not make you special, special. Prostrate yourself!"'

Okaaay… Clearly not pleasing *this* crowd. Maybe somehow they know in reality my mum's posher than the front row at Ascot and my dad's so quiet, half the time you don't even know he's there. Ah, who am I kidding? Audiences aren't bothered about the truth. They just want funny.

I look back at my mark who's quivering under the hot glow of my attention.

'No, babes, if you want this, you got to want aaaaalll of this. I'm not just a snack, I'm all three courses!'

No cheer – again. Fine. Tonight's crowd are so chin-scratchy and right-on, they're probably worried laughing at this big, black beaut isn't PC. Honestly, political correctness'll be the death of comedy.

'Anyway, that's all from me. My name's Abi Akingbade because I'm – bad aiiiye!'

Some laughter, some half-baked applause but as it's all that's on offer, I'll take it. I hand the mic over to Dina, the MC, and I'm done. Even though this is an unpaid, open-mic gig, she usually pulls in a decent crowd at the Comedy Cabin so I'm pretty sure tonight's stuffy vibe is a one-off. At least I hope it is because playing good rooms like this is what's going to ultimately get me where I want to go – walking out on stage at the Athena Theatre. In all its three-thousand-seat glory, the

Athena is where dreams are made, the comedy Olympus only true stand-up gods grace; and it's where the BBC shoot *ShowTime at the Athena*, which even my humour-free mother has heard of. From international superstars like Yolanda B. Rockwell to homegrown heroes like Mark McGuinty, when it comes to the Athena, only the greats need apply and one day, someday, I want to be up there too – making that huge crowd bust out laughing. That's the dream, anyway, but until then, I'll keep singling out skinny guys in the front row of open-mic nights all while juggling gigs, my temp job and, of course, dating. *Sheesh.* That whole area has been a long ting. Trying to meet someone who gets me and isn't just looking for salad-munching arm-candy, someone who's into the whole package, not just the wrapping; it's no joke – especially when you're a busy babe like me, so tonight I'm multitasking. I'm on a date and I've brought him to the gig so he can hear my routine, a shameless declaration that he needs to accept me for who I am. No subtlety or subtext with Abi. What you see is what you get. I just hope Sam, my date, was taking notes. I see him lurking towards the back of the room looking hella cute, a stocky Damson Idris, his ebony complexion glowing like a polished gem, gorgeous eyes set to a permanent smoulder. I've never dated a smoulderer. Well, I nearly did once, but turns out he had a squint and just needed glasses. I grab my stuff and head over to him. Man, his hotness should be illegal.

'All right,' I say, trying to match his smoulder with a smize.

'Hey,' he says, eyes swivelling to me before being drawn back to the next act on stage.

She's funny and thin. I glare at Sam, wondering what's captivating him more, her material or her thigh gap. For my own sanity, I stopped trying to compete with size tens years ago but the idea he finds someone else funnier, man, that pricks at all my insecurities. I work hard to force them down and instead wait patiently for him to bring his attention back to me and, you know, our date!

'Shall we sit?' I say, 'tude pushing through, not that he notices.

'Sure,' he replies, finally coming back to Planet Abi.

We squeeze onto the end of the comedians' bench, him taking a long, slow drink from his beer. Me, just … waiting. I've been off stage a whole eight minutes. Isn't this where he tells me 'well done', 'interesting ideas', 'nice lighting'? Something, anything. Us comics may look all-conquering on stage but in real life we're fragile AF. Finally, I cave.

'So, what did you think?'

'I'm no comedy expert,' he says, shrugging.

Okay, let me help you out. 'You know how sometimes comedy has, like, a message …'

He looks at me. 'Oh that. Yeah, it was a bit …'

Come on, man, spit it out.

'… much,' he says with a half frown, before his gaze flits back to the stage.

Urrrgh. This is the story of my frigging life. From my mum to my teachers, bosses to boyfriends, I've been told the same thing a million times. I want to collapse in on myself, my Spanx the only thing holding me up. I mean, have any of these people ever thought, maybe I'm not too much? Maybe they're not enough! I should screech this in Sam's stupidly gorgeous face but instead I bury it. Yes, I'd love to blast him with a keynote speech Michaela Coel would be proud of about how he needs to appreciate me for who I am but for some reason I'm still clinging to the hope there might be something between us so instead I smear on a smile. 'Why don't we have another drink?'

At the bar, I regroup, ordering Sam a zero-alcohol beer, the best low-key clapback I can think of that won't actually derail our date. Though it's on life support, I'm not calling time of death just yet. But I've already done the most. I've let him see me perform, got a banging outfit on, I've even done a bikini wax because, well, you never know. He needs to do some heavy lifting now.

Returning, I plant myself and our drinks down. Sam leans in, eyes on the skinny girl who's approaching the end of her routine, and he whispers, 'To be fair, you were funnier than her.'

And just like that, Sam Agyefong, you've earned yourself a reprieve.

Chapter 2

I stare at the four outfits laid across the pull-down bed in my tiny Islington studio. Renting in these ends was a feeble attempt to prove to my mum I'm a success but, in reality, this place is so small, I'm scared to put the front door key in too vigorously in case I smash the kitchen window.

In the background, as always, my laptop browser is on the Comedy Buzz channel where reruns of *ShowTime at the Athena* play on a loop. Every second or third act pulls my attention as I watch in awe, jealousy, but mainly bewilderment, wondering how my comedy will get me there when I'm still struggling to get my first paid gig. However, before the pity party club classics start up in my head, I go back to the task at hand, picking my get-up for tonight's date with Sam.

Truth be told, as it's a Monday, I should be gigging – maybe testing out a new joke I wrote about how my thigh gap has slipped down to my knees (I came up with it after watching skinny girl so, silver linings and that) – but on my deathbed, will I regret trying out a banger or banging a hottie and finding love?

After multiple changes due to make-up smudges and a popped button, I make a dash – well, fast walk – for the bus and an hour later am standing next to Sam in the lobby of the Disraeli private members' club. Seeing him again, and in a place as plush as this, I can't help feel excited. *This* is a proper date and I almost want to kick myself for bringing him to that open-mic night. Anyway, no time to sweat it. We're here now and those fancy cocktails aren't gonna drink themselves.

'Hey, Sareeta,' Sam says to the supermodel receptionist as he proffers a slick, matte-black card.

Without even looking at it or her computer screen, she smiles. 'Welcome back, Sam. Go right on in.'

As Sareeta greets more guests, I notice her almost computerised, transatlantic accent. Maybe this place is so boujie they have robots. I want to poke her face to see if she's real but before I can Sam ushers me up the spiral staircase and into the club. On the first landing a ceiling-high mirror confirms to me that my outfit choice of glittery gold top, leggings and black mini was on point. We slide into a velvety two-seater with a view of the bar and Sam smoulders, whispering, 'You look incredible.'

'Thanks,' I smile, feeling hella validated.

The last time I wore this top, my mum said I looked like gold bullion. The woman is cold. Shaking her from my mind, my eyes drift to Sam's shoulders, his crisp, pale blue shirt, sleeves folded twice revealing lean, strong forearms, his solid jaw and oh, that mouth. Man, I wanna lips him so bad but I guess when we finally kiss it'll be worth the wait. And though he's not that much chattier than the other night, his body language is speaking volumes. *This* is the Sam that made me swipe right. Clearly he needed to be in his own habitat to feel comfortable and that is fine by me. Just as I start to visualise those arms wrapping around me, a waiter comes over to drop off our menus, tearing me from my fantasies.

Sam and I glance through the selections making small talk while I try not to blanch that there're no pence on any of these prices. It's just deconstructed whatever – *twenty quid*. La-de-dah bavette – *forty-five quid*. No messing. And what the hell's a burrata? I thought that was some type of gun. The last time I went somewhere with a pence-less menu was when we celebrated Dad's retirement from the university.

'Ready to order?' the waiter asks.

I look up with a cheeky, conspiratorial grin. 'Can't lie. I'm fully baffled. How's about a bit of a taster menu?'

Sam's expression turns to concern. 'They don't really do that—'

But before he can finish, the waiter's face breaks into a grin too. 'I'll see what we can do.'

And he heads off.

'Impressive,' Sam says, with a surprise I choose not to be offended by.

'Oh, you know, if you don't ask and all that,' I say, as I let my hand gently brush against his.

His smile widens and I reply with a flirty wink before settling back, assured. No one can resist my Classic Abi charm.

On cue, five minutes later, the waiter returns with drinks and lets us know a taster menu is on the way.

'Aaaaayyyyyy, ayyyyy!' I grin, sashaying in my seat.

'Yeah, result.' Sam raises his glass, edging closer to me. 'To getting what you want.'

I feel his magnetism draw me in. Oh, mate, it is *on*. And even though my lacy thongs are slicing me up like a block of Edam,

I'm so glad I wore them. I clink my glass against his, a little louder than I mean to but, hey, nothing's dainty with me. Then, following Sam's lead, I pretend to savour the wine in the way people do on Saturday morning cooking shows.

'Mmmm, you can actually taste berries,' I say with a discerning head tilt.

The waiter hears this and looks well pleased, like this plonk is from his own personal vineyard.

'At what point do they actually add them?' I ask and the waiter's face falls – as does Sam's.

'Joke!' I say, giving Sam a nudge, and he exhales a relieved laugh.

'Funny,' he says, wagging a finger at me. 'Funny.'

I smile to myself, quietly pleased. I am crushing this date. I've been charming, witty, and by the way Sam's hand is now softly grazing my shoulder, I must be giving off pure hotness. Peak peng, baby. My tummy flutters as I realise I don't want to blow it with this handsome, dark-skinned brother with moonlit pool eyes and a laugh as smooth as his skin. Yeah, it's only our second date but I'm thinking – he might be a keeper.

Soon, an array of dishes arrives and as we pick at them, fork-pointing in approval at the really delicious ones, Sam asks, 'So, tell me about this comedy thing. How do you write your sketches?'

Hmmm. I love that he's asking about my life but the question makes me bristle. My comedy is a routine, it's stand-up or a bit, as American comics say. It's not a *sketch*. It's not four middle-class Oxbridge pals in women's wigs, corpsing at in-jokes during a student cabaret night. But I can't be mad at Sam for not knowing that, especially as tonight is going well. At least he's interested. I've been on dates where the only question the guy's asked is how I want to split the bill. So I shake off the light irritation and tell him about the open-mic circuit which I hope to soon graduate from, about coming up with material but how performing is my strong suit and, of course, about the gig I run.

'It's called Wisecrackers.' I beam, filling with pride at just saying the name. 'Me and a couple of mates set it up. Guarantees us stage time, every Tuesday.'

'Makes sense,' Sam says. 'So on top of that and your other gigs, you work full-time?'

'Yeah …' and my heart dips as I remember my daytime Clark Kent existence, 'but it's a temp job, month by month, just until I get enough paid gigs to go full-time as a comic and get off this open-mic tip.'

'Cool,' Sam nods. 'So how many paid gigs have you had?'

I congeal as I tell him, 'None.'

And he nods again. 'You know what you should do, that BBC Athena show.'

My toes curl into a foot fist at hearing yet another person say this – like it's as simple as applying to be a contestant on *Pointless*. Silly me for not thinking of that before. But I'm polite as I set him straight. 'You get invited to do that show. You have to earn it, basically.'

'I see, so what are your prospects with stand-up?' he asks, spoken like a true city boy.

Though I've fantasised every possibility, I swirl my glass, trying to cherry-pick the answer I think will impress him. 'Well, if you get a break, sky's the limit: TV appearances, your own sitcom, tours, movies but … since I was a kid, all I've wanted is to make people laugh, make them … happy.'

My eyes fall to the linen tablecloth as an unwelcome image floats into my mind, of the one person I've never managed to crack. My dad laughs at pretty much everything I say, at times just to be encouraging. But Mum, she's a much tougher nut …

'Well, nuff respect, putting yourself out there with no idea if it'll work out. I'd need a clear path of progression, know where I'm heading,' Sam says, his free hand jutting towards his inevitable future success while the other pumps my shoulder. 'Must be rough.'

I'm sure he doesn't mean this to be condescending but it really is.

'Well, rough would be *not* putting myself out there,' I say, attempting to rally, but it feels like I'm trying to convince myself more than him.

Bill paid, Sam slides out of his seat to standing, and seeing him head to toe sets my pulse racing again. His trousers fit close, in a way only expensive designer clothes can. His shirt skims his body just enough to reveal he's hench but not so tight that buttons are straining – and those arms. It's a chore to drag my eyes back to his face but I have to because I think he's speaking.

'Do you want to head upstairs?' he repeats, eyebrows steepled into a suggestive arch.

I flush as thoughts of undoing those buttons crash around my mind. I was down for waiting to have sex but he's hot, has been giving me signals all evening – and if they've got rooms on the floors above, who am I to stand in the way of our obvious natural chemistry?

'Do you have a condom?' I vamp, smizing to the point I can barely see.

Sam's grin evaporates. 'There's a bar upstairs. I meant, we could have a nightcap.'

'Totally!' I blurt, grabbing at my jacket, to hide my embarrassment.

'I mean … let's see where the night takes us, yeah?' Sam adds, an attempt, I'm guessing, to be gallant and breeze past my humiliation.

I get my shit together and we head up yet another flight of stairs, going deeper into the Disraeli. Finally having shaken off my cringe, I wonder to myself where this night is going. Obviously doing the wild thing is off the cards, but as Sam takes my hand, it does feel like a kiss might still be in play. He leads me through to the bar and I allow myself a coy smile.

'And may I scan your card?' a new waitress asks.

I think she might be AI as well because like Sareeta on the front desk, she too is stunning – in a robotic, man-made way. Sam hands over his card and we settle into a cosy corner sofa. Once again he slips an arm along the seat back and I shuffle into its crook. Observing all the beautiful people having beautiful people tête-à-têtes, I wonder if they're looking at us thinking *we're* beautiful people too. Sam and I share a simmering look, and I realise his gaze keeps dipping to my mouth. Man's looking at me like he's thirsty and I'm the only thing he wants to drink. This is it. I close my eyes, and lift my lips to his. But just at the moment of magic I hear, 'Sam!'

He pulls away and as he looks towards the source of the voice, a group of guys at the bar, I feel him stiffen, and not in a good way.

'Friends of yours?' I ask.

He gives an 'Mmmm,' that would take a Bletchley Park code breaker a month to decipher.

'If you need to say hello …' I offer, gesturing towards the group, one of whom is beckoning Sam with a tumbler of something syrupy and, no doubt, expensive.

I look down. Sam's hands are no longer on me and somehow there's now a gap of several inches between us where before you couldn't slip his fancy membership card. Sam gives his friends a half-wave. An ambiguous 'go away' or maybe a 'give me a minute?'

'It's fine,' he says, distracted.

But now I'm distracted. I look over at these guys, all various versions of Sam. A hive mind of shredded city types wanting to kick it with their boy who, since their appearance, is somewhere else. I take a deep breath. I've been here too many times. Neatening my skirt, I look at Sam.

'Are you embarrassed?' I ask, listening for the answer I don't want to hear.

It's not even the answer, more the quality of it. We all know the sound of a true, say-it-with-your-chest response or an apologetic gurgle hiding an unwanted reply.

'Course not,' he says, holding my gaze, and I really want to believe him. 'It's just …' He peels his gaze back to his friends, 'You're not what I'd normally go for. They won't understand. It's … you're different … in a great way.'

'Different?' I say, my arms crossing tight.

'Thing is, Abi,' he says, trying to hold my hand with both of his, 'you're more … effervescent than other women I've dated.'

'Effervescent – what, like a Berocca?'

'It's a good thing!' Sam insists.

'Soooo, I'm fizzy,' I say, eyebrow arched. 'What else?'

He lets go of my hand. 'It's just, you can be a bit pushy. You know, the taster menu and … asking if I had protection.'

'That was a general enquiry!' I bleat with indignation.

'It's just all a bit … much.' And if that wasn't enough Sam waves his hand in a circle, putting me firmly in the centre.

Over at the bar, his friends are getting impatient, one mugging confusion that Sam hasn't already come over.

'Look, it was nice to meet you, yeah. You're fun, but this isn't for me. Sorry. See you on *ShowTime at the Athena*!' Sam says, rising.

He pats my shoulder with commiseration but before I can tell him I hope the bottom falls out of his stock portfolio, he's over with his mates. Unbe-frickin-lievable, I seethe, my body pulsing with hot anger as Sam clinks glasses with his cohorts, disappearing into the bowels of the group like the absolute shit he is.

Chapter 3

Still reeling, I down my drink and gather up my stuff. I need to get away from Sam – to where, I haven't got a clue. I'm about to march off when I spot his abandoned bar card. Without hesitating, I stuff it in my bag and stomp towards the stairs. Tears blister but I will not let them fall. And I have to fight to swallow a scream I feel rising in my chest. Why did I suggest a second date when he'd all but called me 'too much' at my gig? What was I thinking?

The Disraeli is a warren of staircases and in my urgency to put distance between me and Sam – and locate the nearest loos – I find myself stumbling into a rooftop bar. Its open skylights let in warm, summer evening air which I gratefully inhale to steady myself. Around me, aside from some Shoreditch types debating the morality of commercial space travel, the bar is all but empty. I spot a velvet corner-couch and flop onto it, eyes drawn to a waiter clearing glasses on the outdoor deck. Beside him a gaggle of smokers congregate by an ashtray. As their smoke billows up, a morose cloud descends over me. Is this as good as it gets? Forever braced for the 'You're a lovely girl but …', 'You're stunning, it's just that …', or whatever line the guy comes up with to do the backtrack slide. Either I'm too loud, too funny (er, that's my job, nobhead!), I'm too big (I curdle remembering the fella who told me if I lost a few pounds he could really fancy me), or, of course, when I get angry, surprise, surprise, I'm too emotional. Why do men get to decide what's too much?

And how did my kid sister Kemi and my mum find their person, their other half, who loves them as they are? Knowing those two, it damn sure wasn't by shutting up and being less than. If anything, it's Kemi's husband Felix who's done that. And it's got to be how Dad's survived thirty-four years married to my mum. I sink even deeper into the couch. I can't keep jumping through hoops only for next man to chat 'bout how I'm too big, too black, too whatever. Because then, irony of ironies, my too-muchness means I'm never enough. I turn Sam's card over in my hand, still wanting him to want me yet knowing I'm already old news, tomorrow's anecdote over scoffed sushi with his stupid, city-boy mates.

With no other salve to hand, I scan the menu. It might be time to try that pence-less Châteauneuf de Surf de Boeuf courtesy of Sam Agyefong's bar card.

'I recommend the wings.'

I take my gaze from the menu to the floor and see a pair of pristine black Converse, ones I've noticed all the staff wearing. So, this joker is suggesting chicken wings – because I'm black? I'm about to give him both barrels for racially profiling me when I look up and see a mixed race guy with short twists – the waiter from the smokers' deck. He wipes my table and smiles.

'Er … good, are they?' I ask.

He gives a playful nod before putting down a bowl of fancy nibbles. 'Wouldn't recommend them otherwise.'

I take him in, towering over me with his dusting of stubble, long face and story-filled eyes.

'What else would you suggest?' I ask, literally feeling not just my pupils dilate but my whole damn self.

'Live your best life, take each day as it comes and never trust a bruddah in socks and crocs.'

I bust out laughing, not expecting that. After four hours with humourless Sam, it's a blessing to laugh again. This guy laughs too and though it's just shy of midnight, it feels like the sun came out. But then I come to my senses. He isn't hitting on me. He's doing his job. Charm is part of the package here, along with their 'welcome backs' and 'lovely to see you agains', all done to make guests feel like esteemed old friends. I withdraw to the menu and the business of running up a mahooosive bar bill for man-like Sam.

As I seek out the most expensive cocktail, my waiter says, 'I'm Will, by the way.'

I smile despite myself, replying 'Abi,' while trying to ignore his cuteness.

'I haven't seen you here before.'

'I've been … I'm not … Prison,' I blurt, flustered by his attention.

Thankfully he laughs then asks, 'What were you in for?'

'Grand awesomeness,' I reply, composing myself.

Lightly crossing his arms, he nods with pretend gravity. 'Yeah, my cousin got a few years for that. Let out early for bad-ass behaviour.'

I mirror his serious nod before we both giggle which eventually melts into an easy quiet – not an awkward, brain-whirring search for something to say, just stillness. This is the most relaxed

I've been all evening – so much so, I don't notice Will pick up the bar card from the table. Before I can stop him, he's tapped it on his reader. My stomach spirals.

Deadpan, he says, 'So, what'll it be … Samuel … Agyefong?'

Shit. My career as an identity thief, over before it's begun.

'The thing is …' I blabber, braced to plummet through the riff-raff trapdoor this boujie joint must have under every seat.

In fact, there's probably a security guard watching my every move, fist poised over a fat red knob that will open a chute, dumping me outside the nearest Matalan. Will turns the card over in his hand and I notice how slim and delicate his fingers are.

'I know what's going on here,' he says.

I'm so tense even my eyebrows feel rigid, prepared for whatever punishment a private members' club metes out to blaggers like me. Is tasering off the table?

'I suspect,' says Will, 'you and Samuel got your cards mixed up. Happens a lot.'

I study Will's face. Is this a trap? I give a noncommittal, 'Mmm-hmmm.'

'So why don't you order and we can figure this out tomorrow? Everything's always clearer in the morning.'

'Yeah,' I sigh with relief.

'Let me fix you something special,' Will smiles and heads to the bar.

I flump back into my sofa, its big velvety cushions enveloping me as I unscramble tonight's events; a disastrous date, shocking identity-theft fail and now this last-minute curve ball – Will, who's defo a solid nine and a half. He's tall too. Much taller than me so, side-by-side, we wouldn't have that 'perfect' ratio thing going on like you see in movie posters and old postcards of Charles and Di. No, if we stood next to each other, we'd look like a lower case d. And there's something delicate but not wilting about him. He's strong but in a way you don't see in many men, like he'd totally cry at *Waiting to Exhale* but his favourite movie is probably *Training Day*.

Before long, Will returns with my drink and shortly after that, a plate of wings.

'Enjoy,' he winks, and I raise my glass.

But, sitting here alone, in this emptiness, it doesn't feel like a win.

'Why don't you come sit at the bar?'

I look up and Will has taken a few steps back towards me. 'That'd be great,' I say and he scoops up my drink and food, leading the way. I settle in at the marble counter and take a sip of my cocktail. It's delicious and, most importantly, plenty boozy. Will glances over, his face breaking warmly. Though I want to deny it, it sure does look like he's into me but even if he is, eventually won't he be yet another guy to give me the you're-too-much talk? A heavy sigh billows from me. Why can't I be me? Why are my options either being rejected for who I am and facing a life of chronic singledom, or dimming my light for someone else's benefit? And what will that get me – ending up like my mum and dad, two satellites orbiting each other, paths barely crossing?

Will takes off his apron, folds it into a neat triangle on the bar and scoots round onto a stool next to me.

'Wait, did you just quit?' I joke.

'Oh, I've got something way more spectacular planned for that. You seen *Jerry Maguire*?'

'I love that movie,' I beam.

'Well, I'm taking all the fish!' Will declares and we crack up, bouncing quotes back and forth.

I'm shocked that he does a surprisingly good Tom Cruise impersonation. His Renée Zellweger isn't too bad either – which is weirder. Eventually, after barrelling through multiple movie moments about being shown money, the weight of human heads and who's completing who, we land into a comfortable chat.

'Can I tell you something?' says Will after a while.

I'm not sure. If it's *Jerry Maguire*-related, I'm down, but from the tone of his voice, I don't think it is.

'Sam's a regular and … he's really not worth it.'

I say nothing but my shameful, thin smile speaks volumes. Sam's got form but I'm the last to know. Will's hand hovers before he softly places it on mine.

And once again, I'm fighting tears. 'He's my third date in as many weeks and it's been the same story every time.'

'Well, he needs his brain and his eyes tested,' Will says, sitting back to take me in. 'You're gorgeous.'

My cheeks flush. 'You're a joker, innit.'

'If Sam doesn't see it, *he's* the joker. Serious.'

'Or maybe I'm the joker, sitting here by myself,' I reply.

'But you're not by yourself,' says Will as he gently, so gently, strokes my hand. This guy …

I look around as wait staff in their civvies bundle through the employees-only door and nod goodnights to Will.

'Are you closing soon?' I ask.

'Up here closes in ten but downstairs is open till about two,' he says peering at his black-strapped watch. 'Staff stick around for drinks cos Monday is our Saturday night.'

I watch Will, enjoying his quiet, fluid glide. It's there in everything he does – including making a move on me. And I'm torn, wanting to brush off his advances, certain this will go the way things always do but wondering, could this be different? Will adjusts, resting his elbows on the bar. 'So come on, what's the deal? What's a funny, gorgeous woman like you doing with a wasteman like Sam?'

My chest compresses at the memory of being discarded earlier with barely a backward glance. 'I thought he was special but, same beat, different dancer. All my life I've been told I'm too much and it's getting to be a lot, you know.'

Will nods but I doubt he, with his neat put-togetherness and natural ease, would understand.

'You know what, yeah, if you're too much then so am I.'

As sweet as it is, my eyes roll at the idea. 'You think I'm gassing. Trust me, fam. This is real. I get told it *all* the time.'

'I'm gonna need empirical evidence.'

'Well, we can go downstairs and doorstep Sam,' I say with Annalise Keating levels of side-eye.

My brittle edge glides off Will, as it would someone so smooth.

'Serious, give me examples and I'll let you know.'

What? He's gonna rate my very being? This guy's clowning me, hard.

'Come on, try me,' he says, swivelling on his bar stool.

My eyes narrow. So, instead of going on a date with this character where, at the end, he tells me I'm too much, I'm offering it up on platter before we've even WhatsApped a time and a place? Fine. Bring it.

'When I was a kid, wherever I went, I was always the loudest – at home, at school, at Brownies. When Mum picked me up, she said she could hear my voice from a hundred paces.'

I cross my arms, more than satisfied with my opening offer.

'Pah!' Will smirks. 'In the school choir, I was so loud I was the entire tenor section.'

My crossed arms tighten. I'm irritated but also impressed.

'Okay,' I say, with a metaphorical finger crick. 'When I was a kid, I had so much energy, one school lunchtime, I ended up dancing, on my own, in the assembly hall for the whole hour, sweat dripping off me as my entire year group lined up for afternoon classes. I was busting such crazy moves my mate thought it was a dare.'

Will gives an appreciative nod, then says, 'Well, in my twenties, I was always the first on the dance floor.'

'Ha, that's not too much. That's a public service. You're getting the party started,' I say, with a dismissive wave.

'Oh, I didn't *dance* on the dance floor . . . I did backflips, caterpillar, the works.'

'Whaaaat?' I squawk, going in for a high five. 'That's a lot.'

We laugh as I feel my defences slip away. And that icky, high-school memory suddenly doesn't feel so bad after all.

'So, is that all you've got?' he says, beckoning my reply like he's in *The Matrix* dojo.

'Okay. I was obsessed with Blackstreet. I listened to "No Diggity" on loop for two months straight. My sister had to hide the CD.'

Will lets out a big, joyful laugh, clapping his hands. 'I love it but check this out. One time, I saved up for a drum kit but could only afford a bashed-up snare, kick and old cymbal. Played the riff from "Fight the Power" until I had blisters. Drove my mum and dad crazy!'

I rock in my seat, laughing hard, picturing a young Will,

teeth pressed into his lip, thrashing out his beats. As I lean back, my stool wobbles and, impulsively, Will reaches out to stop me falling.

'I've got you,' he says, eyes fixed on mine.

'Thanks,' I say, feeling his firm arm around my waist. 'I think we're neck and neck – can you handle any more?'

Will moves closer with a gaze that penetrates my soul and a smile that could melt ice caps. 'My stomach muscles may hate me for this – but yeah, Abi, give me more.'

We never make it downstairs to the staff drinks, instead staying in the rooftop bar swapping more stories. It's amazing to laugh about things I've always felt so judged for. And I love that Will has his own too-muchness inventory although he soon concedes I'm the champ. We mark it with a shot.

'Nothing like the burn of sambuca at one thirty in the morning to make you feel like a winner,' I say, proffering my glass.

'Too much?' he says with a cheeky wink.

'Not enough!' I declare as we clink glasses and down the sugary liquid.

Our faces contort in playful regret as the sambuca scorches our throats and it takes a minute for all the giggling to subside. But eventually it does and we land in a place I don't recognise. Now what? My mind whirs. As much as I can feel us drawing closer, him making a proper move still feels a long way off. I mean, if I had my way we'd be back at mine an hour ago – why waste a good bikini wax – but I'm not sure that's his vibe.

'It's getting late,' Will murmurs, an ambiguous smile dancing on his lips.

'It is,' I say softly, hoping to draw him in …

'Can I call you a cab?'

The offer feels more practical than passionate.

'I … er … It's fine. I'll get the night bus,' I say, disappointment cascading through me.

Will frowns. 'At least let me walk you to your stop.'

And with that, hope flickers.

Outside the Disraeli, the Soho streets are all but dead as Will and I head towards Charing Cross Road. We're close but not touching, quiet but not silent – communicating something; maybe the shared desire to ask, What next?

We reach my stop. The indicator says my bus is coming in … two minutes. Damn you, TFL for scuppering a girl's love life.

Will leans against the shelter, hands wedged into his pockets.

'Your jeans are cool,' I say, reaching to fill the void and instantly cringing.

I might as well have just told him *I carried the watermelon*, like that girl in *Dirty Dancing.*

My bus is one minute away, this can't be how we leave it.

'I had a great time tonight, Abi,' Will says, taking my hand.

'Me too,' I flush.

Chrrrrist, I wanna kiss him. Screw it, I'm going in. I plant my free hand on his solid chest, a timpani drumbeat within. I lift up onto my tiptoes. His lips part but as I'm about to make touchdown he says …

'Abi, uh, I need to … I've got to get back – I haven't finished my shift …'

I adjust, mid-manoeuvre, and pick at some invisible fluff on his shirt.

'Totally! I was just … you had something on your … there. I think I … got it,' I fluster, covering.

'Great, cool – thanks. Look, let me get your digits, yeah? Maybe we could link up?'

I see the silhouette of my bus approaching as Will pulls out his phone.

'Sure,' I say, plastering on a laid-back expression, tapping in my number.

'I'll text you,' he smiles, squeezing my hand.

'Cool. I'm down. Whatever!'

And before I can gabble anything else, my bus pulls in, I get on and the doors close. Will waves and as I watch him jog back to the Disraeli I wonder if I'll ever hear from that drummer boy again.

Chapter 4

I'm doing my best not to think about Will but failing miserably. Thank God it's Wisecrackers night so I can distract myself with laying out chairs, sorting petty cash tins and all the other unglamorous tasks no one tells you about when you set up your own comedy night. Though, in theory, I run the weekly gig with my friends Frank and Cassie, I usually do most of the graft. I swear, Frank times it so he arrives just after this preshow faff but it's cool, I guess. He has a grown-up job and Cassie's got that and kids to worry about. I flick the lights on as my nasal passages adjust to the pub's backroom 'aroma'. Thea, the landlady, says she misses when people smoked as it masked many foul-smelling sins. She's not wrong.

I get stuck into moving tables as another wave of embarrassment hits at last night's failed kiss attempt. It's probably good that I haven't heard from Will. If my oversharing didn't put him off, me being a Kathy Keen probably did. I practically #MeToo'ed the guy. Best to forget about him and focus on the gig.

It's 6.45 and Cassie's now also late, which is standard. Knowing her, she's probably got stuck in traffic heading to the wrong show or lost track of time yarnbombing her local park. Truthfully, the lateness does vex me sometimes but the upside is, at least I'm doing this with mates and I get all the compering time I want. Who's gonna argue when it's me doing the lion's share? Plus, it was my classic Abi charm that bagged us this venue in the first place. And seven years on, here we are, still going.

'Sorry I'm late,' Frank says, giving me his usual three air kisses. 'Oh, you've already moved the tables. I would have helped.'

''S cool,' I say with a quiet kiss of my teeth.

Frank puts his leather satchel in the tech booth at the back, then slips off his jacket, shedding his work persona with it – strict teacher at a fancy South London girls' school.

'Wow. Preppy teacher to youth group leader in one move,' I tease as I watch him loosen his tie.

'Daytime casual is for the work-from-home brigade, Abi,' Frank says, clipped and posh, not a glottal stop to be heard. 'They're all, pressed shirt up top—'

'Jammies down below?' I say.

'Exactly, or worse,' Frank eye-rolls and I giggle.

He takes 'dry' to Saharan levels.

I carry on setting up as Frank undoes his top button, surveying the near-completed set-up. We pack the punters in nice and close. That's key for a good comedy room. Low ceilings, no lighting on the crowd so they feel uninhibited, and easy access to booze. I lay out the last few chairs and the microsecond they're in place, Cassie rocks up. A mass of bulging tote bags and wild hair, she's the polar opposite of Frank. Where he's all first-day-on-the-job clean angles, Cassie always looks like she's just been made redundant – even though she's self-employed.

'Sorry I'm late,' she coos with her usual fluster. 'Horatio had his HPV booster this afternoon and projectile vomited over half his maths class.'

She takes in the room with an approving nod before turning her attention to me and her flustering gives way to a massive grin.

'Who is he?' she says, beaming.

'What?'

Frank, who'd been scribbling new joke ideas in his notebook, stops, becoming a pointer detecting a scent.

'Spill,' he demands.

'She's had sex,' Cassie declares.

'No, I didn't!' I shoot back, not sounding convincing at all.

Truth be told, after me and Will went our separate ways, in my head we *did*. It's all I could think about the whole way home. Cassie's probably picking up on my frustration, unrealised illicit thoughts only therapists like her could notice. I haven't spilt the tea about last night with anyone – and can I even say there is tea given nothing happened? It's been a whole twenty-four hours and I still haven't heard from him. I throw them a titbit, hoping it'll satisfy.

'There may *or* may not have been some flirting yesterday.'

'I knew it!' she squeals.

'No, you didn't,' drones Frank. 'You thought she'd had sex.'

Cassie shushes him, pulling up a chair and pointing for me to sit too.

'So … was there a kiss?'

'Not exactly.'

'Ha! Sensors are way off, Cass!' Frank laughs.

'What do you mean, "not exactly"?' she presses.

I shrug. 'I leant in and … he leant back.'

Frank snorts, '*Ehhhh macarena*.'

Cassie gives Frank a reprimanding tap and he zips it as I slump into my chair, desperate to decipher Will's behaviour. I guess if there's anyone I can talk to about it, it's our in-house therapist. And so, without much more prompting, words tumble from me as I describe this beautiful man I felt so at home with, and seen by; who walked me to the bus stop then walked away. 'I felt like there was something but I'm worried he might have ghosted me.'

Cassie bobs her head sagely while I pick at my sleeve. But the snap of Frank's notebook closing pulls my eyes up.

'Abi, it's been a day!'

'I know – but that non-kiss,' I say, covering my face.

'Maybe he really did have to go back to work, maybe he didn't want to get swept up in the moment and then have to leave,' Cassie says, eyes misting at the romance of it all.

'Or maybe he's waiting until you're married,' Frank offers.

'Frank,' Cassie scolds.

'I'm sorry, but she's worrying over nothing. As per. He'll call. Why? Because you're fabulous. You know it, we know it, and if he doesn't then – "New phone, who dis?"' Frank says.

A little chuckle escapes me and I start to feel better.

'It's a full moon – decision-making can be a bit skew-whiff around now. Give him a couple more days before writing him off,' Cassie adds.

'And, one last, important thing …' says Frank.

I look to him, buoyed by these Will-positive affirmations.

'Can we straighten these damn chairs so it looks like a comedy night in here and not one of Cassie's support groups?'

'Francis!' Cassie laughs, taking a swipe at him.

Frank dodges and with little enthusiasm to chase him, she instead pulls me in for a hug, which I savour.

Just then, a punter pops her head through the door, a confused look on her face at the sight of us hugging.

'Is this … the comedy night?'

'See!' Frank barks.

'Yes! Sit anywhere you want,' Cassie says, ushering the punter in before quickly turning back to me. 'You know, it could be he didn't run away from you, he ran *back* to his job after sneaking out to be with you.'

'Huh …' I say as Cassie scoots off to show more people to their seats. There's a thought …

'It's busy tonight,' I say to Frank as we get ready to start the show.

'Yeah, I uploaded a vid to lolz.com and they made it clip of the week,' he says, casually, when actually it's huge.

'Explains why we've got almost twice as many in!' Cassie beams.

I congratulate Frank but can't help think about the hustle hyperdrive I went into just to get our gig listed on *lolz*. And just like that his stand-up is on the landing page of UK comedy's online home? Jeez. Plus, even though half the crowd are here for him, happy to enjoy his banker material, he's still scribbling new ideas? Frank's grind puts mine to shame, always looking for ways to level up. I do have joke ideas and occasionally even write them down, but then I think, why unpick my solid routine for the sake of squeezing in a couple of new punchlines?

'So, what are you going to talk about tonight?' I ask.

Frank completes the biroed notes he's writing on his wrist before answering, 'Kids. They end me.'

He can be dramatic. All it takes is some corridor backchat

from a pupil and they're all Rosemary's Babies. Cassie shifts on the spot, never entertained by Frank's brutal take on children. With five of her own, who can blame her.

'We spent the weekend at Callum's sister's,' Frank expands. 'They left me with all four of her litter while they nipped to the shops and the youngest headbutted me in the balls.'

'On purpose?' I ask, not sure if I'm allowed to laugh.

'Yes, on purpose!' seethes Frank. 'But when Callum and his sister came back, he started crying saying he hit his head on my bollocks! Kids, I just don't see the point of them.'

'"The point of them"?' Cassie parrots. 'There's no *point*. They're simply a glorious expression of life – in motion!'

Cassie plasters a smile on her face but can't mask the insult felt. I put myself in reverse and back the hell away from this convo. I don't have kids, I'm not pregnant (unless dreaming of sex can get you up the duff) and I've no plans to have them any time soon.

'All I'm saying is, things would be easier without them,' huffs Frank.

'Without them – have you seen *Children of Men*?' Cassie pales.

'Oh, you know what I mean,' Frank mutters, probably also realising it's best to back away from this before he gets in any deeper.

It's not unusual for him to be this ice cold but normally he's funny with it. And I start to wonder if something's happened, aside from getting nutted in his man-berries. Maybe school's wearing him down. I would ask, but with a restless audience keen for some comedy, now's not the time for a heart-to-heart.

'Shall we start the show?' I say, hoping to shift both Frank and Cassie's attention, at least for now.

Off their mumbled agreement, I crank the music to clear the funk between them and get the audience focused. Then, completing my pre-show ritual, I plump my boobs, top up my lip gloss and head to the stage, grateful I'm compering so I can swerve any lingering atmos from that hypothetical discussion which felt anything but.

'Hey, guys! How you doing?'

That draws a decent cheer, letting me know they're up for a good show – not always the case.

'Make some noise if you're in a relationship.'

There's the usual semi-enthused sound from the audience.

'OK, give me a cheer if you're single.'

The room seesaws to pure delight as the singletons pipe up. Laughter follows instantly. I briefly wonder to myself, if people are so happy being single, why do we spend so much time chasing relationships? And when I say we, of course I mean me. But there's no time to ponder and after ten minutes of crowd banter, I introduce Frank.

'What's up, mother funsters!' Frank hollers in a heavy South Korean accent and the crowd are immediately onside.

After speaking to him in his regular voice, this switch always jars. Frank gets better with every gig but sometimes it feels like he's cheating when these big laughs he gets come from what is, essentially, a gimmick. Yes, his mum and dad are from Busan but he's as London as tutting a two-minute wait for the Tube. Then again, I don't blame him. After a year ticking along on the circuit, one night he adds a Korean accent and boom, he's away.

'He's good, isn't he?' whispers Cassie.

'The best,' I reply, secretly wishing I could tease that same gasping laughter he draws from the crowd.

Frank wraps up, leaving to rapturous applause. I let the excited murmuring you always get after a great comedian die down before bringing Cassie up. The audience are going to need to adjust.

'Hellllllllo, citizens,' she begins, and the energy in the room seeps away like a slow puncture. 'You know when you're contemplating the perfection of a flower and suddenly comprehend the oneness of all things …'

I wince, thanking the gods Cassie is, at least, a great therapist.

In the darkness, my phone emits a dim glow and I peer down at it.

You free on Thursday? Would love to see you again. Will x

And I literally combust with excitement.

Chapter 5

I see Will searching for me among the South Bank crowds but I stay half-hidden behind an ice-cream van. Man, I haven't had butterflies like this in a minute. It's only two days since he texted me at Wisecrackers but that's been more than enough time for my nerves to go into overdrive. Just then he spots me, and comes striding over.

'Abi!' He smiles, face golden in the setting sun's light.

From behind his back he pulls a posy – tiny pink and purple flowers crowding into a dome, and presents them to me like we're in *Bridgerton* or something.

'I wanted to get you these but, fun fact, the florist is on the other side by Embankment station. I'm not late, am I?'

He glances at his watch, brow furrowed.

I step fully away from the Mr Whippy van, taking the flowers. 'You're bang on time and these are gorgeous. Thank you.'

And then, to calm the fluttering in my tummy, I suggest we walk.

'Great idea,' Will says, and we head off. 'By the way, sorry it took a sec to get back to you.'

'No worries,' I shrug, a casual mask for the somersaulting doubts.

'I had to switch nights.'

'You were on duty?' I ask, flattered he's changed his work rota for me.

'Something like that,' Will says as we reach our destination.

The BFI bar is moodily lit, stylish and way swankier than any cinema bar I've been to. I want to say as much but don't want to sound like a heathen so I just go, 'Nice.'

'Drink?' asks Will, as he catches the bartender's attention.

'Whatever you're having,' I say, burying my grimace when he hands me a bottle of fancy IPA.

'Eyes, eyes, eyes,' Will says, as we toast.

The plink of our glasses connecting is satisfying. I take a sip and am surprised this IPA stuff tastes all right though I hate that I'm concerned it isn't lady-like enough. I'm a lady that likes it and that's all that should matter, but what if drinking beers makes him see me more as a mate, someone to discuss Arsenal's right flank problem with, or which barber does the best fade, rather than seeing me as his new boo?

'You okay, Abi?' Will asks.

'Yeah, it's just …'

'You eyeing up where to have a cheeky lunchtime dance?'

I slap his knee. 'I don't share those stories with everyone, you know.'

He catches my hand, sending those butterflies into a frenzy.

'Me neither,' he says, his grasp becoming tender, as though he already knows his touch floors me.

I try to extract my hand but instead of letting go, his clasp becomes firmer, the exchanged body heat making my head spin.

'I'll let go if you promise to be gentler with me,' he says, the corner of his mouth arching upwards.

Gentler? I want to grab at his shirt and kiss that face till he can barely breathe, and none of it will be gentle. But I resist, just about, and allow myself to enjoy his gaze, those kind eyes searching mine. And as we talk more, I try to guess his age. Perhaps a couple of years older than me, so mid-thirties, but I can see the little boy peering out from within. It's sort of beautiful. And I melt a little more.

'So, what *is* your story, Abi?' Will says, adjusting in his seat.

'You really wanna know?' I ask. 'Once I get started, it'll feel like my Audible autobiography.'

'Course I do. Tell me everything,' he replies, attention so fully on me, I almost don't know where to look.

I open my mouth but then pause. More important than telling him *my* life story, is finding out about *his*, in particular, his relationship sitch – cos I just realised, I don't know what it is.

'You already know about one of my love-life fails,' I tell him. 'Let's hear one of yours.'

Smooth, Abi, smooth.

'Where do I start?' Will shrugs.

'Easy – when did you last date someone?' I say, taking another sip of my drink.

Will lets out a big puff of air and after a hell of a long time, says, 'I haven't really been with anyone for …' he turns his bottle around on its beer mat, 'over a year.'

He seems almost surprised by the answer which causes

him to drift off, the initial fun of the question snuffed out. I want to course-correct. 'And you're in shock that *I'm* single? Respectfully, a guy like you getting no action for one whole trip around the sun – scandalous.'

This brings him back and we laugh. His is modest, mine relieved I didn't completely kill the mood.

'Kat and I broke up but it was … it's complicated.'

I nod sympathetically, knowing the curse of a situationship all too well. I was in one where I only found out it was over because he changed his FaceViber relationship status to 'engaged' – and it wasn't to me.

'Divorce, was it?' I blurt, instantly scolding myself for the lack of chill in my question.

Will lets out an *I wish* snort and now I'm confused. So how complicated are we talking? Celibately complicated, polyamorously complicated? I suddenly sense I'm staring as I think of other varieties of complicated, so I take a glug of beer.

'We never married but separating wasn't easy. When we split I had to buy my own place. That's why I took a second job – at the Disraeli.'

Okay, that makes sense. I speculate that this Kat must have screwed him over financially as well as emotionally which is why he gets that faraway look every time the topic of home life comes up.

'So, if the Disraeli is your second job, what's your first?' I ask, suspecting a change in subject will be welcome.

'Music teacher,' Will says, sipping his beer. 'How about you? When did you start doing comedy?'

I hesitate at his deflection, now feeling as though even Will's career might be a sensitive topic, but I decide to leave it. 'Just before my second year at uni. Once I'd done my first open mic, I knew it was the only thing I wanted to do.'

'That must have felt amazing, finding your passion like that,' Will says, his eyes filled with something I can't quite name: hope, longing – or maybe it's just dust. 'So, what's your style?'

'Hmm?'

'Your style. Your brand of comedy?'

The question halts me. I dunno. If it's funny, I say it.

'Well, I'm kind of a ... one liner, social commentary, stream of consciousness gagsmith type,' I say, labouring the seasoned veteran vibe.

Will's expression flickers but he's sweet enough not to call out my blatant BS.

'You know who I really like,' he offers, changing tack.

My toes curl in dread. If he names someone naff or a magician, I'm out.

'Who?' I ask, braced to grab my stuff and exit stage left.

'Yolanda B. Rockwell.'

My eyes go wide and I want to weep. He has evoked my shero, the beautiful black American powerhouse that is the Queen of Comedy. I swear down, if you look in the mirror and say her name five times, you instantly get funnier. I've devoured all her stand-up specials and practically know each one, line by line.

'I stan her so bad,' I say, and Will offers his palm for a high five.

I slam my hand against his and he winces.

'Sorry! But I frickin' love Yolanda B. Rockwell and I am freakishly strong.'

'No worries,' Will says, pretending to massage life back into his poor hand. 'What's that bit she did about people walking in LA?'

Immediately, I adopt my best Yolanda B. Rockwell pose, chin up, looking down towards the audience. *'In LA, when someone tries to cross the street, LA folks be like, "Look at this asshole – walking. Hey! I'm driving here. Selfish jackass."'*

Will wags his finger in recognition.

'That's it!' He laughs. 'Man, she went hard on LA.'

'She's a New Yorker. What do you expect? How about the dogs-in-handbags bit?' I say and Will instantly gives me his best Yolanda.

'I've never seen so many dogs in purses. Scrappy doos thinking they flyin'. Dogs be like, "Damn, the air up here is rarefied."'

Through my laughter, I applaud Will's perfect recollection.

'I should remember that routine,' he says, 'I saw it live.'

'You saw *LA Loca*?' I ask, my excitement sparking.

Will nods, proud.

'Man, I would have killed to get tickets for that show.'

'Well, next time she does a UK tour, we'll have to go,' says Will.

I try to speak but all I manage is a squeaky, 'Yeah,' because, that's tenth date talk. That's boyfriend–girlfriend talk. That's I'm-bang-into-you talk that makes me swell as I think of me and Will doing 'stuff' together, making plans.

'Is your act anything like hers?' he asks, reaching for his beer.

'Kind of,' I lie, cos in reality I'm light years from Yolanda's radical sets about protests and police and justice. I'm all about boys and biscuits and bus queues.

'To be fair,' I add, trying not to sound defensive, 'I don't think it would suit me to do the whole black power, be-the-change thing.'

'I get that. I meant more like, I don't know, speaking your truth,' Will says.

Speaking my truth? Where do people get this idea that comedy and truth are besties? It's called stand-up comedy not stand-up news. I rein in my frustration, not wanting to get argumentative, especially as he just wants to know more about something that's important to me.

'I love making people laugh and I love being on stage. That's it,' I say, then reach for the menu and a change in topic. 'I need food – whaddya want to eat?'

Thankfully, Will bites and we move on to more important things, like how many dishes to order.

The rest of the night, we drink more beers, pick at our food and bounce around safe, first-date topics with a flow that's lovely. As we speak, I can't help notice just how intoxicating Will's gaze is, his full attention on me almost cleansing.

He moves closer, so close I can feel his breath.

'Can I kiss you?' he asks, now so close, a faint breeze could bring our lips together.

'Yeah, I'd like that,' I whisper and as my eyes close and we connect, I swear, I feel ten thousand volts surge through me.

Now *that* was a kiss worth waiting for.

Chapter 6

A few days later, as tradition dictates, I'm at my parents' house for one of our obligatory family lunches. I can think of better ways to spend my Sunday but, taking a deep breath, I remind myself, however bad it gets, it'll be over in a few hours. Sliding my key into the lock, I step into the hallway.

My shoulders feel heavier when I'm here. It's the one place I'm always reminded that, in some way, I'm a disappointment – guaranteed, like a Royal Mail delivery that needs a signature. My dad's relaxed but Mum is – a lot. She's like, two *first-class* degrees clever, always impeccably put together (we once argued for forty-five minutes about whether business casual was a thing; it's one or the other, according to her), and she runs the most efficient household ever. Some homes have give-and-take, where each person's strong suit gets to shine. Not here. Mum isn't just in charge, she's the Queen. And Dad, well, he's merely a loyal subject. My phone pings with a text.

Hey you, looking forward to seeing you soon. Wxx

And there go those butterflies again, taking me right back to our date on Thursday. The whole night was unreal, but that kiss was … next level. I go to tap out a reply but I'm late so I just write:

Abi is typing …

I love that we already have an in-joke. This is our way of saying, *I would write more but for now, I'm with you, even though I'm not with you.* I savour Will's text for a moment longer before stuffing my phone in my bag.

'It's me,' I call from the hallway as I hang up my jean jacket.

'Abioye?' Mum says from the living room.

Literally our whole family is in this house. Which 'me' does she think it is – that polite burglar who announces themselves before raiding your jewellery box?

'No, Mum. It's Nelson Mandela.'

I say this in what I think is a murmur, but somehow …

'I heard that.'

That's the other thing about Mum, she has the hearing of a German Shepherd.

'You're late.'

And she keeps time like a 1940s train station master. If my key doesn't hit the lock on or before 1.30 p.m., I'm condemned to the lateness naughty step. Okay, granted it's just coming up for two but allow me, man. Meeting Mum's standards of personal presentation adds bare minutes to my prep time. If I rock up wearing creased anything, it's a two-hour lecture on how King Charles even irons his shoe laces.

'We're in the family room,' Mum calls out, her posh name for the living room.

Entering, I soften as I see my nephew and niece, Caleb and Ayesha, scrawling in their respective colouring-in books. No shade but it still baffles me that Caleb is the eldest. Because while Ayesha is crafting her very own Mona Lisa, Caleb's creation is a confusion of blues, reds and oranges so far outside the lines you can barely see them. Maybe someday we'll be able to pass this off as a Basquiat and make a small fortune.

'Abi. Perfect timing,' says Dad who's crouching down with the kids, gently pointing out to Caleb that human faces tend not to be royal blue.

My heart smiles, seeing Dad down on the floor, hands-on, as opposed to Mum who always engages from her single seater – up on high.

'Perfect timing isn't arriving moments before lunch is served, is it, Samuel?' Mum says, her pleasant tone emulsified with the usual scowl. 'You reward lateness and she'll be late every month. Oh, hang on.'

Mum raises a sarcastic finger and I roll my eyes, kissing her forehead with a sweet, 'Love you too, Mum.'

'If Kemi can arrive on time, with husband and children in tow, I'd expect *you*, who remains unencumbered by such grown-up responsibilities, to have no problem, Abioye,' Mum says, and underlines the point by gesturing towards my lil sis and her oh-so-punctual family.

'Yep,' I nod.

I don't rise because this is all part of the Akingbade ritual. Me, Kemi, Felix and the kids traipse out of London to visit Mum and Dad one Sunday every month, I'm always late, Kemi's always mad early because she's the Goody-Two-Shoes of the outfit, Mum makes snide comments, Dad tries to paper over the cracks, we have lunch, it's all kinds of awkward, then we retreat to our corners until the next time. Yay.

Kemi pushes herself out of her seat, giving me an apologetic shake of the head on Mum's behalf, and we hug.

'All right, sis,' she says.

'Special K,' I say, squeezing her and swinging her side to side which I know she loves.

'Stop!' She giggles and I rock her harder.

It's only when we pull away I clock she's wearing a weave – or is it a wig? – that's weirdly in the exact same style as she does her own hair.

'What's with the—' I start, pointing at her head.

'Nothing,' she says, cutting me off. 'What's new with you?'

Noted, I think to myself and park that convo for later. It must be juicy if Kemi's not willing to discuss it in front of Mum who she normally tells everything. Success or misdemeanour, Kemi spills all because whatever it is, it's always met with motherly praise.

That's how it's been since we were kids. One time, Kemi tried to climb a kitchen cupboard, even got a foot on the bottom shelf, until the whole damn thing came crashing down. Ground rice flour, spice jars, tins of tomatoes, everywhere. Miraculously, she was unscathed – other than being covered in gari powder but she was terrified of how Mum would react. Thing is, when Kemi did 'fess up, Mum just tutted and said, 'I've been wanting to get rid of that unit for years.'

I remember my mouth falling open like an empty pillowcase. If that had been me, it would have been a different story.

I let out a snort at the memory and Mum corrects with a quiet, 'Manners.'

But before I can reply, she claps her hands which tells us it's time to decamp to the dining room. As we go through, accompanied by a hum of superficial small talk, me and Kemi hang back and, looping a hand in her arm, I ask, 'You okay?' super quiet due to Mum's sonar hearing.

Kemi nods but her eyes dance with nervous excitement. Oh, I can't *wait* to hear what's going on.

Once seated, we are the uber-polite antithesis of those TV commercial families where everyone reaches across each other to grab their favourite dishes, kids screeching, adults enjoying friendly banter.

'Samuel,' Mum says, gesturing for Dad to carve the lamb which, as always, she has incinerated out of a disproportionate fear of food poisoning.

I look at the charred remains, daring any part of this blackened carrion to be undercooked.

'How are things at work?' Mum asks as we diligently pass dishes.

I bite my lip, wanting to answer, but we all know she's not asking me.

'Good. I've moved to the social housing team which I'm excited about,' Kemi explains.

And marking it with a celebratory wig? I want to say.

At hearing Kemi's news, Mum's hand goes to her chest with a concerned, 'Oh.'

From her reaction you'd think Kemi had just announced she's going on a kangaroo bollock diet, not helping house low-income families. I want to say as much, but even I know better.

'Excellent,' says Dad. 'Great way to make a difference. An architectural firm needs these projects to keep its soul healthy.'

'Exactly,' nods Kemi, half her attention on stopping Caleb wave his knife around like he's a conductor.

'Yes, of course,' Mum concurs with a reluctance I enjoy.

There's a plank-rigid silence while everyone gives Mum a chance to ask about *my* work, even though she never does.

'And how's the comedy world treating you?' Dad finally asks with enthusiasm for two.

I milk the attention, taking my time answering.

'Oh, you know, not bad. Still trying to get paid gigs. There's a promoter, Dina, I told you about. I think she might crack soon.'

A loaded, 'Hmmm,' escapes Mum which Dad masks with even more encouragement.

'Keep going, darling. What is meant for you will not go by you.'

'So, how do you expect to get these "paid gigs"?' Mum asks, the words escaping almost against her will.

I'm so taken aback to hear her talk about my comedy, I'm not even primed with a sarky comeback.

'Just keep doing good open-mic sets and hopefully get offered something.'

'Ah. So, you're engaging the fingers-crossed methodology. I wish I had utilised that for my PhD. It would have saved twelve years of study,' she says, dismissiveness dripping from every word.

'No,' I say, with surprising calm, 'I'm using the method of – opportunities will find me if I'm good at my job.'

A stalemate descends and we both decide to say no more.

'And of romance? Any amour floating in the ether?' Dad asks, attempting to clear the scorched air.

Sometimes I forget how bizarre my mum and dad's turns of phrase can be. I go to speak but all words catch as I see my mum's face distort into cynical knowing. *Of course Abi isn't seeing anyone. Every relationship she's ever had collapses into ashen waste.* That's actually what she called one of my break-ups once.

'Nothing much to report,' I say with a throwaway air.

I'm actually dying to tell the fam about me and Will but I don't because I'm not in the mood for Mum's judgement. Once the conversation moves on though, I smile at Dad and the glint in his eye lets me know he gets it. I don't think of myself as a daddy's girl but the way his smile and words soothe, I've got to be. Kemi can have Mum. I've got this champ.

Across the table, Felix eats, a methodical graze that ensures he minds his own beeswax. He does everything with quiet contentment, the perfect complement to Kemi's zigzaggy energy. Their dynamic is similar to Mum and Dad's but, for some reason, theirs works. They fit. Kemi is the sergeant major and Felix, perhaps he's the mess cook or maybe the chaplain. But the difference between him and my dad is, Felix seems all right with his set-up, letting Kemi lead. Dad, though, seems worn down at times. As he saws through Mum's roast lamb, there's a tiredness in his eyes, like if he was offered a medically induced coma for a week, he'd take it. I give his wrist a squeeze. Without looking up he lets out a little laugh. It's almost nothing but tells me he's doing all right.

'Caleb, why don't you tell Grandma and Grandpap what's been happening at school?' Felix says.

Caleb gawps at his dad as though it's opening night of a play he never got the script for, face blank, mind far from having to deliver progress reports.

'Tyler Worrell's been diagnosed with AC/DC,' he says, hoping this morsel of primary school gossip will satisfy.

'ADHD,' Felix gently corrects as Kemi gives a withered smile and moves the last of her gambling chips to Ayesha being the brainiac of the family.

Around about six, we start saying our goodbyes, Mum nestling inside the door as she doesn't want to catch a chill – even though it's been a steady twenty-five degrees all day. The rest of us amble to Kemi's car and I fall in beside my little sis.

'So … spill,' I demand with cheeky delight.

'What?' Kemi says, pretending not to know what I'm chatting about, tossing the car keys to Felix.

'Babe, don't kid a kidder. The barnet?'

Kemi darts a look back to the house. The front door's now closed, Mum standing like a sentinel at the living-room window, throwing the odd regal wave at the kids.

'Not now. Come over and I'll show you,' Kemi says in a subdued but excited whisper.

I'm beside myself with curiosity.

'Okay,' I say, 'but I swear, if you're emigrating or starting a band, I want in.'

Kemi laughs as the kids chase each other around the car, their shrieks echoing up and down the street. 'We better get these two home. Come over, yeah?'

I start to pretend-sing, bottom lip quivering, our imaginary band already primed for its first show. 'You making jollof?'

Kemi gives a weary chuckle as she gets Caleb and Ayesha into the car. 'Okay, fine.'

'Yaass!' I beam, throwing down an old-school Milly Rock in celebration which turns into a wave to Felix.

He gives me a solid wave in return and then I go to the back window of the car and make faces at the kids right up until they pull away.

At the house, Mum has disappeared from the window and I wonder for a moment about going back inside. I fantasise about a quiet chat in the garden, blanket over our knees, enjoying a glass of wine, me telling her about my work, about this amazing new man in my life, how we met, how he makes me feel, how good our first date was. I imagine Mum sharing heartfelt, hard-won wisdom, wishing us well and telling me how much she's looking forward to meeting this young man. Warmed by the thought, I take a half-step towards the house when I hear Mum tap-tap-tapping on the window.

'You're standing on the grass. Mind the lawn!' comes her muted voice from behind the very finest double glazing.

I take an exaggerated step back onto the path, salute goodbye and march to the station, glad to be heading home.

Chapter 7

It's taken three gigs, two dates with Will and plenty of Primarni retail therapy to decompress from that family Sunday lunch despite it being over a week ago. In fact, it was so intense, I was even glad to get back to my data-entry day job, and that's saying something. If I was being generous, I'd call this work meditative, though brain-numbing is probably more accurate. I peep over my computer to see my boss, Jill, doing another lap of our tiny office. She's searching for her glasses, which are perched on her head – standard. I shiver at the thought that if comedy doesn't work out, that could be me in ten years' time.

Yeah, I tried to make it as a stand-up but I prefer the security of working in this windowless mausoleum of despair.

I look across the room where my two colleagues, who sit in data-entry purgatory with me, seem far less concerned about their fates than I am. Rahima's here on a gap year though I can't think what this would be a satisfying gap from – Guantanamo, maybe. And Bobbie, who's probably in his early twenties but talks like a world-weary eighty-year-old – well, I can't quite figure out his story but everything seems to revolve around conspiracy theories.

I check the clock again hoping it's finally five so I can get out of here. It's a big night tonight because Will's coming to watch me perform stand-up – for the very first time. And not at any old gig – at Wisecrackers. I need to prep – as in freshen up and sort my edges out. This heat is a killer for my hair. I want everything to be perfect. In fact, I've been more worried about him coming to the show tonight than I have about when me and him are actually going to make things bedroom official. Yup, two and a bit weeks in and we still haven't done it but, to be fair, the more I get to know him, the more I can tell, whenever it happens, it has to feel right, special. I'm dying to have a proper talk with Kems about it but what with work, kids and life, we still haven't had time to catch up. In truth, I already know what she'll say – *Nike it, Abi! Just do it.* She says that about pretty much everything even though she's way more cautious in her own life. Felix had to propose three times before she said yes.

So, without Kemi to consult, I make an executive decision to hold off on sex until Will and I have been together at least a month. Siri tells me that's fourteen days, five hours and thirty-eight minutes away – not that I'm bothered ... I shut down my computer, say my goodnights to the others and wave to Jill who looks like she's working but I can see the Solitaire screen reflected in her specs. I switch up my outfit in the loos going for a black romper blinged with bare gold accessories ... well, gold-plated. I'm not on that *ShowTime at the Athena* money yet. I wouldn't normally do all this for a Wisecrackers night but cos Will's going to be there, I'm going the extra mile, even dry-shaving my pits – which stings like a mother. Clark Kent makes quick changes look so much easier. Anyway, once I'm done, I head for the show.

At the venue, I channel my nervous energy into setting up the room. As usual, Frank and Cassie arrive a good thirty minutes after me. Frank doesn't even bother with excuses while Cassie apologises over and over, explaining she forgot she'd sold her car and spent forty minutes looking for it.

As she tells the story, I crack up laughing, while Frank snorts, 'You should do a bit about that on stage!'

Cassie looks baffled. 'Is it funny? I nearly reported it stolen. The new owner would have been livid.'

Frank yelps and I bend double, as Cassie shrugs, no clue as to the comedy gold she's spinning. I needed that. It's defo shaken some nerves free. As our laughter subsides, I decide this could be a good moment to slip in a mention about my special guest without it being a biggie. 'Oh, I forgot to say, Will's coming to the gig tonight.'

Frank sits up straight, face instantly contorted into arch intrigue. Honestly, I'd have got a more low-key response if I'd said I know who shot Tupac.

'Well, well, well,' he says, eyes wide.

'Oooh, I can't wait to meet him – what's his star sign … and time of birth?' Cassie coos, pulling out her astrology book.

'Cassie,' I say, trying not to dampen her puppy-dog enthusiasm, 'maybe save the past-lives regressions until you've met him a couple of times.'

'Yes, you're right. I'll just do a general birth chart. We can still work out compatibility from that,' Cassie explains, going back to her book.

'You'll have Freud spinning in his grave,' says Frank.

'New age and therapy can be bedfellows, Francis,' Cassie says as her eyes sparkle with a new thought. 'Abi, do you have a strand of his hair? Actually, never mind – I wonder if Thea has loose tea behind the bar.'

Before I can answer, she disappears next door.

I turn to Frank and a broad grin oozes from him.

'Go on,' I say, hand on hip.

But Frank says nothing, instead breaking into a tuneless rendition of 'It Must Be Love'. I kiss my teeth busying myself with setting up the welcome table but, once Frank's attention is elsewhere, I smile. And when I see Will walk in and my body starts to glow, I think to myself, Frank might be right.

'So, Abi tells us you're a music teacher?' Cassie says at the end of the evening as she lopsidedly stacks chairs.

'That's right,' Will replies, discreetly straightening Cassie's pile before adding more chairs and dragging them to the side wall.

Even though Cassie insisted we leave her and Frank to the post-gig get-out, Will wouldn't hear of it and watching him help out, I'm buzzing. How a guy treats your friends speaks volumes and Will's saying something epic right now.

'Frank's a teacher as well, aren't you, Frank?' Cassie says, conducting the conversation.

'Year head,' Frank corrects.

'Acting,' Cassie chuckles and Frank congeals at the accidental slap-down.

'Cool, what year?' asks Will.

'Eight,' Frank says, pride returning.

'Fun but tough, eh. Caught between being a kid and a teen. My girl's in the middle of that right now,' Will says with a nod of acknowledgement.

'Your girls? I thought you taught at a boys' school?' I ask, divvying up the door take.

'Oh – yeah. No … Sometimes we have year eights from the girls' school. We've got a bigger music department. They've got a great science block so …'

Frank cocks his head, no doubt looking to claw back some points. He's so competitive, even when it comes to being the most teachery teacher, he still wants to win. Once the room's finally reset, we flip the lights and hand the keys back to Thea. Outside, Cassie offers everyone a lift until we remind her she doesn't have a car so instead, she and Frank head off leaving me and Will.

'That was really sweet of you,' I say, pulling on the edge of his jacket, its suede smooth and inviting between my fingers.

'Anything for you, Abi,' he says, gently bringing his hand to my chin. 'You know that, right?'

We kiss and I press into him, his warmth sending my blood pounding in my veins. We explore each other with gentle, light caresses and I am almost delirious. This evening just couldn't have gone any better. My set went brilliantly, Frank and Cassie really liked Will and now here we are, so hungry for each other, I bet if we asked Siri what to do next, even she'd say *get a room*. And I wonder, should I bin my plan to wait, make tonight the night we officially go horizontal?

As we walk from the bus stop to my place, Will's hand never lets go of mine.

'You were brilliant tonight. I loved watching you. I love seeing you in your element. You're so at home.'

I sigh with happiness, as my bucking insecurities settle. I hadn't wanted to ask Will but I've been desperate to know what he thought. 'Thanks. I just love it and I know I'm not the greatest writer but, in time—'

He cuts me off. 'Abi, you don't have to explain. You're happy and that makes me happy.'

I blink these words in. I don't think anyone, except my dad, has ever told me my joy brings them the same and it's the most beautiful thing I've ever heard.

'Thank you,' I hear myself whisper.

'Thank *you* for letting me come and watch. I know it's a big thing …' he says before kissing me again.

And for the first time I'm actually grateful I dated Sam. If I hadn't, I would never have met this amazing human.

We reach my flat, anticipation leaving me ready to burst as the sparks we started outside Wisecrackers grow into a silent inferno.

'This is me,' I say, coming to a stop.

We draw close, lips meeting for the most satiating kiss.

Will pulls away first, eyes looking down into mine, our fingers entwined.

'Abi, you take my breath away.'

With my free hand, I pull out my keys, letting them jangle tantalisingly between us. 'You coming up?'

Will wavers, eyes flickering back towards the main road. 'I've gotta go …'

And immediately I deflate. Why come all this way, to the brink of my threshold, only to leave?

'Oh,' I mumble.

'Tonight has been amazing but I've got a really early start,' he says, before kissing me one more time and whispering, 'I'll see you soon, yeah?'

'Yeah,' I say, as I watch him head back down the street, wondering what I did wrong.

Once he's disappeared out of view, I jam my key in the lock. Good job I've got a new set of batteries, I moan to myself as I head inside.

Chapter 8

It's been nearly a fortnight since our doorstep kiss and I've been on four more dates with Will – dinner, some mad bar with rocking horses (never again), an aborted cinema trip (subtitles! I thought he knew me) and a walk along the Grand Union Canal – yet we're still not under-the-cover lovers. Waiting this long is a record for me but though my frustration is off the charts, one good thing is, I defo know being into each other is not the problem. I'm so into him and *he's* into me. I roll the thought around, still as novel as that evening our eyes first locked. I cross everything that, even if we don't get down to it soon, we at least move along a couple of bases this weekend. The sun's shining and I'm hoping a lazy afternoon picnic will set the mood. As I enter Clissold Park, I spot Will carrying an actual wicker basket and feel self-conscious of my hastily cobbled together haul – strawberries, hummus, pitta bread and wine stuffed, unceremoniously, into a Tesco's bag-for-life.

'Abi,' he smiles and when I reach him, we draw together for a suitable-in-a-public-place kiss.

'What's up, Yogi?' I grin, pointing at the basket.

'Easy, Boo Boo,' Will laughs.

'So what've you brought?' I say, trying to get a sneaky peek.

Will pulls the basket out of view. 'You'll see. Let's find a spot first. Over by those trees is perfect.'

And in true London style, we hurry over, making sure no other couple nabs our space – or worse, a family with kids – but then I notice an ice-cream van and all bets are off.

'There's no queue!' I yelp, doing a sharp ninety-degree turn and dragging Will with me.

'Ice cream – *before* the picnic?'

'Babes, there's never a wrong time for ice cream.'

A flash of a smile later and we're enjoying a lush vanilla cone with two extra flakes. Will grins as he rests an arm around my shoulder.

'I love it. People just can't help but like you, Abi. Extra flakes, drinks on the house at your gig ...'

'That's nothing. One time I was at this boujie private members' place and I ended up doing free shots with this waiter,' I say, grinning.

'Oh, yeah?' Will laughs. 'Good-looking, was he?'

'Man was peng, bruv. A proper ten,' I say, drawing him in for a deep kiss.

Finally we pull apart and head towards the dappled shade of an old oak to claim our spot. Will unfolds his big blue blanket and starts unloading his neatly wrapped food parcels.

'Brought these especially for you. Happy one month anniversary,' he says, handing me a Tupperware of chicken wings.

I crack the lid, letting their delicious aroma escape.

'Has it been a month – already?' I gasp, like I haven't been counting the days since the Disraeli.

Will smiles. 'Well, one month next week. But, I couldn't wait to celebrate it. Meeting you was a good, good day …'

'It's been a good month, an amazing month.'

'I never thought I'd feel this way and it's only the start,' Will says, his sweet breath tickling my skin.

I so badly want to tell him I love him, that he's my morning thought and last goodnight, that he's with me all the time and I've imagined so many magic moments together but … is it too soon? Is that too much?

'I love you.'

My heart thunders in my chest, not sure I heard him right, but I did. He said it and I feel as though I'm floating.

'I love you too,' I say and as we share a *not*-suitable-for-public-places kiss, I sink into the joy of everything feeling right and very, *very* special.

As the sun arcs over our heads, we settle into each other like nestling kittens, my head resting on his tummy while he puts together a Spotify playlist. Soon mellow beats fade out the park noise – that is until a group of kids start splashing around in the paddling pool, their yelps piercing my bliss. I prop myself up and look over.

'How do you soundproof a paddling pool? Or move it to the other side of the park?'

Will lets out a half-laugh but his face clearly hasn't got the memo that I'm joking.

'If you were a parent, you'd soon get used to it.'

'Easy for you to say. You're surrounded by them at work. Not for me, mate,' I wince and flop back down onto his tummy.

But from behind my shades, I can see Will's not smiling with me. His mood has shifted. If I'm honest, I've noticed it a few times, a cloud that moves in, taking him away until he catches himself and slowly comes back. I'm sure it's nothing but doubt circles. Am I overdoing it with the banter? And I do laugh at my own jokes – a lot. Urrgh. That would annoy me too. Or perhaps, I gulp, he's already regretting saying the L-word. I shake my head and snuggle into him, more for reassurance than anything else. I can't let doubt sweep away the magic of those three little words so easily. He's not acting like someone who's about to enrol in the Abi's-too-much club … But then, what *is* up with him?

'Will!'

We both sit up to see where the voice is coming from. A few yards away, a lady with thick box braids and a massive grin approaches.

'Will!' she calls again, waving as she walks.

He flinches as this whirlwind of colour, braids and teeth heads our way.

'How are you?' she gushes.

'Great, thanks,' Will answers, taking a more formal position – if that's possible on a picnic blanket.

The woman hovers, waiting for him to introduce me, then thrusts out her hand.

'Miss Gilhooly. Sharon. Sharon Gilhooly.'

'Well, hello there, Miss Gilhooly. Sharon. Sharon Gilhooly,' I say, shaking her hand.

Instantly, she laughs, head pulsing side to side like a baby being fed Stilton.

'Very funny!' she snorts, jangling her metric ton of beads and bangles. 'I must still be in school mode. It's Miss Gilhooly to the kids but it's the weekend so, heeeeere's Shar*on*!'

I warm to her immediately, laughing at the quirky pronunciation of her name. She and Will chat amiably about the weather and the approaching school term end while I listen, loving the fact that this is the first person from Will's life that I've met – and I like her. She looks too young to be a former teacher of Will's, unless she started teaching when she was, like, eight, so I decide they must work together.

'And how are *things*?' she asks with a caring tone before bellowing in the direction of the paddling pool, 'Persephone, take your foot off your brother's head. I won't tell you again!'

'Good, thanks,' says Will, moving his hand to mine.

'Oh, wonderful!' she says, clocking this and slapping her thigh. 'Well, you two lovebirds don't need this old hen interrupting your turtle-doving! Really happy for you, Will. About time.' And her face crinkles with care.

'Cheers, Shar*on*,' Will smiles, giving her no more chat to latch on to.

Taking the hint, she rocks on her heels and puffs, 'Riiiight, better get back to my two before Persephone gets us banned from the paddling pool!'

She turns to walks away but then swivels back.

'Oh, and by the way, if your Esme is anything like her sister Elle was, I can't wait to have her in my class next term! They're both a credit to you and Kat.'

And with that, Shar*on* trundles off towards her noisy kids.

I pause – did she just say what I think she said? My … boyfriend, my love, my before-anyone-else, has two kids that he has somehow failed to mention? Will and I sit in silence as I digest the acrid taste of her parting words.

After an eternity, he speaks. 'So, we should probably talk.'

'Actually, I think I'm gonna head.'

I stand to leave, so angry and hurt that I yank the picnic blanket from under him even though it's his. Everything is tight; my lips, my eyes, even my nose has tension – everything except my legs, which have turned to jelly, feeling like what was stable has been whipped from beneath them.

'Abi, please let me explain,' Will pleads. 'I wanted to tell you but I just didn't ... I didn't know how.'

'Well, letting me find out from their teacher should have been bottom of your list,' I hiss, turning to escape.

'You're right but I just wasn't sure how you felt about kids – even the sound of them enjoying themselves seems to annoy you,' he says, gesturing towards the pool.

'That was a joke,' I wail, vaguely aware of onlookers but frankly, not caring.

Will bows his head. 'Look, I'm sorry. I—'

I stop him with a snort, fixing my gaze on anything but him in an attempt to contain my rage. And I'm double angry now: once for the secret and again for him ruining what was turning out to be a really special day. I finally look back and see he's holding up his phone, showing a picture of two young faces, pressed together.

Is he serious right now? I don't want to look at family pics, I want to dash his stupid phone in the water, but somehow I calm just enough to allow my eyes to drift towards the screen.

'This is them,' he says, cautiously. 'That's Elle. She's the oldest. Thirteen. Looks like me, sounds like her mum, and the other is Esme. She's six.'

Their complexions are fair – which would make Kat white or mixed-race like Will. In Elle I see his lean physique and his smile, in Esme, unbridled joy. Damn it, she's cute as a button but I refuse to let Will see that in my face – which I fix in stony determination. I want to leave and Will senses it.

'Abi, I wasn't hiding them from you. I just didn't know how to bring it up. It's not like we met online, my life laid out in bullet points. It was all going so well, and I didn't want to spoil things.'

He rubs his face as though trying to erase his mistakes.

'Yeah well, you did,' I say, caught between wanting to bolt and take him in my arms.

Man, I hate this.

'Look, I'm not asking anything from you. Maybe, just take it one step at a time. You could get to know them, as friends, and go from there.'

'Get to know them? I don't even know *you*, bruv.'

Will's gaze falls. 'I just meant, we can take it slowly.'

'Slowly,' I nod. 'Feels like things are moving pretty fricking fast. This morning I was worried about which sexy undies to wear, now I'm wondering what night you have the kids.'

At this, Will shifts awkwardly and a penny loudly drops in my brain.

'On our first date, I was flattered that you said you had to change your plans. I assumed you meant your Disraeli shift but you meant childcare, didn't you?'

Will's mouth swings open but nothing comes out.

'That's what the faraway looks were whenever we discussed home life, why you said that thing to Frank about "your girl" – you meant your daughter, not your pupils. There were so many times, from jump, you could have told me but you made a choice. Not cool, Will. Not cool.'

And before he can backpedal or churn out more excuses, I walk away.

'Abi, wait,' he calls but I've already put several paces between us and I am not looking back.

Chapter 9

Since I left Will in the park on Sunday my brain has not stopped spinning. And the tedium of my survival job has provided zero distraction, instead allowing the whole sorry mess to play on a loop in my head for three days straight. It's coming up to five and so, with a relieved sigh, I shut down my computer, pushing my water bottle into my bag. Just as I'm about to leave, Jill catches me.

'Oh, Abi, before you go, you okay to confirm another month of temping?'

Ah, this question – as familiar as the pile of dusty documents on my desk, and one I always give the same answer to.

'Let me check my diary.'

I know I'll come crawling back with a yes, but deferring allows me to cling to the hope that comedic success could still be right around the corner.

'Okay. By beginning of next week, please.'

'Yep, got it,' I say, tapping my temple.

Jill leaves the office and once out of sight, I grab my jacket. It's time to escape because in a welcome respite from my life, I'm finally seeing Kemi. I've been roped into babysitting which is happy days all round. She gets childcare for her and Felix's date night and I get to spill with someone who can speak wisdom about the sitch with Will and lighten the heaviness I've had in my chest since the kid-bombshell dropped. I've been on edge and barely sleeping, mainly because when I do nod off, I have weird dreams about meeting up with Will, only each time he has another child and he's like, 'Oh, didn't I tell you about Elizabeth – and Elijah – and Ethan – and Emma?'

I really hope Kemi does talk some sense, or at least distract me, perhaps, by dishing about her hair. She's teased me with drip-fed intel for over two weeks now. It's been like waiting for a new Netflix series to drop. And so, after a fifty-minute Tube ride pressed into a tall bloke's armpit, I'm outside her flat. The door opens and just as I'm about to launch into a rant about Will, I finally see what Kemi has been hiding.

'What the rahtid—' I baulk before she raises a silencing hand.

I force my lips together to stop more curse words escaping.

'Good to see you too, Abs,' she says, leading me to the living room to say hey to the fam.

I stumble behind her, staring at the back of her *shaved* head. Kemi's never had her hair this short or, importantly, *au naturel*, like mine. Suddenly the wig makes sense. If Mum saw this, she'd have an aneurysm.

In the living room, Caleb is practising karate way too close to breakables given how clumsy he can be, while Ayesha's at the dinner table doing sums with Felix.

'Hello, Auntie Abi,' the kids chime without stopping what they're doing.

'Excuse me, you two,' Kemi says, voice heavy with correction.

Immediately they give me a proper greeting, a big squeeze that I bend to gratefully receive.

'Hello, legends,' I say, planting a kiss on both of them.

Caleb winces, playfully pulling away which is my signal to land even more kisses. The kids giggle before slipping my grasp and going back to more interesting stuff.

'Hey, Abi,' says Felix tranquil as ever.

'Hey, mate,' I say, giving him a hug before turning back to Kemi. 'Right, kitchen, please. We need to talk.'

She kisses her teeth and leads the way.

Kemi clicks on the kettle and leans back on the counter.

'So?' I ask.

She runs a hand over her hair that I'm sure still feels unfamiliar.

'I've been wanting to do it for a while and, you know, it was time,' she says with a showcase twirl.

I take her in, the new hair starting to form cute coils. It really suits her. 'You look great.'

'Think so?' Kemi's eyes light up with expectation.

'It's fierce and luckily, you don't have a weird-shaped head,' I say, planting my hands on Kemi's scalp for a closer inspection.

'What do you mean?' she says, pulling away.

'Not everyone suits a bal'head. A woman in my office got a number one cos her kid had nits. Turns out she has a head like a light bulb.'

'Abi!' Kemi says, as our laughter bends us double.

'Serious. She constantly looked like she'd had a good idea. Or like the Electric Company on a Monopoly board.'

I'm certain our howls can be heard from the living room. Kemi carefully wipes away tears to salvage the evening make-up she's probably only just finished applying.

'Joker,' she chuckles, then drops tea bags into our mugs and pours in the boiled water.

'So, when's the big reveal to Mum?' I ask and Kemi almost scalds herself at the thought.

'Er, soon,' she says, regrouping to ladle in my usual four sugars, 'so until then …'

'Mum's the word,' I concur with an elaborate mime zipping my mouth closed, attaching a padlock, securing it, putting the key in a safe and rotating the dial.

'You're so extra.'

'Always,' I say with a bow, laughing off a comment that from anyone else might sting. 'I don't blame you for keeping it on the DL though. Mum would be like, "Ah-ah. You look like a boy!"' I bellow in a heavy, Nigerian accent.

Kemi rolls her eyes at the exaggeration. 'All right, funny girl.'

'That's what she'd say, a lie?'

'Maybe,' Kemi shrugs, a tinge of sadness descending. 'But not with that accent, and you know it.'

'I know but it's funny,' I grin. 'Anyway, don't worry about what her majesty thinks. It's peng, babes.'

Kemi smiles again, running a hand over her head. 'Cheers.'

'And you've got your date-night get-up on lock. Looking good,' I say, clicking my fingers with approval at her outfit.

'Oh, stop,' Kemi says, enjoying the praise.

'Don't thank me. Thank the DNA that gave you that perfect, round head!'

'Yeah, okay,' she says before setting my mug down on the table and wrapping a hand around her own.

She looks into her tea like there's more to share, but then says, 'So come on, spill about this mystery man … who's already past tense.'

Instantly, the hurt and anger from Sunday gurgles back up. My arms splay, flapping hard against my thighs. 'He was perfect, Kems. Literally, the best thing that's ever happened to me – ever – and he had to ruin it.'

'Hmmm. Are you sure he didn't tell you about these kids but you forgot?' Kemi offers.

My eyes go skyward entertaining the idea for a microsecond until I realise it's foolishness. 'Forgot? We're not talking about pet hamsters. How would my boyfriend having two kids slip my mind?'

Kemi retracts the thought. 'Well, then he's wotless, innit. How do you withhold something like that?'

'He said he couldn't find the right time.'

As Will's defence leaves my lips, it sounds hella flimsy.

'The right time is the first time you met,' Kemi says, wedging a hand on her hip.

I think about that first time, when Will scooped me up after the disaster that was Sam and how our conversation, so warm, open and, I thought, honest, had filled me up.

'Maybe he was worried about my reaction, that we'd crash and burn before we'd even got started …'

I look at Kemi whose scowling face is a swift reality check.

'Okaaay – but then he shoulda said something on your first date, your second or absolute latest, your third! There's no excuse. These things need to be aired early doors.'

I slump back against the table – she's right. I wanted wisdom but I forgot how much the truth can sting.

'This brother's justifications are lame. What next? He doesn't tell you your yard is burning down in case you don't like fire?'

Kemi's case-closed tone makes it hard to defend Will's actions. I reach for a rationale but come up short, getting the sinking feeling her point is solid like granite.

'Sorry, big boo, but nah, you feel me? It's a lucky escape. He's only just come out of a serious LTR – with kids – which, no offence, is not your forte.'

Again, no lies there. Even when it comes to babysitting, I've only ever done it for Kemi and it was a good four years before she'd let me do that on my own.

'And lest we forget, you go down this road, you'll always be tied to the baby-mother. Plus what if you and Will have kids, you'll never share that first-time excitement because it'll be his second trip round the block.'

Kemi's arms flail as she gets even more angry at Will than I am.

'And ask yourself, will all the kids get on, will you love them all equally or will you favour your blood and what if they can tell?'

I say nothing and just stare opened-mouthed as worst-case scenarios tumble from her.

'I'm sorry to be all doom and gloom but you've got to ask these questions now or you won't know the answer until it's too late.'

I blow out a long breath. 'But if we love each other then surely …' I mutter, petering out to nothing.

'Abi, you can't start something meaningful on a rocky foundation. He tells you he loves you but he's keeping secrets – that's building your house on sand. Look at me and Felix. We tell each other everything. It's not easy and frankly, I wish I could unhear some stuff.'

'Oooh, like what?' I interject, nosiness distracting me from my pit of despair.

'He rates his movements,' Kemi shrugs and suddenly I wish I could unhear some stuff too. 'Look, point is, that's how you have a trusting relationship. Openness – no matter what.'

My sinking feeling returns. I did trust Will and now it sucks that this great guy might not be so great after all.

'I'm right, you'll see,' says Kemi, hugging me.

In the kitchen doorway, Felix appears. 'Babe, it's six thirty.'

Kemi checks her watch and tuts, discarding her half-finished tea. She takes my face in her hands and I feel my eyes prickle.

'You'll meet someone decent. Promise,' she says and I attempt a rallying agreement.

'Course. You know it.'

Once she's in the hallway though, my façade slips and I let myself fall into the chair beside me. I don't want decent. I want Will. I mean, I want a decent Will, who doesn't hide things. My head hurts; in fact, so does my stomach which has been churning ever since Ms Gilhippy opened this can of worms. Before, I called the sensation in my tummy butterflies but right now I think it's moths – feasting on the tattered remains of what was.

Fifteen minutes later, the kids are in their PJs and Kemi and Felix have their coats on, ready to leave. Kemi catches Caleb in the middle of a roundhouse kick and cups his chin in her hand. 'Teeth by?'

'Seven forty-five.'

'Bed by?'

'Eight o'clock.'

'Lights out by?'

'Eight thirty!' screeches Ayesha, wrapping her arms around her mum's legs before returning to the fleet of dolls and trucks on the floor.

'Ready?' says Felix and Kemi hovers.

'You going to be okay?' she asks me with a forced brightness.

She doesn't need to worry. These kids are my blood. The worst thing that'll happen on my watch is a sugar rush.

'Yes! Now go, man,' I say, shooing Kemi out of the door.

'Okay, sorry. And look, I know it's a gig night so really appreciate this. All right, bye, bye, bye, guys!' Kemi calls into the flat as Felix coaxes her towards the communal corridor.

The front door closes and I hear the elevator ping as it heads to the ground floor.

'Okay, who wants popcorn?' I say, clapping my hands.

The kids yelp their agreement and we spend the next hour chomping through a bowl of salt and sweet kernels in front of the TV. Then, out of nowhere, mid-Corrie, Caleb and Ayesha hop off the sofa and start putting away all their things as though Kemi's guiding them via remote control. Toys are returned to their storage, homework slipped into school bags, the popcorn bowl cleared away and a minute before quarter to, they're in the bathroom cleaning their teeth.

I marvel but I don't know why. Kemi runs an even stricter and tighter ship than our mum. The downside is I never want to get on the wrong side of her but the plus, babysitting Caleb and Ayesha is a doddle. And from there, it's not a great leap to wonder about Will's kids and if they're the same. Not that I'll ever babysit them, but still, I'm curious. Can they peel themselves away from a screen, finish every morsel on their plate without the threat of a withheld dessert, or say 'please' and 'thank you' like they were their first words? I mean, if they were like that, then sure, it would all be so easy. But even if I could get over Will's huge screw-up, I can't become a … stepmum. Even the word is alien to me. I travel light, no commitments – always have. Once I start getting paid gigs, which could be anytime now, I'll be travelling up and down the country and won't be around to be step-anything to anyone. Besides, aren't stepmums old and bitter? Look at how they're repped in fairy tales. In *Hansel and Gretel*, the stepmother is a biiiitch. In *Snow White* – biiiitch. And in *Cinderella*, she's a mahooosive biiiitch. No, it's not for me. I'm much better as an auntie. People love aunts. Aunts do well in fairy tales and on screen. I mean, there's Auntie Em in the *Wizard of Oz*, those aunts in *Sabrina the Teenage Witch*, and who can forget the Fresh Prince's Aunt Viv – she was the best, version one and two. I'm happy to be that, but stepmum – I don't think so. And yet, I don't feel like I can just let Will go …

Since the kids went to be bed, I've tried to be productive, even making a vague attempt at writing, but it's not long before I'm on my phone, searching 'Will Matheson'. Though I know he doesn't have social accounts, it doesn't stop me looking. I get some website hits on Google but then decide not to look and instead search 'Kat' and 'dog trainer' which is what Will told me his ex does. As I type, a wry chuckle escapes at the irony of her name given her chosen profession but before I can get too distracted by that, Bingo. Hundreds of hits including her FaceViber profile which I doom-scroll for an hour. She's pretty with wavy brown hair that always seems to be in a messy bun. She looks older than Will so I concoct a story of her forcing him to have kids due to her ticking biological clock, then scold myself for being mean. Continuing my deep dive, I notice how intense her smile is, almost a grimace as though she's on the precipice of a roller-coaster drop. Before long, Kat's profile leads me to Elle's. Most of it is set to private but there's a handful of public photos and, now in the grips of my curiosity, I study them in forensic detail. I'm desperate to get a sense of Will's kids, their vibe, their attitude. In direct contrast to her mum, Elle barely smiles. Even in the photos taken at parties and events, she has this piercing glare that's so full-on it's almost funny. Esme, on the other hand, who's in a lot of Elle's photos, is a bundle of exuberant excitement, just as you would expect from a six-year-old. I'm just about to swipe out of FaceViber when I see a photo that catches my attention – Elle on stage in front of a mic. Behind her, a sign reads, *Hackney Talent Search.*

'No way,' I murmur, reading her accompanying text.

So, I won the HTS. I'm officially a stand-up comedy legend. Smiling emoji.

Though I want to enjoy the dry humour of her actually writing the words, 'smiling emoji', it's the stand-up thing that sets my mind whirring. She's a comedian? That's a curve ball. The next photo, in direct contrast, is a family selfie, faces smooshed together, hugs and big grins. Seeing this, I then wonder if Elle's stoniness is simply a persona she's trying on, perhaps for comic effect, and though I try to resist, I can't help but like her for it. I close FaceViber but residual, happy-family images persist as I visualise my face pressed against everyone else's, packed together in a group photo. We're happy, laughing, holding each other tight, yelping instructions to squeeze in. Then, I'm at a dinner table, doing maths homework, just as Felix was with Ayesha but instead it's me and Esme, her looking to me for the answer while I patiently walk her through the solution. Then Elle is asking for tips on crafting jokes and we write whole routines together. I pull my knees to my chest as these images wrap around me, a fluffy, fuzzy blanket of family love, far removed from my own, and I ask myself, could being with Will and his kids be like that? Could me and Elle bond over comedy? Would Esme look to me for guidance? I've never been that for anyone, not even Ayesha and Caleb. With them I'm just guaranteed horsey rides and amazing bedtime stories. But maybe, just maybe …

I suddenly become aware of the pin-drop silence. I don't think I have Spidey senses when it comes to kids but something tells me to check in on them.

Their door is ajar and in the gloom, I see the glow of a screen. Stepping in, I find them sitting on Caleb's bed, crammed around his phone, wearing an earbud each. I'm shocked they're still up but whatever they're watching has them so transfixed they're oblivious to my presence.

'Your mum and dad are back!' I bark, flipping the light switch.

They both yelp, the phone flying out of Caleb's hand as

Ayesha dives for cover under her duvet. Caleb squints up at me, pitiful and full of guilt. I want to laugh, not just at his face but how Ayesha's quivering feet are sticking out the bottom of her bedding.

'Care to explain what's going on?'

'Yeah but no, it wasn't just me!' Caleb gabbles, eyes darting to Ayesha's feet which very slowly retract under the Peppa Pig cover.

Before they vanish entirely, I make a grab for them with a big, grizzly bear growl. Ayesha screams as my tickling hands dance around her tiny body. A little jab under the arms, into her tum and back of her neck. Soon, there's just a tangle of kids and bedding as Caleb joins in. Panting, I perch on the edge of Ayesha's bed, kids clambering all over me.

'Wait, wait! Mind my hair!' I holler.

I know I shouldn't get them this excited, on a school night, after ten and all that, but it does feel lovely. And, if they're happy, broken rules don't matter too much. Finally, they calm to just bouncing on the bed so I grab Caleb's phone and open the screen.

'So?' I ask.

Caleb's mouth clamps shut, leaving Ayesha to blurt an explanation, 'We were watching people eat chicken on the internet!'

I'm relieved it wasn't porn but my face crinkles, confused. I play the vid which restarts on a young host egging on their studio guest to, as Ayesha accurately reported, eat chicken. It seems to be causing that person increasing discomfort and the kids find this *hilarious*.

'It's called "Jerk the Week". That's Josh, the presenter,' Ayesha tells me, jabbing his face as though she's trying to pick his nose.

'And he makes people eat hotter and hotter and hotter chicken until they explode.'

'No, he doesn't,' Caleb counters. 'There are guest comedians and they eat jerk chicken then answer questions about celebrities.'

'But it gets hotter and hotter and then they explode!' Ayesha shrieks, arms gesturing in case I can't quite visualise an exploding comedian.

'They don't explode, idiot. They keep going till they can't eat any more and there's a leader board and Millie Ronceros is winning!'

'But she nearly exploded!'

This conversation continues across me for several minutes, Ayesha not letting go of the idea that at some point someone definitely explodes.

'Do you want to watch some?' She grins, a big gap where her right front tooth should be.

As fascinated as I am, if I join them in watching this and Ayesha blabs, Kemi will not be impressed with my babysitting skills.

'Maybe another time. How about one of Auntie Abi's amazing stories?'

In fairness, the kids *could* have sounded less enthusiastic but they would have been hard pressed.

'Come on,' I encourage, 'this one's especially for you guys. The heroes are called Ayesha and Caleb, there's an evil young emperor called, um, Josh, and a kind stepmother who saves the day!'

Ayesha's head cocks with uncertainty. 'But stepmothers are evil.'

'Ah, but this one is good and is going to save Ayesha and Caleb from evil Lord Josh.'

'Is she going to give him a poisoned apple?' Caleb asks as I straighten his duvet over him.

'She doesn't roll like that,' I say, burying my impatience at being thwarted trying to rewrite the narrative on stepmums.

'She'll look at him with her craggy old face and he'll turn to rock!' Ayesha says going rigid then falling back onto her bed.

'Who says she's old?' I question.

'They're always old. They have big noses, and they hate girls. The stepmother should be the evil one. Not Josh.'

'And the parents could save the day,' Caleb suggests.

'Do you lot want a story or not?' I ask, frustrated at their unsolicited story edits.

'Okay,' the kids say as though it's a favour to me.

'But,' says Ayesha, lifting a hand out from under her duvet, 'let's keep an eye on this stepmother.'

I promise to do just that and finally start the story but before we've even left the kingdom and bade farewell to the handsome King Drake, they're both out for the count. Caleb is on his back, mouth gaping, while Ayesha is curled into a ball, a sleeping pup that exploding comics couldn't wake.

I close the door and pull my phone out. A random number tells me I've won a thousand pounds' worth of M&S vouchers but there's nothing from Will. I head to the living room and the comfort of the sofa, turning over Kemi's advice in my mind. I wish I could be all Ariana Grande, like 'Thank U, Next', but I don't know if I can let him go that easily. I still desperately want to hear from him but I'm also still super mad about what he did and so, so confused. Where the hell do I go from here?

Chapter 10

'Guys, ever get tired of being told you're too much? I mean, look at me. I'm eleven stone and five foot four. I'm not too much. I'm compact!'

Ride the laugh. Find skinny guy. Wink. Another laugh. All as planned. No innovation tonight, I just need the familiar warmth of my set going well. I did get in one ad lib though, a line about my thighs looking like that doner meat in kebab shop windows. Biggest laugh of the night, along with a bit of wincing, but that's fine. I know it's sending myself up but better to get in before others say it, right? Worked for me at school so if it ain't broke …

Aaaaand there's the flashing red bike light at the back letting me know to wrap up.

'Anyway, that's all from me. My name's Abi Akingbade because I'm – bad aiiiyee.'

I'm proud of me for making it through my first gig since everything went down with Will. Has it really been over a week? I miss him like crazy but he still hasn't messaged and I've got no way of knowing if this is him respecting my boundaries, or saying we're over.

Off stage, Cassie gives me a huge hug. 'You did it. You're back.'

'Thanks, Cass,' I say, enjoying being enveloped by her patchouli-scented smock. She was meant to be doing her big food shop tonight, so I appreciate her detouring to check in on me after I skipped the last Wisecrackers.

'Feeling more yourself?'

'Yeah, I needed that,' I say, tipping my head towards the stage.

Frank squeezes my shoulder. 'Nice work, Abi.'

'Cheers,' I reply, quietly pleased. His praise means a lot. 'So, what new bits are you trying tonight?'

His face crumples.

'I need to get the not-wanting-kids routine down to five minutes.'

Cassie clears her throat, glaring at Frank before jerking her gaze at me in the least subtle way possible.

'Thanks for the trigger warning, Cass, but I'm okay.'

'And anyway, you can't censor me,' Frank says, indignation rising. 'Accept the facts – not everyone wants kids, Cassie.'

'True, but many do and even those that think they don't often do once they have them!' she says flapping her arms like she's about to take off.

'And many often regret it,' Frank pushes back.

'Like who?'

'I bet Hitler's mum wasn't best pleased,' he replies with a weary sigh, clearly done with this convo – as am I, my post-gig buzz now completely flat.

'You can't evoke the Nazis to win an argument,' Cassie bleats.

'Guys – stop. I beg of you. If you're trying to help me, I'm good. I haven't heard from Will anyway, so none of this even matters.'

Frank glowers at Cassie before taking himself to the opposite corner to work on his set.

She watches him go before exhaling slowly, no doubt trying to purge the bad juju from their spat. Aura finally feng shui-ed or whatever, she turns to me. 'If I might offer one last thought – instead of waiting for a response from Will, life may be inviting *you* to decide what happens next.'

'I s'pose. But right now, I can't see this extended family tip working for me.'

'Mmm. Except maybe you need to change how you see it. You're thinking about what you'll have to give up but have you thought about what you'll gain?'

'You mean, like material?'

'Not everything is about comedy, Abi. I meant what they'll contribute to your life. The joy, the laughter, the lessons. I promise you, life is a whole lot more interesting with children in it.'

I nod, processing. 'I guess.'

Cassie gives me a warm grin. 'Okay … well, I should get going. Solomon's making a miniature portcullis so I need to get some barbecue skewers before Tesco's shuts but you're sure you're okay?'

'Promise,' I say, forcing a smile. 'I'm gonna get a drink and watch the rest of the acts.'

'Good for you. And …' Cassie bites her lip, checking who's within earshot, 'maybe take Frank's material with a pinch of salt. His routine is entirely focused on what you lose – not what you gain.'

'Sure,' I say, but my mind's too addled to draw conclusions from anything right now.

So far my best plan has been a bout of revenge-dating but I thank her anyway and we hug it out one last time before she heads off.

'Whatcha doing?' I say, olive-branching towards Frank.

'Has she gone?' he says, glancing to where we were standing.

'Yup, something about skewers for Solomon.'

Frank leers. 'Catchy. I'll make a donation on the JustGiving page.'

I laugh even though Frank looks far from amused, still smarting from their run-in.

'I mean, who made her the official publicist for children everywhere? Not that kids need PR. Everyone seems to bloody want them, according to Cassie.'

'Not everyone,' I say, giving him a reassuring nudge. 'So – how you doing with your set?'

Now back on familiar ground, Frank's dry demeanour returns. 'It's at five and half minutes.'

'So where's the fire?' I ask.

'Tess Blackman from Callback wants to see it. It has to be a tight five.'

'Wait, Callback Productions? As in *ShowTime-at-the-Athena* Callback Productions?'

'Exactly,' exhales Frank as though that extra thirty seconds will be multiplied by a million and taken off his life expectancy.

'That's brilliant news, mate. I'm so pleased for you!'

And I am, even though his success does sting, not because I don't want him to have it – if anyone deserves the next level it's Frank – but because it's a reminder of how far I have to go.

Sometimes I wish I could have Cassie's outlook, that comedy is simply punctuation in her life. But for me, it *is* my life. It's not just punctuation, it's the words, the spaces, the sentences. And when another comic wins, especially one close to me, I always feel like I lose. At this rate, by the time I hit my forties I'll be a serial spinster still temping and traipsing around the open-mic scene, the acrid funk of failure following me wherever I go. Just the thought creates a bitter swell in my gut. I've got to get my comedy moving forward, perhaps take Frank's lead and finally get writing.

Once he's up on stage I rummage through my bag for a pen. Out of the corner of my eye I notice a pair of scuffed burgundy loafers.

'Wotcha,' comes a voice, in the usual back-of-the-club whisper.

'Hey. Carl, right?' I say, pulling out my notebook.

'Famous at last. Yep, Carl O'Connor. As in, you know, Tom …'

He lets that hang and I want to be impressed for him but being *related* to Tom O'Connor doesn't *make* you Tom O'Connor. Funny bones aren't genetic, thankfully, or I'd be finished before I'd even started.

I take Carl in. His aesthetic is off-duty warehouse manager. A pocket bulges with keys and change while one stubby hand grips a flat pint and he smells so strongly of cigarettes I wonder if he's been eating rather than smoking them. I've seen Carl around but don't know him to talk to. From what I hear, that's a lucky escape.

'Great set you did. You know I run a paid gig up near Brackenfield – at a social club?' Carl says.

My ears prick. He instantly has my full attention.

'Pays well and we get a decent crowd; well, pretty indecent some of them,' he sneers with a wink that would be creepy if he weren't so inert.

'Oh, really?' I say, mustering all the casual I can.

'You'd go down an absolute treat,' Carl nods, lips pursed in certainty.

'Thanks,' I say as my heart starts to gallop, because, holy shit. I think I'm about to get offered my first actual, paid, cash-in-my-hand gig.

'Yeah, that crowd would lap you up, as it were,' Carl says holding up his hands. 'No offence. Never know what you can say these days with the PC brigade.'

I nod in agreement but I don't agree because I don't care. What's on my mind is the PG brigade: *paid gigs*.

'I'd be up for doing your show,' I say.

'Lovely. Well, give me a bell with your dates and we'll get you in the diary.'

'Brilliant, thanks. I'll do that ...'

'Oh, it pays a hundred and twenty for a middle spot. Won't buy you a Caribbean island but that okay for you?' Carl adds.

My breath halts and I have to gather myself. *Close gob, stop staring, try smiling, Abi.* A hundred and twenty quid?! That's more than okay. I scrunch my face, pretending to consider it.

'Yeah ... Yeah, should be fine.'

Carl gives me an A-okay then takes a quarter pint glug from his beer, and ambles off.

My face wants to break into the biggest grin. A paid gig. At last. And tonight, of all nights, I wasn't even *near* my best! But it's happened – my first and definitely not my last. This feels amazing and I can't wait to tell Will. He'll be so happy for me. I pull my phone from my bag but then fall back in my seat as reality crashes in. For one sweet moment I'd forgotten everything that had happened. For one delirious instant, we were together. I deflate into the present – hand still clutching my phone. I'm just about to slip it back into my bag, when I notice a WhatsApp notification and I swipe open my home screen.

> I'm really sorry Abi. I know I've messed up. I want to put things right but I also wanted to give you space.
>
> If you really think this can't work, I'll understand but just bcoz I have children, doesn't mean there isn't still an 'us'. That will always be true – if you want it to be. Wxxx
>
> ps I want to tell Elle and Esme about you so there's no more secrets.
>
> pps sorry for the long text.

I read then reread his message – my mind in a jumble. I wanted to hear from Will so badly, but now I have, it's tinged with a whole heap of sadness. How come you can meet such a great guy only to discover the package comes with an ex and two kids? I close my eyes and breathe, hoping I can come up with a rational reply, but the only thought taking up real estate in my head is that I've fallen for Will and can't stop thinking about him. I'm happier when I'm with him than when I'm not, and I feel there's a piece missing when we aren't together, so … maybe we should give it a chance and just work the rest out as we go because I want there to be an *us* … and I'm not ready to give up on that. Cassie's words come back to me, that maybe I need to see what I gain.

My hand hovers over my phone keyboard, hesitation coursing through every finger and then I tap out the only response I can think of …

Abi is typing …

A blizzard of emojis instantly sweep into my inbox. Laughing ones with a bead of sweat and then hearts, so many hearts, and I clutch my phone to my chest as tearful laughter rocks my body.

Chapter 11

'Hi,' I smile, even though standing further from Will than normal is paining me.

'Hi,' he replies.

We're outside Peckham Rye station at his suggestion and I can't help laugh to myself that I really must like this guy if I'm willing to venture south of the river – on a school night – without a peep of complaint. But even though I'm here, we've had no kiss, no hug, we're not there yet.

'Was the train busy?' Will asks with a nervous shuffle.

'A bit. People rushing to avoid – the rush, you know …' I reply, reaching for something funny to say.

We hold each other's gaze, then after a moment he reaches out to take my hand and I let him.

It's been a week and a half since we were last face to face and I am craving his touch even though I know I can't be too eager. Feelings of happiness and confusion mix as I look at him. He screwed up and before we can move forward I need to know he's not going to pull something like that again.

'I've really missed you, missed this,' Will says, looking at my hand in his.

His words disarm me but I say nothing and instead acknowledge with a simple nod. I missed him too. I'm just not ready to say it.

'I booked us a table at a Nigerian restaurant round the corner. That cool?'

'Yeah, very,' I reply, as we turn to walk, Will clasping my hand like he's scared to let it go.

I feel my cheeks flush at the energy pulsing from him but also at the thought he's put into tonight. I've been out with a few guys from West Indian heritage and lost count of the number of Caribbean restaurants I've been taken to. I mean, the food is always lit, the spot is always jumpin' and the bants about the correct pronunciation of plantain is always jokes but never once did they surprise me with a trip to a restaurant from *my* heritage, celebrating *my* roots. Yet here, with Will, my background feels not just validated but honoured. And so, as I walk across its threshold, *Kaabọ* becomes my favourite place on earth. The space between me and Will is still tentative but maybe, just maybe, we're edging towards firmer ground.

I take in the restaurant and bar, alive with a midweek buzz. Young Nigerians, sharp, yet casual, worldly but local, are dotted around the room which pulses with aspiration and drive.

'This place is wicked,' I tell Will over the Dr SID beats pumping life into the restaurant atmos.

Once we're seated, Will reaches across the table, his hand resting on mine.

'Listen, Abi,' he starts but I stop him.

'Wait, Will ...' I say, struck by a need to get my thoughts

out first. 'So, look, about your girls – I get why you didn't tell me. I might have done the same but one thing I know for sure, secrets don't work.'

He looks straight at me. 'You're right. I'm sorry.'

And I feel my shoulders relax; I needed him to say that.

'I – I just like you so much,' he continues, 'and I wanted to tell you early on, but wanted to be sure you'd be okay with it and that the girls would be too – which, now I think about it, is ridiculous. How can I guarantee everyone's happy when I haven't told them what I'm worried they'll be happy about? It was stupid but I promise, Abi, you know everything now.'

Tears come, they're happy tears, tears of relief, as the pressure of the last week releases itself from me but still, I push them down. I'm not about to sit here blubbing in front of Will. Instead I let my other hand meet his and we sit, in this space, fingers gently exploring each other's skin, touch growing more certain.

'You're the first person I can imagine introducing to the girls, you know,' he says.

'Really?'

'Totally. I know they'll adore you. Elle definitely will. She's a budding comedian.'

'Is she?' I say, with all the surprise I can muster.

'Yeah. She's great too. Dry humour. She'll be itching to meet you. She loves talking about everything to do with comedy.'

At the mention of Elle, Will's face breaks with deep love and though I enjoy the ego boost of his certainty on how things will go with them, a thought lands: from here on in, it will never be just me and Will. I'm now officially their extra wheel.

'And Esme, she won't be able to get enough of you,' he says.

I smile but my butterflies are off again. And I'm not sure if it's worry or hope.

'Ma*dam*, you people want to order or did you bring a packed lunch?' a voice says above our heads.

I look up at our waiter, his round face bearing a broad, welcoming grin.

Will and I offer giggled apologies as we open our menus but before we can even skim the starters, our waiter jumps in.

'Don't worry. Leave it to Emmanuel,' he says, whisking our menus away again, and we watch him zip off between the tables, bantering as he goes.

'I wonder if anyone actually ever gets to order what they want,' I say, amused.

'Don't worry. Emmanuel's golden. He won't let us down,' Will says, sitting back with an assuredness.

Our starters arrive. They look delish and we dive straight in. As we eat, syphoning nervous energy into appreciating the flavours, I can feel we're finding our way back to us and it's lovely. Listening to Will, he seems different, unburdened now he's able to talk about his children. The lifted load has allowed us to go deeper and so I take the chance to tell him about Mum. Though I make light, spinning past moments into funny anecdotes, her caustic asides and judgements are beginning to weigh me down so it feels good to unburden and laugh a little.

'She sounds like a character,' Will says and though he enjoys my stories, the solid grip of his hand on mine tells me he hears what's unspoken too. 'Family, eh.'

'Yeah,' I say into the full silence between us.

It's not an easy topic and when Emmanuel descends with his joyful lightness, brandishing our mains, I see echoes of my dad in him, or what he might be if released from under the tyranny of her majesty. Does Mum suppress a certain something in everyone around her? In Dad but also in Kemi who's too scared to tell her she got a bloody haircut? And then I look at this gorgeous man across from me and fear what Mum may suppress in him too. If even the mention of her can kill my buzz, only Black Jesus knows what she'll do to Will. I'm just super grateful we're not doing any of those meet-the-parents intros any time soon.

'Like I said, Emmanuel will take care of you!' He beams, arranging our plates.

I go to ask which dishes we should start with but don't even get a quarter of a sentence out before he bellows, 'Just eat!'

Then he gives me a good-natured slap on my shoulder and vanishes again. Once he's gone, we crack up.

'You heard the man,' Will grins as he washes his fingers in the bowl of lemon-scented water Emmanuel has given us.

He gestures for me to tuck in first and I go straight for the suya – tasty, grilled beef I pull from the skewer, savouring its succulence.

'This is gooood!' I enthuse, wedging the food in the corner of my mouth to speak.

'Right?' Will says as he puts some roasted okra on my plate then serves himself.

We both work through our dishes keeping a little chat in play which is mainly food focused. Normally, I feel self-conscious eating in front of a guy, too aware of their judgement, but there's none of that with Will. He loves his food and loves that I do too. I point a pinky at the prawns, encouraging him to try them as he scoops Kaabọ's special slaw onto my plate.

'You know what, Abi, I would love to meet your mum,' Will says, a sure thought that sounds like it's been brewing a while.

'Trust me, when you do, you'll wish you hadn't. These prawns are peng, babes. Get involved before I finish them,' I say, a shameless attempt to redirect the conversation because the idea of him meeting my mum is already vetoed.

When she pars me off in front of the family with all her snide remarks, that's bad enough, but that happening in front of Will, nah.

'There's no rush, but are we doing this? Me and you? This is real, right?'

I sit straight, suddenly noticing the complete lack of throwaway in Will's tone. This isn't just casual chit-chat. We're having *a talk*.

'Mm-hmm,' I say, my mouth full of the most amazing moin moin I've ever eaten. Nothing like pounded, bean-based deliciousness to take the romance out of a moment. I quickly swallow. 'Yes, totally.'

'Then let's meet each other's people.'

Around us everything blurs. What about his whole taking-it-slowly thing? I mean, I know we're finding our way back to each other and it feels amazing, but even by Abi standards, isn't this a bit too much, too soon?

But before the thought has any chance to bed in, I hear myself blurt, 'Yes, a hundred per cent. Let's do this!'

Classic Abi. Why go at a hundred mph when you can go at a thousand, right? Warp speed into who-knows-what.

Will cranes across the table and kisses me, his lips pressing softly against mine.

'Great, but listen,' he says as we part, his hazel eyes captivating. 'When it comes to you meeting the girls, we'll find a time that's right for *all* of us, yeah?'

'Yeah,' I reply, threads of tension unravelling as I breathe a sigh of relief.

Of course, meeting each other's people doesn't have to happen this minute. We do it when it works. It might be a couple of weeks, a month, or half a year before I have to even think about meeting the girls, let alone learn how to make nativity costumes or help with times-table homework. I'll start by getting to know them and when it feels right, I'll meet everyone else – including Kat. By then the girls will be so Team Abi, they'll be bigging me up to her and it'll be a piece of cake.

'In the spirit of full disclosure though,' Will continues, with a slight wince, 'there is one thing.'

My butt cheeks tense. I don't like the sound of this at all.

'Kat and I made a pact. Before I introduce the kids to anyone, she wants to meet them first. Is that cool?'

'No worries,' I say, the tone of my voice going almost dog-whistle high.

That wasn't quite how I saw this all playing out but hey, what could go wrong?

Chapter 12

The high of getting back on track with Will has me floating through the rest of the week. Even the daily grind of temping is 50 per cent less annoying despite Jill dumping every complaint about her husband into our mid-morning coffee break. I mean, if loading the dishwasher wrong is such a crime, get a cleaner – or a couples' therapist. And I haven't even minded Bobbie's constant conspiracy theories, the latest being that all vaccines have given our brains 5G capabilities since the eighties. And I was shocked that even confirming another month of temping with Jill because, no, I'm not a full-time comic yet, was kind of okay. But however great I feel about me and Will, it can't take the edge off another lunch at Mum's this afternoon.

I glance at the clock in my parents' hallway. I'm late – again. As soon as I step out onto the patio, the kids charge, flinging their arms around whichever bit of me they can grab.

'Look what Grandpap got us,' yells Ayesha literally in my face as I pick her up for a proper cuddle.

I blow a raspberry on her cheek and she squirms, quickly wriggling from my grasp.

'It's a paddling pool!' says Caleb dragging me over.

'Wow!' I enthuse, stumbling along behind him, saying my hellos to the rest of the fam as I go.

Mum, in her Jackie O-sized shades, turns to me.

'Oh good. At least we can eat now. Not that we've been waiting long …'

Mum's voice is tart and her snide slips out behind an amenable smile that means a lot of people miss it. Not me though. The acidity burns but I ignore it.

'Mummy,' I say, hugging her, feeling her body stiffen at my touch.

Mum's hugs are the worst, like she learned by practising on stinging nettles. On the other hand, Dad's are epic, a blanket of love, scented with cologne, skin cream and adoration. He wipes his hands on the Nigeria Independence Day tea towel tucked into his apron and ambles over, arms ready to receive me.

'Beautiful girl,' he says, and I nestle into him.

'Hi, Dad.'

'Watch the barbecue. We'll be eating cinders if you're not careful.'

That's rich coming from a woman who practically cremates meat when she cooks it. I block out her criticism, as always, designed to cut through our moment.

'It's all under control,' Dad says calmly and my eyes go wide, peering over at Kemi to see if she's also clocked Dad's uncharacteristic backchat.

I catch her eye but she looks away knowing that if she lingers I'll make her giggle. Eventually, Dad's cuddle loosens and I make a beeline for Kemi, giving her my usual bear-hug.

'What beautiful hair,' I whisper. 'Where *did* you buy it?'

She digs her fingers into my ribs, and I jolt. Soon we're both giggling as I rock her side to side.

'Abiiii-ah!' she wails.

An hour later and everyone's relaxed. The kids have changed into some old swimming gear Mum's kept and are sploshing about in the blow-up paddling pool. Having bored of listening to Mum sing Kemi's praises, I decide to join them, rolling up the legs of my patterned dungers. It's lovely to see the kids again but I also have an ulterior motive. Knowing, at some point, I'll probably meet Will's kids, I wanna practise with these little ones so I feel *uber* confident when the time comes.

'Hey, guys, can I play?'

The kids are just kicking around a plastic duck so I assume I'll pick up the rules fairly quickly.

'Yay!' yelps Ayesha sending water crowning in all directions.

With a subtle, calm-down gesture, I step into the pool.

'Right, where's the goal?' I ask as I nudge the duck towards Caleb.

'What goal?' he replies as he pelts the duck which sails by my ear.

'Er, that was a bit high, bud. You could have someone's eye out.'

Caleb screws his face in confusion at this new conscientious Abi but I'm all about 'safety first' now. I need Will to know I can be the responsible adult around kids.

Ayesha ignores me, screeching in delight. 'That was a good one. My turn!'

She throws the duck into the water, kicking it as hard as she can. It clonks Caleb in the middle of his forehead and he staggers back with a pitiful, 'Aaaawww-aaah!'

'Um, guys, I thought you were playing some kinda water football,' I say, trying to bring the temperature down a few degrees.

'No,' corrects Ayesha, 'we're trying to hit each other in the face and I'm winning!'

Just then, Caleb hurls the duck up and on its descent attempts a Cantona-style scissor kick in Ayesha's direction.

He misses, landing in what couldn't have been more of a belly flop if he'd been shot out of a cannon. I get drenched as Ayesha whoops hysterically.

She then scoops up water, hurling it towards Caleb – however, her shaky grasp of physics means most of it spatters onto me. My clothes are sodden.

'OK, you two. Perhaps let's go back to duck faceball?' I whimper in desperation.

'No, this is fun!' says Caleb.

Things feel out of control and my panic rises. If this were a couple of dogs, you'd throw water over them but given we're standing in ten inches of the stuff that's not going to work. I think fast.

'Right.' I lower my voice so they have to come close. 'Shall I leave you to play while I talk to Mummy and Daddy about "Jerk the Week"?'

They freeze, stiffer than if I'd announced a mannequin challenge.

Ayesha shakes her head. 'Mummy will take our iPad away … for a looong time …'

I look to Caleb who just bobs his head in sombre confirmation.

'I see. You know what I'm thinking?' I say, pretending to

ponder, looking over at the small plastic table Mum has put out for them, filled with calm activities. 'It might be time for some very quiet games of Connect Four. What do you reckon?'

They both nod and head over to the table, Ayesha's backward glance radiating betrayal. Welcome to the real world, kid.

She flops down in her seat, grabs an assortment of red and yellow counters, inserting them into the slots. Caleb joins in and though it's instantly clear neither of them know the rules, as long as they're quiet, job done. I feel pretty fricking legendary. I just smashed Responsible Adulting 101.

'Look at you, Super Nanny,' Kemi says, impressed, as I come over. 'You'll have to tell me your secret.'

'Just a knack,' I casual-shrug, overlooking my use of a thinly veiled threat to snitch.

Yeah, I piggy-backed off Kemi's strict parenting but as long as it worked, no harm, no foul, I tell myself, sitting at the big table opposite Felix.

While Dad continues to tend the barbecue, Mum excuses herself, breaking out into a discreet velociraptor-type trot that Kemi and I know means she's going to the loo. It's like Mum can't bear people knowing she performs the same lowly bodily functions as the rest of us.

'Making room ahead of the feast,' I say and me and Kemi crack up, unashamedly regressing to our ten-year-old selves.

'What are you two up to?' Dad calls over.

'Nothing!' we both chime, like butter wouldn't melt.

Once Dad's attention is back on crisping up his spare ribs I turn to Kemi.

'So?' I say, nudging her elbow off the armrest, a low-ball prank but a favourite.

'Oh my days, Abi, you're so bait!' she moans.

'*You're* bait,' I counter, giggling perhaps a little too much but I'm happy.

Kemi's eyes narrow.

'Hmmmm, look at you,' she says, putting me squarely at the centre of her suspicious gaze. 'You practically glided in here on cloud nine. What's that about?'

'I'm just gonna check on Caleb and Ayesha …' I say, rising.

'Abiiiiii,' Kemi rumbles as she pulls me back into my seat.

'Fine,' I huff. 'Me and Will got back together but, look, don't be judging me with your church eyes. I think he could be like, my *person*, my *guy*, my, y'know …'

Still nervous to hear the words out loud, instead I say it with photos, swiping through blissy, cheek-to-cheek selfies Will and I have been taking since we met.

Kemi inspects each one like a pathologist painstakingly studying samples, searching for clues.

'He's peng, I suppose, I'll give him that,' she admits, before some more swift, if distrustful, swipes through my camera roll. 'And … he has a kind smile, I guess … But how do you know this guy's straight up and not just some joker?'

I shift in my seat to face Kemi square on. 'He wants us to meet each other's people. He's a real one, Kems, trust me.'

'*O-kaaaay*,' she says, giving me side-eye, but I can see she's warming to him. She goes back to the photos. 'He *is* fit.'

'Riiiiiight,' I murmur, and we exchange a quick *Wakanda Forever* hand slap and click and then I subtly ease my phone from her grasp before she sees any not-suitable-for-barbecues pics.

'So, when do we get to meet this Mr Wonderful?' she asks, and I grin, so glad she's on board.

'I'm waiting for the right time to drop him into the convo. Then I was thinking … I could bring him to a Sunday lunch …'

'Wait, what?' Kemi silently explodes. '*These* Sunday lunches – with *that* mother of ours?'

'All right, calm down. I said *a* Sunday lunch – not necessarily the next, immediate one.'

'Okay, sweet,' Kemi grins.

Her approval feels good but the fact she was doubtful at first wasn't completely misplaced. My love life's been pretty disastrous to date and there's definitely never been anyone I've felt strongly enough about to put through this.

'You know if you do bring him, Mum's gonna pounce on his weaknesses. You need to get ahead of that, so what's his flaw … apart from the kids?' Kemi says, sitting back in her garden chair.

I gasp, 'Yo, you can't say that. *You* have kids!'

'But they're *my* kids. We made them. If I'd met Felix and he already had children – nah.'

Kemi full-stops the sentence with a grimace and I'm shook. This is brand-new information. I didn't think she'd be this hard-line about it. 'You wouldn't get with someone who already had kids?'

'For what? It'd be a dawn till dusk battle for affection. I couldn't,' Kemi shrugs and my mouth flaps.

'What I mean is,' she says, probably seeing my pained expression, 'I'm greedy. I'd want him to myself.'

I glance across at Felix who's acting like he's not listening but I can see a hint of a smile on his lips. 'It won't be that bad. He only has them one or two week nights and every other weekend,' I say, not sure who I'm trying to reassure more.

Kemi's lips pucker. 'So, potentially he has them up to … 43 per cent of every fortnight.'

Man, I hate how quickly she can do maths.

'Yeah,' I say, trying to sound like I've already thought the whole thing through.

'Well, clearly you're a bigger person than me and look, you might be lucky and none of this will come up with Will.'

'Totally,' I say, wishing I believed what was coming from both our mouths.

'But, sis, whenever you plan on inviting him, even if it is in a few months – tell Mum soon so she can get all her "comments" out of her system before she actually meets him.'

I bristle, resenting the power of Mum's opinion and the sting in her words.

'You're one to talk about 'fessing up to Mum,' I say, flicking Kemi's wig. 'We still doing radio silence about your hair?'

Her lips tighten, an outward show of her inner resistance. 'I will, just not yet.'

'What *is* with the cloak and dagger?' I ask, now almost irritated by the secrecy.

Kemi darts a look to Felix who gives her a your-call face and her gaze floats off into the distance, at trees that canopy back gardens as far as we can see.

'Don't you ever get tired of doing what everyone expects of you?' she asks, finally turning back to me.

'I'm sorry, have we met?' I say, sarcasm lacing the question.

'You know what I mean.'

'No, Kems, I don't. I do my thing and get grief for it all the time whereas people love everything you do.'

And when I say people, we both know I mean Mum who,

right on cue, appears in the back doorway. She makes her way to the barbecue, no doubt to interfere in some annoying and unnecessary way.

Kemi, eyes on Mum, lowers her voice.

'It's like, at work there's all these expectations of me, you know, as a black woman, that I should look a certain way, be a certain way and, I'd had enough. I was at Barbara's, for a trim … then I just thought – screw it …'

Kemi gives an oopsie shrug which shakes free a sad smile.

'So, what *have* you told Mum?'

'I've got protective cane-rows under here to give my hair a break from the chemicals.'

'And then what?' I ask but Kemi's gaze flicks towards our parents and she swallows her answer.

It's mad how scared she is of Mum's judgement when whatever she does is always met with gushing approval. Yeah, Mum will be shocked at first due to her tediously conservative views on gender but she'll get used to it. She did when I got the chop and went natural. It'll be even easier for Kemi. But then my stomach spasms as I remember Mum telling me, 'short hair compromises your desirability'. I wanted to yak, there and then. Who says that to their daughter? But I wasn't *scared* to tell her I'd had my hair cut, just like I'm not scared to tell her about Will. I just want to find the right moment. That's not fear, that's strategy. I'll introduce him when I'm ready.

'I think you should tell Mum,' I whisper to Kemi. 'She should, innit, Felix?'

'All I know is, she looks great,' he says with an unreadable smile then heads to the barbie to help Dad bring over the first platters.

'You should. What's she gonna say, "Put it back on!"?' I argue.

'It's not as simple as that.'

'It's just hair, man.'

Our mum approaches and Kemi deflects, turning her attention to Ayesha and Caleb, 'Come on, kids. Grandpap's made loads of lovely food for us.'

I let it go but it seems mad. If I can get free of Mum's opinions, surely Kemi can.

As we finish one round of food, Dad musters up another. Lamb kebabs, giant prawns and squid! My mouth waters as I fill my plate for like the third, possibly fourth time. I love my dad's cook-outs. Not a burger or banger in sight. This is real outdoor cooking and as much as Mum's jibes grate, at least I always get a good feed at Sunday lunch.

'So, Kemi, have you considered your intentions once this social housing project is resolved?'

Mum almost swallows 'social housing' as though it's a swear word.

At the other end of the table, Felix and Kemi exchange panicked looks before Kemi answers with a stilted, 'I'm definitely taking on a private sector project next.'

'Oh, wonderful!' Mum beams with open relief.

'Of course, I'm already in the private sector,' I joke but with a pointed edge. 'If ever there was a dog-eat-dog meritocracy, it's comedy.'

'That would explain your position,' Mum oozes.

Her comment catches me off-guard and I'm momentarily speechless.

'On the up?' Dad chips in and though I appreciate the save, anger pulses in me as I twist my napkin into a strangled knot.

'You should discuss future prospects with your manager, Adekemi. In fact, I wouldn't be surprised if you were doing his job before long.'

Kemi, who usually revels in Mum's praise, recoils, distracting herself with cutting up the kids' food and sweeping crumbs from Ayesha's lap.

'We'll see. How're things with you, Abs? Were you saying something about … didn't you have a thing?'

Bemused, I watch Kemi flap as she tries to divert the convo.

'A thing?' I repeat, still undecided on whether to yank her from her self-dug hole.

'Yeah, you know, like maybe something worth sharing?' Kemi coaxes desperately.

'Such as the decision to seek meaningful employment instead of pursuing a career as a Punchinello?' Mum scoffs and continues painstakingly de-shelling a prawn with her knife and fork.

I marvel bitterly at how she never eats with her hands. Birthday cake, sandwiches – actual finger food. Unless she can delicately draw it off the end of stainless steel cutlery, she ain't havin' it, and every jab of her fork pricks me even more.

'So, elaborate, Abioye. What's your "thing"?'

I go to speak but nothing emerges.

'You should look to your younger sibling for inspiration. Cultivate a solid vocation, children, a good marriage. Of course, you'd be hard pressed to meet anyone given the current status of your career, or have you finally "made it"?' Mum says, using her cutlery to flick air quotes in my direction. 'Or is your thing that you are going to finish your degree? Oh, I know, is your "thing" finally settling your debt with the bank of Mum and Dad or – don't tell me—'

I've had enough and before she can slice at me again, I spew, 'Actually, Mum, I've met someone. And we're super happy.'

I look around the table. Kemi gawps – even though it was her who egged me on to say it – Felix nods with approval and Dad is beaming. Slowly I pull my gaze back to Mum who's momentarily frozen, only able to manage an, 'Oh. A boyfriend?'

'Yup. A boyf,' I say, intentionally shortening the word to irritate the linguistic pedant in her.

'And does this person have a name?'

'Will. It's Will,' I say, trying to regroup, stand my ground.

Actually, I feel good. It's out there now and her reaction hasn't been horrible, just kind of … muted.

'Magnificent! Be splendid to meet the chap who's making you so happy,' Dad says, hopping out of his seat and planting a kiss on my forehead.

With a smile, he saunters back to the barbecue and the ribs, quietly sizzling. At least my news has put a spring in someone's step.

'I might even bring him along at some point … I think you'd really love him, Dad.'

A grin consuming his face, Dad waves his spatula in agreement.

'Never assume, Abioye,' says Mum, eyebrow raised. 'Will this one even be around that long?'

'We love each other, Mum. He will.'

'Love?' Mum flusters, eyes flickering like she's trying to blink away some stubborn grit. 'That was quick. Well then, perhaps you'll be living together and engaged by the time we meet this person.'

She exhales before taking her attention back to her meal and battling the shell from another king prawn.

No one speaks – the airless silence is heavy and I just sit there, a powder keg, ignited fuse now just inches long.

'I don't see why it's such a surprise that I've met someone who's great,' I say, just able to keep a lid on things.

'Darling, I'm pleased for you. My motherly advice, for what it's worth, is simply enjoy it while it lasts. Just in case. You see, I got the impression you seldom attract the type of man seeking something … serious,' Mum says, brow furrowed with what I'm sure she thinks is care.

'Actually, he's very serious about me – so serious, he wants to introduce me to his kids!' I blurt before I realise what I've done.

'Kids?' Mum says, loading one word with so much judgement I'm surprised it makes it out of her mouth.

'Wonderful!' Dad interjects, attempting to dampen Mum's derision and fend off the mood now threatening to contaminate the whole afternoon. 'Friends for Ayesha and Caleb.'

'Children, Abi?' Mum reiterates.

'Yeah. Two,' I say, straightening in my seat to match what's coming at me but falling short.

'Is that what you're looking for in a man – past failures?'

The table curdles at her comment and I drag my paper napkin back onto my lap, screwing it into an even tighter twist. 'Relationships end, Mum. It happens.'

'Not to everyone. Look at your father and me. Thirty-four years married, still going strong.'

Dad acknowledges but the sliver of a smile on his face could be read in many ways, from *yes, lucky us* to *I would smother you as you sleep, Abosede, if I weren't terrified you'd be an even more unpleasant ghost.*

'Well, Will and Kat weren't married so it's not even the same,' I snap back.

'Not married?' Mum whimpers, clutching her chest as though an aneurysm is imminent.

'We love each other, Mum, and that's it,' I say, trying to inject finality into my tone.

'That word again,' Mum breathlessly scoffs. 'Listen, Abioye, it's fine to make a shambles of your own life, dear, but an entirely different matter when other people's children are involved.'

With frayed nerves, she goes back to jabbing at her food and I'm left ready to blow.

'You may think it's a shambles but Will's convinced I'll get on great with the girls. In fact, as I'll be such a big part of their lives, I probably need to figure out what they should call me ...' I say, my voice weakening as I hear myself.

'Delusional?' Mum mutters with a skyward gaze.

Out of the corner of my eye I see Kemi, agog, but I ignore her, doubling down. I can't let Mum win. 'Actually, once I've met his kids – which should be any day now – I was thinking, we could all come down for Sunday lunch.'

The words leave my mouth faster than my brain can stop them.

'You haven't even met them?' Mum says.

'It's going to be fine. And like Dad said, someone for Caleb and Ayesha to play with. You'd like that, guys, wouldn't you?' I bluster.

'Yeah!' Ayesha says while Caleb just shrugs, oblivious to the familial politics playing out around him.

'The more the merrier,' Dad says, looking around the table to the kids, then Felix and then a gobsmacked Kemi.

Finally, his eyes land on Mum whose expression shimmers in stasis, perfectly balanced between attack and defence. I hold, hiding my bluff yet desperate for her to back down.

'Yes, how wonderful indeed, Samuel,' she says finally. 'I would love to meet this "Will" and his two children. Why not bring them next month?'

And we hold each other's gaze for the rest of the year – or at least it feels that way. It's me who breaks first.

'Great!' I pipe, trying to hoist the edges of my mouth into some kind of smile.

Now I've done it.

Chapter 13

I tilt my head up and take Will in for the millionth time, wishing I didn't have to confess my massive blunder at Mum's yesterday. His lips part, turning to a smile and I so just want to enjoy being in his flat, snuggling on the sofa. It's my first time here and I'm still getting used to its vibe – the pop-up home of a newly single dad. The living room is a practical canvas, still waiting for Will to imprint his personality. My eyes fix on some kids' paintings, splodgy handprints turned into flowers and faces, and in the corner of the room, a brightly coloured box filled with a few toys and lots of books. On the wall, Will has the obligatory Malcolm X-by-the-window poster but the kids have also made a collage of other black icons – Marcus Garvey, Mary Seacole and more – arranged on sugar paper. On the bookcase, there's a photo of Will and his daughters, a frayed edge down one side where no doubt Kat's smiling face once was. Another tiny tell of Will's past life. It must be hard, starting again, creating a home after leaving the one you had.

Will's cat, probably the most homely thing here, adjusts into a doughnut, way up high in his cat tree, and watches us through slitted eyes.

'It takes him a minute to get to know you but he's lovely,' Will says off my cautious glances. 'He came with me after, you know, everything went down. He's called Chapelle. Elle named him.'

At hearing this, Chapelle stretches and turns his back on us.

'Attitude,' Will play-whispers and I giggle.

Animals usually love me but I've had so much side-eye off Chapelle, I feel like I'm in an episode of *Real Housewives.* Well, I'm sure I can win him over with some dazzling Abi charm. I nestle into Will, the warmth of his body; even the brush of his stubble against my face is giving me very impure thoughts but they keep getting derailed by flashbacks to my showdown with Mum. All evening I've been searching for a way to bring up Sunday lunch. How do I invite Will and then get him to invite the girls too – especially after talking about taking it all slowly?

'You okay?' Will asks, squeezing my shoulder.

'I'm – you know – loving this,' I say, one hand resting on his chest.

Just say it, Abi.

I shift my eyes away, picking up a notebook that's face down on the arm of the sofa. I turn it over, and emblazoned on the cover it reads, *Don't Even Think About It.*

'That's Elle's,' Will laughs.

'Got it.'

I exhale a nervous giggle then, carefully disentangling myself from him.

'Abi, what's wrong? Is it seeing all the girls' things?'

'No, no,' I insist, 'it's not that. It's my mum.'

'Your mum? What's happened?' Will asks, concerned.

Unable to hold the truth in any longer, my body sags as I tell him about me, my stupid ego and how I just can't handle letting Mum triumph. And, after a job lot of preamble, finally I blurt out my invitation, braced for his reply. Will sits up, facing me.

'Abi,' he says, his face kind yet serious, 'that's not going to work. It's too soon.'

'But you said they'd love to meet me,' I counter, the looming threat of Mum's ridicule making me nauseous.

'Yeah, some time in the future …' Will says, pushing himself forward on the sofa. 'It'd be weird if the first time you guys met was at your parents' house.'

'Easy fix. Why don't we do something before the lunch – go for a walk, or a burger – or have a movie night!'

'Abi, I'm sure the girls are going to love you, but—'

'But what? You don't have to say I'm your new boo. I could be … your fun friend, Abi!' I tease and Will laughs despite himself.

He's teetering – I think …

'Thing is, it's not just about the girls. There's Kat,' he says, a hardness edging in.

'Oh.' I'd forgotten about the meeting-the-ex part. 'Well … that's easy, she could pop over for tea. Baby-mama cuppa,' I offer with the cutest smile I can drum up.

'Abi,' Will says as kindly as he can, 'that's a hard no. This is my flat. My space.'

'Sorry, stupid idea,' I say, gripping the sofa.

I mean, on some level, it's all a stupid idea.

'When the time comes, we'll find somewhere neutral but, in my mind, all that is way, way off in the future.'

Will's frown is seeping from his face, into his whole body

and it's all my fault. I scold myself again for pushing. Because of my own wants, I've created another typical, Abi-shaped mess.

'Here's the thing – I do want you to meet the girls. I love how things are going with us and I honestly think it'll be great,' Will says, massaging his brow. 'I'm just worried Kat will think it's happening too quickly. From her perspective, meeting new partners was hypothetical – until now.'

Will's point lands – but then a thought occurs to me.

'You and Kat broke up last summer,' I say, taking Will's hand in mine. 'It's been a year, babes.'

No longer driven by my own needs but a sudden clarity about the situation, I feel emboldened and something shifts in Will's expression.

'I love how you two have that level of respect for each other and that the girls are front and centre, but moving on after a year – darlin', that's not quick.'

Will's head pulses in a thoughtful nod, but he says nothing. And I realise I've said all I can and it's time to full-stop the convo.

'You know what? Ignore me. It's too much. Standard Abi! I'll meet them when I meet them,' I say, sweeping up the remote control from the coffee table. 'We don't need to think about this. What we need is to binge watch the new Issa Rae show until four in the morning.'

'You're right,' says Will.

'Exactly,' I say, flicking through the Apple TV apps. 'I've heard it's fire.'

'No, I mean about Kat. You're right,' Will says, face now lined not with concern but realisation. 'I was worried she'd be uncomfortable with it, but if she's like that after a year, would she ever be fully on-board? We've got to go there at some point, so if not now, when?'

The remote slips from my hand and plaps onto my lap.

'Serious?'

'As a tax return,' Will says, an excited glimmer in his eyes. 'And once you've met the girls, it'll mean we can see more of each other cos I won't have to keep things separate. As long as the girls are cool, then it's all good.'

My mouth opens and closes about ten times. 'Well, only if you're sure. I mean, personally I'm happy to wait.'

'Abi!' Will says, pulling me to him, tickling fingers jabbing into my ribs.

I yelp, convulsing as I try to retaliate and find his ticklish weak spots too.

Soon we're a mass of arms and legs. We stop, breathless and laughing.

'Man, I love you,' Will says, chest gently heaving.

'I *think* I might love you too,' I tease, and we kiss, bodies tangled once again as we tug at clothes, hands searching to meet flesh.

'Abi?' Will whispers. 'Before we, you know, I wanna take a quick shower. I'm feeling a bit grubby from the day.'

I sit back, lips still moist from his kisses. 'Okay, I'm not going anywhere.'

He stands, palm outstretched. 'Come with me …'

And my stomach flips as I rise to take his hand.

I want to do this so much but I've barely breathed since Will led me into the bathroom. We undress each other, me pulling his T-shirt over his head, him tenderly unbuttoning my blouse. And before long, I'm wearing only my knickers and a nervous smile. He steps into the shower and I watch his naked body through the misted glass. His back is strong, muscles tensing and flexing as he douses himself. And just when I thought he'd reached peak perfection, under the soothing hiss of the shower, I hear Will quietly sing, voice velvet, like a warm caress. He wipes a circle in the condensation and peers through at me.

'Wow …' he says, and I flush hot, every sense firing, deeply aware this is the first time we've been naked together.

Sure, we've swept past a couple of bases and even added a few tangential ones of our own but we've never been skin-to-skin like this and my pulse is galloping. What if, when he fully sees me, regret seeps in? What if he has a type and I'm not it? Half of me wants to bolt but seeing him, soapy water cascading over his body, I so want to get in there. I push down my knickers and take two slow, steady steps into the shower. Will watches, his gaze making every part of me tingle.

'There you are,' he says, and I edge closer to him but then stop.

'I can't get …'

'… your hair wet,' he says, finishing my sentence. 'I know.'

And I smile, moving closer.

Will carefully switches places, standing behind me to let the warm spray hit my body first then he reaches up to redirect the nozzle away from my hair.

'Thank you,' I say and try to relax into the sensation of warm water splashing my front and the heat of Will's body behind me.

'Can I wash you?' he whispers.

Oh my days, I'm not sure I'm breathing at all anymore.

I nod and Will squeezes a small dollop of shower gel into his hand. I feel it, cool on my skin as he works it into a lather that flows down my legs and spirals into the drain. Will moves down my back and, without a word, kneels, lathering soap onto first my left and then my right thigh, hands teasing. It's beautiful and frustrating. Then he stands.

'Turn around,' he says, face nestled next to mine.

'Okay,' I breathe.

And I let my arms, which have been x-ed across my body, fall by my sides. I don't want to feel self-conscious; I know I shouldn't – not with Will – but old habits …

'Abi, you're so beautiful,' Will says as his hands lightly brush my breasts then move down to my tummy.

I tense, feeling his hands glide over my folds and rolls, self-doubt brimming, but then I realise I'm smiling. We are naked – together! My mind does somersaults as Will's hands take in *all* of me and his desire makes me feel boundless. He continues to wash my body, every touch drawing us closer. Eventually, he rinses away the suds, finishing with a delicate kiss. It's a moment before I return from my delirium.

'Let me wash you,' I say and take the shower gel, squeezing it into my hand.

Pppffffftth. It makes a massive fart noise. Typical! When he does it, it's sexy as hell, but when I do, it turns into a Tyler Perry movie. Will cracks up and I laugh too – eventually. He takes the bottle and squeezes it, hard. The fart noise is even louder this time and we both hoot hysterically. Well, one positive, at least I can stop stressing about trying to write great jokes. All I need is an empty shower gel bottle.

I rub the gloopy blue liquid over his soft, warm chest, up to his shoulders, down each arm, then hover as I reach his waist.

'Enough washing?' I whisper as my thirst begins to peak.

'Keep going,' Will breathes.

And before I know it, our wet bodies are pressed against each other, lips urgent as our hands explore and I am totally and utterly gone – lost to the giddying heat of our first time and a wait that was so, so worth it.

Chapter 14

'We're meeting someone. The table should be under "Kat",' Will says to the greeter, as he does a nervous scan of the restaurant.

My hand tightens around his, trying to send positive vibes because Will is not his usual chilled self.

'It's going to be okay,' I tell him, trying to emit enough calm for both of us.

He lets out a quiet 'hmmm'.

'She agreed to meet, that's got to be a good sign,' I add, doing a nervous scan too, even though I'm not sure I'll recognise her.

'She did, but you saw how many texts it took.'

I sure did. I thought I was the queen of WhatsApp, but even I was like, guys, just pick up the damn phone. But it wasn't my place to wade in with my size fours – so I said nothing.

'Just remember, babes, the agreement was only to meet new partners – I didn't hear anything about having to get sign-off too,' I say, hoping to nudge Will from his funk.

'True say – but this isn't going to work if she's not happy with who's spending time with her kids,' Will says, tension seeping back into his hand and suddenly I'm bare tense as well.

'Your friends are already here. If you'd like to follow me,' the greeter says.

Will and I share a look. Friends, *plural*?

We're led through a warren of tables until we reach Kat, and as the 'friends' comment implied, she is not alone. My brain whirs, trying to figure out wah gwan and from Will's face, I'm not the only one.

'Hey, Kat …' he says, eyes wide, mouth tight.

'Hey, Will,' she replies, detangling herself from her 'friend', who, now I've seen him up close, has to be at least ten years younger than the rest of us.

Standing, Kat points at her companion. 'You remember …'

'Marcus,' Will says, all pigment now completely drained from his face.

Marcus, a cherub-faced guy, surely no more than twenty-four years old, cocoa skin like mine and a recent fade, hurriedly springs from his seat, nudging the table as he does. Coke from his glass spills and in a fluster he tries to soak up the puddle while reaching across to shake hands. In contrast to his chubby face, he's beanpole thin, his outstretched limb reminding me of those massive construction cranes.

'Hi, Mr Matheson,' Marcus stammers.

Huh?

Will and Marcus shake hands as my brain cartwheels to keep up.

'It's okay, mate. Will's fine,' Will says as his composure slowly returns.

'Right. Mr Will. Sorry, Marcus. I mean, *Will*,' Marcus gabbles.

'And you must be the lovely Abi,' Kat says, cutting Marcus off.

'Yeah, nice to meet you,' I power-nod like a mascot on a parcel shelf and reach across to shake her hand.

'Oh, come here,' she says and shoos Marcus out of the way.

He shifts, this time careful not to knock their drinks again. Once Kat's shuffled from behind the table, she wraps her arms around my neck, hugging me, all elbows and edges, just like my mum.

I expel an 'Oh!' at the force with which she limpets onto me then search for the right place to put my arms. But then Kat goes to release me just as I tighten my hold. In response, she tightens hers, so I do the same and cringe as we end up in a sort of mutual Heimlich manoeuvre.

'So lovely to meet you!' comes her voice, muffled by my big hairpiece.

At last I'm released from this sweet hell and as we awkwardly take our seats, I finally get to see Kat face to face. She has that same stretched smile I saw in Elle's FaceViber pics. I sense it's her safe, go-to, generic mask. Her expression is taut, eyes anodyne – like a *Scooby Doo* character's – black, beady dots with whites almost the same colour as her skin. She looks kind but also like she could be the evil prospector scaring away the town's folk to make a quick buck. She's also pretty, which pricks my insecurities, but she looks knackered, like she could do with a nice nap. I suppose dating a young 'un can do that to you.

Meanwhile, directly across the table is Marcus who looks totally bewildered, as though he's just *Quantum Leap*ed into the situation. *Oh, boy.*

'Well this is nice,' I say, taking in the soulless restaurant, which tonight is our Switzerland.

'Yes!' Kat replies.

'So, Will, how do you and Marcus know each other?' I say, efforting to keep things light.

Will clears his throat. 'I taught Marcus music at Highbury Academy, didn't I.'

Kat freezes like this conversation is the T-Rex from *Jurassic Park* and if she doesn't move, it might not notice her.

'Yeah, you were a really good teacher, like, I learned bare stuff,' says Marcus and Kat glares at him, probably because she intended him to be mainly ornamental tonight.

I swivel my gaze to Will whose whole face is furrowed with confusion like a remote tribesman trying to grasp inflation.

'How long has this been ... is this new?' he finally asks Kat, pointing between her and Marcus.

'Not long,' she says through pinched lips.

'Like a month – six months?'

Kat offers vague throwaways while Marcus attempts half-word interruptions which she halts with micro hand gestures.

'Not long,' she repeats.

I find myself horrified, fascinated and suddenly very proud of my relatively normal family. It's times like this I wish I was an anecdotal comedian because this would be comedy gold. I wonder if it would be weird to start taking notes. No weirder than it already is, I'd say.

Will presses his fingers into his temple. 'And are you still teaching ...'

'Yes, he's still teaching piano to Esme. It's fine, Will. It's all good.'

Kat picks up her menu, barricading herself off from the conversation.

'Is it?' says Will, pulling it back down, disbelief etched on his face.

'It's not a big deal. You've met someone, I've met someone. We're all adults.'

Barely, I snort to myself, watching Marcus try to get his mouth around the straw as it bobs about in his Coke.

'I thought we said we'd discuss when the girls met someone new?'

'But Marcus isn't new,' Kat counters. 'Esme already knows him and she really likes him, so …'

Will falls back in his seat.

'To be fair, I mean, it's not even really a thing. We're just … and Esme doesn't know … as such.' Marcus stops, mainly because of Will's glare which could scorch flesh.

'This is not cool,' he says. 'Kat, we made a deal – you spelled it out: "Introduce new partners to each other before they meet the girls."'

'Will, I just … we're going round in circles. You were bringing Abi – I decided to do the same and now it's done,' Kat says, pushing her menu away and folding her arms.

Marcus lifts a hand as if going to comfort her – or possibly start a Mexican wave – but thinks better of it; a good decision on both counts. Meanwhile, I'm adopting Kat's earlier policy of just keeping quiet and staying still. Tempting as it is to join in, my voice is not required here, that much I know. However, Will has gone quiet too – dead quiet – and is just staring at Kat like he's seeing her with fresh eyes.

'You know, we are going round in circles. Like you say, it's done. I'm going to introduce Abi to the girls and if they're down, I want them to meet her family too.'

And with that, Will suddenly has Kat's full attention. 'Oh, okay. I … we should probably, I mean, it should be fine …'

'Oh, I'm not asking permission, Kat – I'm letting you know it's happening – and soon.'

I stare at Will in total awe. He isn't angry or loud, just firm and direct in a this-ain't-up-for-discussion kinda way. Is it wrong that I find this very, very hot?

'Fine. Good,' Kat blusters. 'Actually, Marcus and I are thinking of doing something similar … maybe going to his mum's church.'

Kat squeezes Marcus's thigh for confirmation but he's clearly not expecting it, the shock causing him to sit bolt upright like the chair just gave him a surprise rectal examination.

Will shakes his head and stands, whipping his jacket off the back of the chair.

'Come on, Abi.'

I look longingly at my menu then at his outstretched hand. I really fancy some sweet potato fries but I think making a to-go order might detract from Will's pointed exit so I take his hand, throwing pointless 'nice to meet yous' over my shoulder and we leave.

From outside, I watch Marcus try, once again, to comfort Kat who brushes off his attempts. He slumps in his seat, looking lost, like this situation is well above his emotional pay grade.

'Can you believe that?' Will says, tipping his head towards the restaurant.

'Right?' I say, trying to read his mood.

'I've allowed everything to be on Kat's terms. No more,' he says with a sweeping hand.

'Exactly,' I encourage as Will begins to fill with confidence, reclaiming his time.

'I've been so careful not to rock the boat, have everything how she needs it. But that's done.'

'You handled it brilliantly,' I tell him, still flushed at this bold, assertive Will.

'Cheers,' he says, as we start to walk. 'It's just weird. This isn't what I expected moving on to feel like.'

'It's a good thing, babes.'

Will nods, clearly still processing.

'Yeah ... I guess it's not about me, Kat and the girls anymore. It's me and the girls – and you,' he says, a smile spreading across his face.

I'm suddenly choked as his words fold me into the warmth of this new unit we're making.

'So … when's your next Sunday lunch?' he asks, stopping to check his phone.

I scan my diary … well, random notes in my memo app. 'Next month, the fourteenth.'

'Okay, that's Kat's weekend but we've been talking about swapping cos she's away with work, so, let's confirm.'

Before I can say anything more, Will sends a text salvo to Kat then gives a triumphant grin. 'Looks like we're going to Hertfordshire. And the timing is perfect. Elle's in this comedy talent search thing – you could give her advice. And even come and support her on the day. She will love that, and whatever Elle loves, Esme always loves too.'

I smile, trying not to fixate on the idea that Esme's approval is bound to Elle's. If Elle approves, great – but if she doesn't, then what? My heart skips several critical beats as the reality of meeting his daughters starts to hit home.

'Er, Will,' I say, caution flavouring my words, 'remember

what we said before though, about not wanting the first time I meet the girls to be sitting down to lunch with my whole family?'

Will facepalms.

'Of course,' he exhales. 'After seeing Kat, I feel like it's okay to move on but I'm getting ahead of myself. You're right. We need to sort out an introduction. Only thing is …'

And from the splinter of hesitation in his voice, I know what's coming. 'If the girls say no …'

'We wait. We're not going to rush them, yeah?' he says, taking my hand.

'Totally,' I reply, as feelings of relief clash with fear of Mum's derision and a deep, deep wish I had just kept my mouth shut.

'I'll talk to them tomorrow,' Will says. 'And if they're up for it, we could do something this Friday. Kat's going to a conference so I've got them.'

'But that's… isn't it …' I gulp, as everything starts to become hella real.

'You do still wanna do this?' Will says, clocking my concern.

I look up into his soft hazel eyes that make it feel like everything'll be all right and smile. 'Course. If not now, when?'

Chapter 15

Normally at work, I'm first out the door, especially on a Friday, and even more so after an extra busy couple of days juggling gigs, temping and just life. But right now I'm in full faff mode – tidying my email inbox and arranging photos on my corkboard. However, it's when I start emptying my hole punch that Jill's suspicions are raised and she's like, 'It's five past five, Abi. What are you still doing here?'

'Oh, you know, tidy desk, tidy mind,' I bluster.

The fact is, Jill spreads info faster than high-speed broadband so I'm not telling her the real reason I'm dragging my heels – that today is D-Day – or should I say E-day. Elle and Esme. I'm meeting Will's girls. Apparently, they're looking forward to it, but personally, I'm terrified.

On the way over, I duck into the local minimart at the corner of Will's road, giving real-world consideration to starting smoking, I'm that nervous. But in the end, instead of an extortionately priced pack of cigs, I grab a tub of ice cream, unsure if it's a peace offering, a gift or a bribe. Either way, it feels good not to arrive empty-handed. And what kid doesn't love ice cream? That's bound to earn me a bunch of brownie points before I've even hit them with the classic Abi charm.

I arrive at Will's front door and hear the girls' laughter through an open window above. I knock and instantly the laughter subsides as Will makes his way downstairs. The door opens and we both grin before stealing a doorstep kiss.

'So good to see you,' Will whispers and for a moment, I wish tonight was just us.

'Da-ad!' comes a call from inside.

'Let's go up,' says Will, turning.

I linger, pulling him back, my mouth suddenly dry. 'Wait, should we talk about, you know, what the girls will call me?'

'Er, *Abi* – your name?' Will says with a kind laugh.

'Oh, course! Yeah, obvs …' I reply, feeling dumb.

I guess I wanted a protective shield, a character to play, not to be just … Abi.

'It'll be fine,' he says squeezing my hand and turning to trot, barefooted, back up the stairs.

'Yeah,' I say, following behind, holding stress in places I didn't even know you could be tense. Even my fingernails feel tight.

I have to relax. Kids are like dogs; they smell your fear – and you have to train them not to shit everywhere. I need to treat them as just another audience and if there's one thing I do well, it's crowd work. Maybe this is what my eight years on the circuit has been preparing me for.

'Girls,' Will says as two sets of eyes swivel towards me and my confidence evaporates.

'Hey ya!' I say, waving with the hyped-up enthusiasm of a kids' TV presenter.

'This is Abi,' Will smiles.

Elle speaks first, muted, monosyllabic. 'Hey.'

'Hey, Elle. Lovely to meet you!' I sing-song. God, I want to shake myself. *Just chill, Abi.*

'And I'm Esme!' She's all broad grins and skinny limbs.

Her demeanour warms the coolness coming from Elle, and I take a few steps closer, my mind searching for some failsafe, compering line that'll work a bit of magic – though I don't have many appropriate for this situation. I can hardly ask them to 'cheer if you're single!'

My palms begin to sweat under the intensity of their gaze. Even my bum feels damp.

'Don't worry about Elle, she's just shy,' Will says, teasing his first-born with a ruffle of her hair.

She pulls away with a huffy, 'No I'm not,' as her cheeks blush in the sweetest way.

'She's shy,' Will mouths with a giggle and it feels okay to laugh too, which helps discharge some of my nervous energy.

The air feels a little lighter so I decide now's the time to deal my ace.

'I bought this!' I beam, pulling my fat tub of Ben & Jerry's from the plastic bag and thrusting it towards the girls. They both stare at the container and my hand starts to quiver.

'I'm lactose intolerant,' Esme says, her little mouth still learning to wrap itself around the words.

I slump then Elle adds, 'Plus I'm vegan.'

And I slump even more, cringing at my first hurdle stumble. I was so sure B&Js would be a winner. Didn't think to check dietary requirements first.

'Since when?' Will asks Elle, eyebrow raised.

My misery eases slightly as I realise this is news to him too.

'Since forever.'

'She's going to marry a cow,' Esme declares, pulling a kissy-kissy face and embracing herself in mocking delight.

'At least they don't kill the planet!'

I sense now's not the time to mention the environmental impact of bovine farts.

'All right, that's enough,' Will interjects, turning the temperature way back down. 'I think the minimart has a vegan one. We can pop over in a bit, yeah?'

''kay,' Elle says with an indifferent shrug.

'And thanks, Abi. That was really thoughtful,' he adds. 'Elle, put it in the freezer, please. Me and Abi'll have it later.'

Already feeling bruised, I quietly pray our Ben & Jerry's moment alone comes quickly. Though I'm not accepting defeat yet, I defo feel like I'm on the ropes. Elle glares at Will but when he gives her a *do-as-I-ask* glare in reply, she untucks her legs from under her, pulls the tub from my hand and stomps to the kitchen. 'Fine. When the planet's burning from man's irreversible neglect, you'll need something to cool you down.'

'Exactly,' Will says, absolutely not taking the bait.

'I shouldn't even have to handle these cruelty dependent products,' Elle bawls from the kitchen.

'It'll be vegan ice cream for days next time. Promise. Save the planet, yeah?' I call after her, crossing fingers there'll actually be a next time.

I've been here five minutes and already offended the moral principles of Will's eldest and nearly given his youngest anaphylactic shock. Great start, Abi.

Will catches my eye, his mouth arcing into the gentlest smile – which makes me start to feel better – though the curl-up-and-die option does still seem appealing.

Elle returns, plonking herself back on the sofa. In slight desperation, my eyes scour the room, landing on a pack of cards wedged into the toy box. Raucous games of Uno and War with Caleb and Ayesha are always a guaranteed hit. That's got to be a solid way in with these two as well.

'Hey, how about a game of Snap?' I say, clapping my hands and looking for a place to sit.

'Snap?' scoffs Elle and with one withering retort I'm cut down even further.

'You guys used to love Snap!' says Will, corralling on my behalf.

'When I was like three,' Elle eye-rolls.

'Don't worry, Abi, we can play Snap later,' chimes Esme before jutting her finger towards the coffee table. 'Let's finish Deck of Devastation.'

Whoa. I played that once at uni and it's a proper stoners' card game. Defo *not* for kids.

Will notices my fretful look and reassures me, 'It's the family edition.'

'Daddy, you can deal Abi in!' says Esme, plumping the empty beanbag next to hers for me.

I flump onto it but straight away my arse disappears into its morphing softness and despite my best efforts, I just can't get upright.

Elle stifles her giggle while Esme has no such etiquette. Homegirl just laughs in my face. Even the cat seems to be enjoying the show, rolling onto his back and undulating. Thankfully,

Will scrambles to his feet and yanks me up, swapping my beanbag for his all while Esme rolls on the floor snorting.

'Esme, don't be rude,' Will instructs.

'She fell off!' Esme squeals in reply, snorting some more.

Even I'm starting to see the funny side and what with Esme's infectious howls, soon me and Will are laughing too. And despite her best efforts, Elle can't hide her snickers anymore either.

'She was like this!' yelps Esme as she slides around on her beanbag, imitating me, stoking our laughter further.

So much so, Elle's now weeping, face buried in the armrest of the sofa while Will tries to get Esme to stop but can't because he's laughing too much. Giggles pulse through me as I overheat from the pure release. Elle's the first to compose herself enough to speak.

'No one can get comfortable on that one. We call it the sadsack,' she says, wiping tears with the sleeve-covered heel of her hand.

'Facts,' I say, rogue giggles still breaking free.

We gather around the game and I smile to myself, feeling like I'm actually getting somewhere and that the brief, cold snap earlier with Elle may have passed. With everyone distracted by the business of gathering up their cards, I use the chance to take the kids in. Elle's hair is pulled into an intentionally casual bun, loose with wavy strands framing her face. Her jeans gape across both knees and she's wearing a sloganed jumper I haven't been able to read. Esme is still wearing her ivy-green school uniform; a bandana loops her neck and it's all offset with what looks like a nineteen twenties' smoking jacket – light satin with a swooping dragon on the back. This fashion mish-mash makes her look like a tiny Doctor Who.

Will pushes himself up from his seat. 'Abi, do you want a drink?'

'Oh, yes please, babes. JD and Coke.'

That'll defo help relax me. Will stops, glancing at the girls then back to me.

Oh …

'Are you an *alcololly*?' Esme asks, matter-of-factly, while swishing her skirt.

'It's *alcoholic*, dingus,' Elle scoffs.

'No, it isn't,' Esme insists though doubt creeps in.

Will massages his temples. 'Ez, we don't ask people things like that.'

'Why?'

'Because it's better to quietly judge them than know for sure,' Elle rasps.

I laugh at Elle's quip while being quietly intimidated and hella impressed with how grown-up her humour is. No wonder she turned her nose up at *Snap*.

'Why don't I put the kettle on?' Will says, heading to the kitchen. 'Tea, Abi?'

I nod, trying to shake off my embarrassment.

'Can I have a coffee?' says Elle.

'Absolutely not. It's six thirty. Milky tea or a hot chocolate.'

Will's emphatic and though Elle huffs, she knows it's not going to happen.

'Hot chocolate … with sprinkles,' she says, instantly becoming Will's little girl again, 'And can you use some of Ezzie's oat milk, please.'

'Got it,' Will says, 'And, Ezzie, what you having?'

She thinks for a moment. 'JD and Coke.'

'Warm oat milk it is,' Will says without skipping a beat, heading to the kitchen.

And just like that he's gone and I'm alone with the girls. Immediately I start to flail inside.

Will must sense my panic because he calls from the kitchen, 'Hey, Abi, can you give me a hand?'

Not wasting a moment but also not wanting to look too eager, I manoeuvre up from the beanbag but before I get to standing, Esme puts her arm around my neck, mouth right by my ear.

'Don't worry. Mummy drinks aaaaaaaall the time,' she whispers, spittle dotting the side of my face.

And with that, she releases me and I stumble off, splattered and baffled, behind me, Elle's hissing corrections at Esme about Kat's actual level of drinking.

In the kitchen, Will nudges the door closed and I pace, face contorted with worry. 'I'm a disaster, aren't I? You can say it.'

'Are you kidding?' Will says. 'They think you're great.'

'Elle's barely said two words to me.'

Will throws his head back. 'Trust me, that is Elle liking you a lot. Abi, you're doing brilliantly.'

I search his eyes to see if this is just platitudes. 'Serious?'

'Like … a speeding ticket,' Will chuckles. 'And Esme, wow. I couldn't have asked for it to go better. She adores you – even if you are an alcololly.'

I play-slap Will's arm but allow myself a little smile. 'She got me in a headlock before I came into the kitchen.'

'What? Then it's all over,' says Will in a silly, muted shriek, waving his hands like the ref at the end of a thirteen-round boxing match. 'You're pals for life!'

'Stop it,' I say, wanting to believe him but desperate not to get ahead of myself, especially after ice-creamgate.

'Seriously, I could count on one hand the number of people Esme gets in a headlock.'

'All right, funny guy,' I say, bunching Will's fingers before he actually starts counting them out.

'Babe,' he says, 'you are doing fantastic. Relax. They like you. If they didn't, trust me, I could tell.'

Will props my chin up with the crook of his finger, checks the coast is clear then we share a PG13 kiss and it is delicious. Reluctantly, I pull away first, aware of the girls next door. Look at me and my Responsible Adulting.

It's after seven thirty and Esme is pushing her bedtime with the classic, 'ask the adults lots of questions about themselves'. I don't mind though. They're pretty lowball queries and the chat buoys my confidence no end. I reposition on my beanbag, thrashing around a bit to see if I can make Esme giggle again. She does and it's a joyful sound.

'You're funny!' she declares and I puff up.

'You know that's Abi's job – to make people laugh?' Will says, proud, and I plume even more. 'She's a comedian.'

At this, Elle, who'd been lounging in her spot on the sofa, attention half on her phone, straightens, focus now fully on me. And though I hate to admit it, her gaze is validating. After years of wishing that from Mum, who'd have thought getting it from my boyfriend's thirteen-year-old would feel so good?

'How do you make people laugh? Do you tickle them?' Esme asks, wriggling on her beanbag.

'That's not a bad idea,' I reply, as though giving it due consideration. 'Next time I'm having a tricky gig, I'll try it.'

I offer up my palm for a high five and the tiny plap of our hands connecting is adorable. I look over at Will who smiles, content, arms wrapped around his knees.

'That's what I would do,' Esme continues, 'I would tickle them. Or I would get them to tickle each other then I wouldn't have to do anything.'

'That's stupid,' moans Elle.

'No, it isn't. I'd get paid a thousand pounds to just stand there saying, "Let the tickling begin!"'

'Then what's the point of you being on stage?' Elle counters.

'To tell them when to start!'

Will interrupts, probably knowing this conversation would run till dawn if he let it. 'All right, genius. Bedtime. Get some zeds for that megabrain of yours.'

'Awwwwww,' moans Esme while obediently accepting her fate.

'Kiss n'night,' Will instructs and Esme clambers onto the sofa, thrusting her little arms around Elle's neck, kissing her, and then, to my surprise, she clamps her arms around me too. And I can't help but beam. I may have won over at least one of my boyfriend's kids on my first attempt. *Nice going, Abi.*

'I'll be in to read your story,' Will calls after her, then stretches as he pushes himself up from his beanbag. 'Elle, you and Abi should chat comedy.'

He makes it as casual as he can and I appreciate the assist.

'*Will*,' Elle pleads, her embarrassment resurfacing.

My eyebrows peak at hearing her call him by his first name and I imagine doing the same with my mum, Queen Abosede. I'd be lying in a chalk outline before I'd even uttered the final syllable.

'What?' Will says, unfazed. 'The talent search is next Saturday and you've got a real comedian here. You can pick her brains.'

Elle curdles at being put on the spot. 'I was gonna ask in my own time.'

'Well, I saved you the bother,' Will grins and, ignoring her indignant tuts, takes a red-spined book off a shelf. 'Be about fifteen minutes.'

I shoo him away with an I've-got-this wave and he goes, blowing me a kiss.

Turning back to Elle, I weirdly feel more sure of myself with just the two of us, discussing a topic that's safe ground I know well.

'Whatever you need, advice-wise, I'm here. Don't ask me about boys though, haven't got a clue.'

As the words hit Elle's ears, contorting her face, I want to gobble them back up. Why would I say that? Suddenly, I'm free-falling, my dry mouth going into overdrive trying to explain myself.

'Course, *Will's* in safe hands. Dad's, I mean. As in *your* dad, not all dads. But there's nothing wrong with dads. Not that I'm specifically looking for a dad!'

The rat-tat-tat of my ramblings is like a machine gun in my brain. What the hell, man? A minute ago, we were on safe ground and I was all over this, but I've swerved us into a cul-de-sac and the less Elle says, the more this feels like a ten-car pile-up. Though we've had a nice evening, after that Ben & Jerry's fail, I need a solid win with her and so far, this chat is not it.

''kay,' she mutters.

There's a stilted quiet before I feel compelled to add, 'Obvs, I meant advice about stand-up.'

'I got that,' she says and her nose crinkles, like my awkwardness has an actual odour.

I push on, keen to move past the cringe. 'I'm no expert but I've been on the circuit a few years and picked up some stuff.'

Elle considers me for a moment, probably trying to figure out if I'm a comedian or just a clown, then says, 'I'm not sure they'll be into my style of comedy – at this competition.'

I shift on my beanbag, thankfully with more grace than before. 'What style is that then?'

'Umm … anecdotal?' She shrugs.

Jeez, I've been at this eight years and I don't have a style, yet she's already got hers down – at thirteen. But anecdotes about what? Pocket money not rising with the cost of living, convincing your parents you don't know the F-word?

'It's just, the other kids, they jump around on stage and I just … stand there talking about my life. Isn't that boring?'

I sit up, as best I can, on my quicksand beanbag. 'There's room for every type of comedy. I've seen it all – political, one-liners, story tellers, great performers whose writing, well, it's not their strong suit, great writers who aren't solid performers. There's room for everything.'

She thinks for a second. 'What if *I'm* one of those writers who doesn't know how to perform?'

Shit. That wasn't what I meant. The last thing I want is Will returning to find Elle in floods because I've made her think she's crap.

'Why would you say that?' I say, flipping it back to her.

'Because, even though I'm fun off-stage …' she starts and

I resist querying that, 'on stage, I'm dry like a Japanese fashion brand.'

'Superdry?' I say, chuffed I got the gag.

'Exactly.'

'Listen, dry is not the absence of performance. Dry is a style. Girl, you're only thirteen and you've got it going on. From what I can tell, your brand is deadpan, smart and hella funny. You're sorted. Remember me when you get to *ShowTime at the Athena*, yeah?' I laugh and luckily, Elle laughs too, bashful and sweet, squirming at the compliment but proud nonetheless.

'Thanks, Abi,' she mumbles.

Just then, Will reappears in the doorway. 'Everything okay?'

I look to Elle, legs folded into her chest, arms holding them close but face relaxed.

'Yeah,' she smiles. 'Really good actually.'

'Great,' says Will, planting himself on the floor between us, one hand on Elle, the other lightly resting on me.

And that's how we spend the rest of the evening, quietly chatting.

Later, while Elle is distracted on WhatsApp, Will and I, feeling more at ease, steal a kiss that's lush because it's fleeting. Not fleeting enough, though, because Elle catches us. 'Riiiiight, I'm off to bed.'

'Sorry, Ellie,' Will says as she unfurls herself.

He opens his arms for a cuddle and after a beat of hesitation, Elle crouches down, hugging him.

'Love you,' he says, kissing her hair.

'Yeah,' she says, standing.

'Night, Elle,' I say, knowing not to expect anything.

She hovers, body turned towards bed, face toward me,

expression uncertain. Reading the temperature, I offer my hand for a high five.

Relief flushes her face as she comes in, slapping her hand against mine. 'Night, Abi, and thanks for, you know, the advice.'

Once she's gone, Will folds his arms around me, and we settle into each other.

'That was fantastic,' he whispers.

I look up at him, finally allowing myself to feel proud for navigating this tricky first hurdle. 'It was, wasn't it.'

Chapter 16

'So, how did Friday go?' Cassie asks, leaning on the only chair she's put out since she arrived for tonight's Wisecrackers.

'Great. The kids are lovely and Will's so good with them.'

'I should hope so,' she snorts. 'He's their dad!'

'You know what I mean,' I reply, batting away her response.

'Abi's right, men aren't natural nurturers. I keep telling Callum – it's another reason we shouldn't have kids,' Frank says, as usual head buried in his notebook.

'That's just an excuse and not a very good one. What about male penguin couples?' Cassie says, arms crossed.

I go back to the chairs. I'm staying out of this.

'We're not talking about sitting on an egg for a couple of weeks. It's bath times, school runs, cyberbullying, constant costume-making, jabs, exams. God, it's never-ending,' Frank exhales, arms flapping down on his thighs.

'Just because *you're* not the nurturing type, don't write off all men. My kids' dads are super hands-on – and happily so,' Cassie says, then softens, adding, 'Callum clearly wants to be a dad. You two need a proper talk because this is not going away – no matter how many jokes you write about it.'

Frank snaps his book shut. 'Why have a grown-up discussion when I can shit-talk it out on stage?'

And with that, he disappears behind the sound booth, grabs the mic and mic stand and huffily sets them up at the front of the room. Through the PA we hear a snarky, '*Testing, testing.* Everyone is *testing* my nerves tonight.'

'Ignore him. I sense we've touched on unresolved issues,' Cassie concludes.

'You think?' I reply, my sarcasm whistling over her mess of brown hair.

Cassie steps back, admiring the one row of chairs she's now laid out, like she's just built the Sistine Chapel.

'Well, I'm glad the first meet was a success. People make so many mistakes when it comes to that, so good for you.'

'Thanks,' I nod as my curiosity-and-concern circus rolls into town. 'Mistakes, like what?'

Cassie buries a grimace. 'You said it was great. I wouldn't worry.'

'But theoretically, mistakes like what?' I press.

She straightens, as though aligning with her therapy know-how. 'Well, things like telling them you're boyfriend–girlfriend straight away rather than just friends. Adds unnecessary pressure, doesn't it?'

My lips tighten.

'Oh,' says Cassie, 'never mind. As long as you met on neutral ground.'

My head dips and her raised eyebrows plummet too.

'But you at least held off on the pet names and PDAs …'

I gabble a response but even I can't bear the pathetic whimpers of my justifications. Frank starts hooting with laughter, as he listens in. 'You absolute wally.'

'Hey!' I yelp but he's right.

'You've literally done the opposite of everything you're supposed to,' he says, deferring to Cassie who gives a sad, affirmative smile.

My mouth goldfishes as I try to think of a defence. 'How was I supposed to know? It's not like there are books about this kind of thing.'

'There literally are,' Cassie says. 'And blogs, support groups, therapists, *Psychologies* magazine articles.'

'I heard there's a version of Monopoly based on it,' Frank says, brightening at the prospect of spinning that into a punchline.

'Don't worry,' says Cassie rubbing my back.

'Are you … sending me Reiki energy?' I ask with suspicion.

Cassie looks away with sheepish guilt. 'Actually, I was sending it to all four of you.'

'Wait, wait, wait, speak slower, I'm not getting all this down,' Frank snorts as he pretends to scribble in his notebook.

'I'm glad you find it funny. Ten minutes ago, I was hyped about meeting the girls. Now it seems I couldn't have got it more wrong if I'd taken them machete juggling!'

Frank bends double, laughing, but I'm not in the mood.

'I mean, if you lot know so much, why didn't you say anything?' I whine.

'Er, I know nothing,' Frank says, holding up his hands in defence. 'Exhibit A – my whole routine about not wanting kids.'

I kiss my teeth at his watertight get-out before swivelling to Cassie. 'Well, you've got no excuse. This is literally your job.'

Cassie jams a hand on her hip in a rare display of indignation. 'If I therapised my friends through every situation, I'd never get anything done!'

She's not wrong. Me and Frank, alone, would be a full-time job.

'All I'm saying is, people are great at shouting from the sidelines where there's no danger of getting battered but it's not so easy when you're actually on the pitch,' I moan.

'Slightly dramatic image,' Frank says. 'You should just do what I do – talk it out on stage. That machete line is gold.'

I dismiss the thought with a huff. 'I tried that autobiographical stuff once. Went down like a random pube on a toothbrush. It's not for me.'

'It can take a while to bed in jokes,' Cassie offers.

'Bedding-in jokes is one thing but a whole new style?'

I flick my hand to shoo away the topic as a gurgle of anger froths within. This whole convo is making me feel like I'm failing at everything; meeting Will's kids *and* comedy – which was the one thing I always felt certain about.

'It's worth giving it some thought, that's all I meant,' Frank says, his voice dancing around my irritation.

'Spew my life out on stage? No thanks. What if Will heard? I mean, does Callum know what you say about kids when you're up there and how you talk about his niece and nephew?'

'Yeah,' Frank says, unbothered. 'That's why we get on so well: straight talking – so to speak.'

I'm at once insanely jealous and beyond furious. I've given stand-up my all yet it sounds like they're saying it's still not enough. On top of the evenings at clubs and pubs, the travel, the late nights and tricky crowds, I've now got to change my style? Just like that, I'll become an autobiographical comedian. Boom. New me.

'It was just a suggestion,' Frank says, planting himself in the seat behind the welcome table.

'Trying something new could be thrilling,' Cassie ventures as I notice a flicker between her and Frank. My anger ramps. What is this, an intervention? Have they been discussing how bad my comedy is and tonight has been the perfect in?

'Comedy just has to be funny and that's exactly what my stuff is,' I seethe, defensive and hurt. 'Plus, I do it all without gimmicks.'

'Gimmicks?' Frank says, slowly straightening like a dormant rattlesnake. 'You're referring, I assume, to the accent. But what about you?'

My eyes widen. 'What gimmick have I got?'

Frank's head lolls in exaggerated exasperation. 'The never-ending fat jokes? Pleeeease – 1985 called. They want their lowest common denominator comedy back.'

'Wow,' I say, staggered. 'Well, 2010 called, they want their that-thing's-out-of-date joke back!'

'Comrades!' Cassie yelps, her voice strained due to being unused to shouting. 'This is pure turmoil for my heart chakra. Let's just calm down.'

'That's rich,' Frank barks at me, over Cassie's shrill pleas. 'You're accusing me of using an old joke when you haven't written anything new since pedal-pushers were in fashion – the first time!'

'Why would I need to when I'm a shit-hot compere and I've got a banging ten that kills?' I shoot back, slapping my palm on my chest.

'At shitty open-mics maybe, but it'll never get you on TV, I promise you that.'

'Yeah? We'll see when Tess Blackman watches my set!'

I'm so furious I'm saying all kinds of mess.

'Are you kidding? You think I'm bringing someone from Callback here?'

I go to retort but my brain buffers. *What?*

'Why wouldn't you?' Cassie asks with innocent curiosity.

'Seriously, guys, look at the place,' Frank exhales, gesturing around the pub backroom with its chipped wood panelling and smoke-stained wallpaper.

'It's earthy,' Cassie says with very little conviction.

'Yeah, like dirt. I'm not bringing her here. And if you were auditioning for one of the biggest comedy producers in the country, you'd do the same.'

'I'd stay loyal is what I'd do,' I snap, bristling with indignation.

'You can't even get a paid gig, Abi – how would you know what you'd do?'

'For your information, Carl O'Connor offered me a paid spot—'

'Carl O'Connor?' Frank scoffs. 'That comedisaurus? He hasn't updated his routine since the three-day working week. Any gig of his will set your career back to the Jurassic age.'

'Not everything's about trying to get somewhere, Frank,' I reply.

'Well, if you're not trying to get somewhere, Abi, where are you going?'

Frank's question, though rhetorical, is a killer blow that pushes me down into the nearest seat and I say nothing to him for the rest of the evening.

*

By the time I walk out on stage, I'm a tangled knot of irritation, frustrated at how everyone seems to know what they're about except me. Frank is dry, biting. Cassie is a mad philosopher and even Elle already knows what she is, yet here I am, eight years in, with no idea. And apparently, I don't even know who's a good punt for a leg-up. I'm on the express train to Nowhere.

I go to say my usual opener but something flips. I'm gonna show Frank I'm just as good as he is and I don't need gimmicks to prove it. Sure, I make jokes about my size, but I'm great with or without that material, using any style I want.

'So … my boyfriend has two kids that I met a few days ago.'

I take my first tentative steps onto the slippery ice of autobiographical comedy.

'And I think, what do kids like more than anything?'

A women whispers to the person next to her, 'The internet,' like this is coming from painful, personal experience.

Her friend shushes her but someone behind laughs and I decide, in that ruthless way Frank does, I'm having that.

'I mean, apart from the internet …'

And I get a knowing titter from the crowd. Cool.

'They love ice cream, innit, so I took them some. Turns out, one's lactose-intolerant and the other's just gone vegan. Nice one, Abi.'

Pause. There's a couple of harrumphs. A nod of recognition from Internet Lady but nothing resembling laughter. I press on.

'Yeah, vegan. What's that about? Maybe I should have got her … broccoli ice cream.'

A woman in the centre of the audience calls out, 'There's no such thing.'

'All right, tofu ice cream then.'

I fling that zinger into the darkness but in reply I get, 'There's a soya ice cream. It's nice actually. You can barely tell the difference.'

'Really?' says a guy on the other side of the room.

What is happening right now? It's like my set is turning into some food forum. I was trying to get to the machete line but we're going way off course.

'Guys, if you want vegan food recommends follow Tabitha Brown, yeah? I'm kind of in the middle of something.'

That at least gets a response, not quite a laugh but it's better than nothing.

'So, can I get on or do you have any other questions, mate?'

There's more edge to my voice than normal but my irritation raises another titter, so that's a mini-win.

'Sorry, yeah,' he says. 'What's the name of the brand – the soya ice cream?'

'Seriously?' I snap. 'I'm here for comedy, not to help you transition to a plant-based lifestyle.'

The air goes taut until the man replies, 'Well, when does the comedy start?'

The audience reacts, enjoying his brutal heckle. They're laughing, not with me but at me, and it hurts. I try to rally, salvage something from the wreckage.

'... I was going to say, I'd have been better off taking them machete juggling.'

With no proper set-up, the line splats to the floor like a catapulted turd and I search the back of the room for the light telling me my time is up but there's nothing. I tap out anyway.

'Well, I think you've heard enough from me ... My name's Abi Akingbade and you've been – annoying!'

This gets my biggest laugh which is still nothing compared to the vegan heckler. I step off stage and flounce past Cassie. 'And that's why I don't do autobiographical,' I hiss and she replies with an apologetic frown.

I sag onto the step leading to the sound booth as Frank zips on stage, hurriedly resetting the energy in the room. I really thought I was a good comedian. Turns out I've got no style, direction or prospects and tonight I couldn't even do my full ten minutes. I sag further as nagging doubts push their way in. Earlier, Frank asked where I'm going and honestly, I don't know. Maybe I am on my way to Nowheresville. Even my own mother doesn't believe in me, and it seems my two best friends think I'm rubbish as well. I'm not sure what stings more. And the one thing I thought was going well, that I got right – meeting Elle and Esme – may just be a cat's cradle of emotional tripwires I've set up, doomed to trigger something bad, who knows where, who knows when.

Chapter 17

I wake up in a marginally lighter funk than I went to bed in, relieved I came to Will's last night. Even though he had the girls, he was fine with me crashing and I'm grateful because it meant not waking up alone this morning. I'm still tender from that bruising at Wisecrackers and turning towards him is an effort. In the murky bedroom light, I see he's already awake, eyes glistening as they take me in.

'Morning,' he says, quiet and close.

'Again? Didn't we have one yesterday?' I groan.

Will smiles, his hand tracing my duvet-covered contours.

'It's all going to be okay, Abi. Trust me.'

'Hmmm – even after what Cassie said?'

Will props himself up on one elbow. 'I don't think we messed up. I think we did our best.'

'Yeah, maybe.'

I shift onto my back wishing I believed Will's positive spin as much as he did.

'You know what you need,' he says.

'A new line of work?'

Will brushes my misery aside. 'A fried egg sandwich.'

My head shifts on the pillow. That does sound good.

'Fixes all kinds of problems. Kid not talking to you? Fried egg sandwich. Row with your ex? Fried egg sandwich. Global pandemic?'

'Fried egg sandwich?' I laugh, but then remember Elle. 'Eggs aren't vegan though, are they?'

Will sucks in air. 'We're currently not including them. Kat's worried she won't get enough protein otherwise.'

I nod with understanding though it feels like, being vegan, she won't get enough of anything. But what do I know?

I'm just about to reach under the duvet, my hand seeking out Will's smooth skin, when Esme bursts through the door, launching herself onto the bed.

'Daddy!'

Elbows and knees jut into my body and I try not to yelp in pain, burying my annoyance at Esme not knocking.

'What is it?' Will says, picking sleepy dust from his eye, seemingly immune to the jab, jab, jab of Esme crawling over us, the mounds of duvet becoming terrain to traverse rather than our actual bodies.

'Bagsy the bathroom,' Elle calls from the hallway and the door clunks shut.

It's soon followed by an echoey screech. 'Esme!'

'I caught a spider. It's in the bathroom!' Esme tells Will over squeals for help coming from next door.

Will flaps back the duvet. 'All right, Ez. Get rid of it.'

'But he's my friend.'

'Cool. But he's not Elle's,' Will says, firm but with paternal warmth.

Defeated, Esme skulks out of the room.

As the bathroom chaos begins to subside, Will flops back onto the bed. 'Why don't you walk Esme to school with me?'

My pulse starts to peak. I mean, isn't that a bit soon for us? Shouldn't this part of our relationship be all morning sex, breakfast in bed and quickies before work, not school runs and eggy bread?

'You guys won't want me cramping your style,' I say, reaching for the soft option, still figuring out my place here.

Will rolls onto his front, shuffling towards me. 'Esme would love you to join us. And I would too. Please?'

I look back at this handsome man who loves me, and reality hits again – this is the package. Not a single man but a dad with two daughters. That's the maths. End of.

'You know what? I'd love to,' I say and mean it.

Finally, after bathroom mayhem, breakfast, spider rehoming, some tears (Esme's but they could easily have been mine), book bags searched for and found, Elle waved off, school tie knotted – we're almost ready.

While Will grabs his keys and wallet, Esme charges down the stairs.

'Wait by the front door,' he calls after her.

'Yeah,' she replies, not looking back.

'Can you go and wait with her?' Will asks before disappearing back into his bedroom.

'Sure'.

From the top of the stairs, I crane to see Esme in the front doorway – but she's not there. I quickly shift down the stairs. Out on the pavement, aside from the postie wedging circulars through a neighbour's letter box, there's no one. She's gone. My chest pulses like I'm about to vomit up my heart. How can I have lost her already? We haven't even left the house!

'Boo!' Esme shrieks, popping up from the patio of the basement flat, and I damn near pass out.

Behind me, Will appears. 'Right, everyone good?'

'Yeah,' I exhale, thankful my brown skin hides how flushed I am.

'Then let's go,' he says as Esme clasps his hand, her free one reaching out for mine.

Though Cassie said me and Will did a bunch of things wrong when I was intro'ed to the girls, and let's not talk about nearly losing Esme just now, feeling her soft palm against my own, I can't help think we must be doing *something* right.

Finally, we arrive at the school gates but while Will and Esme have happily nattered all the way here, my mind has been in overdrive, assessing dangers at every turn. I'm fixated on keeping this little one safe so Will's in no doubt what a responsible adult I can be.

'Have a good day!' I call, my anxiety slowly retreating as I watch Esme skip across the playground to join her friends.

Will grins as we thread our fingers together. 'Once again, knocked it out of the park, Ms Akingbade.'

'Oh, you know,' I say, managing a playful bow.

And, for one fleeting moment, I actually start to wish this was my life. No more stress from trying to break into the comedy industry, no more survival jobs or hoping and praying. Just the certainty of kids crawling over you in the morning, of eggy breakfasts and goodbyes at the school gate. Getting a proper job, creating a secure routine. Money, time, family … contentment – rather than this constant craving for my 'what if's and 'someday, one day's. But I know me. I'll always be looking for the funny. The funniest. And the limelight in which to share it. Swear down, I'll die trying even though it leaves me forever teetering between despair and joy. Sometimes I wonder why the universe puts desires in our hearts – just to deny us? All I know is, I can't go back. The only way out is through. I walk with Will to the end of the road where we enjoy a lingering goodbye before going our separate ways, him to school to prep for the end of term, me to another riveting day of data entry.

Chapter 18

I'm contemplating a ten-minute power nap at my desk I'm that bored, when my phone vibrates. I grab it, desperate for a distraction. It's Will.

> Heya, Kat's got a work emergency so I've got the girls again. Fancy dinner with us tonight? I think Elle's hoping you can help with her performance for the talent show this weekend ... between you and me she's had the jitters ...
>
> Let me know – be great to see you, ;) Wxx

I'd already cancelled my open spot tonight, in no hurry to get back on stage after yesterday's disaster. And though I'd question how much assistance I can actually be to Elle, showing willing will definitely help us get to know each other. Plus, being with Will two nights in a row is a no brainer. I ping him a confirmation and try to push through the rest of the afternoon without nodding off.

I feel way more relaxed at Will's this time and knowing Elle wants me to come over has made a massive difference. We're gathered in the living room – Elle folded into her corner of the sofa while Esme tries to balance on the seat back, Chapelle, as ever, keeping a watchful eye from above. I want to ask him how I'm doing but I don't think I'm ready for his response.

'Go ahead, Elle,' I say, with an encouraging smile. 'Ask me whatever you want.'

'Is this an interview?' Esme asks.

'Not really …' Will says, bemused.

But before he can explain further, Esme slides off the sofa and starts rummaging through her toybox. 'I need my glasses.'

'You don't wear glasses,' Will says as Esme turns around wearing specs Flava Flav would call OTT.

She sits back down, squished next to Elle with no regard for her personal space. It's very cute. 'When you do an interview, you have to wear glasses so you can see them.'

'But … you *can* see them,' says Will.

'Shush, Daddy. The interview's started,' Esme says with a quietening hand.

Will laughs, flicking a that-told-me look, my way.

'So,' Esme says, peering over the top of her star-shaped frames, 'are your mummy and daddy funny?'

Just the thought of my parents trying to crack jokes is so ridiculous it makes me laugh out loud. 'I guess they're funny in their own way.'

Esme gives a thoughtful nod. 'Okay, when we come to your house, I'll bring my joke book and I can teach them some.'

I look to Will in surprise. So … it's on?

'Yeah, had a chat earlier and the girls are both up for a little trip to Hertfordshire … if that's still okay.'

Inside, I'm beaming. I hadn't dared to ask so this is more than okay. 'Definitely. I'll give my mum and dad some knock-knock jokes to practise.'

'No, but wait. I haven't finished my interview,' Esme says, shushing us all. 'All right, Abi. This is important. What's your favourite ice cream flavour?'

Elle's face creases in annoyance. 'What's that got to do with stand-up?'

'I just want to know,' Esme says as her glasses slip down her nose.

Elle tuts, her hands a tight cluster of pale knuckles and slender fingers – just like her father's. 'Dad, tell her.'

'All right, Ez, why don't we let Elle ask questions for a bit?' Will suggests.

Esme's face falls as she hands her glasses to Elle. 'Fine. You'll need these.'

Elle buries her irked grimace and just thanks her sister, setting the face furniture aside.

After some thought, she unknots herself and edges closer to me. 'Okay, what do I do if I forget my lines?'

I almost want to burst. This is like doing a pub quiz I wrote the questions for. Babes, been there, bought the T-shirt, took the selfies.

'If you're worried, write a couple of prompts on your hand, just here,' I say, pointing to the crook of my thumb and index finger. 'That way, when you're holding the mic, you can take a quick look and no one can tell.'

Will nods, impressed, as Elle listens in awe. 'That's brilliant. And what's a callback?'

This is the best pub quiz ever. 'It's when you refer back to an earlier comment or joke. They're an easy win because you've already done the set-up so it's pure punchline.'

Elle's eyes shimmer as though mentally scouring her routine, searching for places to plant new callback moments. 'And what about hecklers?'

'There's no way anyone will heckle at a competition but if they do, just say something like, "No more shandy for this one!"'

Elle's face is a vision of revelations and ah-has, her body now fully unravelled from the bundled knot it was.

'And …' she hesitates, 'what about nerves?'

I go to answer then notice her knee pumping ever so slightly, a habitual tick, pointing to hidden anxiety.

'Just take your time. Breathe. Don't rush and they'll hang on your every word.'

Elle studies her lap, taking all this in, and I let myself enjoy the fact that I do have something useful to share after all. The spat with Frank and my miserable fail last night knocked my confidence but just because I don't have producers and agents crawling all over me or paid gigs falling out my back pocket, I have to remember, eight years of gigging isn't nothing. Those are hard yards I should be proud to have done. Most people don't make it out the gate but here I am, still going, still trying. *Open-mic comic* doesn't normally inspire a lot of interest. When people ask what you've been on, they want you to say, *Mock the Week* – not 'a makeshift stage in a musty function room'. So to see Elle lean in, eager to absorb what I have to impart, is more gratifying than I dare admit.

'I want to ask something,' Esme chips in, reaching for the glasses. 'How did you become a comedian?'

'That's a great question, Ez,' Will says, leaning back into his beanbag.

I pretend to think, when in reality I've told my origin story a hundred times.

'It was eight years ago. I was about to start my second year at uni when me and my sister decided to do a cheeky weekend in New York before I went back. One night, we're passing this place called the Comedy Cellar and I'm like, "Have we really done New York if we don't go to a dingy basement in the Village to watch some stand-up?"'

I look over and Will and Elle are completely engaged, her knee, for the time being, still. Even Chapelle has crept closer, curling up on the window ledge, watching. Always watching.

'We go in, my sister Kemi whining about the eighteen-dollar entry and two-drink minimum, all the way down the basement steps. Anyway, finally the compere comes on and they rip the room apart. Pure jokes. I start to feel sorry for the opening comic, thinking, how are they gonna follow that? Then they walk out. It's Chris Rock. Me and Kemi's mouths literally fall open. He, of course, tears the room to shreds. There's two more amazing acts after him, but it's when they announce the headliner, I nearly piss— I mean pee myself.'

Esme gives me a scolding glare dappled with a cheeky grin. 'You said "piss".'

'And now you've said it,' Elle says impatiently. 'Let her finish.'

Will and I share a look and my tummy flutters at Elle's attentiveness.

'So, who was it? Who was the next act?' she asks, practically falling off the sofa.

'Yolanda B. Rockwell.'

I watch as her face breaks open.

'No way,' she says. 'How was she? Did she do that bit about introducing her girlfriend to her dad? And the adopting-a-white-baby routine?'

'I think she was still working on those cos they didn't make it into her specials until three years later.'

'Right,' Elle says, like she's literally updating her mental comedy encyclopedia.

I continue. 'She does some old routines too, like the difference between lesbians and … well, I won't say the word she used but …'

'What's a lesbian?' Esme asks, looking up at Will.

'A girl who likes other girls,' he says.

Esme considers this. 'Why is there a different name than if she likes a boy?'

'Let Abi finish her story!' snaps Elle.

'Because there are names for lots of things. Like chair, cat, comedian.'

'Chatterbox,' Elle sneers and Esme sticks out her tongue in response.

'Anyway,' I say, pushing through the sibling banter, 'she's really good. Relaxed, playing with the crowd. Just … amazing. And the sound of that laughter …'

In an instant, I'm back there, marvelling at how Yolanda so skilfully turned a disparate group of strangers into a cohesive one, unified in that glorious, shared experience – of laughter. What she evoked in that basement is a sound I've been chasing ever since. Pure magic. Pure joy.

'That's when I knew I wanted to be a stand-up comedian. I'd put my first set together before our plane even touched down in London.'

'Wow,' says Will, while Elle sits back, excitement in her eyes.

'And to celebrate, when I got home, I had my favourite ice cream – pistachio.' There's a beat and then Will laughs – a big, generous sound. I turn to Elle. 'And that's a callback.'

Recognition turns to respect, then delight as Elle laughs too.

'Got it,' she says, nodding in appreciation.

Will gives me a well-done wink and I flush with pride.

'Elle, why don't you do your routine for Abi while me and Ez finish dinner? Maybe she could give you some more pointers,' Will suggests.

'I'm game,' I say, looking to Elle.

She glances from me to her dad then back again. 'Cool. Yeah, why not.'

Sitting on the sofa armrest, Elle gallops through her set which is really good but her nervous mumbles take the edge off a lot of her best punchlines.

'That's it,' she says, after stumbling through her closing gag.

I whoop and clap my approval but she's not convinced.

'Honestly, Elle, that was great. Your material is fi-yah. I mean it. You don't need to change a thing, but let's talk about your performance. Now, don't get mad, but your dad showed me one of your clips,' I say, words fringed with caution.

I do not want to see that panicked expression I got last time I mentioned this, especially when we're only days away from showtime.

'Nooooo,' Elle cringes.

'Mate, you were fantastic and he was so proud.'

It's a battle for Elle to let that in but eventually she does – just about.

'I remember you saying you don't like to move about on stage. You really meant that, huh?'

Elle looks towards the door, ensuring Will and Esme are fully occupied in the kitchen. 'It's because – I – I don't always feel comfortable on stage.'

'Ah. And the dry delivery, is that …'

'If I look like I don't care, then no one can tease me. Or get to me.'

'Right,' I nod, touched she's confided in me but feeling for her too.

'None of my favourite comedians are like that though and when I watch ones that are, they're brilliant but … the audience don't like them as much, do they?'

I take a slow inhale, buying myself thinking time. We're on a knife's edge. I want to be honest but I definitely don't want to knock her confidence this late in the game. All I can think of is what I would do in her situation – a charm offensive. Go big or go home. My stuff works best when I use all of me, my facial expressions, my voices and my body, recreating scenes, transporting audience to the top deck of a No. 25 bus or the front row of my school classroom. I propose this to Elle and her expression goes from lost to horrified and I instantly start to second-guess myself.

'Okay, wait there,' I say, disappearing off, returning quickly with a broom. 'All right, up on your feet.'

Elle reluctantly drags herself from the safety of the sofa. 'Dad's pretty strict on indoor Quidditch. It's a real no-no.'

'Very funny,' I say, wedging the broom against the coffee table.

Despite Elle's griping, there's a playfulness to her tone which tells me we're okay.

'This,' I say, with a flourish, 'is your mic. Now, you don't have to do your whole routine, let's just look at your intro.'

'Okaaaaay,' Elle sighs, after much head lolling.

'Great,' I say, stepping into the imaginary wings of the stage. *'All right, guys, please make some noise for the amazing, the hilarious, the inimitable Elle Matheson!'*

And I cup my hands, making rapturous crowd noises. Elle blushes, shuffling towards the mic.

'Now what?' she asks.

'Do your intro,' I instruct, gesturing to continue.

'Now?'

'No, on the nineteenth of December. Yes, now,' I say with an even more emphatic flick of my hand.

'Hi, I'm Elle, I know, a thirteen-year-old comedian. I would have gone for climate activist but Greta got there first plus I'm only a thousand air miles off a free trip to Disneyland.'

She turns to me and shrugs.

'Great,' I say, determined to maintain my enthusiasm even if she isn't. 'Now try it with more … bounce.'

'Bounce?'

'Yeah. Put some energy into it, maybe direct the gag to someone in the audience.'

'Why?'

'Just try it and see how it feels,' I say, channelling my impatience into getting her back behind the microphone.

She exhales an 'M'okay.'

And though she's acting like back-to-back SATs would be more fun, she's sticking with this so I keep going too.

'Come on, Elle,' I say, encouraging her. 'Even if you never do this again, just try it. You've got nothing to lose.'

And something clicks, or perhaps releases. Elle's energy changes and she strides towards the mic. 'Hey, guys! How you doing? I'm Elle. I know, a thirteen-year-old comedian. I would have gone for climate activist but Greta got there first, plus I'm only a thousand air miles off a free trip to Disneyland!'

Then Elle pulls a hilarious, what-are-you-gonna-do face and I crack up.

'That was brilliant! You know what else you could do?' I say, inspired.

'A cartwheel?' Elle offers, sarcasm always reliably close by.

'No, Miss Funny Pants, move the mic stand.'

Elle freezes at the very suggestion.

'But …'

'You're hiding and you know it. Just give it a go,' I coax, aware this is a big deal but also that it will give her so much more freedom as she won't be nailed to that one spot.

Elle steps off then re-enters our stage area, this time moving the stand and cupping her hand like she's holding a mic. She peers down into our imaginary crowd, looking exposed but, I'm hoping, also starting to feel liberated.

'How was that?' I ask, searching her expression for a clue.

'It was … it was good.' And a grin spreads across her whole face.

From there, we carry on working through the routine, finding moments where she can bring in more movement, playfulness, joy. And I am in my element. Elle and I are vibing and she seems to really appreciate my input. Her nerves are making her a little hyper but better that than the upright cadaver she was before. She is going to kill on Saturday.

'I was thinking,' Elle adds, her enthusiasm brimming, 'I can do an American accent – should I use it?'

'Yes! It'd be perfect for that weekday bedtimes bit.'

'When I talk about watching TV with your parents and people on-screen start kissing? Oh, and, that stuff with my teacher, Ms Maroof, I could do her walk!' Elle says, eyes now teeming with ideas.

'Why not? It's your stage, your time,' I say, directing Elle back to the spotlight.

She's just about to try another bit when Esme appears in the doorway, making us jump.

'Dinner's ready!' she yelps before disappearing back into the kitchen.

Will obviously gives her some stern-dad pointers on tone adjustment because a moment later, Esme returns offering a more composed invitation and we go through to the kitchen to join them.

'You're gonna do great,' I say to Elle. 'You're well prepped, you've got brilliant material and your performance is proper.'

'Thanks, Abi. This has been cool,' Elle replies with a quiet shyness.

And inside, I'm glowing.

Even Cassie would have to agree, this has been an out-and-out success. And though I was nervous, tonight with Will and the girls has been a tonic. We're already finding our feet as a four. But also, talking about comedy with Elle has reminded me how much I love being a stand-up. It's in my bones. And whatever wobbles I may have had, I'm defo not ready to give that up yet.

Chapter 19

I can't believe I'm at the Comedy Store. God knows how many times I've seen amazing stand-up here and how many times I've pictured myself on that stage bantering with the front row. Probably as many times as I've emailed their booker to try and actually get a gig. But this afternoon, I'm not here to tear this room up. I'm here supporting Elle. I wonder if she gets how important this venue is. I'm guessing she's more concerned with trying to become Comedy Buzz's Budding Comedian of the Year. I look around and the place is jammed with industry faces. In one direction there's a gaggle of producers, in the other, bookers and agents. I'd kill to get just one of these people to see me perform.

We're hanging out at the back where there's a mass of fussing parents, excited friends and, of course, the teenage contestants including Elle, who's having a low-key meltdown.

'Mum said she'd be here,' Elle says, twisting her sleeve while pacing a tiny square in front of Will whose calm is, frankly, award-winning.

'Elle,' he says after she completes a few more laps of her meltdown square, 'she said she'd *try*. You know she'd be here if she could.'

I look over at Esme, where things are far more straightforward. Using Will as a maypole, she's dancing around him in gleeful excitement fuelled by the electric atmosphere already building ahead of the show. I'm in awe as Will simultaneously talks Elle down from her fretful cliff while his arm is yanked every which way by the six-year-old kangaroo holding on to him. As for me, I stand awkward and slightly apart, not knowing if it's helpful to intervene or if I should just keep shtum, wary of overstepping. In contrast to the other night, Elle has barely spoken to me today. Whatever headway we made feels lost and my pocket of anxiety is growing with each passing minute. I stick to keeping quiet, hoping somehow Will and Elle feel my silent solidarity.

It's about forty-odd minutes before lights up and the buzz in the room is palpable.

'You okay, Ellie?' Will says, placing a gentle hand on her shoulder.

'Yeah,' she says, the tension in her body slowly releasing in his gaze.

Will pulls her in for a hug and I relax too but then notice Elle's pulsing knee, that nervous energy with no place to go. If she can't get a handle on her jitters, she's in trouble.

'Elle, babes, don't forget what I said. If the audience see you're nervous, they feel nervous too. Do those breaths I showed you. From the—'

I don't even get to finish the sentence.

'Thanks, Abi. I think I know how to breathe,' Elle sneers but before Will even opens his mouth to set her straight, she apologises. 'Sorry, nerves.'

'S'okay,' I reply, trying to hide my surprise at her bite, steadying myself by taking those big, full breaths myself.

At least one of us is following my advice.

'You're gonna absolutely smash this. You know that, right?' Will says, a hand on her slight shoulder.

'Yeah. You're gonna smash it to pieces!' Esme says, smacking a scrunched fist into her palm.

At the pap of Esme's balled-up fingers connecting, Elle giggles and now we can all breathe.

'Why don't I grab us some drinks?' I say, wagging a finger towards the bar.

'Good idea,' Will says and we share a look to reconnect and purge some of the built-up strain before I head over.

Resting against its counter, I glance over to the comedians' area, tables that, instinctively, punters know aren't for them … or perhaps don't want because of the poor view of the stage. There, four of the aspiring comics congregate. One is reciting his routine as his mum shuffles through index cards, the stopwatch app open on her phone. I look the kid up and down – skinny jeans, a strategic rip on the knee, expensive-looking leather jacket and a white tee brandishing some ironic meme. He powers through his set, then runs a hand through his asymmetric blond hair as he utters his closing line. His mum stops the clock.

'Brilliant, Brandon! You've got fifteen seconds to spare so you can take your time on the spider-in-the-bath bit,' she says, resetting her stopwatch.

I puff my cheeks, exhausted just watching them. Turning back, I notice a woman a little further along the bar and recognise her instantly. It's Dawn Webb, booker for the Laughing Lemming comedy clubs, a national chain of so-so venues. Aside from the godawful gong show they run, their weekend gigs are jampacked with stag and hen parties. It's tricky to land a punchline when the front row are waving inflatable cocks at you. However, given some comics have earned enough to go pro just on the Laughing Lemming circuit alone, getting in with homegirl here would be a very, very good move. And knowing Frank hasn't played any of their rooms, meaning I might get one up on him, gives me that extra dose of ballsy confidence you need for a cold intro.

'Dawn, right?' I say, overplaying the not-sure-who-you-are thing.

'Who's asking?' Dawn replies, eyes bewildered as though I've just woken her up.

'Abi Akingbade,' I say, pressing on.

Nothing registers, her glance bouncing around the room like the lyrics dot on a karaoke screen. Clearly she's looking for someone, anyone, more interesting to speak to.

'I'm a comedian,' I add, hopelessness seeping in.

But slowly something clunks into place for her.

'Yes,' she says, recognition blooming.

My chest inflates at the thought Dawn knows me. That'll make this a lot easier.

'How's LA treating you?' she asks, now radiating industry affability.

I blink my reply, a placeholder until I can think what to say. 'I ummm … I've never been.'

'Oh God, sorry. I'm thinking of Sandra. Sorry, yes, Abi. Right. You got that Vodafone campaign. I love you in those ads.'

I blink some more. 'Nope. Not me. I wanted to talk to you about—'

Dawn slaps her head as either an apology or brain reset.

'Did you just get a Channel Four sitcom?'

Blink. 'That was Nadine.'

'Did you get cancelled for mocking that MP's lazy eye?'

Blink. 'That's Lindy.'

'Are you JD's cousin?'

Blink.

'Shit. You must think I'm awful. I don't think you all … I know who you all are. Who are you again?'

I draw in a long breath to hold down my annoyance. I understand being mistaken for Sandra. We do actually look alike even though she's ten years older. But Nadine Walters, Lindy T *and* JD's cousin – whoever the hell that is? Dawn's obviously got this sea of black female comedians bobbing around her mind but has never bothered to figure out which is which.

'I'm Abi Akingbade,' I say, trying not to sound pissed.

'Of course you are. Yes! Well, look, lovely to meet you but I'm a judge so shouldn't be fraternising. No favourites but … I hope you win!'

She waves crossed fingers at me but before I can a) remind her the cut-off age for this competition is seventeen, b) be flattered by her mistake, c) ask for a gig, she's gone.

'Tess!' I hear her call behind me because, of course, Tess Blackman is here too.

Eight years in this game and while Elle's got agents and producers giving up their Saturday afternoon to watch her, I can't even get some crappy booker to tell my face apart from four other comedians. Those same creeping doubts I had before start to churn again.

I get our drinks and make my way back over to Will and

the girls. Coke for Esme, sparkling water for Elle and beers for me and Will.

'Cheers,' he says, kissing my forehead, and I start to feel like less of a loser.

'Can I have some?' Elle asks.

'Sure. Once the bubbles have settled – which should happen when you turn eighteen,' Will replies.

'Funny,' mumbles Elle. 'Maybe *you* should enter this competition.'

I stifle my giggle, not wanting to endorse backchat.

'Don't encourage her, you.'

Will juts a finger in my side, my ticklish weak spot. I flinch and we both laugh. A good chuckle works magic and my bruising attempt at networking already feels soothed.

We're just heading towards our seats when I hear my name being called.

'Abi. I was expecting to hear from you about my gig. What's occurring?'

I instantly recoil. It's Carl and though I should be thrilled he's so keen, ever since Frank's comedisaurus jibe, I've been putting off contacting him, because what if Frank's right and doing Carl's crumby out-of-towner will just set me back?

'Oh, hey, Carl. Sorry, you know, busy, busy – with work, life – this,' I say, spreading my arms to include Will and Elle.

Carl glances over at her and nods. 'You got a horse in the race?'

'Yeah, Elle Matheson,' I nod, glad to move the conversation on from talk of his gig.

The awkwardness was starting to make my ears ring.

'Oh well, good luck but listen, bell me about my night. Some acts would chew my arm off for a slot,' he says, then carries on working his way around the room.

Chew his arm off? More like shoot myself in the foot, from what Frank's saying. I groan inwardly at how the one and only paid offer I've ever had is such a dud. Shuffling along our row, I join Will and the girls, sitting next to Elle who now seems more relaxed. At least this feels nice. The four of us. Comforted, I shove thoughts of Carl's gig away, instead focusing on the afternoon ahead.

As we settle, for some reason my gaze is drawn towards the main entrance. I spot the messy brown bun first and then that stretched smile. Damn.

'Mum!'

Elle launches past me towards Kat, flinging her arms around her.

'Lovely to see you again, Abi!' Kat says with forced friendliness.

'Likewise!' I say, straining too as Kat joins us in our row.

Of course, it's great for Elle that Kat's managed to get here, but just as I was settling into *this* dynamic, *this* foursome, *this* version of us, along she comes and now I'm just that useless fifth wheel – and we all know what happens to them: shoved in the boot and forgotten about.

'One of my senior trainers was able to take my afternoon session after all so here I am,' she says, pretend-wiping sweat from her brow. 'I have to get back to lock up but I wasn't going to miss my baby girl's big day.'

Kat tries to ruffle her daughter's hair but Elle dodges, patting her curly mane back into place.

'You don't even like comedy, you weirdo,' she says, trying to regain her grumpy teen composure but failing, obviously chuffed by her mum's arrival.

'But I like you,' Kat counters, bringing Elle in for another hug.

As Esme snuggles up to Will, jealousy pricks me from all directions.

There's only a few minutes until the show starts and Elle's leg is pulsating even more than before. While Kat's presence has elevated her mood, it's done nothing for her nerves.

'I'm not sure about this,' Elle says, eyes landing on the kid I saw rehearsing with his mum earlier.

He's got to be on his third run-through.

'Shouldn't I be doing that, going over everything so it's perfect, especially as I've changed things?'

'Oh, what have you changed?' Kat asks, doing her best to sound interested and not concerned.

'Just stuff. Voices and things.'

'Voices?' Kat asks.

'It's fine, Mum. Don't worry.'

Kat locks eyes with Will.

'It's fine,' he mouths, which would be reassuring except he hasn't seen Elle perform since we made those changes either.

The need to take control surges through me. I feel responsible. I'm the one who coached her and this is my terrain. If anyone can offer reassurances, it should be me.

'We don't want her getting stale. Robo-comic over there is so over-rehearsed, he'll sound like Siri when he's on stage.'

This raises a smile from Elle.

'Honestly, you've got this. Trust me, babes,' I say, offering a tentative fist pound, trying to stay chill as I wait for her to respond. 'Don't leave me hanging.'

She looks at me then taps her fist against mine and we smile.

I sense both parents surreptitiously watching us, their energies wildly different. Will is delighted while Kat seems to have caught Elle's pulsing knee syndrome.

'Hellooo everyone, and welcome to the Comedy Store,' the announcer booms through the PA system. *'This afternoon's show starts in five minutes. Pleeeeease take your seats as the show is about to begin!'*

Kat claps her hands. 'Oh God. I can hardly breathe. Good luck, pumpkin!'

'Chill, Kat,' Elle says. 'I'm going to watch from the dressing room. See you after.'

Before she leaves, Will grabs Elle, smooshing his face into hers. 'Smash this, you smasher.'

And for once, there's no too-cool-for-school brush-off. After a moment, she extracts herself from his embrace, gives her mum a kiss, jabs Esme's armpit making her yelp, and – to the relief of my needy self – fist pounds me again and goes.

At last we retake our seats but somehow, I've found myself in the middle. Will senses my awkwardness and grasps my hand.

'Elle likes you,' Kat says, turning to me.

'She's getting used to me like a fly you can't get rid of or an Ed Sheeran earworm.'

'No, I can tell,' Kat says, circumnavigating my self-deprecation. 'She's really warming to you.'

'Elle's a great kid. They both are,' I squirm, suddenly feeling out of my depth.

We look over at Esme who's standing on her seat, eyes glued to the stage, waiting for the moment her sister will appear.

'It's really nice that you've got something to bond over with Elle. I just hope there are other things you can connect on, you know, if comedy doesn't work out – for either of you ... though I'm sure it will.'

Wow. I reel at the bitter sting of her jibe – and the familiarity of it. That could have come straight from my mum's Little Book Of Insults. I want to clapback so badly but when I look at Kat, her expression is clear, innocent. Weirdly, I don't think she meant it as a dig. But I wonder, does she drip-feed Elle this kind of negativity on the regular too? Maybe Mum and Kat have a few things in common when it comes to parenting. The only difference is that Kat actually comes to gigs where as my mum sows her seeds of doubt from the comfort of her own home.

'Elle is a natural and I've been doing this for eight years so ...' I say, hoping the implied *it's going to work out – FOR BOTH OF US!*, is apparent.

'No, of course. I didn't mean it like that. I'm so grateful for the help you've given her,' Kat blushes.

'No problem,' I say, magnanimous but still vex.

Fortunately, the blare of the show starting blasts out any further attempts to speak. The room goes dark and multicoloured Vari-lites sweep the stage, landing on the mic, before turning a hot, showbizzy, bright white.

'Pleeeeeasssse welcome to the stage, your host, Josh Nwachukwu.'

The crowd erupts but my response to Josh is lukewarm. Of course they got the guy from that stupid 'Jerk the Week' show. I could have compered this standing on my head but as usual, they've gone for celebrity over experience.

'So, who have we got in? Give me a cheer if you're in a couple?' Josh belts and I scoff. This is an audience of kids. That's hardly going to work.

A smatter of cheers go up and then a lone female voice calls out a strangled, 'Yay!'

The crowd laugh.

'Sounds like you're happier about it than he is,' Josh pings back.

Another laugh.

'*She*, actually!' calls the woman. 'We're here supporting our son!'

And at that, about three rows combust. Josh rides out the reaction, surfing it into some more pretty route-one banter, until, at last, it's time to bring on the first comic.

'Okay, guys, please make some noise for your opening act this afternoon – give it up for … Priya Parveen!' He whoops, keeping the excitement levels sky high.

A girl in a floral-print dress walks out, looking more like a flower girl than a stand-up comedian but it's a ruse. Her act totally subverts our perceptions with some interesting and edgy stuff. Opening is a tough spot. She does really well and at the end of her set she exits to solid applause. With the show under way, Josh takes a moment to explain the voting which, mercifully, is down to a panel of judges. Spotlights swivel towards their seats, dead centre of the audience as Josh introduces them.

'Nate Ibrahim from JTW!'

Just the mention of 'Jerk the Week' has the crowd go berserk.

'Tess Blackman of Callback Productions, Dawn Webb from the Laughing Lemming, comedian Carl O'Connor, aaaand Mike Garrett from our sponsors, Comedy Buzz!'

That is a good set of judges. I cross everything that Elle can just hold her nerve.

Three more acts go on, including one kid so nervous she forgets to bring out her ukulele. Then it's time for slick Brandon, with his over-rehearsed routine and meticulously planned outfit. He grips the mic, whipping the stand out of the way before launching into his set, just as he's practised – probably a thousand times over. He's sharp, no spare fat but soulless, a carbon copy of the cool garms and machine-gun delivery he's no doubt seen many times on TV. I sit back, assured. If Elle sticks to the plan, she has a killer chance of placing, if not winning.

'He's good,' Will murmurs, concerned.

I shrug. Yeah, he's good, but there's nothing interesting to hook on to.

'So, listen, guys, I just want to shout out to Fortesmere Year Nines for coming out and supporting me.'

Brandon's fan section goes nuts and he clutches at his heart with earnest sincerity.

'Awwww,' says Kat.

I close my eyes to stop them rolling in derision. Playing the emotional card, Brandon, really?

'But I especially want to shout out to my mums, Liz and Alex!'

The audience *lose it*, whooping with a fervour we haven't yet heard.

'Love you!' one of Brandon's mums calls from the darkness.

'Didn't see that coming,' Kat whispers, her face drawn in intrigue.

So, *Brandon* is the kid with two mums! I stare back at the stage in horror as he launches into one last, hilarious routine about being a fourteen-year-old with same-sex parents who are both cooler than you. No, no, no. This is terrible. This is bad. With one twist of donor sperm fate, Brandon has gone from being good to not just great but *interesting.* I quietly curse Will and Kat's heterosexuality. I want to bellow from my seat, *Elle's from a bi-racial, blended family! Her mum's shagging the piano teacher that her dad taught at secondary school! She knows Krav Maga! You want interesting, it's right here!*

On stage, Brandon leaves to roof-raising applause and for the first time, I start to worry.

The interval goes by in a blur with Kat, Will and me doing all we can to bolster Elle's confidence before she's up – fifth in the second half. I tell her that's the sweet spot but, with her nerves peaking, she's barely able to acknowledge me let alone take solace. Soon, the show's up and running again. The second half opening act is a reliable crowd-pleaser but wonderfully uninteresting; the next, I barely register, there's two more performers I couldn't pick out of a line-up and then, at last, the wait is over. Will and I grip each other's hands.

'Guys, please go crazy, go wild for Elle Matheson!'

Me, Will, Kat and Esme whoop and cheer at the top of our lungs, craning so far we're practically toppling into the next row. Elle walks out, planting herself solidly in front of the mic. This is it.

'Afternoon, everyone. And welcome to I-Wish-I-Had-More-Hugs-As-A-Toddler.'

Laughter.

Will and I exhale but I'm shocked. She must have written that line today as I've never heard it. On stage, Elle grips the mic but she says nothing and I notice her left leg start to twitch.

'Breathe,' I murmur, willing her on as she shields her eyes from the glaring lights.

'Okay … wow,' she mumbles, off-mic.

Move the stand, move the stand, I chant.

Meanwhile Kat is practically out of her seat. 'What's happening?'

'Calm down. She's got this,' says Will.

'Calm down? Our daughter's gone into shock,' Kat hisses across me, before apologising for leaning on my leg.

'No worries,' I whisper, vowing never to sit between these two ever again.

'Here we go with the dramatics,' Will fires back at her.

From the stage, Elle clears her throat. 'Sorry, guys, saw my dad and his girlfriend reverse-cowgirl last night. Bad visuals.'

Time freezes. Will looks at me. Kat looks at Will but I just stay dead still, eyes facing forward despite Kat's appalled glare now burning into the side of my head. Nope. Not looking. Not engaging. Thankfully, a beat later, the joke lands and the room literally roars with scandalised laughter.

Biding her time like a pro, Elle stokes the response. 'That's no game of horsey I know.'

The judges disintegrate. Dawn, head thrown back, is howling, as are Carl and Nate. Tess makes notes and Mike Garrett is laughing so hard he'll need a defibrillator in a minute.

Elle launches into the rest of her set. Nerves cause her to rush at first but within a minute she finds her groove, buoyed by that high risk but brilliant opener. She's flying – mostly with material we rehearsed. I wince at one point, though, when she does an impression of her physics teacher, Mrs Maroof, who Elle had failed to mention walks with a limp. The audience recoil as she Richard-the-Thirds through the impersonation but luckily by the time she comes to her killer finish, it's forgotten.

The second Elle puts the mic in its stand Will catapults from his seat, hollering approval. Kat and I join him and to his right, Esme screeches, partly for her sister but, I'm guessing, partly for the pure release of being allowed to make noise without getting into trouble. I don't want to jinx anything but surely this is Elle's for the taking. The acts that follow don't even come near to what she did. Brandon is the only real competition.

As we wait for the results, the atmosphere is electrified.

'She was so brilliant. I'm blown away,' Will says, excitement brimming, and I couldn't agree more.

'Really good. Really good,' says Kat, her lips stretched as though trying to hold a thought in. 'Yup. Yup. Really good.'

'You okay?' I ask.

'Yup. Really good.'

'She's gotta place after that, right. She—' begins Will before he's interrupted.

'How did she know about … the *cowgirl* situation?' Kat says almost biting the words in half.

My eyes swivel towards the bar but Kat's judgy sternness nixes any notion of a great escape.

'Did you get her to say that?'

'What? No. Me and Will have never … We're not really in a cowgirl kind of place yet. Though there has been some rustling …'

Will gives me a *not-now* glare and I stop talking, though I do feel slightly aggrieved, because, you know, the internet? I'm sure Elle's learned far worse there than anything she'd see in Will's bedroom.

'It's fine, Kat, and look, it got a huge laugh,' says Will, his words swallowed by the cheers that suddenly engulf us because Josh has returned to the stage followed by the contestants.

'So first up, guys, can we give some love to this year's entrants,' he says, windmilling his arm to get the crowd excited.

It's not necessary. The energy in this room could fuel a shuttle launch. Will and I are particularly enthusiastic, happy to move on from the 'cowgirl' convo.

'And here to announce the winner is head judge, Dawn Webb!'

Dawn takes centre stage and attempts a feeble gag that makes me glad she books comedy rather than performs it.

'So, in third place – Lexi Kyriaku. In second place …' Dawn pauses, milking it, 'Brandon Thomas.'

Gasps and cheers ripple around the crowd. I clasp my hands to my mouth. She's done it. I can't believe it. Elle's actually done it.

'And the Comedy Buzz Budding Comedian of the Year *is* …'

Dawn leaves an even bigger gap into which Will, Kat, me and a good forty others pour Elle's name. Quickly, we get a unified chant going and it's joyful and silly. *'Elle, Elle, Elle!'*

'The winner is,' Dawn says, adjusting her glasses for effect, 'Priya Parveen!'

I leap out of my seat to cheer until my brain registers the name. On stage, Elle's face drains of colour and my skin goes cold. I turn to Will but he's more in shock than I am. What. The. Actual.

Chapter 20

Elle flies towards Kat and buries her face in her mum's chest while Will, who's holding a sleeping Esme zonked from all the drama, strokes her hair.

I look at Esme, knowing how she feels and still baffled by the outcome. Elle's set was pitch-perfect, well, aside from that impression of her teacher. This doesn't make sense. I attempt a comforting back rub to show Elle we're all super proud of her but the minute my hand makes contact, she flinches.

'Msss mm urrr frrrt,' she says, words muffled by her mum's, well, mufflers.

'What's that, darling?' says Kat, prising Elle's face up.

'This is your fault,' Elle repeats, looking directly at me.

'I– I – It's …' I start, shock numbing me.

'Hey, hey. Not cool, baby girl,' says Will, handing Esme to Kat so he can properly address the situation.

Bringing himself face to face with Elle, he clasps her shoulder. 'I know you're sad about this, but you did brilliantly. And some of that's down to Abi so instead of blaming her, maybe try a thank you.'

'It was the impression. Everyone hated it. She should have stopped me!'

'I didn't know you were going to …' I stutter.

'I asked you if I should do it, *Abi.* You said, "Why not? It's your stage, your time."'

My legs go to jelly at the venom in her voice as she recounts my words back to me. She's not upset anymore, she's angry and it's all coming my way.

'I even asked if we should go over my routine and you said not to *over-rehearse.*'

This is staggering. Only a teenager could find a way to blame someone else when they do something dumb.

'Brilliant advice,' she mumbles. 'Next time I want to fail miserably, I'll call you.'

'Elle! This is not Abi's fault. You're being childish,' says Will.

'Will,' Kat interjects, 'she's upset.'

'That doesn't mean she can lash out at everyone.'

I appreciate his defence but she's not lashing out at everyone. She's not blaming Kat for giving birth to her or Will for not raising her to be funnier. As far as she's concerned, this is all on me.

'If she's exposed to these high-stress environments, what do you expect?' Kat says, a protective arm still coiled around Elle.

I want to tell them both it's the bouncing back that makes you a real comic, that any Joe can get on stage but it's returning after you tank that sorts the warriors from the weak. But I hold my tongue, just standing there braced for further blows.

'Elle,' says Will, mustering all his parental sternness.

'Will,' she replies, eyes narrow.

'Who went on stage today, you or Abi?'

'Me,' Elle huffs.

'And who wrote the jokes?'

'Me,' she mumbles.

'And who decided to do that impression?'

'Okay, I get it. Accountability. Let's not get all *Sesame Street* about it,' Elle snips.

Will straightens and I see him weigh up whether or not to deal with the sass. Lucky for Elle, he lets it slide.

'So?' he says, looking from Elle to me and back until she finally gets the hint.

'Urgh. Fine. Sorry, Abi,' Elle grizzles.

'No worries,' I say, with an unbothered shrug, my internal and external worlds now completely at odds as deep hurt turns into a swell of anger I battle to squash down.

Elle pivots back to Will. 'Happy?'

'With you? Not how I'd describe what I'm feeling but the gesture is noted. We'll have a proper talk later.'

'At least you gave it a go and now you can put this all behind you,' Kat says, with a consolatory smile that looks suspiciously victorious.

As I try to calm myself, I hear a familiar and, frankly, welcome, voice. 'Hey, Abi.'

I turn to see Dina from the Comedy Cabin.

'Nice work up there, Elle,' she says, patting her on the shoulder.

Elle gives a thin smile in reply.

'I can't believe you didn't place.'

'Better luck next time, eh?' Will says, brushing a soft fist against Elle's chin.

She doesn't respond but given her earlier behaviour, this is progress.

'If she wants there to be a next time, of course,' Kat says, her protective arm tightening its hold on her daughter.

'I hope there will be. And I'd love it to be at the Comedy Cabana,' Dina says.

Wait, the Cabana? Dina's paid gig? I've been doing her unpaid show, the Cabin, for time and just like that, Elle's getting offered the Cabana? She didn't even place in this stupid competition! Talk about a spear in my heart.

Elle's face lights up at the offer.

'Can I?' she begs, doe-eying her parents.

'Wow, thank you. That's a great opportunity,' Will says, no doubt hoping this will bolster Elle's mood.

Of course, it's Kat who pumps the brakes. 'Er, I'm not sure that will work.'

Elle clamps her hands together. 'Please, Mum. Please.'

'What about school?'

'We broke up already!' Elle shrills, her arms flapping up and down.

'Right.' Kat frowns, shaking her head as if trying to dislodge more reasons to say no, 'Thing is, pumpkin, this Cabana place, it'll be who-knows-where, full of adults, drinking, men we don't know. No, I'm sorry. Thank you though.'

Elle instinctively turns to Will, clearly well practised at playing one parent off against the another.

'Dad?'

Will sighs, turning to Dina. 'Sorry, can you give us a minute?'

Bemused, Dina moves off and once out of earshot, Elle goes into full pleading mode. 'You've got to let me do this!'

'We don't *got* to let you do anything, young lady,' Kat retorts.

Elle regroups, realising she has a lot of ground to cover if she wants to get sign-off here. 'Okay, but let's look at the facts, yeah? It's the summer holidays, so no homework. There's adults and booze here and I'm still alive.'

'That's because you have three grown-ups with you,' Kat interjects.

'Okay, so what if one of you comes with me?' Elle offers, a final throw of the dice.

Kat sighs heavily. 'I've got enough on my plate without having to schlep back and forth to gigs, pumpkin.'

'It's not *gigs*. This is one show!' Elle begs.

'It's never just one with you,' Kat says, exasperated. 'And what happens when I'm away with work? Dad already has two jobs, he doesn't need a third.'

'Actually, I don't mind. If you can't, I'll do it. We'll just change my week night with them to whenever the gig is,' Will chips in, a note of defiance in his voice.

'And what about this one?' Kat says, nodding towards the sleeping Esme in her arms. 'What will you do with her when you're ferrying Elle around London?'

Will searches for a response but has nothing.

Flailing for options, Elle utters half sentences, still hoping one of them, once released into the wild, will grow into a fully-fledged solution.

'Okay … what about Abi?' she says, jutting a finger my way.

I freeze like an escaping prisoner caught in the glare of an incriminating searchlight.

'She's already on the circuit. She's an adult. You know her. It's perfect.'

Will's arms slowly uncross as he chews on the idea. 'I don't hate this …'

'I'm not sure,' says Kat, words weighted with misgiving.

'What do *you* think?' Elle says, turning to me, instantly switching from snide teenager to big-eyed innocent.

'Well …' I gulp, the only response I can manage as hopeful eyes bore into me.

'Abi's busy too, Elle. You can't just enlist her like that,' Kat says.

'Especially after you were so rude,' adds Will. 'And don't think we've forgotten about that.'

Listening, I consider the possibilities. If Elle's holding on to any ill-will, surely me saving the day will sort that right out. And taking her to Dina's will also give us alone time to get to know each other better. Hopefully we'll click, and a bonded Abi and Elle means a bonded Abi and Esme and all that bonding is going to make me and Will stick together like glue. And, not to be too self-serving, but it won't hurt my career to hang with Dina at the Cabana either.

'Happy to,' I say at last.

'Yessss!' says Elle, pumping her fist. 'Dad, let's tell that lady before she leaves.'

And she drags Will off with her.

'Thank you,' Kat says, a strained smile pulling her lips thin.

'She's booked me! Thursday, in three weeks. A five-minute spot!' Elle squeals when they return. 'And, Dawn from the Laughing Lemming said she wants me to do the gong show at their Camden club!'

I go rigid. Two gigs … in one night and I can't even get arrested.

'Wasn't she one of the judges? Did she say why you didn't place?' Kat asks, craning to look over at Dawn who's shaking on her jacket, ready to leave.

'They don't give feedback at these things,' I say, a lacklustre attempt to reassert my industry expertise.

'Who cares?' Elle blurts. 'She booked me, plus the JTW producer gave me his number and said to call him.'

Kat shudders. 'Three gigs. We haven't even left the building and … three gigs.'

'The last one wasn't an offer but it's a fair point. We only agreed to one,' Will says, landing back in reality. 'Abi, would you be cool to chaperone Elle to the gong show as well?'

'That's not what I meant,' Kat whimpers but the conversation has moved, at pace, from whatever concerns she has.

'I'm sure we can make it work,' I say, because honestly, it feels like the only way forward anyway.

'You're a superstar.' Will hugs me, and winks at Elle. 'You're on your way, baby girl.'

'Thanks, Abi,' Elle says, biting her lip. 'And sorry about earlier.'

'Old news,' I reply and finally, the atmosphere lifts.

'Right, let's get you guys home,' Will says, with a hand on each of the kids.

'Cool, I just need to nip to the loo,' I exhale.

'Yeah, me too,' Elle says, turning to walk with me.

'My first chaperoning job,' I quip and everyone does that polite afternoon-tea laughter.

It's not a sound I'd normally love but given how things were just a few minutes ago, it's very, very welcome.

As Elle and I weave between the last of the exiting audience,

I decide to check in and make sure the earlier schism is definitely behind us. 'So – you good?'

'Hmm. Yeah.'

Not sure how to read that, I add, 'I was thinking we could get a takeaway tonight.'

'Oh, what, my consolation prize?'

'No, to celebrate how well you did,' I say, face beginning to wrinkle with concern. 'Listen, it doesn't matter what any judge thinks, you did so well and you've already got gig offers which is what it's all about anyway.'

'Yeah, no thanks to you.'

And my head jerks, almost to dodge the swipe. 'Elle – I'm sorry it didn't work out, but, stand-up isn't just about being great. It's about being able to—'

'Urrgh. Spare me the lecture. What is it they say? Those who can't – teach.'

I stumble, rigid with shock. 'Look, if you don't want me to chaperone, just say.'

Elle rolls her eyes skyward.

'If I had *any* other option, trust me, I'd rather the Child Catcher took me to these gigs but my parents have approved *you*. So this is a business arrangement. Nothing more. Get me to these gigs and back in one piece. And preferably without yakking on about how we're connected – which I'm hoping won't be for much longer anyway,' and as one last shot across my bow she says, 'Oh, and please don't call me "babes" or any other stupid names. It's Elle or Eleanora. So – you good?'

I nod, watching her walk away, incapable of speech as I try to work out what in the Black Jesus just happened.

Chapter 21

I've spent the entire night, eyes fixed on the ceiling, clock ticking, dawn creeping in from behind the curtains, Will conked out next to me, trying to process yesterday afternoon.

I did my best to shrug off Elle going all Tony Soprano on me, forced a smile as she chowed through a takeaway *I paid for* in front of a movie on *my* Netflix account but, inside, I was burning. I'm not an early riser but this morning I need to get out of here. I feel trapped – on Elle's turf. I have to spew everything I'm holding on to, and I know exactly where to go to do it. Early on a Sunday morning is the one time I know Kemi will be home – getting the kids ready, batting away protests that church is boring while Felix knocks up breakfast. It's chaos but exactly what my soul needs. I peer at the clock; it's seven and I can hear the girls starting to stir. I make a plan – quick wash, dress and get the hell out of Dodge.

I slip quietly out of bed, grabbing the towel Will has designated mine, and creep to the bathroom just as Elle emerges into the hallway. We stop. It's like when you see a fox on its nocturnal prowl and wonder if it'll hightail or pounce at your face. We stand, gazes fixed. After what feels like an age, I shift towards the door. Elle anticipates and breezes by me, letting the bathroom door clunk shut in my face. From inside, I hear her hum, lazy yet deliberate. Anger courses through me as I go back to Will's room and dress, forgoing a shower so I can just leave. I try to calm down but my venting nostrils give me away.

'You okay?' Will says, half-awake.

I hesitate. Telling him about yesterday could lead to bare drama. What if he sides with Elle, or worse, sides with me and gives her a proper telling-off? That'll make chaperoning fun – in no way whatsoever. I shudder, flashing back to Elle's savage one-eighty, so bewildering I wonder if I actually misread the situation and it was just that super, *duper* dry humour of hers. Or maybe, she was acting out, still upset about losing and it was a one-off, never to be repeated. Blinkered by hope, I decide to leave it.

'I'm fine. I just remembered, I've got a few things to do at home.'

I crawl across the bed to kiss him, my acting skills working hard to cover the mass of emotions spiralling within. It wasn't that long ago Will and I agreed no more secrets but, right now, it feels like this is one I have to keep.

'Okay, see you later?' Will's disappointment pricks at my guilt and I can't look at him as I reply.

'Maybe. I'll message you.' But I know I'm not coming back today, not how I'm feeling.

It's just before nine when I get to Kemi's and it's only when I go to knock I realise it is kind of early for an unannounced visit, even when it's family. But I need my sister, so I flap the letter box until I hear movement. Inside, there's hushed mutters, hallway scurrying, kids ushered away and then the front door swings open.

'Abi?'

Kemi is flustered and not half dressed for church as I was expecting but still in her bed gear, silky dressing gown over the top.

'Have I caught you and Felix, you know …' I ask, twirling my finger at her.

'No,' she says, flapping my hand away. 'What are you doing here?'

'I texted,' I say defensively, squeezing by her.

Technically I did but only as an afterthought, walking from the Tube.

'Do you know what time it is?' she moans, tying the belt of her gown.

'Yes. Do *you*? You're usually halfway through your amens by now.'

'We're … not going this week,' she says with a furtive glance towards the living-room door which creaks ajar.

'Waiting for the second coming at home in case they try to deliver it and you're out. Smart,' I say, heading towards the lounge as I usually do.

'Hilarious,' Kemi says, catching my arm, stopping me going any further.

I look at her, confused, as the living-room door quickly clicks closed. 'What's going on?'

'School project. Fancy something to eat? I'm doing yam, stew and eggs.'

The mention of my favourite Naija brekkie takes me off the scent and, to be fair, is the comfort food I need.

*

'So, come on, what are you doing here?' Kemi says, pulling ingredients from the fridge.

Memories of Elle's antics flood back and I crumple, recounting yesterday's events.

'I really felt like I was getting somewhere with these girls. Honestly, the little one is a gem, and I thought comedy was helping me and Elle connect.'

Kemi shakes her head. 'Ungrateful madam, and after all the help you gave her.'

'Oh, my girl had something to say about that. She went, "Those who can't – teach."'

'Noooo,' Kemi gasps, hand to her mouth in shock.

'Trust me, I felt to check the soles of her feet for the mark of the beast.'

Kemi busts out laughing before she can stop herself. 'Abi! You can't say that.'

Though her words scold, her laughter says otherwise and I feel a zillion times better, finally being able to see the funny side in all this.

Still tittering to herself, I watch Kemi prep veggies for her stew – a sliver of Scotch bonnet, garlic, tinned tomatoes. She heats her oil, tossing in onions. The smell of them frying makes my stomach smile.

'So, what you gonna do?' she asks, stirring in her remaining ingredients.

My shoulders bunny-hop with indecision.

'You know what I'd do?'

'That's what I'm here for,' I reply, sitting upright. 'Lay on that Kemi wisdom.'

'Okay, you need to let Elle know Mamma 2.0 don't play,' she says, clicking her fingers.

'How do you mean?'

Kemi rests her spatula on the side of the pan.

'I know you, Abi. You'll be trying to charm these kids, be their best mate, but if you're gonna be a responsible adult for them, they need to see that side of you.'

I go quiet, still not sure I've got that in me. I once confronted a kid for littering and he told me to go fornicate myself. That was the last time I tried responsible adulting around anyone – other than Ayesha and Caleb.

'They need to get, if it comes to it, you're not scared to set them straight,' Kemi adds, going back to her stew. 'Cos if it's a free-for-all at Dad's house, the mum will constantly be having to reset when they come back to hers. You get this right and, believe me, she'll thank you.'

I'm sure Kemi's got a point except ... at Will's, it is relaxed but it's definitely not a free-for-all. And even though the girls are only six and thirteen, they seem too ... grown up for that type of hard-line parenting. I imagine an alternative, stricter reality where there's no more clambering on the sofa for Esme, firm invitations for Elle to address Will as 'Dad' and swift correction in the face of her backchat – and honestly, I don't love it, or recognise that version of Will.

'You've gotta remember,' Kemi says, 'separated parents shy away from discipline cos they think they've put the kids through enough. You step up and you'll be doing them both a favour.'

'I guess, but what if the girls *are* disciplined? What if the problem is just that Elle straight up hates me and getting all Miss Trunchbull on her is only gonna make things worse?'

'Abi,' says Kemi, 'you can only be the fun adult *after* you set the ground rules. Kids need to know your boundaries to help learn their own. It's parenting 101.'

I let out a long, considered sigh just as Caleb barrels into the kitchen.

'I've finished making boxes – can I go on my PlayStation – Hi, Auntie Abi,' he says, all in one breath.

'Boxes?' I query.

Kemi's face falls, eyes darting towards the door. Now I really need to know what's going on. Our gazes lock and then without a word, I slip past Caleb and gallop down the hallway, bundling through to the living room. Breathless, I halt, taking in the scene before swivelling to Kemi who arrives by my side.

'What is this?'

I look around and every flat surface is covered with small boxes. At the dining table Felix is carefully sticking labels onto little tubs which he then hands to Ayesha who boxes them up with packing foam.

'Auntie Abi, we're in business!' Ayesha screeches, throwing polystyrene chips everywhere.

'Explain,' I demand as Kemi releases a heavy sigh.

'This is what I've been meaning to tell you.'

She seems ill at ease. Usually, Kemi only gets twitchy when Nigeria are in the World Cup and she has to choose between supporting them or England.

'Okay, look at this,' she says, reaching for an assortment of containers.

They're all haircare products I recognise, some of which I use.

'These are meant to be for natural hair but look at how many artificial ingredients they've got.'

She starts reading the names of chemicals – nitrohypgloxinol this, hypercondraxythate that.

'Big companies buy black brands and fill the products with this stuff, then we put these unnatural substances on our natural hair. So …' she says, restlessly rubbing her hands, 'I decided to start my own home-made haircare range.'

'Wait, what?'

Felix clears his throat. '*We* decided to start our own home-made haircare range.'

'So, this is the "private sector project" you were talking about?' I say, as the pieces fall into place.

Kemi gives a nervous smile. 'I love my job but I've spent years hankering for something. I thought that social housing thing would satisfy but it didn't. I need to create – for myself, not just keep making other people's dreams a reality.'

She moves packing materials from the sofa and we sit. There must be two hundred boxes and at least fifty tubs and bottles yet to be packaged by Felix and Ayesha.

'You know there's child labour laws about this kind of thing,' I say.

'They just do it at weekends,' Kemi gabbles, no longer her usual confident self.

'I was messing,' I say with a reassuring hand on her thigh.

Kemi tuts and shoves me with her shoulder. 'This is a big deal for us, Abs.'

And I can see this is coming from deep within her – probably that same place my love of stand-up lives. It's that desire to conjure, take an empty stage, a blank canvas, a nothing, and turn it into a something. Magic. I relish being reminded of that part of me, until thoughts of Mum permeate, of how disparaging she can be about creative expression. Lord knows what she'd make of this, which is probably why Kemi's kept it on the DL.

'So are you going to tell her ladyship?'

Kemi shrinks, throwing a furtive glace to Felix. 'Once things get going. If she sees it taking off, maybe me changing lanes won't be such a shock.'

Well, well, well. How interesting. Kemi has this huge thing going on in her life and for once, I know more about it than Mum. Admittedly, I only found out by breaking and entering but still, I savour how this thing, deeply precious to Kemi, for now only lives between me and her.

'So, which came first, the chicken or the egg head?' I say, rubbing Kemi's buzz cut.

Without the wig I really get to look at this crop of hers. It's gorgeous and almost makes *me* want to do the Big Chop again, experience that exhilaration of seeing the new you. It's not just a haircut, it's a lifestyle choice, a fresh way of being, terrifying and thrilling all at once.

'Sort of happened together. I've wanted to go natural for time but when I started looking at haircare ranges, there were so many chemicals in everything. Anyway, one night, we were chatting about it and ...'

Kemi hesitates and I know what she's reluctant to say.

'It's cool. I get it. God told you to do it.'

Her expression contorts. 'That's not quite how He works, but yeah, he definitely put the idea in my heart.'

I study her face, its lines, her eyes, and I can tell this project means the world to her. Though her side hustle is a risk, knowing

Kemi, it'll also be well thought-out, calculated. And like most things she turns her hand to, bound to succeed. I'm so impressed. I can't even get my main hustle off the ground.

'Well, I'm sure, in you, He is well pleased.'

Kemi scoffs at my feeble attempt to quote scripture.

'I am gonna tell Mum. I just want to get that first sale over the line.'

'Hold the press. You haven't sold anything?!'

Kemi looks at the boxed-up products, shaking her head. 'And it's cost us a fortune …'

'All natural, organic, ayurvedic. Doesn't come cheap,' Felix adds.

I take Kemi's hand. 'It's gonna be fine. Trust me.'

'It better be,' she replies. 'I've handed in my notice.'

And I'm stunned silent.

Chapter 22

It's Wisecrackers night and though my time with Kemi at the weekend did bring some relief, I am just not up to it. Frank's late as per and while that has started to grind my gears, given our spat last week, I'm actually hoping he no-shows. His words were wounding – made worse by Elle now joining the Abi's-Not-Good-Enough choir too. The blunt pain of her comments may have lessened but I am starting to think, perhaps her failure *was* my fault. Maybe we should have done one last run-through, then I could have stopped her doing impersonations of disabled teachers, things would have turned out differently and we'd still be building our friendship. Instead I have a growing clump of dread in my tummy which I just can't shift. Is this what it feels like to be a responsible adult?

Cassie has agreed to compere and I'm thankful, even though when she does, it's never pretty. She's been on stage ten minutes and has already got herself into a comedy cul-de-sac with a hospice nurse in the front row.

'Surely being surrounded by death must take an emotional toll?' Cassie asks with absolute empathy.

'Not as much as for the patients,' the nurse says with a half-laugh, a valiant attempt to inject some humour seeing as the actual comedian seems unwilling to.

I should step in but I can barely cope with the mess in my own life let alone fix someone else's screw-ups. And anyway, according to Elle, am I even qualified to help anyone out of a comedy catastrophe?

'Well, I wish you the very best,' Cassie says taking the nurse's hand as though *she* were the one dying, and with an earnest intensity holds it aloft, almost yanking the poor woman out of her seat.

'Not all superheroes wear capes,' Cassie nods in reverent appreciation and the audience applaud, as much as anything to bring this ordeal to an end.

Awkwardness finally over, Cassie introduces me. This is exactly what every comic dreams of – walking on stage to sober reflection.

I pace towards the front knowing I've got approximately fifteen feet and ten seconds to get my shit together. I pass Cassie who gives me a sweet thumbs up, take a deep breath and turn to the audience.

'Guys, you ever get tired of being told you're too much? I swear, it should be my middle name. Abi "too much" Akingbade. But look at me. I'm eleven stone and five foot four. I'm not too much. I'm compact!'

I pause for the laugh. There isn't much and I know why. Aside from the Siberian chill in the room after Cassie's attempt at warm-up, the deflated exhaustion in my voice is enough to send a group of caffeinated toddlers to sleep. I have to fix this or I'm going to tank. I already feel like that's happening in my personal life; I can't let that happen on stage too.

Suddenly, I'm aware of the deafening quiet of a restless audience. A cough from Cassie brings me back and I slip into autopilot, hoping that will get me through. I look for a skinny guy and give him a wink.

'Honestly babe, with these thighs, I'd break your back.' I try the line anyway but my timing's off so he has no idea what I'm talking about.

He blinks, nonplussed.

'Because, you know, I was saying, I'm eleven stone. My thighs are like vices.'

'What's that got to do with anything?' the front row nurse mutters, then adds, 'And it's "a vice", not "vices".'

In an instant, this rubs my fur the wrong way. It's what Mum does constantly, ignore the point, getting hooked on linguistic pedantry. I want to blank her, but how can I when she's two feet away?

'Expand, babes?' I say with a sarcastic huff, hoping I can use the chat to slingshot back into my set.

'Nothing,' she says, clamming up, an icy full stop to the conversation.

I know the pro thing to do is leave it. We're heading into murky waters and I am too off my game to follow.

'No, go on,' I say, annoyed. 'What did you mean?'

She sighs hard. 'Well … it's fattist, isn't it?'

'It's … *you what?*'

The nurse arches an eyebrow towards her friend as though too weary to explain. 'Nothing. You're great. Carry on.'

Embarrassed, her friend slips her cardigan off the back of the chair and folds it over the crook of her arm. She *might* be cold but most likely she's about to leave and that can't happen. There's already barely anyone here. The last thing I need is to shed audience members – more proof for Frank that I'm a dud. I want to tear this nurse a new one, but I've got to right this ship so I go back to the script.

'I know what you're thinking, eleven stone is a lot but too much? Nah, fam. If anything. It's not enough!'

Pause for the cheer that usually gets ... Okay, nothing this time. Well of course not. Nurse Ratched here has ruined my flow.

'Thing is, I want a man that can handle all of me. No, I'm not just talking about my magnificent rack.'

The crowd murmur among themselves and the first beads of sweat form on my neck. Is it indifference they're feeling or have they leapfrogged over that straight to hatred? There's no sympathy or concern. My slow death is just making them angry and irritable, like greedy relatives waiting for their rich uncle to croak. *Just die already.* I feel the comedy coroner check my pulse. If I have one, it's weak as hell and I'm not sure how much longer I'll survive. I go light-headed, looking out and seeing no love, only frustration, money wasted on services not rendered. In the glare of their disapproval, the clump in my stomach turns leaden. If I lose at comedy, Mum will be intolerable, Elle's friendship unwinnable – and what will I be, a full-time data enterer? Nothing more, nothing less. Comedy has been who I am for so long, the thought of not having it causes a surging panic. Edging on desperation, I make a bid at resuscitation.

'No guys, I'm not just talking about handling my incredible, curvalicious bod. FYI, you girls should be grateful I got given this Nigerian behind. If you had it, you'd topple over.'

'Oh my God,' the nurse rumbles before picking up her handbag, wedging it under her arm.

And that's it. I snap. 'What is your problem?'

The room goes quiet. From the back, Cassie looks up, her face frozen in alarm.

'This ain't the telly, love. I can hear you,' I scoff at my front-row critic.

Normally, that zinger from the comedians' community chest would get something but tonight, nish. My back goes damp with perspiration, the mic slippery in my hand. I've screwed it.

'I know it's not the TV,' says the nurse, 'because you wouldn't be on it.'

The audience ooooohhh at her comment and my body goes cold as I try to cobble together some kind of clapback. 'Ha! This one fancies herself as a bit of a comedian.'

'Perhaps the bit that's missing in you – the funny bone.'

Now I just want to launch myself at this basic biaaatch who's got the nerve to say that to me – at my show! But the impulse peaks and peters before I can even ball a fist. I'm not a fighter. Never have been. Plus, news travels like lightning on the circuit. The last thing I need is bookers hearing I lamped an audience member. Tends to make them less likely to offer you paid gigs. The crowd, if that's what you'd call tonight's smattering, is now captivated in the worst way.

'So, who crowned you comedy connoisseur?' I blurt, a shameless play to frame her as the villain in the audience's eyes.

'I'm no connoisseur but I wish you were. Your entire set is fattist, sexist rubbish. You've got nothing interesting to say,' she snorts.

'It's a comedy night, love. If you want "interesting", read Malcolm Gladwell,' I sneer, trying to lock eyes with anyone to get agreement.

I'm not even attempting to be funny anymore. This is just a primal scramble for survival because Nursey's not done.

'Funny and interesting don't have to be mutually exclusive.'

'Listen to it. "Mutually exclusive", like she's doing a TED Talk,' I interject but home girl just blanks me.

'Look at Yolanda B. Rockwell, Fynn Cooper, Melissa Fong,'

she continues. 'Melissa's much bigger than you and she never mentions her weight – ever.'

'So, you want to pick and choose my material? I'm not a jukebox,' I laugh bitterly, now riled this woman's using the name of my shero, Yolanda B. Rockwell, against me.

With the slightest nod, the nurse whispers to her friend and they both get up, making their way to the exit.

'If you want to pick a track, you can stick your coin right here!' I holler, slapping my behind.

At this, a bloke at the back gives a withering shake of his head and gets up to leave too. Aside from the ringing in my ears, his scraping chair is the only thing I hear.

'You know,' says the nurse, turning, 'you could be funny if you weren't such a try-hard.'

She links arms with her friend and they finally go just as Frank appears from the bar, mouth frozen in a horrified O. The audience are looking at me in pretty much the same way – a kind of stunned disgust. There's nothing more I can do so I call time of death. It's over.

'Well, guys, this has been … an education,' I say as I step off to silence.

Cassie rushes past me, throwing a pitiful look my way as she grabs the mic, searching for what to say to recalibrate the atmos.

'It's not easy, comedy … as Abi has so selflessly demonstrated,' she flusters before adding a sincere, 'Thank you for your sacrifice.'

She makes me sound like some battle-weary soldier who's hurled themselves on a grenade. Then again, that is how I feel – and like I'm the one who removed the pin.

'What happened?' Frank hisses, tone still brittle from our fall-out, compounded by me stinking out the room with my disastrous 'set'.

My shoulders slump. Now is not the time for a post-mortem. 'I died. I'm not the first and I won't be the last. Just leave some flowers and send your condolences.'

Frank's disdain is almost suffocating.

'And you wonder why I'm not bringing Callback here?' he says in that disappointed voice only teachers and parents use.

I have no response, except one that involves sunshine-free places Frank can stick his disappointment, so I say nothing and we just stand there, side by side, miles apart. It's a relief when Cassie finally introduces him. Without another word, he strides to the front of the room.

'Wow, you guys. Did I hear there was a hospice nurse in the house? We needed her after *that* death,' Frank says.

The laugh that follows is instant. It's a singeing betrayal but I'm not surprised. Frank will do whatever it takes for the laugh, including flinging me under the bus.

Outside, it's muggy and the heaviness is unbearable. I start to head off when Cassie emerges through the pub doorway.

'Just wanted to check you're all right.'

I nod, failing miserably to mask my mood.

'Listen, Abi, we all have off nights. You're still amazing.'

At her words, I feel that unwanted tingle in my eyes, and tip my face skywards to stop tears falling. 'According to Frank I'm having an off career.'

'Oh, ignore him. He thinks this is a race, not a journey. We get there in our own time and he's going at such a lick, he's missing the view,' she puffs.

'I s'pose, but knowing your mate thinks you're shit ain't easy – if he still is my mate.'

'Don't be daft. Frank adores you. Besides, you've fallen out before. By next week it'll all be forgotten,' she says, a kind smile taking over her face.

But at the thought of returning to the scene of my death, I wilt, the weight of Elle, Frank and my failing comedy career bearing down on my tired shoulders.

'You'll bounce back, Abi. You always do,' Cassie says with a gentle hand on my arm.

At her touch, I crumble, a loud sob escaping me.

'Ooooh, angel,' she says, arms enveloping me. 'You are fantastic and don't let anyone tell you otherwise, especially some silly nurse. She was dastardly. I bet the patients at her hospice can't wait to pop their clogs with her looking after them.'

A snorted chuckle bubbles up and now I don't know if I'm laughing or crying. Keeping hold of me with one hand, Cassie fishes a scrunched tissue from her pocket and offers it to me. 'It's clean. Promise.'

I take it, dabbing at my tears that just won't stop.

'I know this isn't just about tonight. You're going through some major stuff and transformation can be a bloody business,' she says, rubbing my back.

I give a snotty nod in recognition. 'Feels like a slaughterhouse.'

'Think of it as laughter with an added "s".' Cassie smiles. 'Trust me, you'll look back and be so glad you went through it.'

I'm not so sure but I don't have the energy to discuss so I mumble my thanks and we hug out a goodbye.

'If you ever want to talk, I'm always here, Abi. You know that, right?'

'I know. Thanks, Cass,' I say, heading off.

As I walk to the bus stop I can't help replay my dumpster fire of an evening, trying to unpick where it derailed. With everything going on, I've definitely lost my bounce. Could that have played a part? I start to wonder if my routine is more dependent on my personality than I'd realised. Is that why Elle, who's such a good writer, thinks I'm a joke and why I lost the audience tonight? Is my gregariousness the only thing holding this together, so that, with one yank from that woman, me and my sexist, fattist routine completely unravelled?

And I'm still fully baffled by that too. I only make jokes about my appearance so audiences laugh with rather than *at* me, so I can control the room but now, it's starting to feel like a comedy blind spot I have no clue how to correct or if I'm even good enough to.

I've loved stand-up for the longest time. And for that five or ten minutes I'm on stage, all I want is to help people forget their money worries, rocky relationships, jobs they hate, and have a good night – endorphins, oxytocin and serotonin flooding their brains because I'm their natural high. The thought I might not be a fit for this job is so depressing I can barely stand to have it in my brain. Yet at just thirteen, Elle already has paid gigs and a possible slot on 'Jerk the Week' while all I've had is an invite to a crappy out-of-towner – and I might not even have that. I've put off calling Carl for so long, he's probably struck me off his list. I always thought I was on the right path but standing here now I feel lost, longing for something I can't have with no idea how or if I'll ever get it.

Chapter 23

After another dull day of data entry, I'm finally with Will at the Disraeli. I feel like it's been forever since we did this, a date night – just me and him. The place is fairly quiet and relaxed but I can't ignore this perma-tension in my neck, back and shoulders. It's been there ever since my run-in with Elle which I still haven't brought up. I wonder about mentioning it tonight. Being just the two of us, we'll be able to have a proper talk without any distractions. I let that play out in my head – and grimace as what would have been a fun, chilled-out evening, suddenly gets very serious. Instead of sharing favourite film quotes or picking over gossip from the latest series of *Celebrity Marriage SOS*, we'd be discussing discipline, cancelling Elle's gigs and having stern words about her behaviour. It's been a minute since it was just us, out together, enjoying ourselves. Do I really want to spoil that?

'Hey, you,' Will says, handing me a JD and Coke.

'Thanks,' I say, taking a long, grateful sip.

'You okay?' he asks, getting comfy in his seat next to me. 'It's just, you've been quiet the past few days ...'

I hesitate, teetering between spilling all and saying nothing.

'Still thinking about how awful Wisecrackers was,' I say at last, opting to talk about my grizzly demise instead.

'You're a great performer who had a bad night,' Will says, folding me into his arms. 'You'll bounce back. You're too good not to – I know Elle thinks so.'

'Elle?' I say, straightening.

I was not expecting that.

'Yeah, we were chatting about you the other night – about how happy she is that you're chaperoning her.'

My mind spins. 'Elle … said that?'

'Yeah,' Will says, leaning back so he can see my face. 'You sound surprised.'

'Well, she was so angry with me after the competition and … and I feel like things have got harder with her …'

Will frowns, and I stop myself, afraid I've already gone too far.

'I get it. Elle was bang out of order,' he says, hand lightly stroking mine. 'She's … she's still learning to regulate her emotions, let's say, but she is sorry. And knowing Elle, she wouldn't want you to chaperone if she was still holding on to something. So if you're okay to, I think you guys can move on from this.'

I jam my face into something resembling a smile but actually, I'm not ready to move on at all. Is this what being a responsible adult means – putting your feelings aside? Letting shit just *sliiiiide*? You'd have to be so zen, you'd practically need a course in Buddhism for this. And now we've just decided it's all in our collective past, will I ever be able to tell Will what happened?

Or do I just have to ride it out until madam learns to 'regulate her emotions'?

'How about wings – for old times' sake,' Will says, bringing me back to the room. I look up at him, his gorgeous eyes fixed on me, and exhale out my concerns – for now. If letting it slide even for one night means I can enjoy my time with him, it might not be the worst thing in the world.

'Old times' sake? Can we say that after two months?' I laugh.

Will moves towards me, lips close, breath hot and moist. 'Sometimes I wish it was longer cos of how I feel about you.'

'I know. Same,' I murmur, as all worries, at least for tonight, dissolve into a long, slow kiss. Eventually, we part and our gaze meets. 'Abi, I want to tell you something.'

The intensity in Will's voice draws me closer. 'What is it, babes?'

His eyes dip for a moment as he gathers his thoughts. 'How I feel about you, I wasn't expecting it. To be honest, I was kinda done with relationships but then – you came along and, you changed everything.'

'Oh, wow,' I say, lost for words, savouring every one of his.

'And my dad said, if you find something special, cherish it.'

It's probably too early to mention that Beyoncé said if you like it, put a ring on it so I keep quiet and just listen.

'There's something I want to ask you,' he says, reaching into his pocket. 'Do you … want keys to my flat?'

I almost burst as he hands me a newly cut Yale and Chubb linked together on a simple gold hoop. Now I'm *really* glad I didn't say anything about Elle.

'I do,' I say, a massive grin consuming me as our lips lock once more.

'Mmmm. You do something to me, Abi,' he smoulders.

'I'll add that to my comedy bio,' I chuckle, turning the keys over in my hand. Funny how, with these two, tiny objects,

I suddenly feel more part of something, probably because, if I ever do feel on the outside, now I can let myself in.

'Sorry about this,' Will says with a nod towards the front of the room where a singer sits, tuning their guitar. 'If I'd known it was an acoustic night, I'd have suggested somewhere else.'

'No, this is great,' I say, taking a sip of my drink, eyeing Will.

Where he was relaxed earlier, this unexpected unplugged event has left him bothered. I run my hand up and down his back a few times, hoping my touch will chill him out.

'Honestly, I'm excited. Whenever I see live performances, it makes *me* want to go on. I just have to see someone play piano and I want to do the 'Chopsticks' duet with them,' I laugh, enjoying the fact that the spark that propels me on stage is still quietly there.

Will nods but I feel him retreat inside himself. I go to say something but then the ambient music comes down and the compere turns a soft spotlight towards the stage. The show starts and I decide to save it for later.

'Evening, everyone. Welcome to the Dis Unplugged.'

There's about thirty of us in what, once upon a time, would have been a drawing room, its period mantelpiece tonight's grand backdrop for the acts. Half the room give golf-clap applause, the other half, too cool, just single-nod an acknowledgement. On stage, everything's as laid-back as the audience. In fact, after their introduction, one of the acts gets up from the front row. I'm loving this vibe that's cleansing away the concern and drama that's reared its head this week. And watching these artists, some working with just a mic and perhaps one instrument, I feel inspired, remembering the joy of being a creative, doing things not to get someplace, but to be here, now. And sitting with Will, his keys nestling next to mine, his words of love imprinted on my heart, a calm washes over me. I'm not even concerned about Frank. We've had cross words before. It'll work out. And as for the girls, like Cassie said, building a relationship is a long game. In a year, maybe two, we'll come out the other side of this, older, wiser and, with any luck, happier.

It's the interval and after I grab us some fresh drinks, the compere comes over. Will rises to greet him.

'Ehh, Nick. What you sayin'?' He clasps hands, going in for a shoulder-to-shoulder hug.

'Good to see you, bro,' says Nick, genuine delight in his voice.

As they pull apart, Will slips an arm around me. 'Nick, this is my girlfriend, Abi. Abi, this is Nick.'

'Nice to meet you,' I say, glowing.

I don't think I'll ever stop loving the sound of that sentence coming from his mouth.

'Yeah, likewise,' says Nick, whose perfect, dark coils are held in place with wax and cool, his olive skin so flawless I have to make sure I don't stare but it's not every day you meet beautiful people.

'So, listen, bro,' says Nick, hands spread expectantly. 'Seeing as you're here, fancy going on?'

Will deflates, his face hardening. 'I don't know, we're just having a quiet night.'

'Mate, you've felt the vibe. Strictly no-pressure. The room's warmed up and they'd love a song.'

Wait, *what*? I knew Will sang, and gorgeously too, but I didn't realise he was get-on-stage good?

'Appreciate it but you know I'm done with all that,' he says, sitting, but Nick is not letting this go and I'm now thinking, done with all what?

Nick drags a tattered footstool over, planting himself opposite Will. 'Mate, I need you. Shola B was meant to do a set but she got a spot at the Jazz Café. We need something melodic to break up the spoken word, you feel me? Maybe do one of your covers, "Killing Me Softly"? "How Deep Is Your Love"? Could sing it for your girl here.'

Nick gives a hopeful grin and I try to hide just how much I would love to be serenaded. Meanwhile, Will's gaze searches the room for a watertight excuse.

'I don't even have a guitar,' he says, sinking back in his seat.

Hang on, he plays the guitar? This is insane. I search Will's face and can see he's teetering. Something within him wants to go on yet there's some other voice saying, don't. I bury my disappointment at the thought that voice might win.

'Brah, I've got you. You know that sweet custom-made ting Keisha has, it's in the staffroom. Let me go get it.'

Nick springs from his seat but is halted by Will who slams his glass onto the table. 'I said, no.'

His voice is jagged, sharp and not the melted chocolate tones I know. Clearly he wasn't teetering at all. He wipes spilt liquid from his hand and, without looking back, marches towards the stairs.

'Mate …' Nick calls but Will's gone.

I give Nick an awkward smile. 'Maybe he's googling the lyrics.'

Nick doesn't laugh. 'I've got to start the second half. But, listen, tell Will I didn't mean to pressure, it's just, he's really good.'

It's the first time Nick's *Blue Steel* veneer has cracked. It clearly pains him that he's upset Will.

'I'll get our bill and go tell him,' I say, rising.

'Don't worry about that,' Nick says, waving his hand at our half-empty glasses. 'On the house. I just want to know he's okay.'

He glances around the room at the audience, fidgety for the gig to restart. 'Tell him, it's all love, yeah?'

'Sure,' I reply and Nick heads back to the stage.

I find Will outside in the smoking area and watch him through the floor-to-ceiling windows, just as I did the night we met. This evening, though, he's sitting alone, staring into the dark sky. I step out onto the decked patio, drag over a chair and sit next to him.

He tilts his head to me with a sad smile then takes his gaze back to the starless heavens, tinged orange from the street lights below. We sit in silence for a while before I ask, 'What's going on?'

Will shifts in his seat but says nothing and I tighten. I hate when people clam up. Shouting and hollering I can handle, but the silence of someone I love, shakes me. It's what Mum used to do, still does. Shutting down, denying access, making it impossible to penetrate her thoughts, transform the situation. I hate it with her just like I hate it now.

'Sorry,' he says, eyes still searching.

'Nick told me to tell you, it's all love.'

This raises a smile and finally Will looks at me. With a weariness, he plants his hand in mine and lets out a long sigh.

I resist the urge to start wittering – making jokes or trying to fix things. I need to let Will find his words, in his time.

'Nick got me the job here,' he says at last.

I nod as though I've understood the deeper meaning of that. But then stop nodding in case there is no deeper meaning and my nodding makes me look mad.

'We met at music college, started a little collective, mellow, soul vibe. Aloe Blacc, India Arie, Corinne Bailey Rae type of thing.'

Will lets the memory encase him and smiles.

'We were good. Started getting some airplay. Not big time but we did some decent festivals. Things were going well and after we graduated, we carried it on. But then I realised, being in a group, I was hiding. I'd always wanted to go solo so, after a couple of years, I did. The others kept it going. I'd see them at shows and that.'

Will's face creases as guilt surfaces over his decision.

'It was tough for them though. I was the voice, you see, so in the end they just faded away but I kept at it. Took my music in a new direction, acoustic, kinda like a Michael Kiwanuka feel, and things really started happening. Anyway, then, uh …'

He pulls his hand away, rubbing his palms together as I hang on his every word.

'Then I met Kat and, well. Here was this fantastic woman who loved everything about me except this one thing – my career choice. She couldn't even bring herself to call it a career.'

I work hard to stop my face betraying the annoyance I feel. How can you love someone and not their dreams?

'We carried on dating but she just couldn't make peace with my music. When we moved in together, she didn't even like me rehearsing at home. She said she was worried about the neighbours,' Will says with a bitter laugh.

I know too well how easy it is to let one person's reality become yours in a relationship. Until I met Will, I let one guy after another have me believe I was too much.

'We kind of found this work-around but it was only ever going to be temporary. She didn't say as much but she wanted me to choose. Us or my music.' Will's gaze drifts towards the floor. 'I chose the music. Packed my stuff ready to move out. It felt good, you know, the right thing. Anyway, while I was waiting for my flat to come through, that's when she found out …'

'She was pregnant,' I say, his whole situation suddenly coming into sharp focus.

'There was no way I was leaving her so …' Will shrugs. 'Straight away, I sold all my music gear, used the money to buy the best baby stuff I could. I swear down, Elle's pram was like a Formula One car. Matching bottle bag, phone and cup holders, dummy pouch, the works. I figured, if I'm going to let music go, let it at least give my child the best.'

I bite my lip to hold back tears. I always thought Will was special but hearing this makes me love him even more fiercely.

'I haven't picked up a guitar since. I wanted to tell you all this but, I also wanted to leave it in the past. Talking about it reminds me what I gave up. But I've gotta tell ya, seeing you on stage, following your dreams, it makes me so happy.'

We both fall silent. Though my mind whirs with questions

I say nothing and just rest my head on his shoulder as he cradles my face. His hands are soft and haven't done the work they were built for, for too long. And that thought opens the floodgates. As I wipe my tears away, a determination rises. This amazing man deserves someone who loves him from his fingers down to his toes, who wants him to get all he desires from life, not dampen flames because of their own fears. And I know I can love him that way. And if that means making it work with Elle, that's what I'll do. I'll start over, be what her and Esme need too. I get it. Will comes as a package. For our relationship to work, the whole stepmum sitch has to work too and I'm all the way in.

Chapter 24

Now that I've decided to clean the slate and really make it work with Elle and Esme, things feel simpler and there's a bounce in my step again as I walk down the supermarket aisle picking up ingredients. Me and Will are having a quiet Saturday night in making pizzas and though for me the joy of pizza is someone else prepping it and bringing it to your door, he's convinced me this will be fun. I'm in my fave low-cut, black velvety top, boyfriend jeans and suede ankle boots. Bod's looking banging. Maybe a little overdressed for my local Tesco Metro but when you've got a leisurely seduction planned, is there really such a thing as 'too much'?

I chuck the usual suspects into my basket and head for the wine aisle, picking a bottle from the second shelf down. It's over a tenner and has a gold rosette so I assume it's decent. Pizza prep paid for, I head over to Will's.

Before I even get a key to the lock, my first time using them, I hear a sound that makes my skin turn cold: Elle and Esme's playful shrieks spilling from an upstairs window. Have I got my dates wrong? I thought Will had the girls *next* weekend. It's etched in my mind because that's the Sunday lunch they're coming to. I check my phone. I'm right, this was supposed to be a kids-free weekend. I've even marked it in my calendar with bra, wine glass and aubergine emojis.

Another layer of disappoint smothers me. I shouldn't be so pissed off his kids are here. That's the opposite of who I'm trying to be – the understanding girlfriend ready to embrace *everything* in Will's life. I try to shake off the irritation and reset before knocking.

'Hey, babe,' Will says as he opens the door. 'Forgot your keys?'

'Still getting used to being able to let myself in,' I lie.

The truth is, it feels too weird waltzing in now I know the girls are here.

I rise up to kiss Will, wanting to lose myself to it, but a question sticks in my throat. Will pulls away.

'You okay?'

'Yeah, no. Really good,' I nod, knowing my eyes tell a different story.

Will takes my hands. 'Abi, what is it?'

'I … I thought it was gonna be just us tonight. No biggy,' I say, but that brightness he first greeted me with dulls.

'Oh … Sorry. Kat asked if I could take them. I should have said. Last minute work thing, I think.'

Again? That's the second time this has happened.

'No, no, it's fine. Honestly,' I say, trying to breeze over it.

No big deal, let's make pizza, but Will wedges his hands into his jean pockets with a stifled huff.

'I didn't think it would be a problem. I thought you wanted to get to know them.'

He tails off, leaving airtime I'm supposed to fill with 'of course's and 'totally's. And yes, I do want to get to know them, but I also want quality time with bae. Is that so unreasonable, even if he is a fully engaged, hands-on father? Stupidly, I guess I hadn't accounted for him being that always, every day, whether he's scheduled to be with his kids or not. I know plans shift, that's the deal with being a parent, and his ship will always change course when they need him. I just can't help feeling stranded when it does.

'You do want to get to know them?' Will asks into the silence I should be filling with pleas for *more* quality time with them.

'A hundred per cent,' I say, but my enthusiasm is too late to paper over the crack this convo has created.

'Cool,' Will shrugs and he goes upstairs.

I follow, eyes pinned to his back, never having felt more distant from him.

Once inside, I'm relieved to feel his energy transform back to fun-dad mode as he calls out, 'Right, who wants to make pizza?!'

'Me,' squawks Esme, darting from her bedroom, Elle not far behind.

'Hey, girls,' I say, attempting cheery but not quite landing the shift as effectively as Will.

Esme stops, flickering a deferring look to Elle before giving me a cool, 'Good evening, Abi.'

'Hey,' Elle says, and with a hand on her sister they both move past me into the kitchen.

My anxiety creeps up as I follow them through. I know

I've got work to do with Elle but I wasn't ready for Esme's coolness. Maybe she's trying on a character. She is prone to oddball behaviour.

'Right,' says Will, peering into the fridge, 'first things first. Ingredients.'

Great, I'm all over this. I start pulling stuff from my bag – pizza dough flour, fresh herbs, anchovies – I nearly bought pineapple – as a joke – cos, obvs, no sane human puts fruit on pizza, and I position everything on the counter like a shop window display.

'Tah-dah,' I say with a final flourish.

All three of them stare. Will breaks first, his smile kind. 'Okay, I see why I should have told you the girls were here. We're doing vegan pizzas.'

Elle lets out a quiet snort while Esme looks at me pityingly. Patronised and humiliated, my frustration starts to build. Elle's not even a proper vegan. Someone's eating chunks from the Gouda in Will's fridge and it ain't me. And how can you have a *vegan* pizza anyway? Isn't the point the indulgent joy of bread, tomatoes and herbs all bound together with intestine-clogging cheese? Vegan pizza is an oxymoron, like 'crash landing' and 'silent scream', which is what I want to do right now.

'Shall I throw all this away?' Elle says, pointing a lazy finger towards my shopping.

'Don't be silly. Me and Abi will use it some other time, yeah?'

'Yeah,' I say, pulling my mouth into something resembling a smile, but I am properly pissed off.

Until twenty minutes ago, I was in a bra, red wine and aubergine kind of place, not smiley-faced pizzas and fizzy pop. This has totally put me on the back foot with the girls. And it could have all been avoided if Will had given me a heads-up. If he had, I'd have picked up enough vegan ingredients to start a commune, and it would show Elle and Esme I'm thinking of them.

'Right, let's get the oven on,' Will says. 'Me and Elle'll make the sauce and you and Ez can do the dough. Sound good?'

Esme gives Elle that same deferring look then says, 'I want to make the sauce.'

Will's lips purse. 'Not sure I want you at the stove, Ezzie. Tell you what, why don't you and Elle make the dough?'

Esme looks to her sister who gives the tiniest nod.

'Okay,' Esme says.

I'm crushed and it's a battle to hide it. *Et tu, Esme?* 'Back in a sec, just gonna nip to the loo.'

Already lost to the task at hand, the distracted acknowledgement I get from Will and the girls as I leave punctures me further. I close the bathroom door and breathe. Through the wall, I hear the happy chaos in the kitchen and wonder if they even care I've gone.

An hour later, despite my best attempts to engage with her, Elle's said a total of four words to me and they were, 'I don't like oregano' – just as I was about to sprinkle some into the sauce.

But what's baffling is, Will seems oblivious to it all – including Esme's recent frosty turn. Well, I made a vow to figure this out and I'm not a quitter. I will turn things around. And in a few months' time, when it's worked itself out, I'll tell Will everything. Until then he'll be none the wiser, even if my silence is beginning to feel like martyrdom.

At the kitchen table, we get a bit of a production line going. Esme slops sauce onto the bases before Will flings slices of vegan pepperoni across them followed by a flurry of so-called cheese grated by Elle.

'So that cheddar is completely vegan?' I say, confused it's making me salivate.

'Yeah, it's made out of coconuts,' Esme excitedly explains before Elle shoots her a glare.

Esme slaps her forehead, pulling her hand down her face. And for the first time, I genuinely want to laugh. Even when she's supposed to be giving you the cold shoulder, Esme's sweet and hilarious. But my enjoyment is short-lived as Elle starts picking off the mushroom I've just added.

'You like mushies,' Will protests.

'Gone off them,' she replies, letting them plap onto the table.

'Well, don't waste them,' Will says, piling the discarded mushrooms onto his pizza. 'Honestly, what's with you today? Chucking out food left, right and centre. What happened to Save the Planet?'

He doesn't wait for a response, more focused on getting everything in the oven. Elle watches, arms folded, her expression turning stony the moment she catches my eye, and I wilt. This is excruciating and my dread deepens at the prospect of her coming to Mum and Dad's. Sunday lunch is just over a week away, and in danger of being such a catastrophic car crash we'll need all four emergency services in attendance.

Perhaps it's not too late to cancel, admit defeat, but the thought is so distasteful I can barely tolerate it. Seeing Mum's smug grin slither across her face would slay me. She'd say nothing but her expression would speak a thousand words, all block capitals. WHAT A FAILURE.

As I drift back from my depressing daydream, Will pulls the pizzas from the oven. He shakes them off the baking tray onto colourful plates and sets them out. We gather around his tiny kitchen table but, where normally it feels intimate, tonight it's claustrophobic.

'Let it cool down,' Will tells Esme who's ready to hoover her pizza up.

'Oh yeah,' she says and huffs over her plate like she's blowing out birthday candles.

Finally cooled, I pick at my coconut cheese pizza hoping for some comfort but, as good as it is, I'm just not hungry. Having your date night gatecrashed by a thirteen- and a six-year-old can do that to your appetite, and having to hide your spiralling misery behind smiles and banter doesn't help either. Man, I hope Cassie's right about this getting better with time because at the moment, it's grim. I'm not sure what's worse, the girls cold-shouldering me, or Will's lack of awareness. Right on cue, Elle glowers across the table at me, a sinister curl in her lips that says she's just getting started. And this is before we've even begun the chaperoning. The first gig isn't far off and if it's as frosty as tonight, I'm going to get chilblains.

Chapter 25

At the other desks, everyone is half working, half guessing the cash-builder question on the radio quiz. But me, I'm in data-entering cruise-control, mind obsessively sifting over how things are with Elle and that unexpected vegan pizza hell-scape five days ago. I deserve a Pride of Britain award for persevering with this kid. From my handbag I hear the insistent *brrrr* of my vibrating phone and slip it from its side pocket. It's Will so I scurry to the stairwell at the end of the corridor to take the call.

'Thank God you rang. Bobbie's eating pistachios again and the noise is driving me mad.'

'Abi, I can't stay long. I need your help.'

I straighten at the urgency in Will's voice.

'What is it? What's up?'

'Ez was at her holiday club this morning, that garden camp, and she got stung by a bee. She's had quite a bad reaction.'

My breath shortens as I imagine worst-case scenarios – anaphylactic shock, fat tongues and blue faces. 'Is she okay? Has she gone to hospital?'

'She's fine. Threw up a couple of times though so we want to get her home. Problem is, Kat dropped her off early this morning before getting a train to Manchester. She's on her way back but won't get to Ez for a couple of hours. I would go but there's barely a skeleton staff at the Dis so I agreed to stay till Olive comes in—'

I stop Will, mid-flow. 'I'll pick her up and take her to yours.'

I sense him flood with relief. 'Thank you. Are you sure?'

'I've got you. It's not even a thing,' I tell him. 'Just leave it with me.'

'Abi, you're a life saver. I'll call you in a bit,' Will says and we hang up.

I don't think I've ever come to anyone's rescue before and the thrill of this newfound responsibility is dizzying. Getting into action mode, I dart back to the office and grab my things.

'You all right, Abi?' Jill asks, fishing a soggy digestive from her tea.

'No … It's … my mum. I've gotta go,' I say, careful not to catch Bobbie's eye.

If anyone's going to root out a fib, it's the in-house conspiracy theorist.

'Oh, hope she's okay. Do you need us to book you a taxi somewhere?' Jill asks, phone receiver already in hand.

'Would you mind?' I say, hoping it's coming out of the company dime rather than my scant wages.

'No problemo. Where to?'

'Little Green Fingers Day Centre and Garden camp,' I say without thinking.

Jill's hand pauses over the phone buttons. 'Sorry, where?'

Bobbie looks over, eyes narrowing.

'Long story. Gardening accident, rakes, pitchforks!' I babble, waving my hand for Jill to carry on dialling.

Thankfully she does and soon a cab is ordered. I say flustered goodbyes and promise to send updates as I back out the door.

In less than half an hour, I'm pulling up outside the centre. I rush inside.

'Abi Akingbade, here to pick up Esme Matheson,' I say, breathlessly, to a white-haired woman at the front office.

'Oh, yes, your partner called. We don't have you on the system as an Approved Pick-Up so do you have your code word?'

'It's "Chapelle".'

'Great,' the lady replies, pushing back from her desk. 'She's in the nurse's room. Feeling a bit sorry for herself.'

She leads me down a wide corridor covered with finger paintings of multicoloured animals and collages of leaves stuck on faded green paper. From rooms either side I hear kids playing, learning languages, doing art but all I can think of is poor Esme and my pace quickens. However, as we reach the nurse's room where the receptionist hands me off, I start to wonder, what if Esme is still following Elle's orders and blanks me? That's going to make this whole thing super awks.

'Abi, right?' the nurse says, ushering me in.

Her voice is calming and she seems way kinder than the one we had at my school who I'm sure was only in it for the pension. As I walk in, I see little Esme dozing on an armchair, a thin grey blanket covering her.

I crouch down. 'Esme.'

She stirs then slowly sits up, confused, dragging a hand across her eyes to wipe away the sleepy haze.

'Had a good sleep after all that excitement,' says the nurse, leaning against the doorframe.

'Where's my mummy?' Esme asks, bottom lip wobbling, and my heart begins to gallop.

This is it. This is where she tells me she'd rather eat a cat litter sandwich than hang out with me. And to be fair, part of me wants to back out anyway, take a Responsible Adulting sabbatical, but she needs me and I promised Will so I press on. 'She's going to meet us at your daddy's later. He asked me to take you home. Is that okay?'

Esme thinks for a sec then gives a sleepy nod, tiredness still heavy in her body, and I do my best to hide my pure relief as I slip on her muddied blue and pink wellies.

'So where did that big, bad bee get you?'

She holds up her palm, staring at the wound with a gravity that is adorable. 'It wasn't a bad bee.'

I inspect the red welt bang in the middle of her hand. 'Oooh, it got you good.'

The nurse lets out a little chuckle, her brown cheeks creasing into dimples as she watches us. 'I applied some calamine and gave her five mil of Calpol.'

'Great,' I say, with no clue what that is.

It sounds like some Eastern European organisation, but I make a mental note anyway so I can tell Kat later.

'So, what happened?' I ask as Esme's bleariness clears a little.

'She was being a proper Bindi Irwin, weren't you?'

'I was holding the bee in my hand and it got frightened so it stinged me but it didn't mean to.'

My heart melts as me and the nurse share a look. Esme is the sweetest.

'Well, I'm sure the bee was very sorry,' I say, helping her up.

She's still woozy, so without a thought I scoop her up, planting her on my hip. Her arms slip around my neck and I glow at her touch.

'All right, Esme. Feel better and hopefully see you next week,' the nurse says, waving us off down the corridor.

Esme waves back then rests her head on my shoulder. 'You know what would make me feel better?' she says.

'What's that?'

'*Proper* pizza.'

'Well all right then,' I say, and we head back to Will's.

As soon as we arrive, I order our lunch. I'm not sure a Four Seasons is the best remedy for a bee sting but by the rate Esme wolfs it down, it's defo what's wanted.

'So, what *does* happens when you eat cheese?' I ask.

'Farts,' Esme says, gleeful and with a full mouth.

'Well, good job I asked for the vegan stuff, eh,' I say, booping her on the nose.

She boops me back and we do that for a good minute and a half, getting sillier and louder with each one. Our game ends in a giggly truce as Esme turns to me, suddenly sincere. 'Sorry I wasn't talking to you before.'

'How do you mean?' I ask, opting to play dumb.

'Elle made me,' she blurts. 'I didn't want to.'

I let out an, 'Ahhhhhh,' and try my best to reassure her while biting down my annoyance at Elle.

'Do you want to do a dance challenge?' Esme says, hopping off the sofa.

I'm thrown for a moment by the gear-shift. Seriously, you could get whiplash at how quickly things shift with kids. A couple of hours ago, she was too knackered to stay upright and now we're about to try and go viral.

'Don't you need to rest?'

'It'll help me get better,' she argues and before I can protest, she's dragging me from the sofa and scrolling the iPad looking for a video of the dance she wants us to learn.

Even though my full tum would rather I lay prostrate for an hour, I'm game and actually the time goes by in a flash. I'm slower to pick up the moves than Esme, no surprise there, but eventually we get our routine down and after several attempts, mainly due to my missteps, we manage to record it too.

'That was the best one!' yelps Esme as she replays our vid.

We bump fists and though I'm sweating like an Olympian at a drugs test, I'm chuffed. Not just about getting the dance routine down but about hanging with Esme – this feels good. We're vibing and I start to feel like, perhaps I'm better with kids than I thought – little ones at least. Teenagers are a whole other story.

I snap out of my self-congratulations, though, as I hear the doorbell and sneak a look out of the window. It's Kat. I go down to let her in.

'Hey,' she says and we hug.

It's awks as per so I'm relieved when we disentangle and I head upstairs, Kat following. Inviting her in does feel weird as it's Will's yard but I try not to make it a thing.

The moment Esme sees Kat, she darts over, throwing her tiny arms around her. In reply, Kat smothers Esme with kisses, a motherly hand going straight to her brow for a temperature check.

'How you feeling?'

'I had pizza and did a dance with Abi,' Esme beams.

'No cheese,' I say, stepping in to cover my arse.

'It's fine. It just gives her wind,' Kat smiles with an eye-roll.

'She did mention that.'

'So, let's have a look at your hand,' says Kat turning back to Esme who offers up her palm for inspection.

On seeing the swollen bump, Kat kisses it better then works her way up Esme's arm towards her neck, drawing out peals of joyful giggles.

I look on in wonder at what a mother's touch can do, a little sadness rising as I think of my mum but I push it down.

'Oh, the nurse put calamine on the wound and gave her five mil of Calpol,' I say, remembering.

'Good to know. We can give her another dose in a couple of hours if she needs it,' Kat says, brushing Esme's hair from her brow.

'Yeah, that's what I was thinking,' I blag, with a confident nod.

'Do you want to see our dance?' Esme says, wriggling from Kat's grasp and swiping open her iPad.

'I'd love to!' Kat smiles.

'You don't need to put Mum through that,' I say, squirming at the thought of Kat watching me try to pop, lock and slide through the routine.

'Don't worry, I've had to do a million of these. You can't be any worse than me,' she laughs, sitting on the sofa.

'Hold my beer,' I joke, joining her and I swell, not only at making Kat laugh but also at Esme asking me to do something she normally does with her mum.

Esme plonks herself in the middle and hits play, straight away mirroring the moves. I'm quietly proud but keep my appreciation to a subtle head bop.

'Oh, well done, Abi,' Kat says, sounding genuinely impressed. 'I told you you'd be better than me. Elle calls my videos Kat-astrophes.'

'Ouch,' I wince. 'But nice word-play.'

'That's my girl,' Kat laughs.

Esme flicks through some more videos, Kat chuckling at past Kat-astrophes and I realise she's not quite as devoid of humour as I thought. I've been so fixated on my feelings, I hadn't thought what adjusting to all this must be like for Kat – a new person in her kids' life, things moving on even if you're not ready. Perhaps if I was dealing with that, I'd hide behind tight smiles and awkward hugs too.

After another ten minutes glued to the iPad, Kat gives Esme a nudge. 'How much screen time has that been today?'

'I am poorly, you know,' Esme huffs, feigning weariness before giving up the ruse and rooting around in her toy box for something more wholesome to do.

Satisfied Esme's otherwise occupied, Kat turns her attention to me. 'And how are you doing?'

'Fine, thanks,' I answer. I mean, I thought I was fine but now I'm nervous, wondering what Kat's about to hit me with.

'Really, though, it can't be easy stepping into the middle of … this,' she says, her hand arching to indicate just about everything.

Ahead I see two roads. One where I tell her it's been a breeze and I can do this in my sleep. The other, where I tell the truth.

'It's been … lessons,' I say, and we both laugh.

'*Yeaah*. People always talk about how rewarding kids can be. Not so much about the "lessons",' she says, air-quoting it.

And the laughter of recognition is a tonic. Over in the corner, Esme is now building what looks like a new best friend out of Lego so I figure it's okay to speak a bit more freely. 'If I'm honest, it was a little rocky with Elle … but we're working on it.'

Kat's brow furrows and I panic. Have I misread the room?

'I'm sorry to hear that. She's only ever said lovely things about you.'

'Oh,' I say, more than surprised. 'That's nice. I – I think it's mainly me, acclimatising, wanting to get this right, you know?'

I'm gabbling now, trying to claw back ground, but luckily Kat smiles, like she gets it. 'Think that's what we're all trying to do …'

And in a brief moment of connection, something in me settles. I've always assumed parenting was instinctive and that if you messed up, you were clearly no good at it, but perhaps it's more about finding your way, never letting the fear of stumbling stop you trying.

Kat sighs, getting up from the sofa. 'All right then, we should make a move.'

'Is Abi coming?' Esme asks, abandoning her Lego girl.

'Not this time, but I'll see you at the weekend, yeah?' I say.

'Yeah,' Esme replies.

And at the top of the stairs, I hug her goodbye.

'Thanks again for today, Abi. And thanks for being so good with the girls. I can't even begin to tell you how … it means a lot. As I'm away with work quite a bit, it's so much easier knowing I don't have to worry.'

Kat squeezes my hand and I squeeze back.

*

At around six, Will walks through the door.

'I got you these,' he says, producing a beautiful bouquet. 'Thank you for today. You are incredible.'

'I only did what had to be done,' I say, downplaying it, but delighting at being in his grateful arms and covered in adoring kisses.

'You made dinner too!' Will smiles, pointing towards the coffee table, already set with plates and wine glasses.

'Welcome to the nineteen fifties, baby,' I chuckle, pouring our drinks. 'Should be ready in about twenty minutes …'

Will draws me back into our embrace, his tone soft. 'You can stay here whenever you want, you know that, right?'

'Cos I made you dinner? I wouldn't get used to it,' I scoff, even though I know Will's feminist credentials are on point and he doesn't roll like that.

'Abi, if you were here more often, I'd make you dinner all the time,' he says, voice dipping to a gentle murmur. 'When I come back to an empty flat, I miss you.'

'I miss you too …' I reply.

'You have keys. Just come and go when you want – zero cooking required.'

'Careful what you wish for, Mr Matheson,' I say before kissing him, tender at first but soon passionate as my hand slips under his shirt, hungrily clawing at skin.

Chapter 26

Will and the girls in tow, we arrive for Sunday lunch just about on time. But even then, we're still the last to get here. I swear Kemi has an underground tunnel directly from her yard to Mum and Dad's. Still buoyant from my time with Kat and Esme, I feel like things have shifted. Me and Esme are pals again and my convo with Kat has even thawed my heart towards Elle, who, with no lieutenant by her side, is being a little less frosty. We're defo not out of the woods, and who knows what she's going to make of Mum, and vice versa, but, right now, I'm focusing on the positives. Top of the list being that I finally get to introduce Will to Dad and Kemi.

We go through to the garden where, due to promised sunshine all weekend, we're having another Akingbade barbie. It's exactly what I was hoping for, casual and relaxed rather than that pass-the-salt dining-table formality we usually have.

'We're here!' I say, as we step through the French doors and down the decking steps.

'Greetings!' Dad calls from his brick-built barbecue.

He wipes his hands on his favourite tea towel, scurrying over to give me a papa bear hug then thrusts a hand towards Will. 'Good to meet you!'

'Good to meet you too,' Will says, matching Dad's enthusiasm.

'And who do we have here?' Dad enquires, craning round Will to see the girls who are hanging back.

'This is Elle and my youngest, Esme,' Will says, filled with pride as he gently ushers his daughters forward.

'Hi,' they say, shyness muting them.

I give Esme a big smile and Elle a thumbs up, trying to make them comfortable, but Mum soon cuts across the cordiality.

'Aren't you going to introduce me to your latest friend – and his children?' Mum says from her garden chair a few feet away.

'I was about to. Mum, this is Will. Will, this is my mum,' I sing-song to hide the tension building across my whole body.

She slides forward in her seat as though about to get up but then doesn't, wrongfooting Will. He just about covers his stumble and shakes her hand.

'How do you do?' Mum says with the thinnest of thin smiles.

'Very well, thank you, Mrs Akingbade. And yourself?' Will replies, relaxed and unfazed while I'm quickly becoming a shoo-in for a stress-related heart attack.

'Wonderful,' Mum says before slipping in, 'Of course, a curiosity of the English language is that the correct response to "How do you do?" is actually, "How do you do?" Isn't that quaint?' she simpers, relaxing back in her seat.

Man, I wish this was an old school cartoon where a person-sized anvil would whistle down from the sky, landing on her. Then we'd get to enjoy the afternoon, Abosede silenced aside from the odd, squished groan from under the metric ton of cast iron. But it's not a cartoon. It's the real world – unfortunately.

'And this is Elle and Esme – Will's daughters,' I say, smile strained.

At hearing their names, the girls shuffle forward for their audience with Queen Abosede.

'Hello, young ladies,' Mum nods but I half-expect her to proffer her ring to kiss.

With a nudge from Will, Esme and Elle both chorus, 'Thank you for having us over.'

Those intros done, I flush with relief when Caleb and Ayesha bound towards us, Kemi and Felix not far behind.

'And Will, girls – this is my sister, Kemi, her husband Felix – and their kids Ayesha and Caleb.'

After more hellos, Ayesha grabs Elle and Esme, taking them to the other end of the garden. My guess is all four are beyond happy not to be around us boring grown-ups. I'm a bit surprised Elle is going with it considering she's several years older but if they're getting on, it's all good.

'Sis,' Kemi says, arms opening for a hug before whispering in my ear, 'He's a snack and a half.'

'Mate, he's the whole meal,' I reply and we pull apart, pounding fists with a cheeky grin.

'Will, how are your barbecuing skills?' Dad calls.

'Er, not bad,' Will stammers, 'though I'm more of a pizza and pasta guy, to be fair.'

Dad laughs. 'Well, no one's perfect. And tell me, are you vegan too? Abi gave me prior warning so I've got lots of lovely meat-free options and plenty of salads and such.'

'That's really kind,' says Will, 'But it's just Elle.'

'No problemo. Let's rustle up something yummy. How about today you be my sous-chef?'

'Love to,' Will says, rubbing his hands.

What a sweetheart. He's got on his favourite shirt, a short-sleeved number with a leaf print, and he's wearing proper trousers (he insisted, wanting to make a good first impression). He's going to get covered in barbecue gunk but there's not a peep of complaint. He just gets stuck in. And I'm so grateful to my dad for making him feel welcome.

After a few hours my nerves settle, seeing everyone find their groove. The kids dart around the garden, engrossed in a game that involves getting told to calm down by Kemi every fifteen minutes. Felix is gazing up into the trees, occasionally commenting on some tit he's spotted, while Will and Dad exchange thoughts on the perfect lamb marinade. Soon, we all gather around the table and my tum could not be more pleased. I'm starving.

'So, Will, what do you do for a living?' Mum says, splicing the chat as we pass dishes around. 'Are you in jestering too?'

My face remains serene but I feel my toes bunch. Mum has called what I do clowning, burlesque and even a side show. Jestering is a new one though.

'I wish I was as funny as your daughter. No, I teach music at a secondary school,' Will replies with a pleasant smile that gives nothing away.

Thank God I warned him about Mum. At the time I thought I was being harsh but seeing her Abosede-ing on both cylinders, I might actually have held back.

'Hmmm,' she says, her lower lip curling as if she's just applied ammonia lip balm. 'And to what end? I mean, maths opens a world of opportunity, as does English language and literature. History is the gateway to many paths. The sciences, their value goes without saying but … music? You teach it – to what end, dear? More music teachers?'

Table chatter falls away as Will shifts in his seat. This is so unfair. I was ready for Mum to pull apart *my* career choices but Will's? He's in education, just like she was. I thought she'd leave that alone yet she's still found a way to disapprove. Will brushes a bead of sweat from his brow and goes to speak.

'Musicians.'

Everyone looks at my dad.

'Will is helping create musicians, Abosede,' he repeats.

Mum says nothing, instead pulling a chunk of mushroom off her kebab stick and cutting it into unnecessarily small pieces. Somewhere, an imaginary umpire chalks up the point courtesy of a beautiful assist from Dad.

Fifteen–love, Will.

And under the table our hands slip into a brief clasp.

'Abi tells me you met in a bar?' Mum says, rallying.

Will wipes his hands on a napkin, this time ready for the volley. 'Not quite a bar. I work part-time at a private members' club, fitting in a few shifts around school and the girls.'

I try to focus on my food but my eyes keep zipping from Will to Mum and back again.

'Goodness. So many questions. Aren't you concerned someone from your real work will see you?' Mum prods.

'Honestly, no. Plus, membership at this place is three thousand pounds a year. On what we earn, there's no chance I'll see any teachers there.'

'Which also explains why you need to supplement your income, right?' Dad says.

'Exactly. It was either that or try to flog my marinade sauce on *Dragon's Den*.'

'Ah yes, very good!' Dad laughs.

Thirty–love, Will.

Mum's expression curdles.

'And what of the mother?' she murmurs with pretend discretion as though it's cool to sift through Will's life story over chargrilled chicken.

'Mum,' I protest.

'It's a fair question,' Will says, graciously. 'We have these beautiful girls, so we keep things civil and co-parent the best we can. Elle and Ez are with me one or two weekdays and every other weekend but we keep it fluid as their mum's often away with work. To help with that, I decided to stay local, but places aren't cheap around there so …'

Will spreads his hands.

'You took a second job. Very mature,' Dad says, waving his fork in admiration.

Forty–love, Will.

Kemi and I share a look. This back and forth is doing nothing for my blood pressure. Mum jabs at a piece of corn on the cob and we watch, mesmerised, as she slices off kernels before scooping them up.

'Very mature indeed. Although don't expect much of that from Abioye and she's never been great with children. Her sister has only just started letting her babysit alone, isn't that right, Kemi?'

Forty–fifteen.

'It's not like that, Mum,' Kemi splutters, caught off-guard, and I shrink with embarrassment.

That was a low blow, even by Mum's standards.

'You see, Abi's a feet-first type of person. And you'll discover, when it comes to nurturing, she won't have a clue. She won't have a clue,' Mum says, directing her repetition to Will with that pinched, drawstring smile of hers.

Forty–thirty.

Feeling she's on a roll, Mum continues, 'There's so much to think about, Abi. Their health, enrichment, education – not that you fully appreciated the efforts your father and I put into trying to ensure your academic success.'

'University of Life,' I say, attempting a lob, but Mum cuts me off with a sneer.

'I'd be intrigued which legal firm or architectural practice accepts degrees from the "University of Life". How does one gain entry – attending the "School For Hard Knocks"?'

Deuce.

Mum leans back, pleased with her little 'joke' while, at my end of the table, I quietly rage. This is beyond brutal and way past the horrors I'd pictured. And she's not done.

'I'm sure you're already considering higher education options for your eldest,' Mum says, turning to Will, her fingers interlaced into a judgemental steeple.

Will sets down his water. He's been diligently alternating it with wine and is, unlike me, still sober enough to handle Abosede with grace.

'She's only just started thinking about GCSEs and, to be honest, all bets are off at the moment seeing as she's doing so well with her stand-up.'

Mum lets out a spluttered choke.

Advantage Will.

'Stand-up comedy? Like you?' Dad says to me, eyes brightening.

Mum looks at Will, her face pulled into a disbelieving frown. 'Not like Abi. Surely she's good?'

'Mum!' Kemi says, flapping her napkin onto the table.

'It's fine,' I say, putting a hand on Kemi's wrist.

Mum's taken her best shots and, for her efforts, she's shedding audience. The kids have left the table, bored, Felix is here only in body, leaving Dad, Kemi, Will and Elle, who's been quietly tracking the whole conversation.

'Abi's really good,' she says, and all eyes swivel to her. 'She helped me with my routine and is going to take me to gigs.'

'Abioye – is coaching you?' Mum says, hand pressed into her chest in baffled amazement.

'All right, Mum. You're saying it like you heard Stevie Wonder's become a driving instructor,' I tut.

'Really, mocking the infirmed? No surprise your humour reaps few dividends,' Mum snips and I sink down in my chair vowing to only speak again when we're four hundred light years from here.

Deuce.

I give Elle a grateful nod acknowledging her attempt to support but even when a thirteen-year-old offers herself as a human shield, Mum doesn't relent. I need to escape her noxious vapours so I wipe my hands with my napkin and go inside.

Advantage Abosede.

I hear someone follow and hope it's not Will. I'm hurt and humiliated. He can't see me like this.

'Ignore her,' Kemi says.

I suck in air to fight the tears that want to come. Not today, Black Jesus. Not today. But a tear bounces down my cheek nonetheless, its saltiness slipping into the corner of my mouth.

'Why does she do this, Kems?'

Kemi kisses her teeth, resting a hand in the middle of my back. 'If I knew, I would tell you. Will's doing great though. And Dad really likes him.'

'Dad likes everyone,' I scoff.

I don't mean to be dismissive but Dad's affections are pretty much guaranteed. All I wanted was one day where *Mum* gave me a 'well done, look at you, all grown up'. Instead, I'm practically breaking my back dodging her side swipes.

'I know it's easier said than done but don't let her get to you. She loves you. It's just all fear. Trust me.'

Kemi bumps me with her hip which shakes a tiny smile from me.

'And what fear would that be? Fear of being nice? Does she have pleasantaphobia? Hmm, hmm? Does she, Adekemi? Does she?'

I feel a silly energy bubble up, the madness of the afternoon going to my head.

'Maybe, Abioye, maybe, hmm, hmmm!' Kemi says, joining in my silly moment, pulling faces with me until Caleb barrels through the French doors, bringing the best news I've heard all afternoon.

'We're having cheesecake!' he bawls and disappears back into the garden.

'Now we're talking,' I say and dab at my eye make-up with the edge of my little finger.

'Mum's not so bad, Abs. She's just not good with people like you are.'

I take the compliment but then ask, 'If Mum's not so bad, how come you haven't told her what's under that wig?'

Kemi flounders.

'Or about you quitting your job and starting a new business?'

She glances out to the garden. 'Let's get some cheesecake.'

Exactly, I think to myself as we re-join the others. *Game Abosede.*

We decide to have dessert inside as there's a chill in the air – its cause partly meteorological, partly matriarchal. Things mellow once we're in the living room, helped by wine and my decision to ignore Mum for the rest of the evening. Meanwhile, the kids are becoming firm friends, Elle and Ayesha bonding over a love of 'Jerk the Week'; Caleb and Esme locked in a deep discussion about how much chocolate they could eat without throwing up.

After a while, Elle returns to the table, sitting with the adults. As smart as Ayesha is, five-year-olds speak a language your brain soon tires of translating.

'So, Elle, what do you talk about in your comedy?' Dad says, eyes sparked with interest.

'Just stuff really. School, teachers, parents. Life, I suppose,' Elle replies with a shy shrug.

'She's selling herself short, Dad,' I say jumping in, looking to repay her earlier assist. 'She's a brilliant writer.'

'Really?' says Dad, intrigued. 'How wonderful and from one so youthful. Then again, the wisest words often come from the youngest mouths.'

Elle blushes, twisting herself into a bashful cluster.

'You must show us some. I'd love to hear it,' Mum says, indicating for Elle to take the floor.

Shock bubbles in my chest. In the eight years I've been doing stand-up, Mum has enquired if I'm up-to-date with my smear tests more often than she's asked to see my act. This is a trap. She'll get Elle to perform only to pull the rug from under her in some typically arch way.

'Your living room isn't exactly set up for that, Mum,' I say, trying to protect Elle from the inevitable.

'Nonsense, this can be your stage.'

Mum hops out of her seat and starts rearranging furniture as Kemi watches, bemused. I turn to Elle, hoping to allay her fears, but when I look, I see a glimmer of a smile. Wait, does she *want* to do this? She may think so but once she has Mum's judgemental glare on her, burning with the heat of a thousand suns, she'll feel otherwise.

'Mum, the middle of your Persian rug is not the place to do stand-up. You need the right conditions!' I bleat.

'No, *you* need the right conditions. I'm sure Elle can handle this,' Mum says with a dismissive wave.

And like that, I'm raging again, the combo of Mum and Elle causing me emotional chaos, squared.

'It's okay, darling, you don't have to if you don't want,' Will quietly offers Elle, and for a moment she hesitates.

In the vacuum, Caleb seizes the opportunity for some attention, shouting, 'I know a joke!'

Kemi tuts. 'Do you know the punchline this time?'

Caleb deflates like a day-old party balloon.

'I'll do it,' says Elle, her coy façade falling away.

'Very good,' Dad says with an approving nod and Will gives me a gentle squeeze but all I'm thinking is, *Don't say I didn't try to help, Elle.* You're about to perform in front of the harshest of them all – Simon Cowell, Craig Revel Horwood and Judge Judy all rolled into one. However, despite my foreboding, I realise there's another voice that's been whispering to me since this started and this voice wants Elle to flop. It's not clamouring for an on-stage death but it also doesn't want her to be great. If Elle falters, Mum will see it's not that easy. Failure here won't hurt Elle but it will help me. I feel awful for letting that thought in but before I can shoo it away, she's already launched into a routine I've never heard – about when parents break up. Will and I exchange glances as she skilfully teeters along the tightrope of indiscretion and confession, with a raw, rough-around-the-edges bit about life after your parents separate. And it is … brilliant, making Abosede machine-gun out her laughter, a noise I've *never* heard her make. Meanwhile, Kemi is sniggering, hand over her mouth, unable to help herself. Even the kids are screeching, though they're mainly taking their cues from the adults as the jokes whistle over their heads like an RAF flyby.

'*I mean, they don't need to stay together for our sake. I was starting to feel like the odd one out at school anyway, and in thirty years' time, I'll have something to talk to my therapist about.* That's it,' Elle says, her persona shifting back to its quiet default.

The room breaks out into rapturous applause, way beyond that recognition-for-taking-part type all kids get. This is awe. Reeling, I plant my cheek onto an upturned palm, the pressed folds of skin representing my misery piled on misery. My family's cheers for Elle are painful juts in my heart. When have I *ever* had a roundhouse of support in Mum's living room – or *anywhere* – from them? Mum won't even come to a gig, let alone invite me to perform on her best rug after Sunday lunch.

'Well done, dear!' she says, clapping the loudest.

'I love it,' Will beams. 'I mean, obviously you're grounded but, good job.'

Elle gives a little laugh then bows as Dad throws some 'bravas' her way.

'Thanks. There's more about parenting and how Mary, Joseph and God were, like, the original blended family, but I haven't figured it out yet.'

'Oh, how clever,' Mum simpers, while Kemi looks on with a hint of disapproval.

'And how often do you perform?' Dad asks.

'Well, I've done a few shows for kids but I've got my first proper gig coming up. I think it's called the Comedy Caravan. Or Campervan.'

'Cabana,' I correct.

'Yeah, on Thursday,' Elle says.

'Oh, Abi, you still okay to take her?' Will asks, still vicariously enjoying the triumph of Elle's set.

My chest pulsates at the ease with which he asks me. For the first time in a long while I'm angry at him and his blissful lack of awareness at how, for a good week, Elle completely froze me out. And though I offered to chaperone, this deal seems to be good for everyone but me. I'm becoming as much of a doormat as the rug Elle is standing on.

'Sure,' I say, wanting Mum's luxurious upholstery to swallow me whole.

I'm proper done with this day. Every time I think I'm getting somewhere, every time I decide to try and make things work, turn the other cheek, life just slaps me down. I feel so battered, it's making my head spin.

Chapter 27

Last night I dreamed I went on stage, no material, the entire audience made up of Elles, slow-handclapping me. There's no getting away from her, even in my dreams – and definitely not tonight, because the dreaded day is here. I'm finally chaperoning Elle to the first of her gigs. I'm picking her up from Will's and as I walk there, I tap out a message to Kemi, looking for some last-minute advice. My phone pings straight away.

She may be funny but don't take any sass.

I snort-laugh at Kemi's reply but she has a point. I shouldn't be letting a tweenager run rings around me. I'm the adult and the one doing Elle a solid by taking her to these shows. I should be calling the shots. At that thought, I feel a fraction more galvanised for the night ahead.

'Hi, Abi, I'm just going to get my notebook,' Elle says before zipping back to her room.

'Thanks again for doing this,' Will says but his words barely register as I'm completely distracted by Elle's pleasant demeanour.

'Is she okay?' I say, wrong-footed.

'Ah that,' Will says, edging us towards the living room, out of earshot. 'I wanted to leave it a while but we finally had words – about a couple of things, to be fair, and cleared some stuff up.'

'Right,' I say, aware that the dull pain in my neck is slowly easing.

Maybe Will did sense something and, without me having to snitch, has dealt with it. Thank God I kept my mouth shut. This is a much better outcome and will definitely help me and Elle with our relationship. I'm disappointed I couldn't get here by myself but at the end of the day, it's done and now we can move forward. Just then, Elle emerges.

'Okay, ready,' she announces, before turning towards the door.

'Er, something you want to say?' Will prompts, expectation in his voice.

Elle shuffles back, slightly embarrassed. 'Oh, um. Yeah. Thank you for tonight, Abi. I'm really grateful.'

'No problem,' I blink, wanting to quip about where the real Elle is and who's this imposter but I'm pretty sure that'll kill the vibe.

'Good girl. Can't wait to hear all about it,' Will says, planting a kiss on Elle's forehead.

'She's gonna be great,' I smile and we leave.

The front door closes behind us and we pace towards the bus stop. 'Can't believe you're playing the Cabana, it's such a good—'

But I instantly go quiet as I look over at Elle who has a rigid finger resting on her lips, 'Shhhhhh.'

Stunned silent, I say nothing else because, honestly, I've never seen anything more sinister. Of course all that stuff before was an act. Of course she still hates me. Of course this was all to keep Dad off the scent. On the way to the show, Elle and I share less than ten words. Even when I ask if she has her Oyster card, I just get side-eye.

I've never actually been inside the Comedy Cabana. It's smaller than Dina's other gig, the Cabin, but has that special something, an atmos that promises great comedy. The doorwoman directs us towards the green room but as I yank its heavy door open, Elle halts. 'I don't want to go in there.'

'You should meet the other acts,' I say, resolving to kill this situation with kindness even if it's the death of me.

'I'm fine,' she says, slipping into a seat on the end of one of the rows.

Before I can reason with her, she presses open her notebook, knee juddering like a piston.

'You okay?' I ask.

'Can you get me some water?' She says, eyes focused straight ahead.

I want to kiss my teeth so loud they hear it in the street. Who does she think I am, her personal Deliveroo? I have to dig deep to take the high road.

'Please?' she mumbles.

And I stand down, soon returning with a fizzy water because

I know she prefers that to still. As her shaking hand takes the bottle, all irritation fades. 'Are you sure you're okay?'

She twists off the cap then points at her notebook. 'I'm trying to concentrate. You go to the green room if you want.'

And just like that my fur bristles again. But as much as I'd love to just walk away, I can't escape the fact that tonight she's my responsibility, so I slide into the seat behind – away from her stinky 'tude but close enough to keep an eye, fantasising about the Five Guys burger I'm going to reward myself with after this nightmare is over. Just as I start picking my condiments – tomato, lettuce, hot sauce, obvs – the heavy door leading to the green room opens and Frank walks out. Our eyes meet.

'Frank, hey.'

Though we've had a couple of Wisecracker nights since our bust up, Frank's been proper elusive, arriving late, leaving early, giving us no time to speak, well, not properly.

'Abi. What are you doing here?' he says, zero warmth.

'This is Elle, my …' But before I accidently spill on what, or rather who, connects us, she glares at me and I quickly change tack, my body stiffening. 'She's on the bill. I'm chaperoning her.'

'So, *you're* the middle spot?' Frank asks her, glancing between me and Elle, quickly joining the dots.

She nods, suddenly not aloof or distant but shy. 'I watched you on Lolz. You were brilliant. Are you doing that routine about school staffrooms tonight?'

Frank's shoulders inflate about fifteen per cent while mine deflate by the same, hearing her compliment him.

'No, I've got a new set because someone from Callback is here to watch me,' Frank says, gaze lazily scanning the room.

I try to catch his eye to offer congrats but he doesn't look my way and I shrink further. So much for Cassie saying this would pass in a few days.

'Right, well. Good luck,' Elle says, awkwardness rearing.

'Sweet,' Frank says with a little scoff. 'See you next week, Abi.'

All I can manage is a quiet, 'Yep.'

He moves off towards the bar and I sag back into my seat, stung and angry. I was willing to put things behind us, get back to how we were, but the way he's just been, on top of the things he's said about my act and chucking me under the bus that time, homeboy's taking my goodwill down to the wire.

In front of me, Elle goes back to writing in her notebook so I occupy myself by doom-scrolling Insta. Immediately, I'm bombarded with dynamic images of comedians doing better than me. I'm in danger of falling into a self-doubt death-spiral when I spot Dina doing her usual pre-show tour of duty. She eyes everything with an air somewhere between proud parent and territorial big cat.

Down but not out, I brighten, wondering if I can engineer a casual chat, even persuade her to put me on the bill sometime. That'd show Frank. If I can find my moment, it's worth a shot.

I glance up at Elle and notice that as showtime approaches, her whole body seems to be vibrating, nerves threatening to consume her.

'They'll be getting started in a sec. You ready?' I ask, braced for my head to be bitten off.

There's a moment of something I can't name and then her eyes soften. 'What do you think I should open with?'

The question surprises me. After the talent show, I never thought she'd ask my comedic opinion again.

'Er, well, don't tell your mum but I'd go with the cowgirl thing. It killed.'

'Yeah,' she says, enthused, before remembering to keep things chilly between us.

'You're gonna do great, Elle. This crowd won't know what hit them.'

She gives me a shy smile and though I'm on my guard given how violently the wind blows from hot to cold with her, it does feel like a moment.

'I didn't want to go in the green room because … everyone will be looking at me. This is my first paid gig, with adults at a proper club. It's so …'

'Real?'

She nods.

'Thing is,' I say, daring to come round and sit by her, 'the comedy world is a bit of a family. There's petty beefs, sibling rivalry, falling-outs and that but there's also a lot of love. If you want to be a comedian, it means being one of the family. You'll be the baby sister.'

Elle sits with this and I'm suddenly aware of how small she is. Not frail or weak but just very small and I can't help wanting to protect her.

'Okay,' she says simply, and collects up her things. 'Let's go meet the Fockers.'

I chuckle, following her through the green-room door.

Not long after, the gig starts with Frank opening the show. Out the gate, his swagger gets on my wick. This Callback audition is the worst thing that's happened to him. He was normal amounts of cocky before but now he's taken it to Steven Segal levels. In fairness, he is killing it, bolstering his kids routine with some new brilliant but brutal lines.

'I hate children. I wouldn't want one, not even for the potential spare kidney.'

As that gag drops, from backstage, Elle and I hear the audience explode with outrage-filled laughter.

Part of me wants to cover Elle's ears. It feels like Frank's going extra hard on the kids material tonight. I'm not sure if it's to big himself up to Tess or bury Elle, the upstart. Maybe a bit of both.

'You know the worst thing about kids? They're useless. In my country, by eight years old, children have two jobs. Like, paper round and Minister of Finance. Kids here? Hey Siri. How do you do ten times ten? Help me, I'm dumb!'

Frank now has that rolling laughter where all he has to do is tickle it to generate more. Meanwhile, Elle's face is fixed in a grim expression listening to Frank double-down on his impression of UK kids.

'I need to win a TV talent show so I can work from home and eat avocado on toast!'

Finally he finishes, leaving the stage to rapturous applause. Elle's up next.

'Break a leg,' I say but she's already gone.

A moment later, Frank returns to the green room, letting out a self-satisfied puff as he stops his watch like he's just run a personal best.

'Well done,' I say, battling the surge of wounded envy that wants to keep my lips clamped shut.

'Thanks. I didn't get through everything because they were laughing too much.'

'Nightmare,' I say but Frank misses my sarcasm, his mind already on linking up with Tess to secure his comedy future.

Though I know it's futile, I hover, still hoping for Frank to connect with me – ask how I'm doing, how things are with Elle, something. But his attention is miles away and it burns to be with someone I'd normally spill all to, yet unable to say a word. Because despite everything, I don't want it to be like this, a heaviness where our friendship used to be, a stranger in place of the Frank I used to know. But as bruising as this is, I can't do anything about it right now because I need to make sure Elle gets off to a good start. I slip out into the main room, tucking myself down the side aisle and crossing everything this goes smoothly. Elle has already positioned herself at the mic but is just staring into the crowd. Is she pretending or has she really gone into shock this time? An uncomfortable murmur grows and a lone voice calls out, 'Tell us a joke!'

He's quickly shushed by others in the audience.

Elle pulls the mic out of the stand, takes a long, deep breath then exhales. 'I would, mate, but my uncle Frank stole all my best ones.'

There's a moment of silence, just like at the competition, as the room realises this girl has just delivered a great opening gag that's not only a callback but also a clapback at the previous comic. The crowd erupts.

'Yes, Elle,' I say, with an appreciative nod – feeling a mixture of shock and relief at how strongly she's come out of the gate.

Whatever nerves she had evaporate as she riffs off Frank's lines one after the other, the crowd eating out of her hand. She's doing great and so, safe in the knowledge she's smashing it, I decide to quickly seek out Dina. I spot her at the back of the club and shuffle over, casually positioning myself a few feet away, like I'm just a sistah trying to get a better view of the stage.

'She's good, huh?' I whisper, nodding towards Elle who's striding around like she was born to perform.

'Very,' Dina says in agreement.

'I helped put that routine together.'

I let this precious intel slip from the corner of my mouth as though escaping without permission.

Dina looks at me, an eyebrow arched. 'You should write like that for yourself.'

And I crumble on the inside while still trying to stand tall. I doubt Dina meant to hurt me but, coming from someone I respect, the slight is gutting.

'I am,' I lie, crumbling further.

'Great,' she says. 'Let's see more of that and less pandering and we can talk about putting you on here.'

'Nice one,' I whisper, trying to play it cool but really wanting to punch the air. This is the closest I've got to playing the Cabana, to finally showing Dina what I can do in a paid room and I am trippin'.

'How's about we start with a five after the interval?'

'Huh?' I say, my mouth trapdooring open because – I think she just offered me a spot – tonight!

'Frank cut his ten spot short so there's a five-minute slot going – if you want it?' Dina chuckles with an edge of impatience.

'A hundred per cent. I won't let you down,' I yammer, though I panic wondering if she's expecting that Elle-quality material I claimed I've been writing.

Fact is, I haven't written anything new for ages and if I try and come up with something before I go on, it'll be a car crash.

I go to speak but Dina smiles. 'Don't worry. If the new stuff's not ready, just do your tried and tested.'

'Great,' I exhale.

'I'll let the compere know. You'll be on after the second half opener.'

I give her a thumbs up and she heads off. This is epic. In an instant, chaperoning has become the best career choice ever.

On stage, Elle is finishing up her routine. She delivers her last gag and gets deafening applause which, lucky for her, covers her awkwardly fumbling the mic back into its stand. *Always do it before your final line. I've told her this. Not such a pro after all, Miss Thing.* Anyway, I'm glad she did well. As she leaves the stage, I make my way to the green room to meet her.

'Nice work. You pleased?' I ask.

'Yeah, it was amazing,' she beams. 'What did you think?'

I hesitate, choosing not to admit I didn't see her perform cos I was bagging a slot off Dina. 'Great, as always.'

'Thanks. So, where do I go to get paid?'

I share a look with the other comics, like, *bleeeesss*. 'It doesn't work like that. Your dad will send them bank details. Should come through in a few weeks.'

'Right,' Elle says, crestfallen as she shoves her rolled-up notebook into her jeans pocket, heading for the door.

'Oh, hang on, Elle,' I say, drawing her back. 'So, amazing news. Dina offered me a five-minute slot in the second half.'

Elle stares back. 'Er, I don't think so. I need to leave.'

I double-take her to check this isn't a wind-up. 'You what?'

'Sorry, Abi. Tell Dina you'll come back another night when you're not working.'

I see one of the other acts look over, smirking, and my body goes rigid with the shame. Not only am I getting owned by this kid but in front of other comedians who, a moment ago might have seen me as a peer, but will now just think of me as some minion. It can't go down like this. Elle pulls at the door handle and I press it shut, ushering her away from prying eyes and flapping ears.

'We won't have to stay long. I'm on straight after the opener.'

Elle crosses her arms. 'Which means we won't leave for another hour.'

I pull in some air, hoping that, as well as nitrogen and oxygen, it contains a big dose of patience. 'Look, I already said yes so if I pull out now, I don't know when Dina will ask me again.'

'Wait, so when *did* you ask her, while I was on stage? You're supposed to be chaperoning me not scrounging for gigs!' Elle hisses.

'Being your chaperone doesn't include listening to your routine every single time. You said it yourself. My job is getting you here and home in one piece.'

'Then do your job,' Elle snips, throwing her hands wide. 'Or should I get myself home? Good luck explaining that to my dad.'

Elle cocks her head in defiance and I want to … I feel my chest heave; breath pounding. And suddenly, Frank's comments about hating kids isn't just comedy, it's scripture.

'Okay,' I say, with a calm evenness that frightens me.

I work my way through the interval crowd, Elle following, with audience praise not far behind. Some pat her on the shoulder, others recite lines back to her, one even tells her she should be on *ShowTime at the Athena* and my stomach churns. After giving

Dina a half-baked excuse about Elle feeling unwell, we leave, travelling home in silence.

I've put up with so much brattery from this tween, been nothing but nice, agreed to take her from gig to gig, helped with her comedy and this is the sucker punch I get?

In the deafening vacuum between us, my skin tingles with anger. I want to be as far away from her as possible, leave her to get home alone and, while she's at it, find some other mug to ferry her around. But though the thought is intoxicating, I know if I go down that road, everything will have to come out, it'll be carnage and God knows who'll be left standing once the dust settles. Am I really willing to take that risk? Because at the end of the day, whatever Elle loses, I know I'll lose way more. Man, I wish I didn't love Will so much.

Chapter 28

I hate myself for thinking this but since the grimness of my evening with Elle, I've been desperate for some kid-free time, just me and my man, an opportunity to decompress, regroup and, frankly, lick my wounds. For the price of my silence about Elle's behaviour and giving up my time to chaperone, is that too much to ask? But no such luck. Why? Because it's Will's birthday and long before I was on the scene, he made a promise to the girls that despite his separation from their mum, this day would remain a family affair, as it always has been. So even though I'd love to have planned something awesome, a night away, a spa trip, anything, I can't because we're here, at the Dis, with not just Elle and Esme, but Marcus and Kat too. *Frickin' fab.* I plaster a smile on my face as I scan the Sunday brunch menu. This situation is far from optimal. Yet another thing you don't anticipate when you get involved with someone who has kids, the constant splicing of time, sharing, always sharing. I sigh to myself as I sip my virgin Margarita, wishing it was full-fat booze despite it being eleven thirty on a Sunday morning. The only vague plus here is, it's nice to return to the Dis, the home of our origin story, although right now, surrounded by Will's BA life – Before-Abi – it doesn't feel much like ours. Even Marcus has known him longer than me.

On the next sofa along, Elle and Esme play on their iPad while the adults chat. Our waiter arrives with a tray of nibbles, fist bumps Will with his free hand then places the tiny white dishes on our table.

'Happy birthday, bro,' he says.

'Cheers, Jamal,' Will smiles, indicating for the girls to tuck in.

Esme ravages the vegan sausage rolls as though she hasn't been fed in a week.

Meanwhile, Elle inspects the dishes with the disdain of a cat who's suspicious about how gourmet their food really is. For the briefest moment we catch each other's eye. I venture a smile to see if she'll reciprocate. Nothing. Instead, she carries on picking at the food and playing on the iPad with Esme. I literally vibrate with indignation that Elle thinks she's got more right to be mad at me than I do with her. Okay, it was opportunistic to try and wangle a gig while she was on stage, but I've got to live my life too. It's like, everything is about compromise with kids. I'm not allowed to detour whilst on child-minding duty, even for an amazing opportunity, just like I can't whisk my boyfriend away for a fun birthday treat because he's already promised to his girls. This is feeling harder and harder with every passing day.

'So, I hear Elle's first paid, er …' Kat searches for the right term, 'gig went well.'

It comes out with the force of a hiccup she wants to suppress.

Elle looks over at me, then to her mum and back down at the iPad.

'Abi said she smashed it,' Esme offers, stretching her arms out just because.

'That's brilliant,' says Kat with that slightly mad smile of hers. 'It's good to get it out of your system.'

'And Abi's been brilliant with the chaperoning,' Will adds.

'Yeah, you have,' Kat concedes. 'This wouldn't be possible without you but surely you've got your own comedy career to think of. Last thing we want is Elle getting in your way, hey, Elle?'

Elle's eyes snap up, her face frozen. 'What?'

'I'm just saying, Abi's got a career too.'

'I know,' she bristles.

I let the tension hang for a moment, my indignation rallying. Yes, I've got a career too, albeit a faltering one in danger of coming off the rails. Still, it's good for Elle to be reminded what a favour I'm doing her, that I'm giving up gig nights to chaperone. I lean back, letting the corners of my mouth curl upwards until they reach peak magnanimity. 'It's fine. Anything I can do to help.'

Will takes my hand. 'You're the best.'

But before I can get carried away with my own back-patting, Nick from the unplugged night comes over.

'Eeeeeeh!' he says, holding out a hand.

Will springs up to greet him and they fall into a bro hug. 'What's up, man? And what's this?' Will says pumping Nick's upper arm.

Nick crumples laughing then throws playful one-two jabs in Will's direction. 'I'm just trying to keep up with you, cuz.'

I give Nick a wave that's more girlish than I was hoping. I'm pretty sure I look like a competition winner. He waves back then spots Kat.

'Shit. Kat. How you doin'?' he says, and she nods in that way parents greet friends of their kids' they just don't like.

Nick fist bumps the girls and sits opposite Will, slipping into an easy chat which is lovely to watch. Actually, it's lovely to watch Will do anything – talk, eat, cook vegan pizzas. I swear I would watch him go to the loo. Strictly number ones, of course. I don't love him that much.

'So, I hear this one's tearing up the stand-up scene?' Nick says, tapping Elle's leg with the back of his hand.

She tries to play it down but her flushed cheeks betray her.

'I tell you what, star, you ever want a gig here, just give me the word,' Nick says, leaning towards Elle. 'All kinds of names watch the show. Could turn into something.'

'Thanks, Nick, but this isn't going to be a long-term thing,' Kat says before Elle can make any kind of noise either for or against the idea.

'I think Elle can decide that, don't you?' Will says with a joyless scoff.

Immediately the air around the table changes. What was starting to feel relatively relaxed becomes tense, a minefield strewn with incendiary emotions.

'No, I don't,' Kat snips back. 'You may be comfortable with her gallivanting across London in the middle of the night, but I am not.'

Will snorts. Gallivanting does sound a bit extra, like we're marauding through town on white steeds, swinging cutlasses at strangers, when actually the most excitement we've had is when I accidentally double-tapped my Oyster card and the guard had to swipe me through.

As though looking for back-up, Kat pumps Marcus's thigh,

causing him to flinch like she's just tasered his balls. Ignoring his swallowed yelp, she presses on, 'It's not a joke, Will. You're all about chasing dreams but then I have to clean up the mess when it goes wrong.'

'That's bullshit and you know it,' Will says, battling to keep things light, if that's even possible when you're sitting with your ex, her young lover, your two kids, your good mate and your girlfriend – on your birthday.

'Please don't swear in front of the kids,' Kat says, voice sharp.

'Which kids? Elle and Ez, or Marcus?'

Daaaaaammmmn. I felt *that.* Will's brutal shot ricochets off the rest of us and hits Kat, causing her mouth to fall open like a broken letter box. Beside me, the girls become fully engrossed in their iPad game, braced bodies the only sign they're actually totally aware of what's unfolding.

'Listen, it was just a thought, yeah. I didn't mean to cause any …' Nick begins, his hands raised in innocent surrender, the classic gesture of a guy who keeps his life strictly drama-free.

'No, no,' Will interrupts, 'Elle's up for it. When's the next spot?'

'Dad!' Elle scolds.

'See, she doesn't want to do it,' Kat counters.

'Mum!' Elle says in bemused shock. 'I never said that either.'

'Maybe you should try being supportive sometime instead of suffocating them,' Will says, scooping up his Virgin Mary and taking a hard glug.

Kat's lips furl, tightening like a melting crisp packet. 'I'm protecting them. Maybe *you* should try that instead of setting them up to fail like you did.'

That's a knockout blow which hits Will squarely in his spirit.

He recoils so far into himself we'll need to call an air, sea and land rescue squad to retrieve him. Just then the lights dim, and we see a flickering yellow glow over by the far door. Shadows dance across the walls as Jamal approaches with a huge two-tiered cake dotted with candles.

The other floor staff begin to warble Happy Birthday as they gather round us.

In a half-hearted drone, the rest of our table join in, though, from our faces, you'd think we were at a wake. Will stares, the candles' up-light carving deep shadows into his face as Esme bounces on her chair. 'Make a wish, Daddy.'

Jamal hands Will a small plastic cone to blow out the candles. With a big puff, he does, the tiny flames flickering out as everyone cheers. Will offers a few perfunctory 'thank yous' but avoids catching anyone's eye – even mine.

'Well, I should leave you guys to it,' Nick says which we all know is British for, *This is too awkward. I'm out. Sorry, (not sorry).*

'Course,' Will says rising with him. 'And you know what, if there is a spot, I'm down for it too.'

I look up at Will. Kat's eyes swivel in his direction as well.

'Serious?' Nick asks.

'Totally,' Will replies, looking to me with a smile that radiates from his soul.

He's back. My baby's back.

'Cool. You got a guitar or you still want me to sort you out?' Nick says, enthused by Will's shift in demeanour.

'Ah-ha!' I say. 'Wait there.'

All morning, I've been holding out for the right moment to give Will his present.

Retrieving it from Jamal who helped me hide it the day

before, I trot back, beaming. The way Will's been singing more and more around his flat recently, I know he's ready for this. As soon as he sees me emerge, his eyes go wide.

'Abi.'

I hand over my gift and, from its padded case, Will pulls out a refurbished Taylor V-Class acoustic six-string guitar. I rock backwards on my heels very, very pleased with myself.

'Abi, wow …' he says again as he turns the guitar over in his hands. 'This must have cost a fortune.'

'Nice,' Nick grins. 'No excuses now, brah.'

Will rests the guitar on his lap and gently plants his fingers on the frets while his other hand hovers over the strings.

'What do you think, girls?' Will says, turning to Elle and Esme.

Though Esme is yelping for Will to play her favourite K-Pop tracks, Elle's face has turned to stone.

Will strums a chord, his fingers extending over to Elle to coax her back out of herself.

'Stop it,' she mumbles.

Will croons a silly song but Elle's having none of it.

'Will,' she says then looks to Kat. 'I thought he was done with all this …'

'Not now, Elle,' Kat says, ramping up the iron in her voice.

'What?' Elle whines. 'It's like you said – it wasn't good for him and now she's brought it all back. Cheers, Abi.'

Elle falls back into the sofa, arms crossed, and my face tingles with embarrassment at what drama my grand gesture has caused. Seizing his chance, Nick makes a pantomimic display of checking his watch.

'Yo, I've gotta bounce,' he says then quickly fires out goodbyes before darting off.

My whole body slumps as I look to Will.

'Abi, it's amazing. Thank you,' he says, setting the guitar down and kissing my cheek.

The softness of his lips lifts my mood but not by much. I get that Kat has a thing about Will being a musician but surely just having a guitar, the chance to make music for his own enjoyment, can't be a bad thing? And of all the people that should get that it's Elle. Jeez, this family.

'Look, this doesn't mean I'm about to turn into a struggling musician,' Will says to Elle who pivots from him huffily, trying to snatch the iPad from Esme.

'Elle!' Kat barks and she stops.

I want to disappear. I'm humiliated, angry, confused, plus I need a wee.

Everyone is quiet.

Picking at the cuff of her sweater, Kat turns to Will. 'Just so you know, that's not what I said. Elle asked what happened between us and … well, I thought she was ready for a grown-up conversation about it. And to be honest, I was worried because I know certain things can run in the family and I remember how the whole music thing made you so …'

She looks over at the girls, trying to find an appropriate word.

'Depressed,' Elle says flatly and I say a little prayer.

Dear Lord, if there is such a thing as an interdimensional portal, please open one up and let me fall in. Best regards, Abi.

'I mean, in fairness, it all happened before you two were …' Kat whimpers.

'But he *was* depressed! And it was all because of *that*!' Elle spits, pointing at the guitar. 'Everything was okay after Mum told you to give it up.'

I sit frozen, suddenly grateful my mum never had any of these grown-up convos with me.

'Elle, no – that's not … Your dad chose to give up music,' Kat blusters, defending herself. 'It was too much. You know, the ups and downs were taking their toll.'

'On me or you?' Will levels. 'Music didn't depress me. Giving it up did.'

'We were starting a family. We both had to let things go …' Kat says, desperately going between trying to keep the peace and stating her case.

'Really, what did you give up?' Will asks.

'Whatever. This isn't good for you,' Elle sneers. 'And can't you see, Dad, Abi's trying to make you into a failure, just like she is!'

We all fall silent, and before anyone can reprimand her, Elle flees to the bathroom. At our table, no one moves. I look to Kat who suddenly seems drained. 'I'm so sorry, Abi. That was—'

'Bang out of order,' Will says, his chest heaving with fury.

Still reeling, all I can do is take short breathes to stop myself screaming. But soon that's replaced by an eerie stillness. I'm vaguely aware of Kat and Will falling over themselves to apologise with promises of swift discipline – grounding and phone confiscation. But what I hear loudest is the piercing whistle of Elle's accusation – that I'm a failure. Shame radiates. Is that how *everyone* sees me, a flop dragging those around me into my pit of underachievement? No, that can't be my story. I've worked too long and too hard at comedy to go out like that. I am not a failure. I'm not.

With a shaky hand, pulsing from anger, I grab my phone, pounding out a furious text to Carl. Like Kat said, Elle shouldn't be getting in the way of my career. It's time I focused on getting it moving, starting with my first paid gig. Regardless of what Frank or anyone thinks, I can make it – and no one, especially not Elle, can tell me otherwise.

Chapter 29

It takes twenty minutes and two JD and Cokes to steady my nerves ahead of Carl's gig. After firing off my anger-fuelled text, I didn't hear back for days and when I did, I thought he'd offer a date in maybe a month or so. However, desperate for a replacement after one of his middle spots pulled out, Carl drafted me in just a day ahead of this evening's show, and I snatched at the chance like a hungry *Oliver Twist* extra. It was only when I'd hung up, and the tickle of nerves began to grow, that I wondered if I'd done the right thing. Yes, I wanted the gig, prove my haters wrong, but did I actually *have* a solid twenty-minute set? Burying looming doubts, I've been trying to convince myself it'll just be some piddly, back-of-beyond show, however now I'm here, I can see, I couldn't have been more wrong.

This place is massive, like two bars massive – a main one then a temporary overflow at the back. There must be three hundred chairs here and Carl and a couple of staff are setting out more. There are staff! My nerves start to crest. I haven't been on stage since my implosion at Wisecrackers. This could be horrific.

⋆

With the audience finally crammed in, the show gets started. They seem nice, laughing in the right places and well behaved apart from the usual lone drunk bloke, but still, I'm glad I'm not on until the second half. I just need a minute to get myself together. Though Carl's certain this crowd will love my humour, given he also thinks mother-in-law jokes are funny I can't rely on his comedic sensibilities. I mentally reshuffle my set and hope to God for a following wind. I need this to go well so I can look Elle, Mum, Frank, and anyone else who thinks I'm a failure, in the eye, and know I'm not. The first half flies by and before I know it, I'm being introduced and am heading for the stage. I go with one of my standard openings where I move the thin, black mic stand to one side and say:

'My skinny twin.'

Huge laugh.

Then I dive straight into material about my hair.

'Honestly, guys, when I was a kid, my little afro looked like a microphone. My sister would come up behind me and go, testing, testing, one, two, one, two!'

I do a mime and they love it, giving me another massive laugh for free.

'Wow, I've never been here. Brackenfield is so nice. Not like where I grew up. You know your manor is rough when it gets a shout-out in Drill tracks. That's not happening around here, is it. Can you imagine.'

And then, as always, I throw in a silly little rap, inserting the name of whichever quaint town I'm in.

'Shop in Waitrose, never Farm Foods,

Then golf with my girls from the Brackenfield Crew.'

Another big laugh as they enjoy their town getting a namecheck. I let out a laugh too, enjoying them enjoying me, but then, slicing through that bonhomie, the lone drunk guy yells, 'Aciiiiiiiiiiid!'

A few people shush him and it lifts me, knowing the crowd are on my side.

'At least when the police come to get him, we can tell them what he's taken.'

Big reaction. I am flying.

I decide to go hard into my Nigerian material, really trowelling on the impersonation of my mum.

*'And it's weird, the things she pronounces differently like, cucumber becomes coo-*coom*-ba. It sounds like a dance on* Strictly*.'*

Over the laughter, I do a little ballroom shimmy, causing the wave to peak again.

Drunk bloke raises his pint and calls out from the back, 'SeveRRRN!'

There's a few titters of recognition but mainly tutting as everyone tires of his interjections.

'Mate, 2016 called, they want their Strictly *catchphrase back!'*

That gets a loud cheer. The tide of support is fuelling me. This is going well. I don't need to spend more time on this joker than necessary.

'Guys, you ever get tired of being told you're too much? I swear, it should be my middle name. Abi 'too much' Akingbade. But look at me. I'm eleven stone and five foot four. I'm not too much. I'm compact!'

Lovely response. Carl was right. I can really feel they're on my side as I head into the home straight. I look down at my ever so skinny mark and grin.

'Honestly, babe, with these thighs, I would break your back.'

The guy turns beetroot as his friends nudge him.

'Crush me with them ebony thighs anytime!' comes a voice we all now know.

His comments carve through the vibe sending murmurs fluttering around the room. I look over and see Carl speaking with the heckler who's doing the usual placating hands of a drunk person promising to keep quiet.

'I don't know about crush, suffocate would be good.'

My ad lib gets a cheer but it's a hollow victory. He's killing the buzz.

'I've never had a black girl!'

'Shut up, mate,' someone calls out.

'And you never will.'

More applause which I use to springboard back into my routine.

'Babe, you couldn't handle my incredible, curvalicious bod. FYI, you girls should be grateful God gave me this Nigerian behind. If you had it, you'd topple over!'

This hits nicely because it seems improvised. Ah, the magic of comedy.

'Marry me!' calls out my drunk friend, before wailing a tuneless rendition of 'Ebony and Ivory'.

Finally, Carl has had enough and I don't hide my relief when he escorts him out, his slurry serenade fading as he's marched away. The room is now filled with a strange, swirly weirdness which I have to set straight. I sigh and put the mic back in the stand with a shake of my head.

'Yup. I remember my first drink too.'

The joke pricks the tension and laughter is once again released. I say a silent thank you to the comedic community chest for these one-liners, there to use with impunity whenever we're in dicey water.

'Anyway, that's all from me. My name's Abi Akingbade because I'm – bad, aiiiye!' The roar of approval is instant and almost knocks me back. I bounce off stage, head high, feeling every inch a success – finally. I realise how much I've missed this over the past couple of weeks, the buzz of hearing the audience's laughter, feeling them on your side, knowing it's your words that did that. I wish I could bottle this, then waft it under Elle and my mum's noses so they could experience the scent of my success too. With one whiff, surely Mum's doubts would evaporate, and Elle, well, maybe she'd start to respect me at last.

Carl gives me a lovely back-intro as he resumes his MCing duties and I head to the back of the room to watch the rest of the show. On my way, a woman at the end of a row taps my arm as I pass. 'You did so well with that idiot. He does that every week.'

'Cheers,' I whisper. 'How come they keep letting him in?'

The woman tips her head towards Carl with a weary sigh. 'Because it's his brother, Kevin.'

I splutter a shocked laugh.

'Both of them are a bit odd, to be fair, letting everyone think they're related to Tom O'Connor,' she tuts. 'Anyway, you were fab. Well done.'

'Thanks ...' I say, shook by that little revelation as I settle in next to the bar.

When I think about it, Carl has never actually said he's related to Tom O'Connor, he just points to the shared last name, leaving everyone to make the connection. Weird, the thought someone is so desperate for success they'd fabricate an association. Not me, I want to make it, for real. And tonight has shown me that can still happen. On stage, the final comic has taken the mic, a seasoned circuit act who's a fitting end to a great night. After, Carl wraps up and when I get one last shout-out, my cheeks practically catch fire at the warm reaction that receives. Show over, the room quickly fills with the chatter of a satisfied audience but before I can get lost in my own fuzzy feelings, I see Carl's brother, Kevin, zigzag towards me through the exiting throng.

'Listen, I just wanted to say sorry about earlier. You were brilliant.'

He's still pretty drunk, speech laboured and spittley.

'It's cool,' I say with a fixed smile.

'And, and, when you talked about your Nigerian behind, I *loved* it.'

'Great,' I reply, eyes plotting an escape route if he doesn't bugger off in the next thirty seconds.

'And your mum sounds hilarious. Telling the monarch to kneel for her,' he says, compounding my discomfort with an impersonation of me impersonating my mum who doesn't actually talk like that anyway.

'"Come on, your Highness! A crown does not make you special, special!"'

I grimace, hearing my material yakked back at me, only able to manage a faint, 'Yeah, nice one,' in response.

Just then, the woman from earlier passes behind Kevin, mouthing to me, 'He does *this* every week too.'

I stifle a giggle. At least that was funny, unlike this guy bastardising my set with his boozy, Thames Estuary drawl. As sweat patches form on his shirt Kevin tells me four or five more times how much he loves my behind and my mum until finally Carl scurries over, shunting him away.

Well oiled, Kevin has little resistance and so stumbles forward, ricocheting off the odd chair which he waves at with a lazy fist.

Carl lets out a tired sigh. 'Sorry again about him. He gets a bit overexcited when we have anyone … different on the bill.'

'Oh,' I say, starting to feel like a ticked box on a diversity form.

'I mean, I *love* variety. Give me a box of Quality Street, I'll even eat the coconut eclairs. That's what was great about that Comedy Buzz competition. So much variety.'

'Yeah,' I nod, baffled by Carl likening a group of highly talented teenagers to budget confectionery.

'And by the way, really unfair what happened with your Elle.'

I bristle at the mention of her, reminded of the stinky 'tude she's had since that day.

'She was fantastic,' Carl continues, 'but we just couldn't place her cos of that cowgirl joke. Them's the rules – no rude material. We even reminded them before the show.'

Wait, what? Did I hear him straight? All this time I've been beating myself up about that result – and it was Elle's fault she didn't place. My head spins as I think of the nights I've lain awake what-if-ing a different outcome, imagining I'd gone over her routine one last time like she suggested, checked and rechecked every joke, and now it turns out none of that would have mattered. It was Elle who messed up, pure and simple. I feel beyond vindicated and kind of furious at how I've been second-guessing my every move ever since that afternoon.

'Well, like you say, those are the rules,' I rumble and after we say our goodbyes, I powerwalk to catch the last train, emotions surging at this revelation.

As the guard bumps along the carriage checking tickets, my mind is a jumble from an evening with more plot twists than a Christmas episode of *EastEnders*, the biggest, of course, being that I'm not to blame for Elle losing the competition after all. I decide to wedge that little factoid in my back pocket till I know what to make of it. Because though that intel has left me hella indignant, something else is bothering me, a pebble in my shoe I can't shake, an irritation that swells as I recall Kevin reciting my material back to me. It's that uncomfortable holding, a rigidness in my body I always get when someone is teetering on unwittingly saying something ugly about race. Like the time a teacher compared my skin tone to her daughter's badly done spray tan or when a saleswoman at a make-up counter told me my foundation colour looked 'muddy' against her pale tones, but on me would 'be lovely'.

Micro-aggressions. Was that what Kevin just did? All unintended but diminishing just the same. Picking over my encounter with him as he sweatily blasted my material back in my face, I deflate. Yes, I felt diminished, but … he was only repeating what I had already said. Yet hearing my jokes coming from him – they felt eggy, old and out of touch. I go cold at the realisation. Is that why Carl is the only promoter who'll book me for a paid gig; why Dina was so pleased I'm writing fresh material and why that bloody nurse said my stuff was rubbish? Because it *is* dated and out of touch. And maybe that's why Elle thinks I'm a failure and Mum has no faith in me either. As the train rattles past deserted platforms, I glare into the blackness and can't help think of Elle and how different the response to her comedy is – rolling laughter, never groans, all coming from a place of recognition. It's like, by Elle telling her truth, she's speaking everyone else's into existence too. My comedy never does that. My hand clamps over my mouth in horror as

I realise … I'm a hack, who's saying nothing for The Culture; in fact, I might be doing damage. At the thought, I take involuntary gulps to push down the acid burning my throat. Anyone can be a clown but to write about yourself in a way that reflects the audience's lives, damn, that's practically art and that is definitely not what I'm doing. Suddenly I feel like a piece of Rubik's cube trying to slot into a jigsaw. I don't belong in this industry. I just don't have what it takes. And after eight years, what am I actually doing? Though I've been denying it for the longest time, Mum might have seen what I've been missing all along. There's a reason no one pays me to do stand-up – because it's not worth paying for. Frank and I always laughed at journeyman comics we'd see at open-mic gigs doing their same, old routines. We'd snicker at their lack of self-awareness, oblivious to how the circuit had no use for them other than as padding or a designated driver for remote gigs. We'd laugh at how these hopeless fools spent years trying to make it, all while holding down a day job, unwilling to accept comedy was never, ever going to be their bread and butter. We laughed but maybe I'm one of those sorry souls, deluded with no sense of when to give up. Some people are naturals, like Elle and Frank, and some people, like me, no matter how many hours we put in, how passionate we are, how much we long for it, aren't a fit. We're just try-hards, destined to be the creative asphalt, paving the way for those who can – for the Elles and the Franks of this world. How is it, on the night I smash my first paid gig, all I feel is a despair that eddies in the pit of me, thrashing so deep down I can't even bring myself to cry? No. Tears don't dwell in this kind of sorrow but new life choices do. I stare out of the window, for the first time feeling like being in the funny business isn't very fun at all.

Chapter 30

I wake with a restlessness that even snuggling closer to Will doesn't ease. It's six a.m. and I've barely slept – eyes jolted open time and again by the same nightmare – Kevin, face of a parrot, squawking my routine in my face while Elle and my mum point and laugh. A grim cloud moves in as I recall the previous evening. What should have been a triumph is, instead, the dawning of something that's been staring me in the face for a long time. Either me, my material – or both – suck. Man, this is awful. It's Saturday morning, for Christ's sake. This should be about fry-ups and lie-ins, not languishing in this misery ditch, but the realisation I'm a dud clings so tightly I can barely move. I try to bolster myself, thinking of the pluses, but what are they? I did material that's an embarrassment, in front of people who lapped it up, and the thought of that leaves me feeling grubby. But what am I supposed to do? Rewrite my routine and create a new one, switch up my whole style? It's not that easy to— I stop, remembering that's exactly what I asked of Elle – and she did it. Even at changing lanes, she's more accomplished than I am. Jesus, I really do *suuuuuuuck*. Ugh, I need a distraction from thoughts of narrowing career prospects and squawking parrots. It's Carnival weekend which can normally take my mind off *anything*, but even the anticipation of guzzling a cold Red Stripe and yamming some freshly charred jerk chicken over in West London can't bring me out of my funk. In a tangle of soft sheets, I roll towards Will but he's still asleep. I flop onto my back.

It's been a week since his birthday and you wouldn't need a thermometer to gauge the frostiness between me and Elle. But since her outburst at the Dis, her punishment has felt token and hella lenient, almost like the whole thing's been brushed under the carpet. Perhaps Kemi was bang on about how separated parents fear being strict. I mean, Will says they had words after the comedy competition but look how things have been since then. And if I bring up how Elle's been, will that get brushed under the carpet too? It's so frustrating because, though no one's said it, setting her straight, in any way, just isn't my place. But then what is? Where do I belong in this puzzle made of pieces that don't quite fit? Man, why is this so hard? Why can't we just be nice to each other? Play Deck of Devastation on rainy days, go for walks in the sunshine, make pizza, watch shiny Saturday night shows and Sunday morning cooking programmes? Why does Elle have to try and get one up on me all the time, undermine me? Why does she have to be such a … My chest pounds as I picture, not for the first time, the moment I tell all, detailing for Will just how shitty Elle has been and him fuming, thanking me for having such grace under fire— but then my tumbling thoughts brake hard, slamming into those grand assumptions about where I stand in Will's affections. I really don't know who he'd side with and that's painful to admit. Next to me, Will stirs. I look across, meeting his bleary eyes.

'Morning,' he smiles as an arm rests on my chest.

I push myself towards him and he presses against me in reply. I so want to feel him want me, to connect and satisfy him in the most primal way. Though the girls are preoccupied in the living room, Will and I keep the noise to a minimum. And there's something insanely hot about the restraint. Every contained moan feels exquisite, every brush of his lips against my body, stolen. I'm taken by an urgency as I swing my leg over his hips and move him into position. I need to feel Will now, his love, the intensity, to give him something only I can and carve out my place so I become as critical in his life as anyone else.

'Whoa, slow down, what's the rush?' he whispers.

'I thought ...' I say, tipping my head towards the rising noise of Elle and Esme next door.

Will lets out the sardonic laugh of a seasoned parent. 'Don't worry about them. If they've got the iPad, we don't exist.'

'Right,' I say, mustering a knowing nod even though I'm aware they'll never not exist for me.

There's not a moment I'm not thinking about them, measuring myself against the girls, testing to see how drowned I'd have to be before Will swam back to save me because – am I really his bae, his *before anyone else*? But thankfully, I'm drawn from those thoughts as Will pulls me to him and our lips meet, blooming into a full, passionate kiss. Beneath me his hips begin to rise and fall and just as the sensation of that sweet thrust takes me to another place ... the girls crash my reality.

'Daaaaaaad! Tell Elle!'

Before I get to reach back and pull the duvet over us, Esme has barrelled into the bedroom.

'What are you doing?' she says gawping at me straddled over Will, the duvet barely covering my butt.

'Your daddy had something in his eye,' I flap.

'They were having sex,' Elle calls from the other room.

'Which is why I've been asking both of you to knock before you come in,' Will says, zero embarrassment in *his* voice.

I slip down beside him and cover myself with the duvet wishing I *was* now invisible to them. Asking the girls to knock clearly isn't enough. A *Do-not-enter-until-Dad-says-so* sign might be more appropriate, with actual consequences if they ignore it? Maybe *this* is why stepmothers are so cranky – they never get to shag Daddy in peace! But as always, I say nothing – because it's not my place.

'What if there's an emergency?' Esme says, clambering onto the bed.

'Like what?' Will asks, folding her into his arms.

'I was kidnapped?'

'Then you wouldn't be here to knock,' he counters.

'What if my head fell off?'

'Then knocking on the door is the least of your problems.'

'Exactly,' Esme says, like that solidifies her argument.

Will's brow furrows. 'Exactly how?'

'Because if I knock, you'll know my head hasn't fallen off,' Esme explains for Will's simple brain.

And in the face of this unbridled cuteness and despite my frustrations, I can't help but smile listening to them continue down this logic-free rabbit hole. It takes me a beat, but soon I shed the crankiness and instead ponder how relaxed they all are about the whole sex thing. I mean, it's not like there's a viewing gallery for the kids but there's also not the uptight squirm-fest bordering on revulsion I grew up with.

Eventually, Will and Esme's conversation runs aground, mainly due to her boredom, and she leaves. Will slips from under the duvet and nudges the door closed, eager to get back to where we left off.

'So, you've had the birds and bees chat?' I ask, impressed.

He nods though if his face were an emoji, it'd be that smiling one with a bead of sweat. 'It was more like the foxes and the vixens, to be honest. Saw a couple of them "stuck" together. That prompted most of the questions. Ez was like, "Why is that fox trying to get a piggyback from the other one? Is their leg bad?" We had the talk that afternoon.'

'Yo,' I say, a fisted hand going to my mouth to stifle my laughter.

'I mean, given where kids come out of when they're born, you'd think this conversation would be easy, but hey,' Will says, sliding back under the mess of bedding.

I shimmy down next to him but just as we're about to get back to it, Chapelle noses the door open, pouncing onto the bed. He stares for a minute, flashes his bum hole at me then starts kneading the duvet like an angry *Bake Off* contestant.

'All right, fella,' Will says, nuzzling Chapelle before throwing on some trackie bottoms and a T-shirt. 'Let's get you fed.'

He winks at me then follows Chapelle through to the kitchen. I look at the light seeping in from behind the blind and catch a glance of Will's retro alarm clock – 6:58!

Bloody hell, I groan, don't these people do lie-ins?

The short answer is, no. Will has the girls for the whole bank holiday and with Carnival starting tomorrow, it's gonna be a jam-packed weekend. We've come up with our plan for navigating Notting Hill but, though I haven't missed a single Carnival since I was fifteen, this year I'm actually in two minds. I love being there – wining in the street alongside the sound systems, enjoying the costumes, finding secret toilets no one else knows about, but do I really want to do all that with Will's kids in tow – especially when one of them is barely talking to me? But, as always, there's no time for hand-wringing reflection when the girls are here so I shelve those thoughts and focus on the now – breakfast, getting dressed and then heading over to South Ken to check out the museums. There's a black history exhibition the girls are keen to see and, as it's one I've been meaning to check out too, I'm game. Plus I'm hoping there'll be enough to occupy the kids, that the chill between me and Elle won't be noticeable.

As I look around the hall, I'm aware I've never really known how you're supposed to 'do' exhibitions. At least nowadays they've made them interesting for kids – just push, pull or poke something and it's bound to make a noise, let out a puff of smoke or, at the very least, babble some commentary. But what about us adults? How long do I look at an exhibit for, do I have to read every plaque, is it okay to skip a floor? While I'm worrying about all this, Elle and Esme are having no such doubts, tearing around shouting out facts about any of the black historical figures they recognised.

'Look, Marcus Garvey!' says Elle and the pair race over to an animated bust of him speaking intently about the Black Star line.

Will rests his arm on my shoulder and steals a kiss. 'You all right? You seemed a bit quiet on the Tube.'

'Yeah, I'm good,' I say and give him a squeeze but I'm tense.

We haven't all been out together like this in a minute and somehow Elle and I have silently agreed to pretend we're cool, while saying practically nothing to each other. The worst thing is, we both know she's got this gong show coming up when I'm supposed to be chaperoning her. How are we gonna plan that – using BSL? It's not exactly ideal. However, seeing as the alternative is being blasted with Elle's fury, as a stopgap Coventry will have to do. I smile up at Will, still blissful in his ignorance of all this, and for once am thankful he's none the wiser. The truce between Elle and me isn't peace but at least it isn't war either, and right now I'll take that.

Will and I catch up with the girls and we gather around some artists' impressions of black merchants visiting Britain during the Roman Empire. Then Elle and Esme race ahead again, past drawings of African attendants in the court of Henry VIII, through the sixteenth-, seventeenth- and eighteenth-century rooms, straight to the Equiano section. Around us, it's mainly black families but there are quite a few white ones taking their time to absorb information – the parents pointedly getting their kids to pay attention to *everything*. One mum carrying a sleeping toddler gives me a look of apology mixed with solidarity. I'm guessing she's just come from the slavery section. It'll do that to a person – although, I'm glad that area doesn't dominate the exhibition given that's not where our history began. She gives me an earnest nod and says, 'Of course, on some level, black history is all our histories, isn't it?'

Her face bears folds of unnecessary guilt so I double tap a fist to my chest in sincere thanks and quickly move on to the next section.

'Look!' Esme gasps, pointing ahead.

We go over and find several seaside-style cut-out boards but instead of buxom couples in fifties' swimwear, they're black historical figures.

Esme thrusts her head through the hole where Mary Seacole's face should be, instantly adorning herself with a long, Victorian gown.

'Daddy, stand in this one,' she says, and Will becomes Olaudah Equiano.

'How's that?' Will says, pulling his most noble expression.

Me and Elle laugh and off that brief, shared moment, my tension eases.

'Take a picture!' Esme instructs, determined to capture the occasion.

I pull out my phone.

'Wanna get in on the action?' I say to Elle, venturing a smile. 'That Lillian Bader one has your name all over it.'

'I'm good,' she says quietly.

'Take the picture, Abi,' Esme squawks and at her instruction, I frame them up. 'Say, Black Excellence!'

'Black Excellence!' Will and Esme chime.

Memory saved for posterity, Esme takes Will by the hand, yanking him towards the next part of the exhibition.

Meanwhile, back with Elle, I search for something to say but am surprised when she speaks first.

'I'm sorry about last week.'

Elle's fingers knot, gaze barely able to meet mine. My eyes

narrow. I mean, an apology? I need to get the BBC Newsroom on the phone. This should go in the evening bulletin.

BONG – teenager apologises – unprompted. Our family correspondent is at the scene now.

'Thank you. I appreciate you saying that.'

Elle smiles. 'And I'm glad we're all here today …'

'Yeah, me too,' I agree.

'So …' she says, eyes fixed on Will and Esme, 'are you still cool to take me to the gong show next week?'

I waver, as everything, including time, seems to slow to a crawl. 'I … yeah, sure. That's fine.'

'Brilliant, thanks,' she says and then paces back towards her dad.

I watch them, the Mathesons enjoying some family bants, Elle nestling in beside Will, and my insides coil into a rancid cluster. Did I just get played?

Chapter 31

I'm desperate for some Will-and-Abi time but recently it's seemed as though something always gets in the way – it's his night or weekend with the girls, he's got to collect or drop them off at a play date, their friend's house, a birthday party, an escape room. And if it's not that then one of them is due a dentist check-up or … it's never-ending. And though I knew it was part of the deal, it's like, everyone expects me to just smile through this. Even spending more time at Will's hasn't helped because once he's done running around after the kids, there seems to be so little of him left. Nothing feels quite right in my life at the moment. It's already Wisecrackers night and I'm still unsettled after Carl's gig. Part of me wishes I could cocoon myself away, emerging later as an iridescent butterfly with a ton of new, meaningful, killer material – but even I know the only way I can overhaul my set is by putting in the graft. Except that, when it comes to writing, that's just not something I've ever really done – like sat down, pen in hand, scratching my chin, head turned to the sky for inspo. I've always just made it up on the hoof. If it gets a laugh, it goes in the set. If it doesn't, I add a silly face and paper over the cracks with a load of Abi. As I yank the pub door open, I'm aware how much I really want to talk to Frank. Not only is he one of my best circuit pals but he's the person I always turn to when I want to talk comedy – probably because he's so good at it. Man, I hate that things are strained between us. I really miss our trio, the pre-show heart-to-hearts, the banter. Though harsh words were said, I want to move beyond this. We should just apologise and let that be the end of it, because I need my mate.

'Comedy not on tonight?' Thea says, stacking steaming pint glasses from the dishwasher as I head through to the back room.

Bless. She often gets the days mixed up – which makes it a nightmare to play April Fools' tricks on her.

'Why, am I the first one here?' I say with a quiet tut.

'Yeah. I thought you'd cancelled,' she replies, tucking a column of glasses under the counter.

'No, it's still on,' I say, pacing through to the darkened function room, anger beginning to churn.

It's ten to seven. This is the latest I've ever arrived and I'm still the first to turn up. In fact, I can't remember the last time Frank or Cassie got here before I did. Everyone seems so comfortable with me being the dogsbody, whether it's setting up this gig or schlepping Elle around town. Is this how people see me? Good enough to sort out the furniture or fetch a glass of water but never destined for the spotlight. Coils of resentment start to unravel in my gut. With a grizzled sigh, I begin getting the room ready, each slammed down chair loosening some frustration.

'Sorry I'm late,' Cassie says, sweeping in with her usual, chaotic bluster. 'Horatio found what he *thinks* is a Roman coin and we—'

I swivel towards her and my face tightens. 'I don't care.'

She instantly falls silent, then, looking around with a sheepish bewilderment, sets down her bags and goes to fetch more chairs.

'There's already enough out,' I tell her then disappear behind the tech booth to retrieve the sound gear.

Her hands flop beside her and she just stands there. I don't offer pointers as to what else needs doing. If she were ever here on time, she'd know.

'Frank not arrived?' she says eventually.

'Unfortunately, I didn't have a TV producer or comedy agent to bait him with, so no,' I say, shoving the lead into the bottom of the mic causing a loud feedback whistle to blast through the speakers.

Cassie clamps her hands over her ears.

'Sorry,' I muster.

She approaches the stage with the caution of someone trying to ensnare a stray dog.

'Shall I give him a call, see if he's nearby?' Getting little from me, Cassie pulls out her phone, then pauses. 'I hear things aren't great with him and Callum. I think they might have broken up.'

I clutch the mic stand, my knuckles taut.

'That's too bad but we're trying to run a gig here.'

'Abi,' Cassie says, taken aback.

My lack of sympathy shocks me too but as much as I want to reconnect with Frank, I'm also fed up. 'Sorry, Cass, but I've had enough of doing this by myself. Frank only gives a shit when there's something in it for him, but when it comes to pulling his weight, crickets!'

'Well, Frank has the new term to prep for and—'

'Yeah, it must be tough having a month and a half off work over the summer while the rest of us are still hustling. Stop making excuses for him. Every week it's the same. Why am I always the first to arrive?'

Cassie recoils, sadness brimming. 'Well … I've got a lot on my plate too. Horatio's been banned from his wrestling club for an inappropriate hold – he swears it was a genuine mistake – and Shay wants to find his birth dad again so I—'

'Enough, Cassie,' I blurt. 'I've had enough. There's always something. Horatio found a World War Two shell, Shay thinks he has early onset dementia, Solomon got his heart broken and now he wants to join the army.'

'He's filled out the application.'

'Good for him! Though I'm not sure the army are taking eight-year-olds right now,' I say, pulse surging at finally expressing what's been brewing for months.

Cassie nods wordlessly and I step down from the stage, approaching her. 'This gig was supposed to be for all three of us. Remember why we started it? To get guaranteed stage time; yet now Frank's getting better gigs elsewhere, TV on the horizon, he doesn't want to know. He's that ruthless I bet he's glad him and Callum broke up so he can mine it for material. He may think he's better than the rest of us but if you reach the top by constantly chucking people you care about under the bus, you're just a … a self-serving hack.'

'Abi!' Cassie interjects.

And I'm silenced. Are therapists allowed to shout at people? But then a hole opens up inside me as I notice her gaze, fixed on the doorway. Before I even turn, I know Frank is behind me.

'Evening, ladies,' he says with serial-killer calm.

'Frank, I was …' I start but my mouth dries.

'Sorry I'm late. I was writing some hack bits about my break-up,' he says with a joyless smile.

'Frank, I'm sorry, I didn't mean it like that.'

'Give a shit, Abi. I'm done with this,' he says, waving a hand at the whole space.

'No, Frank, what do you mean? You can't,' Cassie pleads.

'Why should I work with someone who thinks I'm a …' Frank's barely able to say the word.

'Well, why should I work with someone who thinks I'm a failure?' I hit back.

Frank's mouth gapes. 'When have I ever said that?'

'You … you implied it. Like thinking I'm not good enough for paid gigs when I did one last week.'

'Which you only got cos I pulled out,' Frank sneers.

I stagger back at this body blow. 'If you think Carl's gigs are so shit, why did you book one?'

'It was in the diary from ages ago. Placeholder until something better came along.'

Wow, so what was a lifeline to me was just disposable filler for Frank. I reel, almost too snared by my own hurt to see Cassie start scooping up her stuff.

'Where are you going?' Frank and I snip, at last noticing.

'I'm sorry, you two, but I don't want to do this anymore. Abi, you asked why we started this gig. Yes, we wanted stage time, but we also did it because we were friends, because we wanted to walk this path with best buddies by our side, and because it was fun. This is not fun.'

Cassie walks out, knocking chairs as she goes, leaving me and Frank in a deathly quiet. After what feels like an age, I take my gaze to him and am met by his steely glare.

'That was your fault,' we both say in unison, and despite the stress pulling at every part of me, I laugh.

Then Frank laughs too until we return to a quiet that has just a little more room. I pull up a chair and plonk myself down, clutching a knee to my chest. He sits opposite and I take him in, my first proper look at Frank since he arrived. His eyes are puffy and bloodshot, shoulders fixed, like he's trying to stop himself collapsing into a heap.

'So, is it true? You and Callum broke up?'

Frank tries to blink his tears away, only for more to replace them. Elbows wedged onto his thighs, he buries his head in his hands. 'Bloody kids. It's always about bloody kids.'

I reach over and rub his back, but he shrugs me off.

'Don't,' he whimpers, 'it'll set me off again and you don't want my Viola Davis crying.'

So I just listen.

'Callum wouldn't let it go and we ended up getting into it on Friday.'

So that's why he pulled the gig. 'What happened?'

'I finally told him, point-blank … I don't want kids,' Frank says, trying to inhale his sadness but getting drawn back to the moment. 'Of course, that's when the yelling started, him saying that comedy is more important to me than him, that I always put it first.'

He brushes more tears aside.

'Is that true?' I venture, not sure I should dare ask.

Frank looks up at me, shocked. 'Of course it's true! But he knew that when we met. Comedy is my life.'

And we both sit, letting that truth bomb land as it brings up deep questions within me about my life. Frank has a single-mindedness that's inspiring, going for what he wants with zero compromise. Yet it's terrifying too because it means he's willing to tank his relationship with a man he's waited his whole life for, and I know I don't have that in me. Furthermore, looking at Frank, wallowing in misery, I can't help feel it's too high a price. I mean, what's the point of that big win if there's no one to share it with? But then I wonder, without that ruthlessness, that unbending determination, can I ever taste those big wins?

But also, why is this whole thing so either/or, demanding we choose love *or* success, a family *or* being a creative, security *or* chasing your dreams? At least, that seems to be the truth everyone has bought into, even Kemi. Stable job *or* explore your passions.

Frank sighs as the immediate despair finally releases him. 'Well, I've got no excuse now, have I? I've got to make a success of it.'

'You are, mate. You'll get an agent in no time and Callback will come knocking sooner than you think. It'll work out.'

Frank stares at the floor, then, after a while, looks back at me. 'I think it might be already. I got signed with Meagan Leslie last week. And Tess really loved my set so she's booked me for *Comedy Zone Live*.'

'That ...That's epic, Frank!' I say, springing out of my seat to hug him. 'Aren't you excited?'

'Excited, thrilled and bricking it,' he says through a nervous smile.

'You're gonna smash it. Wow, *Comedy Zone Live*. You know the next step is the Athena, right?'

Frank's smile flickers. 'If I do well, they've told me it could happen.'

'Oh, my days, congrats, mate,' I say, sitting back in a stupor.

I'm genuinely happy for Frank though I can't deny the sting of him sailing into my dream gig, leaving me waving from the dock.

'I mean, it's not a given but thanks. I'm made up,' he says, as a sadness creeps in and he shifts uncomfortably in his seat. 'Thing is, Abi, with all that's going on, I can't run Wisecrackers anymore. It's taking up too much time. I need to focus.'

'Right,' I say, swallowing down simmering emotions, keeping my head high.

'It's shitty timing given Cassie just flung in the towel too,' he continues, 'but I need to make this my last night. I'm really sorry.'

I gulp, still not able to form thoughts, so Frank fills the silence.

'And I want to say, sorry for what I said before. You are a brilliant comic and I've been a shit friend … Sometimes I get so one-track minded. I just really, really want to be … great.'

He practically whispers that final word, as though it's too precious to be spoken. Suddenly I see what's driving Frank, but also what it's cost him.

'I understand, and listen, I'm sorry too, for everything. You are not, and never have been, a hack,' I say and we hug again.

As Frank's arms loosen, he looks at me, eyes serious. 'Abi, I want to tell you why I said what I did. You're an amazing performer, and lord knows you've got the energy to light up Oxford Street but I also know how much writing scares you and I just wanted to, I don't know, jolt you out of your rut. I've gigged alongside you for seven years now and your confidence and skill on stage is incredible but to get where you want to go, you've got to lean into those places that terrify you. It's time, baby girl. It's time.'

I nod, tears prickling at his words.

'You're right,' I sniffle. 'But listen, when you're doing the

Athena or being the funny one at the end of the couch on *Graham Norton*, you won't forget us, yeah?'

'Forget you? Babe, who do you think is heading up my entourage?' Frank grins.

I gulp down happy tears, half laughing, half crying. 'Well, good job I've got a banging wardrobe for all that schmoozing.'

And we hold each other tight. 'Love you, mate.'

'Love you too, Frank.'

Chapter 32

I've never done a gong show, mainly because it scares the blackness out of me. Imagine the most intense, gladiatorial event – comedian versus gong, with a braying audience who've come for blood. And it doesn't matter how good a comic you are, you could still be left battered and broken by it. Are you too smiley, too posh, too weird-looking? Somehow the crowd's brutal hive mind makes a collective decision, and if they no-likey, it's curtains.

Even if you arrive feeling confident, once you see the montage of comedians tail-spinning to their doom edited to 'Another One Bites the Dust' playing on monitors around the venue, you'll soon change your tune. I try to block the screens from my peripheral view to allay my worries but Elle's pre-show pacing keeps them stoked. On stage, a lanky Australian guy with a hollow face is slowly winning the crowd over. They're clearly into him because thirty seconds later, a sound effect of jubilant trumpets rings out. He's beaten the gong. Lasting the full five minutes, he'll now go through to the next and final round later tonight. The cheer as he exits is generous, if peppered with a few 'G'day mates' and a raucous rendition of 'Down Under'.

Elle looks over to me with unease. I offer a smile back, still trying to gauge the true lie of the land between us. Since the exhibition and her suspiciously well-timed apology we have, at least, been back on speaking terms but there's a way to go before you'd call things friendly. She's twisted into her usual nervous ball, eyes glued to the stage where Glenn, tonight's MC, is chatting with the front row, effortlessly mining jokes from seemingly innocuous ore. It's impressive and a telltale of his many years on the circuit.

'Right, let's get another sucker ... I mean comic out here,' Glenn chuckles, his dense Geordie accent adding a playful warmth to the jibe. 'Please give a Laughing Lemming gong show welcome to Malcolm Unwin-Cordell!'

Glenn hands the stage over to the next comedian, a young guy in a baby blue T.M. Lewin shirt and chinos.

'Hi, I'm Malcolm. Friends call me Malc and I'm a second-year law student from Richmond!'

He gets no further, the instant boos sending him staggering back off stage with the force of an atomic blast. Glenn can barely hide his mirth and my concern for Elle begins to skyrocket. If I was mad at her, my revenge could never be crueller than putting her on in front of this lot who are getting rowdier by the minute. I decide there's still time to intervene. I open my mouth to speak but am cut off straight away.

'I'm doing it. It's fine,' Elle says.

That nip in her tone I've heard many times before has returned but I ignore it. I've got to do the right thing here, even if she hates me for it.

'Elle, this isn't a normal audience. These people aren't comedy fans. They're here because they love the smell of death and the beer's cheap.'

'I can do this.'

My head droops in exasperation. Do I have the power to pull the plug? Can I overrule and just say she's not doing it? Is that within my paygrade or literally am I just here to take her bloodied, broken body home after the bell? I take a deep breath, trying not to sound like a terrified supply teacher, but before I can even formulate a thought that might change her mind, Glenn calls her up.

'Now, be nice, she's only thirteen,' he says in a hushed voice as though Elle's going to be brought out, asleep in a bassinet.

In response, the audience let out a collective *aaaaaawwwwwww* and my stomach spasms. I can barely watch as Elle takes to the stage. She shakes hands with Glenn and plants herself in front of the mic.

'Hi, my name's Elle and yes, I'm only thirteen … which means child protection are watching this gig. One wrong move and you'll be in front of a judge quicker than you can shout "Tell us a joke".'

'Tell us a—' someone from the audience goes to call out but Elle has, in one move, short-circuited the impulse and instead, the audience catcall the lone voice which recoils, humiliated.

I sigh with relief. Her first joke has landed which is more than poor Malcolm Unwin-Cordell managed. I edge closer, my protective gaze set on Elle, ready to step in if it starts to unravel. But by two and a half minutes in she's going well, riding the laughter even though it's coming in places she isn't used to. At this rate, she might actually make the full five minutes. Clearly enjoying the crowd's goodwill, Elle looks down at a young guy in the front row and I waver.

'You look younger than me. What's your name?' she asks.

'What … is … she … doing?' I hiss to myself.

Crowd work, at a gong show? No, Elle. That's the MC's job. I shudder, silently mouthing my protests. I can see the back of the young guy's head. He doesn't want to engage. It's completely thrown Elle's rhythm and she knows it.

'Come on, what's your name?' she asks again, doubling down instead of backing off.

He giggles to his friend before answering, 'Mike Rack.'

'Mike Rack?' Elle says, face tangled in bemusement. 'That's a weird … Okay, cool. And what do you do for a living, Mike Rack?'

At hearing her say the name, the audience snigger. Now they're no longer with Elle but laughing at her – and I'm frozen, not knowing what to do.

'Come on, Mike Rack. What's your job?' she says, looking to others in the audience, still not understanding the laughter.

'Doctor,' he says, barely able to hold it together.

'Dr Mike Rack?' Elle says, and the audience fall into hysterics.

It's the biggest laugh she's got but she's lost them. Elle's brow furrows, her mouth open in confusion, and then I see it – that left knee slowly starting to pulse. Can I just go up there and yank her off stage?

She tries to push on but they're not listening. Now visibly shaking, she grips the mic like it's the edge of a sinking life raft and when she speaks, her voice is thin, uncertain. The audience, now no longer enjoying the demise but pitying it, mercifully, red card her, and she's gonged off. For a moment she stares out at them as though her brain is lagging behind current events. But when the speakers emit a second gong, its comedic clang cracking up the crowd and finally snapping Elle from her reverie, she hurries off, humiliation complete.

*

'What … what did I do wrong?' she asks, robotically lifting one arm then the other as I help her into her jacket, face etched with bafflement.

I smile as kindly as I can. 'Mike Rack … My crack. He was winding you up and you missed it but I promise, you were doing so well up until then.'

Elle sags at the realisation. I'm guessing this is her first proper death and though it comes with the territory, the last thing I want is someone so young going through it, and definitely not like that. I want to throw a protective shield around Elle, pull the misery from her but she seems so numbed out, I'm not sure she'd even hear me. I decide to say nothing, for now, gently leading her towards the exit. We're about to walk out the main door when I see Dawn, the booker we met at the competition, come over. Wearing her usual all-black outfit and blonde nest of hair, in this comedy club gloom she looks like a floating head.

'Love, what a shame,' she coos to Elle, her face ridged with pity. 'Listen, come with me, let's have a chat.'

Elle and I exchange glances as we follow Dawn down a labyrinth of corridors.

Once we reach her office, she plonks herself into a big, black, swivelly chair, fingers interlocked, tutting sympathetically. 'Elle, Elle, Elle. You were doing so great … until that audience stuff. You've gotta leave that to Glenn. It's what he's there for.'

'Yeah,' Elle replies, simply.

'But chin up,' Dawn pipes. 'You know all those screens around the club?'

Elle nods.

'We show clips of past comics during the breaks. Fancy seeing yourself up there?'

And Elle's face transforms. 'Seriously?'

'Yeah. We're re-editing the reel this week so we could get a clip from tonight slotted in, no bother. By Saturday, you could be on screens across all twenty-four of our clubs,' Dawn says, pulling out a scrunched piece of A4, thrusting it towards Elle. 'Just need to sign this release form.'

From nowhere, my full-chaperone-mode kicks in. 'Er, sorry, Dawn. Elle can't sign that. It has to be a guardian or a parent,' I say, trying to keep my shoulders broad, chin up. 'And before I sign, is this clip for the gong show montage or the one you play on normal club nights?'

'Who cares, Abi?' Elle hisses.

I ignore her even though her glare is boring into me like a pneumatic drill.

'I can't say for sure but, Elle, don't you want to be on screens across the biggest comedy network in the country?' Dawn says as she attempts, unsuccessfully, to raise a botoxed eyebrow.

I brace, unsure whether to continue, but Kemi's words about being 'the responsible adult' and 'boundaries' come back to me. Isn't this why I'm here, to protect Elle, make the right decisions even if she doesn't agree?

'I'm responsible for Elle,' I say with new-found confidence. 'I'll sign if you agree not to use the bit where the set tanks.'

'Abi-aaah!' Elle growls.

Dawn stares back at both of us.

'Fine,' she says with a derisory snort, folding up the release form and putting it back in her desk drawer.

I knew it. She's not trying to give Elle exposure, she just wants the rights to plaster her on-stage death all over their clubs with impunity. The cynicism makes my nose wrinkle in disgust.

'No, wait. I'll sign. I don't mind which bit you use,' Elle wails but Dawn has swivelled away from us, not even pretending to be doing something else.

'Close the door on your way out,' she says, without so much as a half glance at us.

Elle stares at her back for a good ten seconds before I finally convince her we need to leave. She darts down the corridor, vanishing through the exit and out into the street. I have to haul ass to catch her.

'You're not in charge,' Elle says spinning around, practically spitting the words at me.

'You know what, for the most part you're right, but here, tonight, I am. When it comes to rights and stuff like that, you have to be careful.'

'What would you know, your face has never been on any TV screen,' Elle yelps.

I do my best to side-step the attack. 'Listen, your parents only agreed to let you do these gigs if an adult came along.'

'And I got you,' Elle scoffs.

'Yeah, you did, and I'm not just here to ferry you about or bring water when you click your fingers. I'm here to make sure things like that don't happen, promoters exploiting you,' I say, standing my ground. 'Look, I know you're upset but trust me, you do not want to be in that reel.'

'Why do you have to spoil *everything*, just because I'm better than you?' Elle screeches, eyes bright with tears.

And I stagger back with no answer, no words, as Elle marches off, silhouette shrinking into the distance.

Chapter 33

Elle's old enough to make her own way home. It's four stops on the Tube then a bus ride so I refuse to feel guilty. *She* stormed off from *me*. In fact, her storming was so categorical, it should be named by the Met Office and given a mention in the evening forecast – *reports of a nasty isolated squall in the Islington area*. But though I know I'm not in the wrong, panic grows, thinking about what might happen if she doesn't go straight home. I call her phone but get her voicemail and pray that means she's on the Tube, going back to Will's. Although, even if she is, I need to get there first, give my side, otherwise who knows what she'll say, the state she's in. I swipe open my phone and order an Uber.

Twenty minutes later I pull up at Will's but it's all in vain because Elle is already there. The second I open the door I hear her voice upstairs, muffled but jagged. My throat closes as I walk into the living room and catch the tail end of her testimony.

'And … and I think …' she says, inhaling a spittley breath, 'she's doing it all on purpose!'

I gawp, unprepared for the sobbing and gloopy snot pooling around her nose and worse, the look on Will's face as he's completely drawn in. My heart plummets. I'm too late.

'Abi, where have you been?' he says, springing to his feet.

'Elle, you got back okay. Thank God,' I fluster, a futile display of concern.

'She came home by herself, Abi. What's going on?' Will asks, the press in his question making me tremble.

I open my mouth searching for answers, but Elle slithers into the paper-thin gap my hesitation leaves.

'I was on … the … the Tube, and I was scared and all by myself and there … was … this … maaaaan!' she cries, her sobs reaching new peaks. 'And he was looking at me!'

Instinctively, Will pulls Elle to him and she weeps into his chest, eyes shut tight.

'What did Elle tell you about why she left?' I probe, seeing if, by some long shot, amidst the tears, she told the truth.

'That you tried to mess up my gig like you've been doing from the beginning,' she whimpers, pushing back from Will, her voice cracking from the upset, but still sharpened to wound.

'Ellie, I need to talk to Abi alone. Can you go to your room, please.'

'Why am I being punished?' Elle wails.

'I'm not punishing you – I just need to speak to Abi.'

I look at Will, jaw clenched as he struggles to maintain his calm.

'*Uuurgh*, you always put her first when all she does is hang around and spoil everything. And you just expect us to like her! Why couldn't *you* take me, just once, instead … instead of …'

Elle's pointed finger is a poisoned arrow that pierces my heart, striking me dumb. I search Will's face but his focus is entirely on her, trying to console as she pulls from his grasp, steaming out, slamming doors as she goes.

His total investment in her version of events is now a barrier – him and Elle on one side, me on the other. I look from the empty space where she was back to Will as he draws his hand down his face and lets out a long breath. Through the wall we both hear Elle's quiet sobs and then the sound of Esme, comforting her sister. That mental image makes my spirit ache and feel even more on the outside than ever. Will closes the door and leans against it as if the life has been sucked from him. 'So, what happened?'

'I … I …' But I falter as his expression transforms to one I've never seen before, like I'm an interloper he has to protect his loved ones from. I can't help it. Tears brim.

'I'm serious, Abi, what happened? Why did Elle come home by herself?' Will's voice has an urgency that jolts me, a stinging reminder that even my tears mean less.

He moves to sit on the arm of the sofa, and I perch at the other end but feel so at sea, no idea where land is or in what direction. 'She had a bad gig …'

'Right …' Will pushes, the strain in him palpable.

'And the booker wanted to use clips from her set on their screens.'

'And she said you refused to sign the form?'

Thankful of the slight question in Will's voice, I pray that means he's open to a different interpretation of events from Elle's.

'Yeah, because she … she tried to do some banter and … this guy made a fool of her and she … I was trying to stop the booker taking advantage.'

Will rests a hand on the back of his neck. 'Look, I get where you're coming from, but … Abi, that's not your call.'

I open my mouth, searching for a reply. Isn't that *exactly* what I was there for, to protect her? Responsible adulting 101, right?

Off my confusion, Will then asks, 'Don't those forms need a signature from a parent?'

'Yeah, a parent or a guardian, so I—'

'Well, that's not you. You're not her guardian or her … You're …' he says, hands landing on his lap with an exasperated flap, and my heart breaks a bit.

I'm what? I want to ask, but I'm scared he's already given the answer by not speaking. I'm nothing. Not family, not their friend, just a stop-gap for when Mum and Dad are busy – whereas Elle, she's his everything, his life, to the point that, when she's hurting, his vision becomes so tunnelled he's oblivious to all else. I try to catch his gaze, a hopeless attempt to connect, but his eyes keep flitting to the wall that separates us from Elle. Of course he can't hear what I have to say. He's not even in the room with me. Eventually though, Will comes back, his brow furrowing deeper as if gathering thoughts he doesn't want to think. 'What's going on with you and Elle?'

My skin goosebumps and I cringe at the sound of my fake innocence. 'How do you mean?'

He kneads his forehead, eyes tired, body drained. 'I'm not blind. Things have been off between you for weeks. I hoped it was a blip, that the chaperoning would help you figure it out, but you haven't.'

What? *I* haven't? Like, it's all on me. What about Elle? She's not exactly been a cherub. I don't know if Will meant to load that sentence with accusation but that's all I hear. I press my lips together, hoping to stop myself saying something angry or unhelpful, stop a sob breaking free.

'I'm trying, Will, it's just …' I say, my voice splintering with pain – because I am trying. I've been trying for months yet whatever I do only seems to make things worse.

'It's just, what?'

I want to hold back. I do.

'She's a nightmare,' I whisper, eyes fixed on the floor, not ready to look at Will. 'She's been a nightmare ever since the Comedy Buzz competition. She takes potshots all the time, undermines me every chance she gets. She's embarrassed of me. At gigs, she doesn't even want me telling people how we know each other. I'm basically the help. And I have tried, Will, given everything I can to be a mate, to support her, protect her, but she just blows so hot and cold it makes me dizzy.'

I dare to look up. The silence is brittle, Will's face unreadable as he digests these revelations.

'Perhaps let's take a break from the chaperoning, yeah?'

My body goes numb as the sense of failure grips me. 'Okay … but now why do *I* feel like I'm being punished?'

A heavy frown moves across Will's face. 'You just said she's a nightmare. Problem solved. Stop chaperoning.'

I turn squarely to him. 'Will, the chaperoning is not the problem.'

'So, what is?'

I can't believe this. After everything I just said, he has to ask.

'It's Elle. Elle's the problem. You have to speak to her.'

'So, what are you saying? You *do* want to keep taking her to gigs?' Will asks.

The sarcasm in his voice is slight and perhaps even he hasn't noticed it, but I do and my irritation simmers.

'No, Will. I want you to talk to your daughter!' I say, face tightening as I realise the girls are probably on the other side of the wall, ears pressed against it, straining to listen. 'Talk to her about how she's being – like you said you would after your birthday but then you did barely anything.'

Will lets out a slow and deliberate exhale, his manner strained. 'Look, I know she can come across as grown up but she's only thirteen. She's been through a lot this past twelve months with the break-up and everything. And yeah, maybe we could do more when it comes to discipline but truth is, with kids, sometimes you just have to let things go and be the bigger person, cos you're the adult.'

I'm staggered. Is he for real? '"The bigger person?" Babe, I've been so big I could change my name to Hagrid. Did you know, this whole time I've been wracked with guilt about that competition, blaming myself for what happened? Turns out Elle didn't place because of her cowgirl joke. It was her own fault, but she's been taking it out on me ever since. So instead of telling me to be the bigger person, how's about taking care of business and having my back for a change!'

A sob bursts from me as despair scores my face. Shocked, Will falls silent as I wipe salty tears away with my sleeve, sinking back into the sofa. And we stay there for a good while as the energy dissipates.

'I'm sorry. I should have stepped in,' Will says at last. He takes my hand but something in his touch feels off. 'Sometimes I worry I've played this all wrong. Like, when you first met the girls, going to your parents so soon, giving you a key to their home – it was a lot. But I s'pose because it felt so good and it seemed to be going well, I didn't always think about how it was affecting them. And I love how you've done all you can to make it work but perhaps it's just too much. D'you know what I mean?'

I stare at him, open-mouthed. Oh, I know what he means because I've heard it a million times before but the last person I expected it from was Will and I'll be damned if I'm gonna stay to hear any more.

'Cool, got it,' I say, voice trembling with hurt.

I jump up and one-eighty to the bedroom, stuffing clothes into a bag. Will follows but I push past him to the bathroom, snatching up toiletries. I probably don't need depilatory cream but I'm that angry I'm grabbing anything.

'Abi, what are you doing?' Will pleads, hands pressed either side of the doorway.

I duck under his arm.

'Going where I'm wanted. If you, of all people, think I'm too much, then …'

On the other side of the hall I catch a glimpse of tiny eyes peeping from the girls' bedroom and my neck goes damp with a cold sweat. But this thing is on rails. I can't retreat. Instead I thunder down the stairs, Will right behind me.

'Abi, that's not what I meant. I never said *you're* too much. I meant the situation. Abi, wait, this is not how family works. You can't just run off at the first whiff of trouble.'

'It's not the first whiff, Will. It's been stinky for months. I'm tired of feeling second best and only appreciated when I'm doing something that helps you – chaperoning or picking up Esme when you and Kat can't sort out childcare. I'm trying my hardest to fit in to *your* family but when am I ever a priority? I know I made the right decision at that club tonight but if you can't see that, then you don't have my back at all. What is it you texted me after I found out about the girls – "just bcoz I have children, doesn't mean there isn't still an 'us'". Well, where's that "us" now?'

I tug the front door open and walk out. But with every step, I desperately want Will to come after me, grab my arm, turn me around, kiss me and say he'll fix everything because he can't bear to lose me. But he doesn't and as I walk, tears fall that I'm scared will never stop.

Chapter 34

I wake up to insistent snuffling around my left ear and for a second forget where I am and who the phantom snuffler is. However, the minute I feel a leathery paw on my face, I know. It's Cassie's dog Mitzi probably wondering why his favourite spot on the sofa has been given over to me. He cocks his head like I'm a problem to figure out and I pull the thin blanket up to my face, suddenly feeling the need to protect my modesty. I swear down, this guy will hump *anything.* Undeterred, Mitzi decides to make himself comfy on my chest. For a little dog he's surprisingly dense and the weight of him forces me to exhale.

Chapelle never got this close. He'd always just glare from his cat tree, tracking me like an aerial assault was imminent. A sad laugh escapes as thoughts of Chapelle lead me back to Will and the awfulness of last night. I check my phone for the eighteenth time, turn it off and on again, even switching from Cassie's ropey broadband to my 4G just in case, and then go through my DMs. There's nothing. Not even a new like. But it is only six thirty in the morning so I cling to the thin hope Will might message later when he knows I'm up and about.

How did I get here? I shudder, recalling the sharp jabs Will and

I exchanged last night. Just the thought makes me want to bury myself under these covers and never come out. In fact, I would if it weren't for the slight whiff of Parfum d'Mitzi. Still, I'm grateful that when I turned up on Cassie's doorstep, the thought of my empty flat too much to bear, she took me in. There was not a word about how things were left between us after that last Wisecrackers. Instead she just gave me a big cuddle and an even bigger glass of wine. And all that reminded me what a great mate she is and that at least one person has my back.

I hear creaking floorboards upstairs and quickly dress, throwing on yesterday's clothes. I'm not sure what mornings at Cassie's are like but given she has five kids, a menagerie of pets and live-in exes, anything's possible.

I just finish pulling my top on as Del, Solomon's dad, thumps downstairs, planting himself at the dining table.

'Mornage,' he says, flapping open a newspaper that looks a year old.

I try not to gawp but he's fully dressed from the waist up, wearing nothing but swimming trunks down below, his scruffy hair jutting in whatever direction the pillow decided on while he slept.

'Del, are you ready?' Cassie calls.

'Yup,' Del says without moving.

Ready for what? I wonder as one of the kids walks in wearing a woollen hood over his entire face.

Cassie emerges shortly after, bundling her two youngest into the kitchen.

'Horatio's going through a balaclava stage,' she explains. 'I can't get him to take it off.'

'When society collapses, you'll be thankful of all that military gear,' Del says with a knowing nod.

'Del, please get dressed! You can take your kecks off when you get to the beach, not before,' Cassie moans, chucking a balled-up pair of cargo shorts at him.

He catches them, then eyes me intensely. 'Always prepared.'

I keep forgetting Del's a prepper, ever ready for the fall of civilisation. How disappointed will he be if that happens this afternoon when he's in Margate. While Del loads his pockets with all he'll need for a day at the beach (if that beach were Normandy circa 1944), Cassie gives me an embarrassed smile, whispering, 'Sorry, they'll be gone soon.'

And not gonna lie, I'm grateful. Though her kids are sweet in their own way, I don't have the energy for anyone under thirty right now. I'm still so stung by everything that's happened. Because of Elle I might lose the best thing that's ever happened to me. In fact, I may well have already.

Soon, Del and the kids head out but as their voices trail off, Cassie's left staring at their dirty plates and half-drunk mugs of tea with a sad longing – she already misses them. I've never had that feeling – missing kids – even with Caleb and Ayesha. I enjoy them loads but I'm hella glad when they've gone. There's a plummeting sensation inside me as I question if I'm even built for a life with children – especially someone else's. And could I ever explain those feelings, those thoughts to Will? That I'm scared I don't have it in me to be any kind of responsible adult; that, at times, I'm insanely jealous of his bond with the girls, their love – one that's uniquely theirs and theirs alone; that I've had moments where the thought of spending the evening with them makes my heart sink and that, more than once, I've … wished his daughters didn't exist so I could have him to myself.

Wow, that makes me sound like a keeper. My skin goes

cold as I ask myself: if Will knew any of this, could he still go long-term with someone like that, someone who would literally wish his kids away?

'Penny for them,' Cassie says as she fills the kettle.

I shake my head, at a loss. 'How do you do it? I mean, isn't it ever … too much? No diss but it feels like constant chaos – in your head, in your heart … in your kitchen.'

Cassie lets out a little laugh. If I have offended, she doesn't let on.

'And what is chaos but life in motion in ways we're yet to understand,' she says looking off wistfully at Mitzi who's giving the eye to a worn old ottoman.

'Chaos is too complicated, loving a man with kids is too complicated,' I moan, jamming my chin onto my hand.

Cassie pulls a couple of mugs from the cupboard. 'Not complicated, complex. You ever been to dinner with a group of friends? You order drinks, have your starters, get chatting, your mains arrive but then someone turns up late, or somebody unexpectedly joins you. What do you do?'

I look at Cassie, perplexed. 'I don't know, shuffle round, ask for an extra chair or whatever.'

'Exactly,' Cassie says waving a spoon in acknowledgement. 'You don't tell the person to leave. You don't say, "Sorry, no space." You find a way. You can always make room at the table.'

'Just so I'm clear, whose table are we talking about?'

'Will's. Yours. Whoever's. But if it is yours, how can you let Will sit down and eat without letting the girls join as well? And how can you sit at Will's table without understanding the girls belong there too?'

Hmmm. The idea that my life, my heart, has more capacity

than I'd thought and that loving people is not a one-in, one-out type of thing, quietens me. But doubt still lingers.

'I just don't think I'm right for this, you know, being a step-mum.'

'How do you know?' says Cassie dunking our tea bags.

'Because I woke up sleeping under your dog's blanket,' I say.

'Yes, sorry about that. The guest one has moths.'

'It's fine. I'm grateful, mate, but doesn't the fact that I'm here and not there say something?'

She stirs our teas, thinking, then hands me one. 'Thing is … you're *not* a stepmum, you're Will's girlfriend.'

I go to speak but as words come, they wither on my tongue. I really want to give a 'yeah but …' or a 'what you don't get is …' but she has a point. And the tightness that has been gripping my shoulders for weeks releases me just a little, just ever so.

I sit in a quiet contemplation as Cassie potters. I'm not a stepmum so why have I been going all the way extra trying to be one, be more than was ever asked of me? Being too much in all the ways that are helpful to no one. Why have I never felt like I'm enough? Turned myself inside out trying to be? The thought plucks at a raw nerve and before I know it, my face is damp with tears at finally being able to discharge the pressure that's been accumulating inside.

Cassie sits at the table but says nothing. And that space she holds for me is everything. My body rocks as waves of sobs break. It's the relief of letting go of trying to get life right, be just the perfect amount. Not too little but definitely not too much. Yet always feeling like I've missed the sweet spot, my best self.

Eventually, through bleary eyes, I look at Cassie who's just nodding, like she knew all along, tenderly sifting the poison and pain from my soul so I can be whole again. I search her gaze. She just keeps nodding, steady and sure, wordlessly letting me know 'you're okay, you're okay.' Finally, my tears subside, those last drops of sadness wrung from my body.

'Well done,' she says with a quiet serenity.

And something about that makes me laugh, subdued at first but then hysterically, big howls erupting from me, making Cassie laugh as well.

'That'll be eighty pounds please,' she says and we both crack up even more.

I wipe my face with the heel of my hand. 'Oh my God, I needed that.'

Once our laughter has ebbed away, Cassie asks, 'What do you want?'

I search within for answers but nothing comes. My mind is scrambled, any authentic response buried under piles of strategies and strong suits, and attempts to be charming, liked or wanted. 'I don't know, Cass. To not lose the guy I love?'

'Do you want my opinion?'

'Is it going to make me cry?'

'It's hard to predict in my line of work,' she smiles. 'But if there's one thing I know for sure, children, whether they're yours, you've adopted or they're your partner's, will bring out anything in you that's unresolved, bring out those wounds you've long kept hidden. Guaranteed.'

'Oh.'

And the penny drops as my mind immediately goes to my mum. How could I ever offer anything approaching maternal to Elle and Esme when my example growing up was Queen

Abosede, with the motherly warmth of a polar bear's arse? Our relationship is my unhealed wound, a cold war that's been going on for more than twenty years. It's Sunday lunch this weekend. I was dreading it but maybe this is an opportunity for me and Mum to finally figure our shit out so I can be who Elle and Esme need – that's if I'm not too late.

On the doorstep, Cassie and I share a long hug that fills me up. I'm still tender but surprisingly okay. 'I have no idea what you did but wow.'

'Glad it's helped but look, I know it just felt like lots of crying but today was a big release. Take things easy. Don't do or say anything impulsive.'

I give Cassie a cheeky 'who me?' grin but her teacherly glare soon nixes that.

'Got it,' I say with a little salute. 'And, Cassie, thank you.'

She gives a no-problem shrug in reply. 'Scant repayment for everything you did at Wisecrackers.'

And at that, I wilt, embarrassed at my harsh words and mean behaviour when she's only ever been sweet and kind to me. 'Look, I'm really sorry about that night. I was out of order. You've been such a great mate. Always there for me, pulled me out of my funks, given amazing relationship advice …'

'That you ignore,' she says with a chuckle.

'I'm processing,' I protest playfully.

'True. You get there in the end.'

'But seriously, queen, thank you,' I say, feeling tears blister once more.

'Oh, don't, you'll set me off and I've got a client soon. What will they think, seeing their therapist in floods?' Cassie says, dabbing at her eyes.

‘They’d be honoured to see a superhero without their cape on.’

And at that, we both cry, happy, healing tears in each other’s arms.

Chapter 35

Though it's been a couple of days, I'm still experiencing the after-effect of my morning with Cassie, like some calcified crust has broken away, releasing insight after insight. My thoughts spiral and at the centre of it all is – Mum. Emotions jagged, I get lost in memories of all the times I've laughed off her lack of support. All the times I've made it my mission to succeed just to show her and how much energy that's sapped from me. It's a mad ting. But no more. Today, I want a proper talk. Not jibes, just a real conversation.

'No Will and the girls?' Mum oozes the moment I walk through the door, sickly snide dripping from every syllable.

I try to ignore it, to push through and instead propose an honest exchange that will stand us on new ground but before I can, she drips in a little more toxin.

'Or have things run aground on that front?' she asks, her query caked in cynical expectation, and I buckle, instantly tossing reconciliation aside.

'They're gone,' I say flatly, then off Mum's concerned expression, 'Witness protection.'

I suppose, where being mean is Mum's factory preset, cracking jokes is mine – no matter the cost. Perhaps neither of us can help ourselves.

'What a peculiar sense of humour,' Mum says, with a dismissive roll of her eyes, indicating for Dad to carve the lamb roast.

'I know a joke!' yelps Caleb.

'Go on then, son,' Dad says, trying to inject some levity before giving me a little supportive smile.

'What do you call a cat with three heads? No, wait. Yeah. What do you call a cat with three heads?'

Everyone, except me, pretends to think, offers guesses – Ayesha the loudest, screeching things like, 'Three cat head!' and 'Meow face!'

'No, it's cat, cat, cat!' says Caleb then falls about in hysterics.

The whole table, including Mum, gives a generous, well-done-for-trying laugh. Are you kidding me? I'm turning myself inside out to be a better comedian and you lot are cracking up at 'cat, cat, cat'. And Mum thinks *I've* got a weird sense of humour.

The rest of the day lumbers on in similar style. Eventually Caleb and Ayesha peel off to the living room while the adults chat – polite, superficial. It's not long before afternoon doziness sets in for Dad and Felix but not me. My veins are coursing with righteousness.

'You're quiet today, Abioye,' Mum says, in passing.

'Mmmm,' I reply, adding mumbled excuses but nothing to latch on to.

'So how's Elle getting on with her comedy?' she asks.

Opposite, I feel Kemi's glare. She's had an eye on me all afternoon. It might be because of the half bottle of wine I've sunk or, as Mum's so keenly observed, my teeming silence, a powder keg ready to blow, her words, the fuse.

'She's doing as well as a thirteen-year-old can,' I say eventually.

'So talented,' Mum replies, ignoring the arctic in my voice.

Around the table a quiet descends that's full and brooding because, as we're all aware, the next natural question for Mum to ask is, how's *my* comedy going, but we also know the British Museum giving back their nicked loot is more likely.

'Maybe it's time you stepped aside, for the young ones ...'

I stare at Mum. 'Step aside?'

'Yes, this comedy of yours – you've been doing it so long. Perhaps you've had your time. Why not speak to your sister, get advice on a new path. Kemi's made such great choices with her career.'

Mum gives me a thin smile which transforms into nodding approval of Kemi, and my skin prickles. Across the table Kemi stiffens, a pleading in her eyes, but I don't feel particularly sympathetic today.

'I'm not "stepping aside", Mum. There's room for me and the "young ones", as you put it,' I say, grabbing my wine glass and necking a big gulp.

Mum scoffs, taking her look from one person to the next as though there's something everyone knows but hasn't said. 'Oh, Abi. It's clear comedy isn't for you. Let Kemi help you find your way. It's a chance.'

'A chance at what?'

'Making something of yourself,' Mum says, almost baffled by the question.

I snort in response before turning squarely to her. 'What's the point of making something of myself when you see everything I do as a failure? Not gonna lie, Mum. Feels pretty shit!'

'Abioye. Words!' Mum exclaims.

'"Shit" is a word.'

'Abi, maybe now's not the time …' Kemi says but I'm not listening.

This isn't how I imagined it but maybe now's exactly the time for me and Mum to finally get real.

'No one wants to support your comedic aspirations more than I. However, unlike Kemi, success appears to continually elude you. I'm simply suggesting you take inspiration from her.'

My eyes dart to Kemi who in turn throws her gaze towards the door.

'I think the kids are tired,' she mumbles, going to get up, but I raise a hand, stopping her.

'Look what you've created, Mum,' I say, despite imploring glares from Kemi.

Mum looks confused. 'What do you mean?'

I reposition myself in my seat, almost savouring the moment.

'A daughter too scared to tell you that maybe *she's* taken inspiration from *me* and found her own creative path!'

Mum looks almost bewildered, an involuntary laugh escaping her. 'Kemi wants to be a comedian too – is this one of your jokes, Abioye?'

'Her *own* creativity, Mum,' I throw back. 'Kemi has set up a haircare business, but she's too scared to tell you.'

The words trip out of me with an ease that feels hella satisfying. I sit back as Mum's fraught gaze zigzags from me to Kemi to Dad and back again.

'Adekemi?' Mum says, her voice muted with shock.

Kemi almost has to drag her eyeline up to meet Mum's. 'I was going to say … I just wanted to get it off the ground first.'

Mum's mouth flaps silently.

I pour myself a top-up, putting the wine bottle down with a heavy clunk. Crockery and cutlery rattle in reply. I didn't think seeing Mum lost for words would feel so good.

'I want to hear more about it, sounds exciting,' Dad enthuses but even he can't cut through the jutted atmosphere.

'It is exciting. She's even quit her job to do it,' I add, taking yet another glug of wine.

'Whhhhaat?' Mum says, clutching her chest.

'Pardon is more polite,' I simper, waving my glass at her, but my enjoyment wilts when I see the betrayal carved across Kemi's face.

I gulp down my guilt while, at the head of the table, Mum's expression changes from sad and open-mouthed to hardened as she regroups.

'So,' she says turning towards me, 'you knew about this?'

My eyes golf-ball in shock.

'Wait, Kemi lied to you and you're cross with *me*? You know she cut her hair off. She's got a fade under there that Stormzy would be proud of!'

'Shut up, Abi,' Kemi hisses with that no-nonsense menace she often uses on the kids.

But I ignore her because I'm not one of her kids. I'm her sister who's been taking the heat for too long.

'Go on, tell her to take that wig off. She hasn't got a protective style under there. She's got a number three!'

Mum is now no longer concerned with me, her attention fully on my bal'-headed sister.

'Adekemi?' Mum whispers.

Kemi gives me daggers across the table as she slowly pulls her wig from her head, revealing a neat crop which she massages back into shape.

'Oh … my …' is all Mum can manage before Dad jumps in.

'You look beautiful, my dear. Doesn't she, Abosede?'

Mum tries to show agreement but it looks a lot like she's choking.

'I'm sorry but I'm tired of being the failure while Kemi gets to be the angel when the truth is, she's not.'

Instinctively Felix puts a protective hand on Kemi.

'That's enough,' he says, his voice quiet, firm.

'You're right. It is enough. It's enough of Kemi being the goody-two-shoes and me always taking the hits. Kemi and I ain't that different, Mum. She just hides things better. And, for the record, *she's* the one that mashed up your lipsticks that time, *she* filled the washing machine with bubble bath and *she's* the one that burned a hole in the lounger cushion and it wasn't with an incense stick, it was a cigarette!'

The litany of revelations hits Mum like a machine-gunned villain in a Tarantino movie, pinning her to the back of her chair. No such response from Kemi though, who dashes her napkin onto the table. 'You're an arsehole, Abi.'

But I'm an honest one. I may be dropping bombs but it was a load I couldn't carry anymore. And it's all thanks to Cassie. I would never have had the guts to do this without our talk the other morning. I mean, I know she said not to do anything impulsive but this feels right, maybe even *necessary*. These old wounds needed airing out.

'I'm just sick of being the scapegoat. Mum, I don't want you to be mad at Kemi. I just want you to give me a break.'

The words choke me as they meet my lips. It's unexpected and I have to battle to push the feelings down.

'Give us both a break, me and Kems. You know why she lied about all that stuff? Because of how she's seen you treat me. That's why Kemi's uptight. She's scared of what will happen if she isn't perfect. When you see a flaw in someone, you treat them like they're broken, and shut them down like you do with Dad, or make them feel a failure, like you do with me.'

'Maybe we should take a breath,' Felix says.

Mum dabs the corners of her mouth, slow and deliberate. 'I do not treat you like a failure. I encourage you constantly. You just don't listen.'

'You don't encourage me; you tell me to try different careers. You've praised Elle more than you have me!'

'Practical guidance is part of firm parenting and if that's such a disaster, how have Caleb and Ayesha turned out so well? Polite, good grades, obedient. If you had your way, they'd be running around like Victorian street urchins.'

I snort-laugh at yet another compliment for Kemi. I swear down, Mum can't even hear herself do it half the time, it's so automatic. 'They're not as well behaved as you think. They stay up late all the time.'

'No, they don't,' Kemi snaps.

Felix clears his throat and all heads turn towards him.

'Actually, I let them stay up sometimes and to be honest …' he hesitates, picking his words with care, 'they don't always respond to the strictness so …'

Kemi flounders, her whole reality falling apart around her.

'But they're the best-behaved children in their class. Ayesha gets a merit badge practically every week,' she stammers.

'I buy Caleb extra data for his phone and Ayesha, well, she loves Pokémon, so …'

'*You* bought her all those cards?' Kemi says, crushed.

Felix nods, the atmosphere so raw even I'm out of smart comments.

'I'm sorry, Kemi, but sometimes you are too … stern,' Felix says, kind but steady. 'And I could see it start to happen, that same thing you and Abi have … with your mum. Caleb taking the blame for the little things Ayesha does. You seeing him as the clumsy one and Ayesha as gifted. I wanted both of them to know there was someone on their side.'

Kemi's eyes widen as she takes this in.

'I am on their side,' she whispers, eyes damp with pain-filled tears.

'I know. That's not how I meant it,' Felix says, taking her hand, but she flinches, pulling away.

'We should get going. I'll get their shoes on,' she says before leaving the room.

Ignoring the kids' protests, Kemi soon has them ready. As she heads to the car, she looks drained. And in an instant, guilt sweeps aside any righteousness I felt earlier. I dash after her, desperate to explain, to put this right, but she refuses to look at me.

'Kems – I had to say something, I *had* to – I was doing it for both of us …'

'Whatever, Abi,' she sighs and before I can say anything more, she gets in the car and they're gone.

At the living-room table, Mum arches her fingers. 'Well done, Abioye, literally driving everyone away.'

'No, Abosede,' Dad says drawing our attention, 'well done, *you*.'

Mum's face contorts with shock and embarrassment at the reprimand. In their thirty-four years, I don't think I've ever seen Dad push back like that and I'm almost as shook as she is. Reaching for a reply and coming up short, she springs to her feet, picking up her napkin only to toss it back down again in flustered indignation. With no retort forthcoming she strides out into the hallway and up the stairs, two at a time, slamming their bedroom door. As angry echoes fade, Dad shuffles his chair towards mine, putting an arm around my shoulders and I crumple.

'Oh, my darling girl,' he says softly.

'I'm sorry, Dad,' I say, clinging to him, hands grasping at folds of his sweater.

He kisses my forehead.

'Don't apologise. I rather enjoyed it,' he chuckles. 'Nothing like a bit of drama to shake things up. Besides, no one would be this upset if we didn't love each other.'

And I sink further into his embrace. That's exactly what it is, why this kills me, because I love Mum so much. And though I get support from Dad who's always texting links to articles about never giving up, from Kemi who still tries to come to gigs despite everything on her plate, and even Felix who forwards scripture memes hoping to inspire, so often, none of this registers. Of course it doesn't because the one person I want support from never gives it and it draws up a pain I can hardly endure. No matter what I do, it's never good enough. I'll always be Abi the failure, a disaster where my only job is not winning but being a cautionary tale to stop everyone else losing.

Chapter 36

I do mean to go straight home after Mum and Dad's but when I think about returning to an empty flat, I can't. So instead, I head south, and after a train and a Tube ride, I'm in the West End, standing at the foot of Eros where buskers, nomadic foreign students and drunk Londoners congregate. As dusk gives way to evening, I watch a street performer gee up the crowd for him to do what will basically amount to a backflip. Even this guy, who doesn't enjoy the luxury of performing under a roof, probably earns more than I do with comedy.

I let out a long, grizzled sigh. When I've been like this before, Will's instantly made me feel better by giving me a pep talk, telling me I'm great and that it'll all work out in the end – but it feels like that is a million miles away. Nonetheless, I check my phone again. Still nothing from him and the silence slays me, feeling more and more fatal with every passing day. I open up the messenger on my phone, wondering if I should send an olive branch, but then a wave of embarrassment washes over me as I replay the moment I essentially snitched on Elle like a whiny brat. Of course I haven't heard from Will. Who wants that energy in their life?

I pocket my phone, trying to shake this heavy funk. But then Kemi floats into my mind. Thanks, brain. The image of her wounded expression is something I'll never forget. At the time, I felt justified; however, now there's just a sinking despair. Jee-zus, all this because I'm so desperate for approval, so needing to be loved that I'm willing to wreck every relationship I have. And is that what my stand-up is, just a desperate cry for love? My mouth goes dry at the thought. Is the last eight years and wanting the Athena gig just me searching for a gigantic pat on the head? I move on just as the street performer does his backflip. He lands in front of his collection hat, quickly proffering it to a now-uninterested crowd who dispel like mist, like my career, like everything I've ever wanted.

As I pass him, I chuck in a quid and then walk, trusting my legs will take me where I need to be. After about fifteen minutes I turn down a side alley and am soon outside Oublier, one of my favourite comedy clubs in London. For me, performing here is almost as much a pipe dream as playing the Athena. Tiny in size but mighty in reputation, Oublier is for established comics only. Even circuit regulars struggle to get on here. Touring comedians, TV talent and international stars flexing their stand-up muscle – that's what Oublier is about. And despite never listing its line-ups, the place is so renowned, shows sell out weeks in advance. On the day, the only way in is if you're a comedian who's mates with Deon on the door. Then you can usually wheedle a standing-room spot at the back. And after, most of us head up to the comedians' bar on the mezzanine. Here you might get to hang with a comedy icon or at least someone off the telly, looking down on mortals below, kidding yourself you're in the entourage and not just a fan with a pass. As an open-micer there aren't many perks, but rubbing shoulders with comics who've truly made it is one. I reach the entrance and pound fists with Deon. He's been sneaking me in to Oublier since I started out.

'Hey, babes,' I say, stepping towards the rope barrier, but Deon juts an elbow, his giant frame almost blocking out the light.

'Sorry, Abs,' he says, 'sold out.'

My face scrunches. 'On a Sunday night? How come?'

Deon pulls his lips tight. 'Can't say.'

Which, obvs, means now I really want to know. 'Come on, fam. I've had a stinker of a day and … I think I might be quitting comedy.'

My insides congeal hearing out loud what, up until now, I've only been thinking. After everything that's happened, giving up is starting to feel not just like a possibility, but perhaps an inevitability so tonight I just need to laugh, to see people at the top of their game and forget I'm at the bottom of mine.

'You serious? Thought you were in it for the long haul,' he says with genuine concern.

'Maybe the haul is too long, fam,' I say, trowelling on my genuine despair for effect.

Deon sighs, then shakes his head, unclipping the rope barrier. 'All right, Gloomy Tunes, get in there.'

My eyes go wide. 'For real?'

'With that face, you stay out here, you'll put punters off coming in,' he says with a kind laugh before reclipping the rope behind me. 'I hope you find what you're looking for.'

I do too.

*

The show is about to start, and being in this basement steeped in comedy history, I already feel better. I grab a JD and Coke, nestling in between a couple of other comics, exchanging nodded greetings. Tucked into the end of the row I spot Carl O'Connor and give him a wave, batting away thoughts of *that* gig, the last time I saw him. Then my gaze floats up to the hallowed mezzanine floor which, during the show, doubles as a green room. Straight away I see a black woman with a perfectly shaped afro and my breath catches. Is that …? I want to ask someone but I'm scared in case it *isn't* my favourite comedian – of all time.

The show gets under way and after two solid acts, the compere announces Yolanda B. Rockwell, confirming what I'd only dared hope was true. I legit think I might faint from joy overload. The crowd erupts, with me whooping so loud comics either side are giving me funny looks. But I don't care. This is the GOAT, Yolanda B. fricking Rockwell. My comedy shero. The person whose footsteps, if I could, I would follow, stride for stride. This woman is my archetype, my blueprint. And I am mesmerised, watching her prowl around stage, head-to-toe in faded denim, wide flares, a bashed-up jacket peppered with protest badges and a T-shirt that declares she is her ancestors' wildest dreams. And this is all topped with Yolanda's iconic bold lip. Straight out the gate, the audience are loving her, from the characters she brings to life to her deep yet hilarious insights, she handles every topic with a skill I can't define. I guess that's why she's the best. And you can tell because around me, all the comedians who normally hold back when watching others perform, are bent double with wipe-tears-from-their-eyes, thigh-slapping laughter. Well, almost all the comedians. Carl's face is screwed up in confusion like he can't work out why a brown comic isn't doing impersonations of their first-generation parents and talking about how strict they were. My tummy sinks. That's my bad. Well, me and a few others. On stage, Yolanda is closing out with a bit about her neighbour's kid who, though he's only fifteen, keeps giving her the eye. On the surface it's a routine about this very forward teenager and Yolanda's social awkwardness with that but underneath it's a biting commentary on masculinity. She did this routine in her last special and if she were taking requests, it's what I'd have asked for. It's an amazing end to a blistering set.

After the show, a conga line of comedians heads upstairs, me amongst them, borderline stanning Yolanda as she graciously navigates copious, unsolicited feedback – mainly from male comics, including Carl. I try to edge closer but honestly, I'm just so happy to be in her orbit, sharing air is enough. I see a few semi-famous faces do laps of the room, making sure we all know they're here. Meanwhile, I, due to the constant ebb and flow of bodies, somehow find myself in a circle of comics discussing comedy. Carl and the others happily pontificate but I simply bob my head as though at any moment I may say something, knowing damn well I won't, because what can I offer? I see Yolanda edging through the crowd, eyes on the exit, when one of the guys in the circle stops her.

'Yo, Yolanda, sick show. You were fi-yah!' he says, snapping his fingers.

And I want to chew my own face off. Hearing posh white guys do their blaccent is beyond cringe.

'So you've been doing this a while, yeah,' he says without

a shred of irony given Yolanda's probably been gigging since before this guy could even say 'microphone' let alone hold one, 'and we were discussing how many gigs it takes to be a comic. What do you reckon?'

Though clearly trying to make a discreet departure, Yolanda is polite enough not to show it as she considers this, all while I freak out that she's joined our group.

'I don't know. Whatchu think, sis?' she asks, looking across the circle at me.

I blink in response like her gaze is a thousand-watt spotlight. This is a development I did not see coming. I scan the other faces, checking there's not some other 'sis' she could mean. There isn't. I look back at Yolanda who raises an expectant eyebrow and smiles.

'How many, a hundred, a thousand?' she says, giving me time to think.

I've heard comedians discuss this a lot and they always pick a number that's fewer than they've done, elevating their position and, at the same time, reducing that of aspiring comics who've obviously done less.

'I think …' I say, bolstered by her attention, 'it's … one.'

'Say more,' she asks, intrigued.

'If you've done one gig, you're a comedian. Same as if you've written one thing … Like the saying goes: "If you wake up in the morning and can think of nothing but writing, you're a writer."'

Carl rocks on his heels as though in some French literary salon exchanging philosophical ideas.

'Hmmm, *Sister Act Two*,' he says sagely.

'Rilke,' corrects Yolanda, the 'idiot' implied by her tone.

I let out a little laugh and as the others rib Carl, Yolanda takes the opportunity to extricate herself with quiet goodbyes. Some reply as if it's no big deal, as though hanging with the likes of Yolanda B. Rockwell happens on the daily. But for me I have no such chill and instead slot in beside her as she heads towards the stairs.

'You were great tonight,' I blurt.

Not the best opening gambit but I couldn't let her leave without telling her.

'Thanks. You a comic?' she says as we descend to the main room where a few patient punters loiter hoping for a photo.

'Yeah. No. Sort of. I'm not sure.'

She snorts. 'Well have you done your one gig?'

I laugh self-consciously at the callback. As the waiting fans flock to Yolanda and before I can say more, I find myself drafted in as the official photographer, taking one phone after another, shuffling people left and right to get that good lighting. After several photos, I sense Yolanda's restlessness. Finally, the crowd disperses, swiping through camera rolls, satisfied with their photographic evidence of having met *the* Yolanda B. Rockwell.

'Is it always like that?' I ask.

'You Brits are pretty chill. After I do an *SNL* taping it's like I'm Rihanna or some shit. Crazy.'

'I bet,' I say, having exactly zero idea what that could possibly be like.

I walk with Yolanda to the door. Once outside, she orders a car and I wonder if that's my cue to bugger off. This is already above and beyond what I expected from meeting her. The only thing that could top this is a photo but weirdly, I feel as though asking would spoil the vibe, so I leave it.

'Well ...' I say, knowing I need to say goodbye but not wanting to.

Yolanda looks up from her phone. 'You wanna grab a beer?'

I can still feel the half bottle of red wine sloshing about inside me from lunch, but this decision is a no-brainer. I try to suppress the grin threatening to take over my whole face. 'Sure!'

A little while later, we're sitting in a cordoned-off section of the Disraeli. Where the rest of the bar is packed, people looking over each other's shoulders at who's walking in, this area is roped off with just three small groups chatting – Yolanda and I being one of them. Though I know Will doesn't work Sunday nights, I scan the room before relaxing.

'So, for real,' Yolanda says picking at her fries. 'Your burgers here are ashy as hell.'

Her laugh is big and generous and makes her seem ageless. I know she's in her mid-forties but honestly, at times she looks like she could be ten years older or younger than that.

'They're all soft and shit,' she says, flopping the bun aside. 'Y'all need to get into brioche.'

She's not wrong. They're not all terrible but the UK burger tip is defo hit and miss.

'The wings are pretty good here,' I offer and she raises an eyebrow.

'Like British good or real good?'

'Fair point,' I laugh, but we order some anyway.

'So, tell me, little Abi, why'd you get all in a spin when I asked if you were a comedian?'

My shoulders deflate as I try to give Yolanda the abridged

version of events but end up spinning it out till it's longer than the *Lord of the Rings* trilogy.

'And this young 'un is how old?' Yolanda asks, her face pulled in quizzical wonder.

'Thirteen.'

'Damn. I'm just thinking what I'd achieved by thirteen and it wasn't a lot.'

'Yeah,' I scoff in agreement even though that makes me feel like more not less of a failure. *That's me, Abi Akingbade, successfully failing for more than three decades.*

'Thing is, that shit yo mamma said, you buying into it, talking like shawty taking your spot. But it ain't work like that. You know that, right?'

'Yeah …'

'She's doing her. You gotta do you. You're on completely different paths, totally different styles of comedy.'

I try to absorb as much of Yolanda's wisdom as I can, still in awe that I'm here with her at all. I know big comedians need to decompress after a show, let the adrenalin subside, but the fact she's doing that with me and not a swarm of security, managers, stylists or whoever celeb types hang with, is blowing my tiny mind. I grab a clutch of fries, chewing them slowly to steady myself. 'It's just, I feel like I'm never going to make it to the next level.'

'And what level is that?'

I knot my fingers as nerves take hold. Am I really about to share my biggest dream with this woman, this megawatt star?

'We have a programme here, *ShowTime at the Athena*. I want to be on it.'

'Oooooh,' Yolanda says, as she leans back into her seat. 'You talking levels like *that*.'

She cocks her head for emphasis. I'm not loving this reaction and part of me wants to retract, offer up a different dream that won't make her look at me like I want to be the first penguin in space.

'Girl, when you talk levels, you need to start with levelling up with your comedy. When I started out, I ain't look like this, I didn't talk about what I talk about. Back then I straightened my hair so I'd be like the white chicks – "acceptable" – and I'd do routines about "strict parents" or "going to church". Stupid, clichéd shit. Yeah, it was loosely based on my life and it made people laugh but it wasn't *about* anything and it definitely wasn't for The Culture, you feel me? But the minute I realised you can be funny *and* have something to say, everything changed. So, Abi, what do you have to say, because when you find that and become the best comic you can, then all that stuff, the big shows, the TV spots, that'll come.'

I nod, letting her words sink in.

'On the way over here, when you were telling me about your comedy, it sounded good, except, look …' she says, fully facing me. 'You an intelligent, black, plus-sized beauty but when you cut yourself down like that, you give people permission to do the same. And I know what you about. It's a good plan: say it before they think it. But we ain't in that time no more, you feel me.'

I gulp. It's true. I'm not at school and this isn't the nineties.

'That's why this Elle kid is doing so well. She authentic, just telling it like it is through thirteen-year-old eyes. She's about the truth. You about … pandering. Tell the truth. Don't mean people will like you but you'll start to like yourself a whole lot more.'

Just then a bowl of wings and two more beers arrive but I just stare at it all.

Pandering? I've heard that before. Is that the difference between what I offer audiences and what Elle is giving them? Is she the truth-sayer to my court jester? And is truth that special something Yolanda has? Sometimes when I watch her routines, I search for the magical formula but in all these years, I've never figured it out. Perhaps because it's so simple, so completely obvious, that it's been hiding in plain sight. She tells the truth. Even the routine about her neighbour's kid is based not on hack lines but a reality about the effects an unstable household has had on this kid's view of women. In fact, now I think of it, the best comedians are always telling a made-up version of the truth, the truth about being human. But that's definitely not what I've been doing. It's just, I've been in this groove so long, I don't know how to do anything else.

'By the way, thanks again for earlier,' Yolanda says, picking a wing from the bowl.

Glad of the topic change, I flush at the acknowledgement. 'No worries.'

'I could feel another wave coming of white guys mansplaining my act to me so I was thankful to have a sistah in the crowd. Earlier, I got cornered by this one guy, Carl, talkin' 'bout how I should do more accents!'

'Nooooo,' I gawp, glad I missed that bit.

'Oh, yeah. Even showed me. Sounding like Mammy from *Gone With the Wind*,' Yolanda smirks and we both crack up.

'Well, you were very sweet, how you dealt with everyone,' I say.

'To be honest, it's nothing I haven't heard before. But after working on my new set tonight, and then all that, I did need to clear my head so I appreciate you and I appreciate your company.'

Yolanda raises her beer bottle and I clink mine against it. 'Anytime.'

Outside the Disraeli another black Merc awaits, hazard lights blinking.

'Okay, Abi,' Yolanda says, opening up for a hug.

I practically fall into her arms. 'Thank you. You have no idea what this means to me.'

'All right, all right, I ain't the next messiah. I'm just a girl standing in front of an audience, asking them to laugh until they pee a little.'

I giggle and Yolanda chuckles to herself.

'Listen, just do me one favour?' she says, as she steps into her waiting car.

'Anything.'

'Find your greatness … But never let it become more important than love. What an audience gives you can feel like the most epic kind of love … but it ain't the same thing, okay?' she says and her face flushes with sadness.

She closes the car door and as it silently peels off into the Soho traffic I realise – she's lonely. That's what she's sacrificed for greatness; that same sacrifice Frank is willing to make. But the thing is, I know that's not how I'm built. I have to find a way to be as good as I can without paying that same price because I love to love and be loved, and I don't mean by audiences, but by people I care for, and nothing is more important than that.

I pull out my phone realising there's a text I've been putting off sending that I can't delay any more. I tap it out, short and sweet.

> Hey …

I stare at my screen, willing a reply to come through. Finally, I see the three, shimmying dots.

> You are literally the worst sister in the world. I demand a refund.

I cry-laugh at my phone. That is the best reply ever.

Chapter 37

I rap my knuckles on Kemi's front door, so glad she invited me over but nervous to see her after everything that went down. Even though we've been texting all week, in-person is a totally different energy. I know I still need to make amends.

'Who is it?' Caleb hollers from the other side of the door.

'Homework police,' I reply in a gruff, Cockney accent. 'We've had reports of children playing Minecraft instead of doing their Citizenship assignments.'

'But it's Sunday!' Caleb says, panic climbing.

'Don't matter, young man. Open up.'

I hear Caleb freak out, whispering to Ayesha to shut down the computer as the sound of grown-up footsteps approaches.

'Don't be silly, Caleb,' Kemi says opening the door.

On seeing her, contrition contorts my face into a pathetic grin.

'Well, if it isn't Clive Myrie with the news headlines, spilling the tea on the hour, every hour,' Kemi says, a hand on her hip.

'How long did it take you to come up with that?'

'About as long as it's going to take you to make up for what you did,' Kemi scolds.

And I instantly adjust my tone, sheepishly taking a couple of steps forward, playing up the trepidation of wanting a hug. She lets me pull her in and after a moment of resistance, hugs me back. I swing her side to side as I always do. And just as she always does, Kemi protests.

'Abiii-yah. My bladder's bursting. You'll make me wet myself!'

Of course, this makes me rock her even more.

'Hey, Auntie Abi,' Caleb and Ayesha squeal with excitement, now assured they're *not* about to get bundled into a white van by the Homework Police.

'Come and play with us,' Ayesha insists, trying to drag me towards their room.

'Slow your roll, bud. I can't,' I say, pumping the brakes.

'That's right,' says Kemi, with the smugness of a teacher doling out a juicy detention. 'Because Auntie Abi is here to pay penance for what she did. We learned about that in church earlier. Do you remember what it is?'

Ayesha shakes her head, half interested.

'It's what naughty adults have to do when they blab each other's secrets.'

Kemi gives me an exaggerated stern look and I bow my head. I know she's playing but I also know the penance vibe is a real ting.

I follow her through to the living room where hair product hell awaits me.

At the dining table, Felix is at his laptop.

'Abi,' he says with a firm nod.

I sense we're not back at the hugging stage yet given I indirectly dropped him in it too, so I just mirror him. 'Felix.'

'Right, we've got a new online ad going live tomorrow which

I'm hoping will generate our first sales. So, these seventy-five tubs need labelling, front and back, boxed and added to the inventory before then,' Kemi says like a huffy shop steward.

'Are you sure there's not something else I can do – decorate the hallway, babysit for a month?' I whine.

'You want to make things right, get labelling.'

Without a leg to stand on all I can do is plonk myself on the sofa and crack on.

'Snack?' Kemi asks, lingering at the door.

Felix flaps down the screen of his computer. 'Sounds excellent. Do we have any of those chocolate chip cookies?'

'We do. And I'll bring some of that carrot cake,' Kemi simpers but before I can even lick my lips in anticipation, her expression turns to granite. 'Fruit for you. Don't want you getting a sugar slump before you've finished.'

She bowls off towards the kitchen and I shrivel. 'Jeez, how long is this going on for?'

'I'm sure it won't be for long. Till Christmas?' Felix says, chuckling to himself.

'Great,' I moan, taking my first of what feels like a million tubs and smoothing a sticky label across its side.

'Oh, and Kemi forgot to mention, you need to put these tamper seals on the top too,' Felix says, flinging a wad of them my way.

I catch them then collapse into a miserable heap. My sis got me back good.

An hour later and my evil employer allows me a break. I even get to join them for some afternoon cake.

'So have you spoken to She-who-cannot-be-named?' I ask, savouring my well-earned treat.

'You mean – Voldemum?'

'The very same,' I reply with a dramatic sneer.

Kemi sighs and the playfulness ebbs from her.

'Yeah, we spoke. Or to be more accurate, she spoke at me. *Why can't it just be a hobby? Speak to your director about rescinding your resignation.* And every time I told her I'd thought it all through, she just talked over me. You know she'd even calculated how long it would take to grow my hair back. That's when I hung up.'

'You hung up – on Mum?'

Kemi nods, proud.

'Oh my days!'

'You were shaking at the time,' Felix chips in.

'True. But I have to say, after I put the phone down, I got where you were coming from. That conversation was a fraction of what you've been putting up with for being "too much", while all this time, I was hiding in the background – being too much too. You protected me,' Kemi says, pushing down simmering upset.

'I mean, I didn't really think of it like that, it just happened.'

'You kept secrets you didn't have to, even when it cost you,' Kemi says as a tear breaks free, tumbling down her cheek.

'No point both of us getting steamrolled,' I joke, trying to brush off her acknowledgement, trying to keep myself from crying as well.

'It's like she had this idea of what we were supposed to be and anything that didn't fit, she squashed. The only way I could handle that was doing everything on the DL and you *always* kept my secrets.'

'Until now,' I say with a sad smile, another surge of guilt washing over me.

And as I watch my sister, this rock of a woman, wrestle with her emotions, I'm filled with adoration. Tough as it is for me being in Mum's critical glare, at least I'm fully out there, unlike Kemi who feels forced to hide who she really is. That must be awful and the thought inflates my guilt. 'Listen, Kems, I'm sorry for what I did. It wasn't my place to say those thing and definitely not like that.'

'No, it wasn't,' Kemi says quietly, 'but I am glad you did.'

At hearing that, I sway with surprise. The idea that in some twisted way my selfish act did some good, is a balm to my remorse. I reach across the sofa and our hands lock as whatever had knocked us out of kilter resets, and we ease back into alignment.

Kemi leans an elbow on the sofa arm. 'I was always jealous of you, doing your own thing, not caring what Mum thought, while I toed the line.'

'I did care!' I protest. 'I just couldn't live not doing my thing. You know, the acting, the poetry, my tagging …'

'Ha! You were a graffiti artist for, like, a week!' Kemi laughs.

'True say,' I concede.

'My point is, I was jealous but I also wasn't ready to be "me". I didn't even know what that meant. Then I got so good at pretending that when I did discover what it was, I didn't know how to speak it, to be it around Mum. If you hadn't said anything, I'm not sure I ever would.'

I grip Kemi's hand even tighter, filled with overwhelming love for my one and only, brilliant sister. Then I grab my bag, rummaging through it. 'I got you something.'

'Better not be another reed diffuser,' she says, 'or a Jo Malone candle. I've got them coming out of my ears.'

'Like I earn Jo-Malone money. Here, it's a good luck pressie, for your business.'

I shove the package into Kemi's suspicious hands and she tears at the wrapping. 'A T-shirt?' she says, bemused.

'Read it.'

Kemi does as she's told, laying it out on her lap, and as she mouths the printed words, her eyes glisten.

'Oh, Abi – it's perfect,' she whispers, tears now freely flowing.

'What does it say?' Felix asks, craning to see.

Kemi holds it aloft, pride at full beam. '"I am my ancestors' wildest dreams".'

'And don't you ever forget it,' I tell her and she comes in for a big hug, this time rocking *me* from side to side. We tumble back on the sofa, and laugh and laugh, just like we used to.

Felix heads off to put the kids to bed while me and Kemi get a cheeky takeaway – honest food for an honest day's work. As Kemi places our order, I look around her living room. Seeing it with fresh eyes, I notice how much 'family' fills every crack and crevice. Yes, there's the standard kiddies' paintings on the wall, height measurements on the doorframe, space rockets made of cereal packets, rows of colourful books on shelves, toy boxes chocker with goodies only accessible once chores and homework are done, but there's also love – a place at the table for everyone and it is chaotic but it's also beautiful.

Down the hall, I hear Felix deep into story time.

‘Everything okay between you two?’ I ask, tentative, just in case.

Kemi curls her legs underneath herself. ‘At first, I was super mad.’

‘I’m not surprised. That was one hell of a reveal,’ I say, still not sure Kemi’s ready to joke about how her parenting style wasn’t as on lock as she thought.

She rubs the back of her neck. ‘It shook me. I mean, am I really that strict?’

‘Naaah. Although you did once threaten to “end Caleb” because he spilt orange juice on the sofa.’

‘You can’t play the Floor is Lava with a drink in your hand!’ she exclaims. ‘But seriously, am I that bad?’

I purse my lips. This is still a sensitive subject. When Kemi was pregnant with Caleb, she so wanted to get being a mum right, they couldn’t have printed child development books fast enough to keep up with her need to read them. I have to choose what I say wisely.

‘Let me put it like this – loosening up won’t do the kids any harm.’

Though I’m trying to lessen the blow, Kemi shudders all the same.

‘Shit. I really am my mother’s daughter.’

‘You’re not *that* bad. At least you let them talk at the dining table. I was twenty before I found out people actually have conversations over dinner. I was on a date and the bloke kept yammering on. I was like, “Mate, shut up, I’m trying to eat!”’

At this, laughter splutters from us both, as we remember all those silent supper times we had as kids.

‘Thing about Felix is, and don’t you dare tell him this,’ Kemi says, lowering her voice, 'though he doesn't say much, when he does, he's usually right.'

'Daaaaaaamn,' I whisper.

'I'm serious,' Kemi says, wagging a finger. 'You say a word and you'll be boxing hair products for a decade!'

I mime zipping my lips closed and cross my heart for good measure. 'You got a good one there, a lie?'

'He's a real one. I mean, I knew that but recently I've seen how much he, I don't know, just lets me be, makes room for all of me and never judges. He just rolls up his sleeves and says, "What do you need?"'

'That's what Will gave me too,' I say and my tummy flutters at the thought of him, a bittersweet reminder of what we used to have and how he made me feel.

'So … is it really over?'

'Do you know what, sis, I honestly don't know.' And we drift into a thoughtful silence.

Chapter 38

I'm sitting in the lunch room at work but everyone in my section is out because it's the first sunny day we've had in a while. Even Bobbie left after he found out some promotions girls were giving away free ice creams near the Tube.

So here I am, on my own, with an hour to try and write. Staring at this blank page, I have to pinch myself that the reason I'm even doing this is because of Yolanda B. Rockwell who's now not just my shero but my comedy saviour too. She has no idea what she gifted me that night. I can't let her down. So, pen poised over an A4 pad I swiped from the stationery cupboard, I sit, waiting for inspiration.

Right, Abi, I say to myself. *No more pandering …*

My pen starts to move across the paper as I allow thoughts to cascade, hoping I'll fish something useful from the stream of consciousness that's flowing.

Mum has no belief in me, she'd be prouder if … what?

Everyone I know seems to be killing it on the stand-up circuit while I've been relegated to cheerleader – and no one wants to see me in those skirts—

No, Abi. No pandering.

I waggle my pen, praying it'll antennae in a punchline … But nothing comes. Why is this so hard? I push on, trying to get myself out of the way so ideas can flow. Forgetting about punchlines, I decide to just look for stories, moments, loose threads I might weave into something. Picnics and black history exhibitions, piano teachers and walks to school, baby mamas and bee stings, feelings – so many feelings – anger, jealousy, sadness, guilt, love … uncomfortable, unexpected love, and vegan pizza. Brain starting to cloud, I read back my notes which look more like scribblings of the criminally insane than comedy gold. I tear off the most rambling pages, scrunching them into a ball, still not sure I can extract this greatness Yolanda seems convinced is in me. I close my eyes, trying to conjure up comedians who speak their truth – and Frank pops into my head. Though the accent is fake, his gags are brutally honest. The funny voice is simply a sweetener to help the medicine go down – whereas I've been all sugar and no substance. I need to find *my* authenticity and depth. My truth. But even if I do find it, how the hell do I make any of it funny?

I chuck the paper in the bin and as I crack the lid of my lunch box, Bobbie passes, double-fisting a couple of mini Magnums.

'Want one?' he says, looking like he wants to do anything but share his loot.

'I'm good.'

I can't. It's such a tenuous thing but ice cream always takes me back to Will, to lazy afternoons in the park, nights in curled up on the sofa, of summer when everything felt possible – until it didn't. I peer at my phone. Still nothing from him, the void now leaving me numb. I don't want things to be over but what do I do? Reach out, try to see if we still have a pulse? But what would I even say? My thumb hovers over my phone's screen but before I manage to formulate any kind of thought, a text pops up.

Can you do a paid ten at the Cabana tonight? Dina

Wait, what?? After reading then rereading the text about eighteen times, I leap from my chair and break out into a Milly Rock dance, punching the air in pure joy. A paid spot at the Cabana? This has *got* to be a sign, I giggle to myself, scanning my notes for anything vaguely salvageable. The comedy gods are shining on me now and I'm not wasting this opportunity.

I get to the gig early to settle my nerves and go over notes I'm still making. I'm not sure you could call it material yet but it's a start. Dina spots me and comes over, hands wedged in her pockets. 'Hey, Abi, good to see you.'

I sit up like the head teacher has entered the room. 'Likewise and thanks again for tonight.'

'Glad you could step in,' she says, shifting her stance. 'So – I heard about what happened with Elle last time you were here …'

I wilt. That testy exchange was just superficial green-room gossip for others but for me, it was a painful and embarrassing window into my relationship with her. Dina gives me a gentle pat on the back. 'Sounds like a tricky situation. I hated my stepmum. For years me and my brother called her Toast cos of her awful fake tan. Get on brilliantly now.'

Dina's comment raises a smile though I dread to think what Elle calls me behind my back.

'And just remember,' she continues, 'no matter how bad it gets, you can always get an Edinburgh hour out of it.'

'Yeah,' I snort, imagining I could probably wring *two* Edinburgh shows and a tour from what I've been through.

'So, how's the writing going?' she asks.

I look down at my notes, still just sifted topsoil rather than that deep excavation I need to do and barely any jokes to speak of.

'I'm getting there. Got a couple of new ideas,' I say, lifting my pilfered A4 pad, 'but I think I need to go with tried and tested tonight, one last time ...'

I search Dina's face for approval. This isn't pandering, this is ... well, it's clinging to the life raft until I know it's safe to swim.

Dina gives a thoughtful nod. 'It's tough letting go of the safety net.'

'Yeah,' I say, catching the knowing in her eyes.

It's not just tough, it's terrifying.

'Anyway, I'm sure you'll figure it out. Have a good one,' she says before heading off to do her usual perimeter patrol.

And I relax, feeling like I have Dina's blessing to stick with what I know, just until I'm ready to say goodbye to my old material. After that, there really will be no going back. No letting Yolanda down. No letting myself down. Only pushing through to the next level.

I'm so glad to be here, an oasis in the emotional tundra I've been schlepping across for the past few weeks. The crowd seem nice and if I can keep a grip of my nerves, this should go well. Smashing it would be great but just having a *good* show would be plenty. I'm the middle spot in the first half, safely nestled between solid acts. So after the MC warms up, and the first comic goes on, it's me.

I start with one of my go-to openers, staring at the mic stand.

'Look at this skinny bitch – this ain't a double act!'

Then I sweep the mic stand out of the way.

The audience are warm and go with it, so I plough into my set. I kick off with a routine about my mum, going heavy on the accent, and the crowd are with me. Then I remember a joke I thought of ages ago about my thighs. It fits perfectly.

'Honestly, you lot, they look like kebab shop meat. You know that massive elephant's leg they have in the window, that's me!'

YOU AN INTELLIGENT, BLACK, PLUS-SIZED BEAUTY ...

I'm put off for a moment as Yolanda's words elbow their way into my mind. I know, Yolanda, but I've got a plan. It's tried and trusted tonight but as soon as my new stuff is ready, I'll go all-out – promise.

'I'm making your mouth water, innit?'

AND I KNOW WHAT YOU ABOUT ... SAY IT BEFORE THEY THINK IT ...

Yolanda's words barge back into my thoughts, jolting my concentration. I look out at the crowd and notice a group of lads. They've been murmuring behind cupped hands and, I begin to suspect, tagging my lines with cruel and unkind private jokes of their own – that I've set up.

WE AIN'T IN THAT TIME NO MORE, YOU FEEL ME?

'Sorry, guys, what was I saying?'

A light-skinned, black woman in the front row with a natural hair puff looks up at me, unimpressed.

'Something about breaking that "skinny guy's back",' she says, crossing her arms.

I look at her and for a moment all I see is Yolanda. My stomach lurches.

DO ME A FAVOUR ... FIND YOUR GREATNESS.

Without thinking, I pound my heel onto the stage, trying to kickstart my brain.

'Sinkhole!' calls one of the lads.

The audience groan a response and my cheeks burn. It's not that long ago I would have made a similar joke myself but now it makes me feel sick, embarrassed. Not only for me, but for all big girls. Because I've armed idiots like this for no good reason, just so I'm liked, just so I have a routine.

Then and there I decide to dump all that material – for good. I'm better than this and can do better by people like me so we're no longer the punchline.

'What did you say?' The confrontation in my voice is unequivocal and causes the mouthiest of the guys to throw his hands up in defence.

'Ignore me. It's all good. You're funny.'

'Mate, I know I'm funny. I've been doing this for time. Eight years, in fact. I've got bare road miles under me so the last thing I need is to look at your wotless mug chatting breeze. I deserve more than this!'

My arm sweeps wide. Because I don't just mean this club. I mean life – all of it.

'Let me guess, you've got a nice, safe job, in a nice, safe part of London and the same friends since school who you go on holiday with and to the pictures and to see comedy. And after, you go home to your nice, safe girlfriend and make plans to buy a house, get married, have kids and tick all the boxes that will make your nice, safe mummy and daddy happy.

'Whereas I've got a mother who doesn't even know how to hug. It's like cuddling an ironing board; a mother who'd probably be more proud if I became an online scammer cos at least I'd have transferable skills.

'A mother who's more impressed with my possibly-ex-boyfriend's thirteen-year-old daughter than she is with me. Thirteen. My mum and dad's fridge is older than her. And you know how I fit into the picture – she's a stand-up and I'm her chaperone. It's like Driving Miss Daisy, *except, we don't even have a car. We have to Uber!'*

The room is still, but I don't care.

TELL THE TRUTH. DON'T MEAN PEOPLE WILL LIKE YOU BUT YOU'LL START TO LIKE YOURSELF A WHOLE LOT MORE.

'So why am I even putting up with that? I hear none of you ask. Yup. For the D. I'm in love and for that, seems I'm willing to put up with a whole bunch of BS. The thirteen-year-old hates me. And I'm pretty sure she's turned their cat, Chapelle, against me too because I only ever get the bumhole end.

'The youngest one's cool but she doesn't have voting rights. And the worst thing is not knowing where you fit in. I'm not their mate, I'm not their mum, I'm not an aunt. Turns out, I'm not even a stepmum. I'm just … there, with no discernible use, like scatter cushions or a dado rail.

'No, I'll tell you the worst part. It's knowing that no matter how much he loves me, if he ever had to choose, I'd be out quicker than you could revenge-cancel a shared Netflix subscription, you feel me?'

I take a breath, about to dive in again, when I see Dina, edging towards the stage waving a flashing bike light.

'Oh … Looks like that's my time.'

A relieved murmur spreads as I turn my attention back to the group of guys who look at the floor, anywhere but me.

'So yes, I'm a big girl in all the places beauty ads and work-out videos tell us we shouldn't be, and I made a mistake. I gave you permission to laugh at that by joking about it myself. Well, I'm done. I'm funny because of what I say, not what I look like, and I'm here to take up space and if you don't like it, you can kiss Chapelle's bumhole.'

I drop the mic to the floor and there's a distorted whistle.

'Sorry,' I say, quickly scrambling it back into the stand.

I leave the stage, crossing paths with the MC who stares at me, open-mouthed. As I return to the comedians' area, Dina marches over and I brace for the heat I'm about to take but I'm also clear in my mind, no matter what she says, there's no going back. I don't know what's next for me but it can't be fat jokes and Nigerian matriarchs. By the look on Dina's face, it's not ten-minute spots at her clubs anytime soon either.

'I'm sorry, but I had to—' I start but Dina cuts me off.

'Finally!' she whispers, excitement pouring from her.

'Huh?' I say, confused.

'Now you're getting somewhere. That's what I'm talking about. I mean, it was a hot mess, just terrible, but it was good terrible, you know? Keep going. You're on the right track.'

Dina shakes my shoulders then heads off and I collapse into the nearest seat, hands trembling with adrenaline. Could I be on the right track? Maybe, if I can make some of that funny and not just an angry rant spewed over the audience. Piece of cake … in no way whatsoever. Well, no one said it'd be easy. I'm entering uncharted territory but the only way out is to keep moving.

A few minutes later, Dina returns, pushing two twenty-pound notes into my still slightly shaky hand. I look at her, at the money. Carl is yet to pay my invoice for his gig so this forty quid is the first payment I've received for my stand-up – ever.

I take the twenties, fold them into a square and hand them back to Dina.

'Keep it on account.'

Outside, I suck in the warm evening air, buzzing that I finally might be moving in the right direction with my comedy, no longer heading over a cliff edge but into the unknown, and it's exciting. Maybe I'm not such a disaster – and maybe, just maybe, I can do the same with my relationship, take it from the brink to solid ground, somehow. One thing I know for sure, there's only one person I want to share my small, messy victory with tonight so I pull out my phone and without hesitating, text Will.

Hi ...

A reply comes straight away.

Will is typing ...

And I smile. Maybe I am on the right track.

Chapter 39

'Hey,' Will says.

'Hey, you.'

It's a sunny Saturday afternoon and over two weeks since I last saw his face. Even though his eyes are masked by dark shades, he already looks different. Up and down the canal path where we've met, couples, dog walkers and groups of friends stroll with a leisurely ease I'm not sure I'll be able to manage.

'You found it okay?' he asks, a conversational placeholder while we get used to being face to face again.

'Left at the Walter Tull mural and down the steps,' I say, repeating his directions.

He smiles and it makes me want to go to him, be in his arms, tell each other it's going to be all right, but I know we're not there, we're nowhere near there.

A beetroot-faced jogger pounds past us, panting in a way better suited to the bedroom than this towpath.

'Hope he gets there,' I say out of the corner of my mouth.

'Sounds like he's coming,' Will replies and we do a bad job of burying our sniggering.

Eventually we grow quiet and I search for what to fill the space with.

'Wanna walk?' Will asks, pointing ahead. 'There's a pub with a nice view of the wetlands.'

'Sounds good.' But walking beside Will, no contact, no hands interlocked, no arm resting on my shoulder, no place to put mine, feels so strange.

'How have you been?'

'Oh, you know,' I say, not knowing where to start. 'Mixed bag. You?'

'Same.'

We continue further, every step, every breath delicate and deliberate, careful not to knock this tentative equilibrium out of kilter.

'Sorry I didn't message sooner. I needed time to think. That night was a lot and to be honest, Abi, after Kat, I promised myself I'd only be with someone who could handle the hard conversations, and not head off at the first sign of trouble. Because I have daughters, that's as important to me as anything I might need.'

I bow my head, ashamed. I thought I was that person but when things got rough, I walked away, only thinking about how I felt.

'Yeah, that's some grown-up business,' I say, a little unnerved by Will's sobriety.

Where his focus was on creating emotional safety for the kids, I was just this yammering approval gremlin desperate for them to like me, validate my existence, same as I do with Mum. And the less I got from them, the more I used my personality as a battering ram, trying to force my way in. And somehow, in the midst of that, I convinced myself I was nailing this responsible adulting. I cringe, thinking back to the paddling pool with Caleb and Ayesha, threatening to snitch to get them to quieten down. That wasn't parenting, that was blackmail. And all the while, with Elle and Esme, I had this background jealousy wrapping itself around my good intentions, creating a constant push and pull. Pulling me to compete with the girls, push, push, pushing to be accepted. On some subconscious level, Elle could probably sense the strain and it repelled her. Just the thought of it makes me want to recoil too.

'Why didn't you tell me how things really were between you and Elle?'

My throat constricts. 'I wanted you to think I could handle it. I wanted it to look like whatever she threw my way couldn't faze me cos I'm so great with kids, a natural or whatever. But she brought out something childish in me – I hated myself.'

My voice trails away as shame mutes it to silence.

'Yep. They'll do that to you. Thing is, you can't force your way in. It's not about being important to them. It's about being there for them,' Will says and my shame balloons.

We pass through a section of path shaded by trees and Will wedges his shades into his collar. Finally, I can see his eyes, but where I expected judgement, there's just understanding, and it's a massive relief. We carry on walking, side by side, though what I wouldn't give to feel our hands slip into their familiar clasp.

'Abi, I want to tell you something.'

We both slow and I brace myself.

'You were not and have never been too much and I hate that you thought I would say that. I was talking about the situation, not you. Never you. I realise now, I should have stepped in instead of hoping for the best, especially as I was the one person that could have put things right. You were in such a tricky situation, trying to create a relationship with the girls, knowing you can't replace any of the ones they already have. I should have helped you with that. I let you down. I was desperate for things to work out between us and so into you, that I didn't take the care I should have – as their dad *and* your boyfriend. So I'm sorry.'

I draw big, deep breaths as this lands.

'Thank you,' I say, overwhelmed by how much hearing this means to me.

At times I felt I was going crazy, bearing the weight of this whole thing, telling myself it was all my failing. Will's words are a salve to that wound. He looks at me, eyes kind and sad all at once, and I can instantly see the man he was before kids and what having them has asked him to become.

'And I'm sorry, Will. I shouldn't have walked away like that. It was unforgivable.'

'You're forgiven. A million times over. This isn't easy and a lot of it was because I totally had my blinkers on so … me and Elle finally had proper words.'

I tense. 'Did she say I was the worst human ever?'

Will exhales a laugh. 'Not gonna lie, that is kinda where we started but once I told her about the competition, and why she didn't place, she got very quiet. Then we were able to have a real conversation. It's obvious now, but none of this was about you. She was scared. Her whole world has shifted in just a couple of years and she has no clue how to deal with it. Where Esme's happy-go-lucky, Elle's always been the sensitive one, but it was no excuse and she gets that now.'

I feel my body flood with relief, the dull ache that's gripped me slowly subsiding, and as we continue walking along the towpath, our strides fall into sync.

'Abi, there's something else,' Will says, gathering his thoughts. 'I can imagine that sometimes this has felt like an either/or situation where I'm constantly choosing between you and the girls. But I want you to know, it's not like that. I love you in such different ways that I never see it as a choice. I've got room for all three of you. It's just, because they're so young, sometimes they need me more urgently but that'll never mean you're not important. Ever.'

He opens his arms. I fall into him and it's the most incredible sensation. I realise, instead of worrying about trying to fit at Will's table, it's time to pull up a couple of chairs at my own – and perhaps even a pair of foldaway ones for Kat and Marcus. It's like those noisy Sunday afternoons we used to have at my Auntie Blessing's house, the place filled with laughter and love, mismatched furniture and trestle tables extended for the extra mouths to feed. Yet despite her tiny flat, she always found a way. And that's what this is, figuring it out as we go, finding a way.

Will and I reach an empty bench and sit, no space between us. We let the quiet in again but there's a calm to it now.

'I thought I'd never meet someone who got me, loved me as I am. And then, boom,' I say, making a little explosion gesture.

'I was "boom", too,' Will says, mirroring me.

'I still am,' I venture, searching his face.

'Me too,' Will says and I almost can't believe we're here, not back at the same place, but somewhere new.

Perhaps we had to go through all this to find ground that's much firmer and definitely more honest.

'I think your weekends with the girls should be just you and them. It's not right that I'm always there. It should be special time for you guys to be together.'

I look up at Will with a resigned but resolute smile.

'All right,' he says, eyes solemn, 'but how are you gonna cope without your weekend vegan pizza?'

I giggle, jabbing him in his ribs. 'I'll work something out, perhaps spread Blu-Tac over a piece of cardboard?'

Then it's my turn to get jabbed, but it's quickly followed by playful kisses. I'm sure my laughter can be heard up and down the towpath.

'Seriously though, balance – and going at a pace that works all round. This isn't a race so let's enjoy the journey, right?' I say, with a clear-headedness I hardly recognise. 'I do want to spend time with the girls, but we have to make sure you all get alone time too.'

Will nods. 'And we do as well. Balance, because nothing's changed between us. This is still for the long haul, yeah?'

'Hundred per cent,' I say, kissing him, loving his lips on mine.

'We're going to be fine,' Will says as we settle into one another on the bench.

And feeling us finally make our way out of those choppy waters, supporting each other, I think he's right – we're going to be just fine.

We stay on the towpath for at least another half an hour, and I think about what 'long haul' means; not walking away from tough convos for a start, truly making room at the table and being there for the girls rather than trying to be important. My God, who needs therapy when there's children?

'How are Elle and Esme doing?'

'Esme's good. She's been asking after you,' Will says.

My grin widens. 'Ah, baby girl.'

'And Elle's had some interesting news.'

'Do tell,' I reply, intrigued.

'Callback are making a kids' stand-up show. They're going to record it ahead of their *ShowTime* tapings.'

'And they've asked Elle to do a slot?'

'Yeah, recording in a month,' Will says, proud.

'That's amazing!' I squeal, genuinely happy for her, because I've decided, if there's one thing I'm going to do, it's not let jealousy shape my thoughts and words anymore. From now on, if someone I care about is winning, I wanna lead the cheerleading not the criticism.

'So,' I say, clapping a hand onto my thigh, 'who's her chaperone?'

And Will and I crease double, laughing.

Chapter 40

Me and Will finding our way back to each other has felt amazing and it's been a real shot in the arm for my comedy now I'm no longer distracted by fretting about our relationship. With Frank and Cassie no longer involved in Wisecrackers, I've decided to park the gig and instead focus on overhauling my set. So tonight, instead of my usual Tuesday evening routine, I'm at the White Lion in south-east London for a new material night. It's a typical working-class boozer similar to where we host Wisecrackers and I immediately feel at home. There're the regulars at the bar cradling a pint, swirly carpets, frosted windows and dark wood furniture throughout. I spot Glenn, tonight's MC, recognising him from Elle's gong show, and go over.

'Hey,' I say, introducing myself, 'I'm Abi Akingbade.'

'All right. Glenn,' he replies, his manner friendly and relaxed. 'Welcome to the gig that time forgot.'

He's not wrong but its frayed edges are somehow reassuring. As Glenn lugs a portable speaker towards the stage, I offer to give him a hand.

'You could do … or you could get us a pint,' he smiles.

Despite his bare cheekiness, I decide I like this guy and get us both a drink.

'Quiet,' I say, looking around.

It's not long until showtime and the pub is dead. I'm all for intimate gigs, especially as I'm trying new stuff, but we need *some* punters.

'Don't worry, it'll fill up,' Glenn says, clocking my concern. 'And so you know, I keep things nice and informal. Exhibit A – the green room.'

I follow his pointed finger to a couple of benches pushed against the side wall.

'Informal is good,' I tell him, planting myself on one of them and opening my new notebook.

Its crisp pages send an excited charge through me. Though I've only worked up a couple of bits, this is now a road map to a place I've never been and it's exhilarating but scary at the same time. Plus it's shown me what a crutch my old material was, making me even more determined to push forward without it.

After Glenn finishes setting up the rest of the room, he comes and sits next to me.

'So, Abi Akingbade. I've heard good things about you.'

'Yeah?' I reply, not expecting that.

'I did Carl O'Connor's gig a few nights back. Said you're a solid act.'

I nod a wordless thanks. An endorsement from Carl isn't necessarily a compliment, especially when it's based on dodgy material I've now dashed.

'Anyway, just have fun tonight. It's a lovely, no-pressure room.'

'Cool.'

Glenn chuckles. 'Well, I hope you're this chatty on stage.'

'Sorry, I'm just a bit – I'm trying something new,' I smile, suddenly self-conscious.

'At a new-material night? Bloody hell, glad I booked *you*,' he says, rising with his empty pint glass. 'Right, what you drinking?'

'Lime and soda?'

'The last of the rock and rollers, eh. Actually, to be fair, I might join you. Their beer's weaker than a tech billionaire's handshake.'

And he disappears off to the bar.

Soon the show gets going and just as Glenn promised, it's a very laid-back affair. He ambles on stage chatting with the audience who have swollen from three people facing the TV to about thirty, eyes on the stage. Glenn's loose, charming, but with whip-smart ad libs that make the whole audience lean in.

'Okey-doke,' he says, clapping his hands, 'let's get started. Who shall we have up first? Abi, you ready?'

Shock jolts through my spine. I knew Glenn said it was informal, but I didn't realise he meant pluck-the-acts-at-random informal.

'Er, yeah, cool,' I call out, my voice thin and unsure.

'Great!' he says.

And next thing I know, I'm at the front of the room, blinking into the dazzling bulbs of four IKEA lamps Glenn has angled towards the stage.

'Hey guys, my name's Abi. So first off, gimme a cheer if you've got stepkids?'

I have to peak my hand over my eyes to see faces, the lights are so bright. I hear a couple of noncommittal murmurs and a much more committed 'no', and I panic. I needed at least one person to say yes for this bit to work. I think fast.

'Yeah … me neither … anymore.'

I couple that with a sinister grin to sell the idea I've offed my stepkids. This gets a minor reaction from a woman at the back.

'Note to self. No jokes about bumping off stepkids.' I pretend to write that down and it gets more of a response than the actual joke. I keep going.

'Anyone in a relationship?'

I feel the collective eye-roll of an audience bored of being asked the same tired questions by comedians looking to shoehorn in their material.

'Try Bumble,' a strained voice calls out.

'I did, mate. Completed it.'

I almost surprise myself with the ad lib and the nice reaction it gets spurs me. I really want to build on this, but nothing comes to mind. The pull towards the safety of my tried and tested set is strong. There's defo gags I could slip in here but as comforting as those laughs would feel, I know, deep down, I'd be the joke and I'm never letting that happen ever again.

'He'll go out with you,' says a girl sitting with a group of friends.

They laugh and I reach for some kind of comeback.

'No thanks, babes, but I'll call you when there's an opening.'

Jeers follow and it takes me a second to hear the double-entendre.

I feel like I'm on a tightrope, sweating from just about every place skin meets skin. I make an attempt to get some control, a quick glance at my notebook, steadying my nerves.

'If you must know, I tried the dating apps but they're not for me. Guys write things like, "Really want an LTR". They want a long-term relationship but they can't even be bothered to write it out in full.'

This gets a laugh but once again I haven't got anything to follow it up with. Damn, this is tough.

'I finally met someone but he's got kids so now the biggest headache is knowing what relationship status to pick. "It's complicated," doesn't really cover it. Should be more like, "Not what I dreamed of when I was eight."'

Then I have an idea.

'When I said I wanted a fairy tale, I was hoping to be the princess, not the gnarly stepmum with chin warts.'

The tag works and I catch a glimpse of Glenn who gives an appreciative nod. I fling out a few more ideas, getting a mixed bag of responses – but there's definitely goodwill. I'm on the right track and I want to do more but as I've overrun, I wrap things up and get off stage to scribble down my improvised lines before they're forgotten.

Wow. That was not easy but, I have to admit, it was fun, and the thrill of unearthing something, mid-set, was – intense. Maybe I *can* do this. My mind teems with ideas that I race to jot down, still buzzing from the adrenalin of not knowing what, if anything, will work, the rush when something does, the dizzying attempts to rebalance when it doesn't. Though it's only my first official new-material night, I'm already addicted and kicking myself I didn't do this ages ago. But I know why – fear. However, now I'm on this path, there's no going back.

I stay to watch the other acts and begin to notice there's

a knack to doing new material, a playfulness and enjoyment at how none of these gags have ever seen the light of day and maybe never will again. At the start, I was almost apologising for what I had to say rather than relishing the sausage-making process. But when you treat it like a game, it becomes play – and that's what I loved about comedy when I first started out. It was playtime where I could do whatever I wanted, say what I felt like and no one could tell me, it's too much.

After the show, I sit for a while, savouring the post-gig high.

Glenn joins me. 'Well done. Though that wasn't quite how Carl described your act.'

I dread to think what he said and instantly feel the need to explain. 'Thing is …' I begin.

'I meant in a good way, like,' Glenn says, off my worried frown. 'When you started talking about stepkids and you weren't doing loads of accents, I thought, Oh, aye, she *is* trying something new. It's good. And look, it's not going to happen overnight, but you'll get the material together. And personally, I'd rather hear about that stuff than how big your thighs are.'

Glenn gives me a gentle shove and my self-belief inflates.

'Thanks. Really appreciate it.'

'See, stand-up's one of the few creative things you have to show the consumer before it's ready. You do a painting, you can let your mates have a look first, write a book, your agent'll have a butcher's before it's printed but stand-up, well, the only way you truly know if it'll fly, is if you jump. Absolute feckin' nightmare,' he says with a huge fatherly laugh, 'so enjoy the fall.'

'Cheers, Glenn,' I say, beaming.

'Nae bother, pet. Come back any time.'

Glenn heads off to mingle with the other comics and I'm suddenly humbled, loving that, despite how competitive the comedy scene can be, it's also a community. There are so many comics like Glenn, incredible circuit acts who'll probably never get any love from TV producers. But without comedians like him, there wouldn't even be a circuit for the rest of us to be on, aspire to, transcend or springboard from towards whatever heady heights lie beyond.

Chapter 41

Despite having a good time at the gig last night, what's had my heart racing all day is the anticipation of this evening – just me and Will snuggling up on the sofa, eating good food, watching Netflix and doing … whatever. We're putting into practice what we've been discussing – carving out space, just the two of us. Who knew a night in could be so special?

I arrive at his flat bang on seven, but hold off using my keys. Given we've only just got back on track, it feels presumptuous so I knock and wait.

'Quick. No time!' Will says, flinging the door open.

He pecks me on the lips then bounds up the stairs, two at a time.

I'm a bit disappointed he didn't comment on the outfit. Jean jacket, cream lace cami, pencil skirt over sheer, black leggings and my fave suede boots got me looking peng even if I say so myself but whatever. I follow him up, taking the steps one at time because, well, heels. In the kitchen, Will is fanning smoke out of an open window as a pot hisses under a running tap.

'Everything okay?' I say, though clearly it isn't.

'This is why I stick to making pizzas,' Will exhales as he wafts out the last swirls of smoke.

Finally he turns, taking me in, and his eyes brighten like we haven't seen each other in a month. A smile dances across his lips as he moves towards me. 'You look amazing.'

'Thank you,' I say, casually, like it's no biggie when, in reality, I nearly made myself late for work picking out these garms this morning.

We kiss, long and lingering.

As we pull apart, I take in the kitchen chaos around us. 'So, what's occurring?'

Will flaps his tea towel down on the counter. 'I wanted this to be perfect. I made the stew, plantain's cut, okra's ready to go and then I started on the rice. That's when it all fell apart. I was cooking my onions and tomatoes, then somehow ended up in this Google rabbit warren of best jollof recipes.'

He shakes his head in despair.

'Babe, schoolboy error,' I laugh, taking his face in my hands.

'I know. I've been all over the place. Nigeria, Ghana, Cameroon, Senegal. Then I started getting into East Africa!'

'Oh, don't start messing with them East-side recipes,' I say with a playful reprimand.

'Right?' Will laments. 'I just wanted us to have a great night and I almost burnt the building down.'

Though he's doing his best to laugh this off, his desire to make tonight special radiates from him.

'We can make our own type of perfect,' I say, pushing my jacket off my shoulder to reveal a lacy camisole strap.

'Ooookkkkay,' he says, his voice low, breath warm and wet on my skin as he kisses my neck.

'Too much?' I giggle.

'Not enough,' Will says and in a tangle of hands pulling at clothes, lips pressing into each other, we head to the bedroom, food now furthest from our minds.

Later, we finally move to the sofa, no TV, just gentle music. I pull my silky robe around me, this exact scenario in mind when I bought it the other day – and lean on Will as he strokes my skin.

'I wasn't sure we'd get through this,' he says.

'Me neither,' I smile. 'It's been a journey ...'

Will adjusts next to me, and I feel a tension seep into his body.

'I'm still mad at myself for dropping the ball like that. I should have realised ages ago how important it was to have time alone for us and for me and the girls. It's so obvious.'

'Yeah, well, like they say, hindsight's 20:20. You're only human, Will. And I should probably have realised too,' I say, sitting up.

He nods though I sense he hasn't fully forgiven himself yet. 'I've got one job, be a good father, and that means more to me than anything. As a black man, I feel eyes on me all the time, plus my dad set such a high bar. You know how some kids wish they could swap their dad for someone else's? Well, the father all my mates wanted was mine. He's the best. But living up to that, it's bare pressure so when I mess up – it's a lot. I think it created fear in my relationship with Kat. I mean, we were both scared. Me of never being as good as my dad and Kat, well, rejection was her kryptonite. Just the thought of putting yourself out there terrifies her.'

Will reaches for his drink and takes a thoughtful sip.

'I think I can see that in the way she smiles,' I suggest, unsure it's fair or even appropriate to chime in.

'That's right. She's scared but also scared of people seeing that, so she tries to paper over it. I didn't notice at first but once I did I couldn't unsee it.'

I laugh with relief at Will saying what I've been thinking since I first met her.

'I remember one time we took the girls to this nice café and there was a coin-operated horsey ride outside. Esme was straight on it, rocking back and forth, nattering away to the horse. She was so happy.'

Will's eyes go misty, remembering the scene.

'Then this woman, all buttoned up with a screw-face, started glaring at Ez and before I realised what was going on, Kat had taken her off the horse and plonked her at our table. Well, Esme screamed the place down, making way more noise than she was before. I don't know what happened to Kat growing up, but if someone puts themselves out there, does something creative, or is just fully themselves, it scares the shit out of her.'

'Is that why you're so supportive of Elle doing stand-up?'

'I can see Kat doing what she did with me, shutting it down because *she's* scared. I can't have that for Elle, especially as my dad always encouraged creative stuff in me. He'd say, "Bwoy, those who can, do. Those who can't, review."'

And though there's a twinge of embarrassment as I remember Elle's 'those who can't, teach' comment not that long ago, I have to give him props, 'That is good.'

'Exactly, and it's how I want my daughters to live. I want them to just do.'

'Yeah,' I say as the idea, of just letting people be, percolates, giving them room to create in their lives without imposing your fears, hang-ups, concerns, judgements. I so want that from Mum but perhaps that's the place for *me* to start. Letting her be who *she* is.

'I've got something for you,' Will says, patting my leg.

'Yeah?' I say as I try to contain my delight. I *love* pressies.

'Wait there.'

While he's in the bedroom, I ponder the story he shared about Esme in the café. It felt all too familiar because what Kat did was how Mum used to treat me, always shutting down exuberance, concerned what others thought rather than just letting me be. And I start to wonder if me doing something creative terrifies her too. So much so, she uses whatever tactics she can to contain it, dismissing my efforts, deriding my wins, maybe even labelling it all … too much. Perhaps that's what Elle thought was happening when I refused to sign that release form, that it was my attempt to contain her. I need to talk to Elle. We could hang out, maybe take her to a show. Yolanda B. Rockwell, perhaps. The tickets go on sale soon. I reach for my phone but then pause. This is what I *always* do: go in feet first, then have to do a clean-up job after. I sit back and, for once, just give myself a beat. I don't have to *do* anything. Maybe I can simply let things be. I relax further into the sofa and as I do, Chapelle slinkies down from his cat tree, eyeing me. He stretches out his long, thin limbs and then, as though he's been doing it all his life, curls up at my feet. A grin spreads across my face at the blissful touch of his soft fur against my skin. Just then Will returns, guitar and a sheet of paper in hand.

'Look, look, look,' I whisper, pointing down at Chapelle, and Will laughs.

'Told you, he just takes a while. Pals for life now,' he says, planting himself next to me and resting the guitar on his lap. 'I wrote you a song.'

My hand rises to my chest in disbelief. 'Shut up.'

'Being with you, seeing you push yourself with your comedy, going on this new journey, it's inspired me, Abi. As well as everything else you do to me, you've lit a fire under my creativity too …'

Damn. I was expecting perfume or some sexy undies but this is … wow. I bloom at the acknowledgement.

'So, am I your muse?' I ask, with a mischievous twinkle.

'You're not just my muse, you're my music, the song I hear in silence – you're everything,' he says as he begins to strum, his soft, velvety voice dancing over the chords, and it's the most beautiful sound I've ever heard. My baby is whole again.

And as the melody fills the room, my face streaks with tears, heart swelling to capacity with each note. Will draws his fingers down, teasing one final refrain from the strings, the sound floating like mist before evaporating.

'Thank you,' I whisper.

Will sets his guitar aside, moving closer.

'I love you, Abi Akingbade,' he says.

And our lips meet, bodies gently pulsing to a silent rhythm. I tug at Will's shirt, guiding his hands under my robe as I rise to meet his touch. We entwine, that pulse, pulse, pulse – so delicious, taking us somewhere else, somewhere new, somewhere together.

'I love you too, Will Matheson …'

Chapter 42

I'm on stage at Coco, a new-material night that pulls in a good crowd, and am starting to relax into my set. After the White Lion last week, I've decided to follow Glenn's advice, treating these gigs more like a game, and I think it's working. Since our chat I've done three shows, each building on the last, each playful in a way that's freed me up to help unearth the funny. So now, instead of desperately reaching for jokes, they're finding me. It does still feel like roller-skating on ice, but the material is starting to seep into my bones. And with a more discerning crowd like tonight's, willing to give us acts the breathing room we need, it's getting easier and easier each time. I've found a way to talk about the girls that doesn't make me sound like some cautionary tale for single dads, and I'm being more honest about Mum. It means she gets fewer mentions than before, mainly because I'm not ready to go there, but that's not necessarily a bad thing. I mean, there's telling your truth and there's spewing your soul.

By the end of my ten minutes, the crowd are completely with me, laughing in all the right places. I even get a smattering of applause for an improvised line and sign off to a lovely response. As I step off stage, I spot Frank and Cassie at the back and can't help but smile.

'Hey, you two!' I whisper as we huddle by the bar.

I've been dying to see these guys for aaaages but with life going at such a gallop it's been hard. Thankfully, tonight, with a bit of fortunate booking, me and Frank have ended up on the same bill with Cassie tagging along for the ride.

'So, we finally got the band back together – at a gig,' Frank laughs.

'I know, right? Why can't we be like normal people and go for a drink?' I say as Cassie gives a motherly eye-roll.

'With you two bunny-hopping from show to show, it'd be New Year's before we'd see each other.'

She's probably not far off but I'm so inspired now, any time I'm offered a new-material gig, I grab it with both hands.

Hugs and how-are-yous done, Frank pulls us into an even tighter huddle, his face suddenly shimmering with barely contained excitement. 'So, girls, I have something to tell you, but I wanted to wait till we were face to face.'

'Oooh,' Cassie says, trying to formulate a guess. 'You've accepted Jesus Christ as your personal lord and saviour?'

'What? Why would I do that?' Frank baulks.

'Well, your spiritual life is somewhat lacking,' she offers with an overly compassionate smile.

'Cassie, shush, man. Let Frank speak,' I moan, curiosity peaking.

He gives Cassie one last glare before a joy-filled grin slowly consumes his whole face.

'I got *ShowTime*,' he whispers.

We stare at him, mouths open, then burst into a frenzy of

hushed celebration, aware we need to keep the noise down as there is still an act on stage. 'Yes, *babes*, that is siiiiiick!'

'Yes, it's truly sick!' Cassie chimes and we bundle onto Frank, smothering him with love, leaping about in delight.

'All right, you lunatics,' he says, as we finally manage to contain our elation.

'Sorry, mate, but it's amazing news. Aren't you excited?' I ask.

'I am but … it's just such a big show.'

Cassie gives an empathetic nod. 'Oh, bless you. *That's* why you're practically tripling up on these warm-up gigs.'

'You can't over-prepare,' Frank insists. 'I just … I can't believe how nervous I am.'

'That's understandable. Just remember, nerves are excitement minus breath. Breathe and you'll be fine,' Cassie says.

'Mate, your set is fi-yah and you're amazing. You've got nothing to worry about,' I add.

'Thanks, guys.'

Frank tries to maintain his usual cool but apprehension flickers below the surface. Uneasy in the warm glow of our nurturing attention, he attempts to deflect the convo. 'Well, speaking of amazing, love the new material, Abi. It's really working.'

'Oh yes, you were brilliant,' Cassie agrees, beaming.

'Awww, cheers, guys. Still finding my way but, you know,' I reply, suddenly coy at their approval.

'How long have you been working on it?' Frank asks.

'Couple of weeks. Did you hear, Dina gave me a spot at the Cabana and I diiiiiiiiiieeed,' I say, contorting myself to exaggerate the awfulness.

'That's hilarious,' Frank crows as Cassie offers giggled condolences.

'Honestly, mate, you could smell the stench of my corpse from Old Street Tube,' I say, clicking my fingers behind me to indicate just how far my death stink travelled.

Frank's laugh crescendos. If there's one thing us comedians love, it's hearing about each other's deaths. Somehow it dilutes the pain of ones we've had and those yet to come.

'Well, it was clearly worth pushing through,' he says once our laughter eases. 'I love your new set. So honest. Given me food for thought. I'm wondering if … perhaps I should drop the accent.'

'For *ShowTime*?' I gasp.

He nods, eyes jittery with nerves.

'Goodness,' Cassie says.

'I don't know. Maybe not,' he back-pedals. 'I literally just had the thought. I mean, if I did go for it, I'd need to do a load more prep to get used to the change. What do you think?'

I puff my cheeks. This is huge. It's like asking Yoncé to lose the wig and wind machine or Jared Leto to act without prosthetics. 'It's such a big night but only you know what's best.'

Frank considers, uncertainty tightening his face. 'Yeah, I s'pose.'

'How long till your recording?' I ask.

'Next month. On the fifteenth.'

My joy flickers. 'They're filming a kids' stand-up show that afternoon and Elle's on the bill.'

'What, you're kidding? Just like that?' Frank blusters, sounding more taken aback than I was. 'So much for putting in road miles on the circuit. If I'd known the quickest way to make it was to be an embryo, I wouldn't have wasted my time.'

Though I've made my peace with Elle's rapid rise, I do get Frank's annoyance and how it could feel like she's gamed the system, being handed opportunities he's toiled years to earn.

'Oh, Frank,' Cassie says, her irritation good-natured but there nonetheless. 'Everyone has a gimmick. It's called "who-you-are". And anything that marks you out as different from the homogenous parade at comedy shows has to be a good thing. Right, Abi?'

'Facts,' I say, and we share a fumbled high five.

Frank huffs, letting this in, and his indignation slowly subsides.

'You're right, I suppose. I guess we've all got a "thing". Mine's the accent, hers is not being old enough to buy superglue. Well,' he says, taking a breath to reset, 'the fifteenth is gonna be a long day for you, Abi. That is, assuming you and Cassie will be my plus ones?'

'What? Serious?' I squeal, squishing him against my boobs with a massive Abi-hug. 'I wouldn't want to be anywhere else.'

Excitement overflowing, we smother Frank with even more love but before we can get too carried away, the compere for tonight's show approaches. 'There you are. You're up next.'

'Okay, cheers, mate,' Frank says before turning back to me and Cassie. 'Right, see you on the other side.'

He heads off with our calls of good luck in his wake. Once he's gone, Cassie and I get comfy at the bar.

'I'm so proud of you both,' she says, a serene smile playing on her lips, 'and I love this new path you're taking. You know what Peter Ustinov said about comedy?'

'Didn't he used to play for West Ham?'

'No, silly. He was a much loved raconteur and he said, "Comedy is simply a funny way of being serious."'

And with that simple little gem, my brain explodes a bit … That's why the truth is so important; it's a way to make the serious stuff palatable. It's what I see in Elle, what Yolanda was talking about, what the greats do, while I was settling for fat jokes and meaningless send-ups of my mum. Suddenly, though, this path feels big, maybe too big for me.

'That makes sense, Cass, but I've still got a long way to go. Like I said, first time I tried it …'

'You died.'

'Like a black man in a nineteen seventies horror movie,' I reply.

'You should write that down,' Cassie says with a knowing laugh. 'The way I see it, good comics have good material, great comics have something to say. They drill down and find the hilarious and tragic truth at the core of the human experience. I think I've got the truth bit figured out. I'm just not great at making it funny.'

'But you still can. I could get you on at the open-mic venues I've been doing …'

But Cassie stops me. 'I'm okay with where I'm at. I was never trying to "make it". I just wanted to say something truthful. Us counsellors, we have to find ways to release the energy we absorb from our clients. Some go dancing. Some have therapy themselves; some smash the shit out of a squash ball. I do comedy.'

I stare at Cassie, speechless as I recall her routines – random odysseys into life as a mum of five, deep dives into the nature of existence and a bit about hereditary bunions. All those times I wrote her off as not having what it takes, she was tapping into something I'm only just finding, searching for a taste of that golden nectar that can only be harvested from the centre of our own souls.

This sparks a fire in me. Where before, my steps along this new comedic path were sometimes tentative, now I'm ready to stride forward, arms swinging. And seeing Frank and Cassie, feeling their support, has made those flames roar.

Look at me. I'm eleven stone and five foot four. I'm not too much. I'm compact!

And all this time I've been thinking I had to turf out the old, but I don't. There's a truth underneath everything, even my old gags.

With these thighs, I would break your back.

You just have to know where to look.

But we'd never be a couple, would we? Because the media doesn't present girls like me as peng. No slow-mo bikini shots or chocolate ads for us. Nah, it's always skinny gyals dem, practically going down on that choccy bar. I mean, why is it always women in these ads, anyway? I know bare man with sweet tooth but you never see them in a cable-knit sweater by a crackling fire, deep-throating a twitty-twatty-curly-whirlathon!

Ideas flow as I grab at them like they're the tail end of a kite rope I can't afford to let go of. I sift through old material with fresh eyes where I'm no longer the butt of the joke. And the wisdom Yolanda shared with me that night suddenly makes total sense.

YOU'LL START TO LIKE YOURSELF A WHOLE LOT MORE.

And I do. I really do.

Chapter 43

I've agreed to meet Will at the venue. I don't say it, but I could do with the alone time on the Tube ride over to the Athena. For the past few weeks, Will and I have been enjoying date nights, just me and him. It's been amazing but also helped us create a foundation so that when I do spend time with the girls again, we're solid. Not a me-against-them but an *us*. It's just, while theorising about that has been easy, now that I'm heading to see the girls for the first time in a minute, and without my usual armour of charm, jokes and efforting, I'm proper scared. So much has happened, so much has changed and I have no idea how this day will pan out.

The train has that weekend busyness – fewer people but more energy because instead of traipsing to work, everyone's in leisure mode. Personally, I'm not sure where I am on the enjoyment spectrum. Yes, going to the Athena is amazing but it's not exactly baggage-free. And it's going to be a long day, what with Elle's performance in the afternoon then Frank's show later this evening. I'm just glad I brought snacks.

I arrive a few minutes after one and there's already a stream of parents, friends and family making their way into the theatre.

I text Will to let him know I've arrived. The plan is, after getting Elle settled, Kat will stay backstage while Will and Esme join me in the auditorium. Then, once Elle's show's done, I'll link up with Frank ahead of his performance tonight.

I pass through the heavy ornate doors into the venue, and my breath catches as I take in its size. Stalls and three sections of seating ascend to the gods, burgundy and red upholstery throughout with gold detail on balcony edges and banisters, looking every bit as plush as it does on TV.

'Oh my days,' I murmur.

'Do you know where you're going, miss?' an usher asks.

This place has been in my dreams more times than I can remember. Even if I didn't know where I'm going, I definitely know where I am – heaven.

'Yeah, thanks,' I say, moving down the aisle and deeper into the splendour.

I find our row and shuffle along to my seat, still gawping at my surroundings. With the upper tiers cordoned off, the stalls fill quickly and I'm soon surrounded by that same excited buzz there was at Elle's comedy competition. My tummy tightens as I think back to that day and Elle's reaction to her loss. What if she has a bad gig this afternoon? Will she react the same way? The one good thing is, this time, she can't blame me – or at least I hope not. But my feelings aside, I just want her to do well, to come away feeling great, like she's good at this. Basically, I want the audience to love her.

'Abi!' Esme yelps as she runs down our row towards me.

I stand to greet her, scooping her up in my arms.

'Baby girl!' I say and give her a big Abi squeeze.

'I lost two teeth and we just played Deck of Devastation and

I won,' she tells me, as though picking up a conversation we started a couple of minutes ago.

'Reaaally?' I say, with delight.

'Yeah. And I got three pounds from the tooth fairy,' she says, before cupping her hand to shield a whispered, 'She's not real.'

'Serious?' I play-gasp and she gives me a conspiratorial nod.

Around us, the excitement for the show ramps up.

'How's Elle doing?' I ask after Will and I share a quick kiss over Esme's head.

'Surprisingly calm. Kat's the one stressing. No surprise there,' Will says.

'As long as Elle's okay, that's all that matters. And how are *you* doing?'

Will smiles, considering. 'I'm good.'

And that makes me happy.

As the audience reaches peak restlessness, desperate for the show to begin, I sit back, a quiet slowly replacing my earlier anxiety. For now, things feel okay. After a few more minutes, the lights go down and, with music blaring from all corners, the host takes to the stage. Deafening screams fill the auditorium and no wonder. It's the presenter from 'Jerk the Week' who hosted Elle's competition. 'Hello, people! My name's Josh Nwachukwu and welcome to the Athena!'

'This guy,' I say, pointing a cheeky thumb in his direction, slightly jealous but also knowing he's probably the best person for the job.

As he bounces around the stage warming up an already piping hot crowd, I look around the venue, still awed by this place. I've imagined being here so many times, but sitting in the auditorium, rather than standing backstage or, better yet, on it, is bittersweet. One day, Abi, I tell myself. If a little black girl from Nutbush can become one of the biggest music stars in the world, surely this one can make it up there someday.

It feels like forever until Elle's on but at last, her moment arrives. As she enters, the follow spotlight tracks her downstage and I find myself shifting forward, willing her to do well.

'Hi, my name's Elle, thanks for coming out on a Saturday afternoon, though it looks like the parents are just glad to be sitting down.'

And she's away.

Elle barrels through her set. Some material I've heard before, some new. I can tell there's a hint of nerves, but she still looks comfortable, assured and so, while Will practically mouths Elle's lines along with her, I sit back and enjoy the show.

'So my mum and dad are both seeing new people. I feel like I'm collecting responsible guardians, I need one of those sticker albums to put them in. "Mum, dad, new partners, Got, got, got. Oooh, gossipy aunt – need."'

Though this flies over the heads of some of the younger ones, the older kids, and the adults, literally fall about. Elle is nailing this. Her ten minutes zip past and soon she's saluting the audience a goodbye, leaving the stage to cheers and applause.

'She was great!' I whisper to Will.

'Yeah,' he says, eyes glistening.

Looking at Will I wonder if, in Elle, he's seeing whatever was pushed down in him finally having the room to shine, and that, somehow, that's allowing him to shine too.

*

After the show, I follow Will and Esme to the backstage entrance but when we get there, I hesitate.

'You okay?' Will asks.

'I should probably give you guys some family time. Let you four enjoy the moment.'

Though nerves about seeing Elle are colouring my decision, I'm also trying to do the right thing. What's the point in us discussing balance, only for me to bowl into the middle of things the first opportunity I get? Will takes my hand in his while a distracted Esme clasps on to his other.

'Abi, we all want you there. Promise.'

'Yeah?' I ask, teetering towards believing him but scared to get this wrong.

'Honestly, on the way over, Elle must have asked about five times if you were definitely coming.'

And at that, my cheeks flush as Will hands me an Access-All-Areas pass. I proudly loop it around my neck and we go up to Elle's dressing room. But as we ascend the stairs, my heart begins to drum louder and louder. Elle's blown hot and cold the whole time I've known her. What if today's no different? Though she was asking after me earlier, what if seeing me again brings all her doubts and fears back up to the surface? What if that sticker album line was her way of letting me know I'm just one of many, easily pasted over? My stomach plummets as it hits me: no matter how much I try to do the right thing, if Elle's not onboard, this ship's going nowhere.

'Knock, knock,' Will says, rapping on Elle's door.

As Kat opens it, greeting us both, Will swoops in, gathering Elle up for a massive squeeze. 'You were sooooo good, Ellie, oh my days!'

'Do you think so? I forgot a bit and I had to ad lib a line,' she says, worried.

'No one would know. You smashed it,' Will says, squeezing her even more.

'He's right. You were … incredible,' Kat beams.

'Yeah. Smashed it!' Esme repeats, skipping about on the spot.

Meanwhile, I stand awkwardly by the door as the family lavish praise on their newly minted superstar. I feel a mighty tug to just turn and go, once again unsure it's even my place to be here, a moment only meant for those on the family page of Elle's imaginary sticker album. My insides curdle at the discomfort. And I decide I'm just going to offer my congrats and bounce. Surely that's best all round if we really are taking things slowly.

Elle untangles from her dad and we catch each other's eye.

'Well done, Elle,' I say, starting my exit countdown.

'Thanks, Abi,' she replies, clasping at a bottle of sparkling water, fingers pale with tension. 'What did you think?'

'I …' I begin, surprised she's asking my opinion, but just by her doing that, something quietens in me. 'You were really great.'

Her feet shift side to side, box-fresh Gazelles, slightly pointing inwards. 'Thanks. And do you think that sticker album thing was too much?' she asks, eyes bright with the need for approval.

'Elle,' I say, shoulders finally relaxing as I take in this brilliant, complicated girl, 'it was perfect.'

And she looks as though she just might believe me.

Chapter 44

It's just gone four, and having been politely ushered from the dressing room area so the team can prep for the evening show, we've descended to the circle bar for a post-gig toast to Elle. After a couple of drinks, Kat declares it's time to get Esme home and we say our goodbyes. I relish the hug me and Esme share and wave until they disappear through the double doors and out into the street.

'Okay,' Will says, rubbing his hands, 'I'm gonna take this one for a celebration veggie burger – she was too nervous to eat earlier.'

Elle blushes at the over-share. 'Jeez, Will.'

'I know, right? He'd make a terrible spy,' I say.

Elle giggles and that warms me. We're on the right track.

Will clocks this and smiles too. 'We'll see you for Frank's show in a bit, yeah, if you still don't mind us joining?'

'Totally,' I reply, waving them off. 'Enjoy the burger.'

With things seemingly going well, part of me wants to go with them, but I resist asking to tag along. Their daddy–daughter time is important, and giving them space for that feels right – plus, Frank has just arrived so I need to get up there and start entouraging. Can't let this peng outfit go to waste.

*

After a flash of my triple-A lanyard at the stage door, I make my way back to the dressing rooms, bounding up the stairs. I'm buzzing to tell Frank and Cassie how well things went with Elle but when I reach Frank's room, I'm met with a vibe I'm not prepared for. Cassie is learning Tai Chi from a YouTube video while Frank is lying in corpse pose on a long purple sofa, a satin eye-mask hugging his face. We're just three hours away from a major league stand-up show and it feels like a Bali beach spa in here. Suddenly I'm self-conscious of every sound I make, almost holding my breath, despite the need to gulp lungfuls of air after barrelling up the stairs like that.

'Hey, Abi,' Cassie says, voice muted so as not to disturb the man of the hour. 'How did it go with Elle?'

'Really good – so far!' I say, waving crossed fingers. 'Kat's taken Esme home but Will and Elle have gone for food then they're coming back for this evening's show.'

'Oh, wonderful. Small steps,' Cassie whispers.

'Totally. And, honestly, Cass, she was so great up there—'

'Abi.'

Frank has raised one side of his mask and is glaring at me with an incriminating eye.

'Oh, right, yeah, yeah, sorry,' I mouth, scouring the room for some kind of silent activity I can do to bleed off this restless energy.

As Cassie continues to 'grasp a bird' and 'carry a tiger' or whatever moves she's doing, I spot a tattered magazine and peel open the cover but as I start to read Frank's feet twitch in irritation.

'I can hear you turning the pages,' he intones.

'Sorry, sorry, sorry,' I say, and put the magazine down, minimising all physical movements, and fighting the urge to chat, even though conversation wants to erupt from me like a spewing volcano. Because today was massive. Things felt good between me and Elle. We all hung out and there was no drama. This is huge progress and I want to talk about it!

Frank shifts on the sofa. 'Sorry, Abi. I can hear you breathe.'

I bite down my restlessness, and get up. 'You know what, I'm gonna leave you to prep and go for a wander.'

Cassie give me a sympathetic smile as Frank raises his eye mask, propping himself up on an elbow.

'Great news about Elle, though,' he smiles before easing back into his corpse pose.

'Thanks, love,' I say. 'And don't leave that thing on too long or you'll have mask lines all over your face.'

'Noted,' Frank says, blowing me a kiss.

Hmm, being in an entourage is not what I imagined. I was expecting way more schmoozing and boozing than this – and a few C-list celebs thrown in for good measure. Still, I do have this triple-A pass so I might as well work it while I'm here. I turn it over in my hand, knowing exactly where I want to go. Following the luminous signs, before long I'm navigating a dark corridor. It meets a metal staircase that leads to a low-ceilinged walkway and I can instantly tell – I'm under the Athena stage. My pulse pounds in my ears as I break into a trot, finally reaching a thick fire door with a red and white sign that reads *STAGE RIGHT.* I yank it open and climb the stairs two at a time, even though my knees are begging me not to. And suddenly I'm in the wings, looking out at that mammoth stage, the bright follow-spot still trained on its centre. The auditorium is empty aside from a few crew, chilling between shows. Upstage, the previous backdrop is being lifted out and, in its place, the famous *ShowTime at the Athena* cyclorama brought in. I'm literally vibrating with excitement and as I stare at the circle of light in the middle, the urge to walk out is overwhelming.

I can almost hear my voice, booming through the monitors.

Good evening, ladies and gentlemen! My name's Abi Akingbade!

And there's a cheer as I dive into my routine, riding waves of laughter as though I've been surfing this kind of blue tube my whole damn life.

The mists in my mind's eye clear and I know I can't pass up this once-in-a-lifetime opportunity. I'm walking onto this stage. What are they gonna do, kick me out? *I'm triple-A, baby.*

But just as I go to take that magical step from the darkness to the light, in the wings opposite, I see Elle. She looks towards the auditorium, her gaze bright with reverence.

'Great, isn't it?' she says, stepping out.

'Yeah,' I reply, taking a couple of cautious steps towards the spotlight.

We're now both clear of the wings, sharing the floor, dazzled by our surroundings.

'How was your burger?' I ask.

'Solid three stars,' she says.

'Cool. And where's Dad?'

'Music shop.'

I scan Elle's face for judgement of this, concern or even fear – but there's none.

'Great,' I say.

'Said I'd meet him in a bit but I wanted to come back here and soak this up one last time.'

I nod in appreciation. 'Same … same.'

We fall silent, looking out from the stage, absorbing as much as we can, creating tomorrow's memories. This is too awesome even for selfies.

'My dad was really … down after you went. Esme too,' Elle mutters, like knowing this is a burden almost too heavy to bear.

That's a lot of stress for someone not even old enough to buy a lottery ticket or a can of spray paint. I want to reassure her but seeing Elle search for what she needs to say, I don't want to interrupt so I just pulse my head, edging a little closer.

'I'm sorry I made things so … hard for you and my dad. I didn't mean to,' Elle continues.

I look into her eyes, regret scorching her face, and I feel a wave of guilt too. All this time I've been thinking about my hurt, forgetting she was stung as well. She's just a kid acting out of survival in a space that didn't feel safe. I put a hand on her shoulder, and she shudders as though barely able to receive my comfort, her remorse so enveloping.

'It's okay,' I offer, but her head slumps and instead of the tiny warrior who a moment ago was surveying her domain, she shrinks to the delicate, sensitive soul she also is.

'I made everything shit,' Elle whimpers, burying her face in the crook of her elbow.

'It was shit but you know what,' I say, rubbing Elle's back, her reddening eyes crushing me, 'I'm the grown-up and I should have done more to make it easier for you. It's just, I had a bit of growing up to do myself. I so wanted to get it right that I was trying too hard, did what I always do, throw a whole load of Abi at it and hope for the best. It was too much and I'm really sorry. You know how you call your mum and dad by their first names sometimes? Well, you have permission to call me Grabby Abi.'

Elle giggles and it's light and lovely. 'Well, in that case you can call me "babes" any time you want,' she counters playfully and I laugh, slightly embarrassed at how familiar I tried to be with her so early on.

And as we give this moment some room, I start to relax. When I first saw her upset, doubt had paced the recesses of my mind. Was this genuine or another play? But as she dabs at her face, cheeks puffed with sadness, I can see she's for real. Pulling the back of a hand across her eyes, she wipes away the last of her tears.

I venture a topic change, to give Elle some space to tidy the little make-up she allowed Production to put on her. 'Good that your mum came. Maybe she's a bit more onboard now?'

Elle gives an exaggerated eye-roll. 'No chance. I'm surprised she didn't have a uni application form half-filled out for when I walked off stage.'

'My mum's the same. She's desperate for me to get a "proper job" and I've been doing this eight years!'

We shake our heads at the craziness of it.

'How come people don't think of this as a career?' Elle asks.

'I dunno. Because it's fun.'

She bobs her head in acknowledgement. 'So how do we handle the doubters?'

I think for a moment, pondering how I've navigated it.

'Believe in ourselves,' I say eventually. 'At the end of the day, that's the only thing that matters, innit?'

'Truth,' says Elle and we turn to leave, but as we do, she clutches at my sleeve.

I look back and she shuffles awkwardly towards me before clamping herself around my waist.

I'm startled for a second but as I feel Elle's grip tighten, I wrap my arms around her too and we stay there, like that, just being.

'Thanks, Grabby Abi,' she whispers and I chuckle, kissing the top of her head.

'All good, babes, all good.'

Chapter 45

'Shit, shit, shit, shit, shit!'

I'm back in Frank's dressing room, still blissfully breathless from giving the guys a moment-by-moment account of how me and Elle ended up hugging it out in the middle of the Athena stage, when the sound of hissed expletives from the corridor outside stops me in my tracks. We all exchange concerned glances then, as one, leap towards the door, pressing our ears against it. On the other side, hastened footsteps pass by as a tinny voice crackles from a radio: 'Have you got eyes on Jimmy yet?!'

Ever the nosy neighbour, I crack the door just as the crew member, a solid guy with a mousy blond topknot, practically skids along the hall, disappearing down the stairs.

'Who's Jimmy?' Cassie asks, picking from the fruit bowl on Frank's dressing table.

'Jimmy Halloran. The warm-up. He should have been here ages ago.'

'Shiiiiiit,' I say, 'that's not good.'

'It's not. I can't go on to a cold audience,' Frank says, his serene calm evaporating by the second.

In the hallway I hear more frantic footsteps and take another peek. It's Topknot now returned with Tess Blackman, going dressing room to dressing room in the desperate hope one of them is harbouring the elusive Jimmy.

Topknot give me a frantic look. 'Jimmy Halloran not in there, is he?'

'Sorry, mate. Just us and some seedless grapes,' I reply.

Frank scoops up his phone, frantically tapping at its screen.

'What are you doing?'

'Trying to find Jimmy. He might have had a heart attack or something.'

'Frank!' Cassie says, appalled at the suggestion but then adding, 'Though he does exhibit many of the early warning signs.'

'What about Josh from earlier? Couldn't he do it?' I ask.

'Blimey, Abi, this is the Athena, not *Blue Peter.* They need a grown-up and besides, he'll be long gone,' Frank replies, face still buried in his phone.

'Fair enough,' I say, quietly enjoying his dismissal of Josh as I join him scrolling our socials for clues.

'I'll check TikTok,' Cassie says.

'I hardly think a man on the edge of a coronary is going to use a dance challenge to signal for help,' Frank scorns.

'No idea is a bad idea,' I say, trying to encourage.

Just then, we hear Tess outside the door and, once again, press our ears to the cold, painted wood.

'He's just got in touch – from a callbox. His phone died,' a panting Topknot informs Tess.

'His phone died,' Cassie repeats to us in a whisper.

'Where the hell is he?' Tess flaps.

'Newport Pagnell services.'

'He's at Newport Pagnell services. Oh, it's nice there,' Cassie relays.

'What?' says Tess.

'Some lady's said, "What?"'

'Cassie, be quiet!' Frank hisses and we all go back to listening in.

'Overturned lorry across two lanes. Says it's bumper to bumper. Wouldn't get here much before nine at best.'

This is bad. For a TV recording to go well, the audience needs to be warmed up – *before* the cameras roll, *before* the acts go on. If there's no pre-show warm-up, the first act, who tonight is Frank, will go on to a crowd whose heads are in traffic jams, rows with their partner, Tube delays and late babysitters. It'll be a disaster.

'We need a replacement, like yesterday,' Tess snaps and both voices disappear off in different directions.

Me, Frank and Cassie step back from the door as though the heat of that corridor exchange has singed us.

'So …' Cassie exhales.

'Are you thinking what I'm thinking?' Frank says with an arch grin.

'Yes. That lady needs to do some Compassionate Leadership training, asap,' Cassie says, with a displeased shake of her head.

'No, dummy. They need a warm-up and who better to work a crowd than …' Frank finishes his sentence with a flourish in my direction.

'What? No. Are you mad? They'll never … I can't,' I bluster.

'They will and you can,' Frank claps back and before I know it, he's taken me by the arm and we're heading to the production office, my heart thundering and me bleating excuses as we go.

Behind the stage door area, down a corridor with a shiny red floor, we arrive at an office. Inside, several people make urgent calls. Someone is on the phone to Jimmy trying to work out how he can travel fifty miles in less than twenty minutes. Meanwhile, everyone else is texting, emailing and calling agents, acts, anyone who'll pick up, to find a replacement.

'Maybe we can delay the start of the show,' one timid production runner suggests.

'Because of a warm-up?' Tess barks.

The runner wilts, going back to making futile phone calls as Frank nudges me further into the room. There's a pull forward, towards offering myself as the solution, but there's also a strong and equal pull the other way, to pretending I've taken a wrong turn and was actually looking for the snack kiosk. However, before I can back away, Tess looks over. 'Hi, Frank, we've got a bit of a crisis here. Do you need us to get you something?'

Even though there's literally no warmth in her voice, he takes that as an invite to approach. 'Crisis averted. Abi's a comic. So if you're looking for a warm-up ...'

Timid Runner stares hopefully from me to Tess and gradually everyone follows suit.

'Who are you?' Tess says, almost irritated this is getting in the way of finding a *real* comedian.

'Abi Akingbade. I'm a comic. Well, obviously. I was with Elle Matheson at the Comedy Buzz Competition.'

Timid Runner edges closer to Tess, muttering in her ear. I only catch the odd word. I hear 'Cabin' but it could be 'Cabana' and I gulp as I've had mixed results at both. Tess's eyes dart to me then she straightens, moving closer.

'Yeah, I've seen you,' she says, giving nothing away. 'You done warm-up before?'

I swallow. 'I've compered loads but …'

'What's the biggest room you've played?'

I want to cheat this and answer in square footage, but I know she means capacity. I hesitate a moment too long and she turns away, clamping her phone to her ear again.

'Okay, look,' I say, daring to take another step forward, 'the biggest club I've played is three fifty, Carl O'Connor's room, but I've run a comedy night with Frank for seven years. I compere all the time and I know how to get a room warmed up. Ask him.'

Everyone stops except for one junior on her mobile. 'I've got Josh Nwachukwu's agent on the line. Josh is free and still in the area. What should I say?'

Tess looks at the junior then back to me and I do my best to hold her gaze. Out the corner of my eye, I can see Top Knot rooting for me. He leans into Tess, murmuring, 'It's not for transmission, just for tonight … Maybe give her a shot.'

'Shhh,' Tess hisses.

'Look, sorry if this is an overstep, but as I'm first up, I have to tell you there is no one I'd rather have doing warm-up for me tonight,' Frank says, slicing through the dithering.

The room freezes, all eyes on Tess, yet still she wavers. Emboldened, I decide to shoot my shot.

'Tess, I can do this. And okay, I haven't played a venue this big before but neither have Frank, Elle or at least two of your other acts, but if you're looking for someone with the energy to fill a room, I'm your girl.'

No one speaks, everyone waiting on Tess's say-so like she's the Man from Del Monte. Meanwhile, my insides are somersaulting with anticipation. It's twenty to seven. Curtain-up is in less than half an hour and through the show relay speaker, we can all hear the excited murmurs of the audience begin to grow. The air crackles with tension, collective breath held, waiting for Tess's decision.

'Okay, fine, get her miced up.'

And for a moment my soul leaves my body, but I'm zapped back to reality just as quickly when the production machine whirls into action around me.

'We need a lapel mic to the production office, stat!' says Topknot.

'No time,' another runner says. 'Get Sound to meet us in Make-up. Abi, if you'd like to follow me.'

In an excited daze, I pace off after them mouthing a thank-you to Frank as I go. He winks in reply. 'You're gonna be great.'

Chapter 46

'Will! Ohmygodohmygodohmygod!'

I'm holding my phone so close to my mouth it might as well be in it.

'Abi? What's happened?'

'I'm warming up! For *ShowTime*!!' I screech, barely able to contain myself.

'What? No way!'

'Way! Are you back at the Athena yet?'

'Yeah,' Will laughs, probably cos he can tell I'm literally jumping up and down. 'We're just getting some drinks.'

'Cool. Cool. Well, I don't want to get in the way of your quality time,' I rush, trying not to encroach.

'We're good. It's all good. We'll grab our seats then see you after, yeah? I'm *so* proud of you, Abi. I love you.'

'Thanks, babe. Love you too!' I squeal, just as Timid Runner takes me into Make-up.

Once I'm out of the chair, as they say, I'm escorted to the wings where Cassie and Frank are waiting.

'So glad you're doing this. You've earned it,' he says.

'Noooo, stop being nice! They've only just finished doing my face,' I flap, sensing the prickle of tears.

'And you look like a goddess,' Cassie says, rubbing my back.

'Cass, are you giving me Reiki?' I ask, suspicion in my voice.

She turns comedically angelic. 'A little bit.'

'Cool,' I chuckle. 'Just checking.'

And as the backstage pre-show energy swirls, ours gently lands, the three of us standing in the wings, looking out at the spotlight, the centre of it all, where I'll soon be.

'On in five,' Topknot says.

'Great, cheers.' I nod to him then turn to Cassie and Frank for a last-minute check.

'Perfection,' Cassie says.

'You'll do …' Frank winks.

I jut him with my hip before we go in for one last group hug and as we part, I look back out to the stage – the sound of the audience like nothing I've ever experienced. The buzz, no longer a collection of individual voices but waves of chatter, excitement, movement. Every hair on my arms stands on end. I'm right where I was two hours ago, when Elle and I saw each other, but everything is different. I feel different. I feel ready. Mic in my hand, I say a silent prayer, a promise – to make the ancestors proud.

'Can't believe you're going out there before I am. Should have known you'd beat me to it,' Frank snarks and before Cassie can even think about telling him off he adds, 'I'm joking. Wouldn't have it any other way – just don't be shit.'

He links arms with me, and I smile, eyes still fixed on that circle of light. 'I'll do my best.'

'I know you will, darling,' Frank says, pecking me on the cheek.

Behind us, a flurry of crew do final tweaks, and making her way towards us, I see Tess, now wearing a Madonna-style headset.

'You ready?' she says, nervously yakking on some gum.

'I am,' I reply but Tess barely looks at me, her eyes searchlighting the immediate area, scanning for last-minute catastrophes.

'There's a countdown clock in front of the foldback monitor. You know to do fifteen minutes, right?'

'I do.'

'And don't talk to the celebs. That's the host's job.'

'You said.'

'And just do what you know will work. I don't want any comedy heroics. Get them going then get off.'

I feel Tess's doubt ooze across the floor towards me, in danger of wrapping itself around my legs, creeping up into my thoughts, telling me to play it safe, not be too much. But as it tightens its grip, I push back. Her doubt, her fears are her problem. Even if I tank, I'm going out in such a flaming blaze of too-muchness they'll see it from the moon.

'I've got this, Tess,' I say and lock my gaze down-stage, centre.

Just then, from the auditorium there's a booming, showbizzy voice.

'Ladies and Gentlemen, Welcome to the Athenaaaaaaa!'

Instantly, my skin shimmers with anticipation as Topknot directs me into position.

'You'll get a countdown, the backdrop goes up, there'll be smoke and then you walk on. Cool?'

'Very cool,' I say as I get in place.

This is it. I'm here, standing on ground as sacred to me as the Vatican, Mecca and Lourdes all rolled into one. I take my hand to my chest to still my heart.

'Ten, nine, eight, seven …'

I'm not a religious person but I fill with gratitude, feeling the need to thank the man upstairs.

'Six, five, four …'

'Cheers, Black Jesus,' I whisper into the darkness.

'Three, two, one …'

The backdrop rises and I'm engulfed in stage smoke. I stride towards the footlights, each step like landing on clouds.

Good evening, Athena!

The roar of three thousand comedy fans almost knocks me off my feet. These folks don't know who I am, they don't even know who's on the bill, yet here they are, looking fly, giving up their night to be here, showering the stage with love and I am so, so thankful to stand in front of them.

As I land centre-stage, I see Elle and Will looking up at me and for a moment, I'm thrown. I want them here, but seeing their faces … his pride, her expectation, I feel a pressure to deliver – for them but also for *me*. I steady myself and remember, I can do this, I am funny and it's more than okay to take up space. I launch into my new, banker material excavated from what once was hack but, with some soul-searching, has become a routine I'm proud of. And soon I find my stride.

My mum has crazy high standards. Everything has to be the best – even her double glazing. It's so good her house is like a Tupperware box. No wonder no one can hear anything, my dad says. He's living in a vacuum.

The laughter is solid, the audience totally with me.

I assured Tess I had the energy to fill this room and I make good on that promise because, in a place this big, too much is just the right amount. Soon I'm in this incredible feedback loop with the crowd. The more I give, the more I get back.

I was single for ages. Didn't stop me joining Costco. But I swear, a single woman with a Costco card is a cry for help.

But then I met an amazing guy – with two kids and … it's the best. I want to mention it all the time. I was in a café and the barista was like, "How do you take your coffee?" I said, "Blended, like my family."

TELL THE TRUTH … YOU'LL START TO LIKE YOURSELF A WHOLE LOT MORE.

I glance at the LED clock counting down my fifteen minutes and it's nearly at zero. The time has flown by. No, it didn't fly, it stopped. I wrap up, the audience replying with long, heartfelt applause, and I want to snapshot every part of this so I can take these memories to the grave. I wave to all corners, up in the gods, the boxes either side but it's when my eyes go to the front of the stalls that my knees almost give way. In the family and friends seats I see Elle, on her feet, clapping and whooping in pure delight. I throw my hands into a heart shape then blow her a kiss. Before the applause subsides and not wanting to outstay my welcome, I give one last salute and head back into the wings. Once off stage, it takes a second for my eyes to adjust but when they do I see that the whole crew are applauding me too, including Tess. I know it's not my show, I know my set is not for broadcast but, for a moment, I feel like a star.

Epilogue

I order a lime and soda from Thea who scowls as she pours a tiny splash of cordial into a half-pint glass (even though I ordered a pint). She then sprays the soda like she's at a shooting range before plonking the drink in front of me.

'Thea, I said I'm sorry.'

But at my apology, her lips thin. 'It won't be the same without you lot. We got used to you being here. Like having the racing on in the background.'

It's not exactly flattering that she saw Wisecrackers as comforting white noise but, to be fair, I'm surprised Thea's bothered at all by us pulling the show. We pay next to nothing for the room and the bar take for a first round FA cup match is higher than on our gig nights. And yet, when I told her we were calling it quits, she was genuinely miffed. Thing is, after stepping on stage at the Athena a mere ten days ago, and having, basically, the gig of my life, I know I have to put all my energy into my comedy. At that show, something in me took flight and just like Frank had seen for himself, the pressure of running a night was getting in the way. Now, I can focus on what I really want – to be the best comedian I can.

'Well, if you ever want to start it up again, you let me know.'

I agree to do exactly that. And after promises to keep in touch, Thea completes my drinks order – a tonic water for Frank, white wine for Cassie, a sparkling water for Elle and a beer for Will. Thea arranges them on a sticky tray, and I take them next door where everyone is setting the room up for the last time. Will hops down off the stage and takes the tray from me. 'Mic's set up, chairs are sorted and the check-in table's good to go.'

'Cheers,' I say with a flutter of sadness and Will draws me close.

I've had such good times here, learned so much, met so many amazing comedians, and though I know letting it go is the right thing, it's still tough.

I see Elle watching and I pull away from Will.

'Don't mind me,' she says, hands raised. 'PDA all you want.'

Will and I laugh but separate anyway.

'I'm gonna gaffer down that cable. You got any tape?' he asks, his sudden pretend-formality tickling me.

'Toolbox,' I reply, copycatting his energy, and he heads off in search as I approach Elle. 'Thanks again for doing our little show. It's really cool to have a big-time TV comic here.'

She blushes as I tease her, replying with a faux majestic wave. 'Well, you know.'

'Seriously though, how you feeling, new queen of comedy?'

Elle scoffs, 'I don't think so.'

'You did great, and you know what—' I begin, ready to launch into a rousing speech.

'Abi, it's okay,' she says, interrupting. 'I am proud of myself. But I've had a lot of luck. Even me doing this gig makes me a bit of a Nepo Baby. If I really want to make it, be a "queen of comedy", I have to put in the work, don't I? There's no other way. I learned that from watching you.'

And I'm choked. After so long on the circuit, at times feeling like I was getting nowhere, this acknowledgement means a lot, especially from Elle.

'Thank you …' I say, lifting a hand for a high five, but instead she opens her arms and we fall into each other.

Holding her is just as sweet as that first time at the Athena and though she's tiny, her embrace is as mighty as her warrior spirit.

'Do me a favour,' I whisper, 'find your greatness.'

'I will,' Elle nods.

'Abioye!'

Releasing Elle from our hug, I swivel on my heels and my mouth gapes.

'You made it!' I say, dashing over to Kemi and Felix who've just arrived.

'Didn't want to miss the big farewell,' she says as I cling to her, glee spilling from every part of me.

After the obligatory rocking from side to side, and yelped protests, I turn to Felix, probing to see if a hug with him might be on the cards too.

'We good, F-Dawg?' I say, arms wide as I approach.

Thankfully he reciprocates and soon we're hugging it out.

'We are,' he says with his usual calming tones, and it feels good to get back to how things were.

'Right, are we doing this or filming an episode of *Long Lost Family*?' Frank says, breaking up the love-in.

'Yeah, let's crack on,' I reply, the realness of it all hitting me. I don't want to say goodbye to this mad, little gig but I also know, closing this door will open so many more.

There's a good-sized audience with late-comers trickling in right up to the last minute. Thea even pops her head through.

And by the time we start, Cassie has had to lay out more chairs, the back row practically turning into the friends and family section. For the last time, I step onto the Wisecrackers stage.

'Sorry for the delayed start but welcome!'

A cheer from the audience who tonight are generously boisterous.

'This is the final show of Wisecrackers …'

I raise my hand coaxing the crowd's playful condolences but then I pause, thinking …

'You know what – Wisecrackers is a really shit name!'

And everyone creases up, Frank cackling the loudest. 'I've been thinking that for years!'

'*Now* you tell me!' I holler, the room enjoying our back and forth.

I let that naturally lead to some crowd banter which tonight is so fizzy and fluid, the gig feels more like a party. I could do this all evening, but I know we have to get on.

'Okay, guys, you sound like you're ready for some comedy. Please put your hands together and make some noise for Frank Cho!'

We shake hands and emotion simmers as I realise we really are saying goodbye to our baby. Frank holds my gaze for that extra moment and I can tell he's aware of it too.

Feeling the bittersweetness of it all, I slide into the empty seat next to Will, his arm around my chair back. But my expression turns to shock as I listen to Frank launch into his act. He has the same acerbic attitude, the same slick delivery but … no accent. In the end, he kept it for *ShowTime*, but I'm so proud that tonight he's decided to perform without it.

His set goes well but just that small change does make a big difference – and I can tell, he's still getting used to the adjustment. At the end, he slots the mic back in the stand and though the outgoing applause is warm, he purses his lips almost in apology. *No, Frank! You did great*, I want to yell. Leaping on stage, I practically strong-arm the audience into giving him a bigger round of applause. Even if they don't know what a big deal that was for him, they're going to act like they do, damn it!

In the second half, Elle comes on for a short set and with no nerves pulling at her, she does brilliantly. She's observational and hilarious. The crowd love her and after two more acts including Cassie, we're done. The only thing left is for me to close out the show.

'So, guys, as you know, this is the last ever Wisecrackers,' and I'm properly moved at the sound of the audience's disappointment. 'I know, I know. We're all gutted but I want to say a massive thank-you to Frank Cho and Cassie Delaney who've been my partners in crime for, wow, is it seven years we've been doing this?'

'Feels like longer!' Frank calls out and everyone laughs.

'Tell me about it. I spent six of those waiting for you to put out the chairs,' I reply and the audience respond with an 'oh no, she didn't' oooooooh then laugh again.

'Thank you to all the acts who've performed at our show, some of whom are here tonight, but most of all, thank you … our gorgeous audience. I know it's a cheesy thing to say but this literally isn't possible without you. Thank you for turning up week after week, some of you, for bringing your sense of humour and leaving your outrage at the door, for being general legends and for never letting us have an empty front row!'

'Here, here!' calls Cassie from the back. 'And thank you, Abi!'

Everyone cheers and I see Will spring to his feet, whistling his support. I'm already choking up but when I look around and see Thea, a wry but grateful smile on her lips, Elle, Frank, Cassie and our lovely audience all rising, I crack. I can't hold it in.

'You guys!' I sob. 'You're ruining my mascara. I'm gonna look like the Joker!'

At that, not wanting to but knowing I must, I hop off stage, moving through the audience, shaking hands with a few of the regulars. And then I see her.

'Mum …' I whisper.

She moves towards me, Dad not far behind, and my mouth is suddenly dry. Around me everyone is in their own world, getting drinks, chatting, shaking on coats and jackets but my eyes are fixed on just one person.

'What are you doing here?'

'Thought it time I finally came along to one of your shows. Sorry we only caught the last section. But you were …'

She reaches for the words, but seems unable to find them. Eventually, after stuttered half-sentences, she pulls her phone from her bag, swipes it open and hits play on a video clip. I'm stunned. It's me – at the Athena.

'Where did you get this?' I say, scrambling to make sense of it.

Mum doesn't answer but I follow her gaze which lands on Will, Frank and Kemi who all wave with guilty-as-charged smiles.

'They always have one camera rolling so I pulled a few strings with Callback,' Frank explains.

'I got it to Kemi …' Will adds.

'And I sent it on,' Kemi says, patting her hair – *au naturel* style out and proud for the very first time, in front of our parents.

I look to Mum but instead of the disappointment I so often see and expect, there's only love in her eyes and I am shoooook.

'Thank you, Kemi. I'm grateful and, by the way, your hair looks … beautiful,' Mum says, before turning back to me. 'And, Abi, my darling girl, you were *magnificent*.'

I'm overwhelmed. When you've wanted something so long, once you do get it, you barely know how to cope.

'The Athena was Elle and Frank's night, really. I just greased the wheels,' I stammer.

Mum smiles. 'Maybe, but for me, you were the main event.'

Where has this come from? And why now? There's a crackle of anger as I wonder if Mum's switch is only happening because she's finally seen me do something that makes me look successful?

'Mum …' I start.

'I know, darling … and I'm sorry.'

And this stops me, dead. I don't think Mum's ever apologised to me. Her face tightens as though holding in some admission she's fearful to make but eventually she whispers, 'I was scared for you. But I didn't know how to tell you so I turned it all into something you were doing wrong, which was … terrible.'

And her eyes shimmer with guilty tears.

'My father was an artist, a painter. Back in Ikeja, there wasn't much call for that, so he did all sorts to make ends meet, made carvings to sell in the market, sold bottles of soda by the side of the road, anything. My aunts would nag Mummy incessantly, telling her that he was no good, but she believed in him.'

'What happened?' I ask, hardly able to bear knowing.

All I'd ever heard about my granddad was he died young but beyond that, he was never a topic of conversation. Mum lets out a long sigh. 'Eventually, he started focusing more and more on the painting, doing less and less to bring money in, but by now there were four of us kids.'

'Auntie Blessing, Auntie Modupe and Uncle Adebayo?'

Mum nods, transported for a moment somewhere else, life in the city as a teenager or perhaps the compound her family lived in.

'Mother took up the slack, of course, as we women do, working all hours. We hardly saw her. Hardly saw either of them. While Mummy was working, my father had commandeered a shack just outside our home. Day and night, he was there, painting.'

'And did he ever …'

Mum shakes her head. 'He never gained success, barely sold any of his work and the whole experience broke him. We didn't talk of depression in those days but that's what it was. He died frail, poor and with shattered dreams never realised. Mother was never the same after that. I suppose in my young mind I decided that the arts …'

She shakes her head again, trying to stop her tears but, finally defeated, pulls out a hankie – fresh-pressed cotton, of course – and dabs her eyes.

'All this, it terrifies me,' she says, her words quivering, face almost shocked at hearing herself this way, vulnerable.

'And seeing this creative side coming out of you as a little girl, reminded me of him. So bold, unafraid to be yourself, stand out from the crowd, follow your passions.' She dabs again at unrelenting tears that streak her face. 'I panicked. It took me back to those dark days that stole my daddy from me. I didn't want to lose you too.'

'Oh, Mum,' I say, as her hardened exterior cracks wide open.

Cheeks damp with tears, we hug, Kemi joining our quiet

embrace that wrings the sorrow from us. And I sense Dad quietly move closer, placing his hands on our backs.

'So, I'm sorry – to you both,' Mum says. 'I just wanted to stop you making what I thought was a terrible mistake but seeing this, seeing you here, I know now, shutting that down would be the mistake because it would mean shutting down the most important parts of who you are, what makes you special. What makes you, you. This is not just your job, it's your calling.'

Sobs spill from Mum but her tears are now infused with love.

'I'm so very proud of you girls, and, Abi, it's not just because you did that big show. It's because despite me, you followed your dreams. That takes courage, more than I showed in watching you on this path.'

And with that, the roar of anger I felt before burns to nothing but a flicker. I know me and Mum can't fix everything overnight but the way she just opened up makes it feel like at least something different is possible, a new way to be – together.

After more tears, hugs and then goodbyes as some peel off to catch Tubes and last trains, I perch on the edge of the stage, taking it all in.

Will plants himself beside me, interlacing his fingers with mine. 'I'm really happy for you and your mum.'

'Thanks,' I say, smiling.

'And I tell you something, your new stuff gets better every time I hear it.'

'Ah, cheers, babe,' I say, looping my arm through his. 'You know … I'm thinking about writing my first Edinburgh show. I feel like I'm ready.'

'Amazing,' Will says. 'What's it about?'

My mouth opens and I hesitate. 'This.'

Will looks around confused but then the realisation hits; that I mean us, our situation. I search his face. I don't see horror but I'm yet to see approval either.

'Course, I don't have to,' I backtrack. As much as we've made strides, we may not be ready for an hour of comedy about it. 'I mean, what do you think? Is it too much?'

'Too much?' Will says, sandwiching my hand between his. 'Abi, and I say this with every fibre of my being, not enough!'

And I laugh, overwhelmed with pure relief.

'Jeez, don't do that. Are you sure? I mean, what about the girls?' I say, now half-scared this might actually be happening.

'Elle?' says Will, beckoning her over.

She prises herself away from Thea who's been trying to persuade her to ditch comedy and become a landlady.

'Yeah?' she says.

I steady myself.

'I'm thinking of doing an Edinburgh show about … being … having …' I reach for what to say, unsure how to describe myself, our set-up, this. I've used 'stepmum' so flippantly but it's not just a title, it's a responsibility I'm yet to earn. 'About getting to know you guys, about the journey …'

'You mean, about being a sort of 'sparent', you know, a spare parent,' Elle clarifies off our scrunched-up, confused face.

'I … well … yeah, sort of.'

'An hour of material, that's so cool. You'll be great,' she says and I goldfish a few more times, still unsure how to react.

I look to Will. Though he appears unflustered, I suspect he's also trying to contain his happiness at hearing Elle gradually letting me in.

'Thanks,' I say, eventually. 'I mean, obviously I'll change names, and really it's about my experiences rather than talking about you guys.'

'Honestly, it's all good,' Elle shrugs as though bringing a new adult into the fold and granting them permission to write an hour-long comedy show about it, is a daily occurrence for her.

'Okay then,' says Will, mimicking Elle's shrug as she walks off.

'Okay then,' I say back and we can't help but laugh.

'So, do you have a name for the show?' Will asks.

'I'm not sure,' I say, looking around the room, struck by how far I've come. It wasn't that long ago I was on this same stage moaning about my singledom, lamenting my too-muchness, and now I've got more than I could ever have imagined. But getting here was not easy. At times I thought it might break me, but somehow, here I am, on the other side. Here we are. I look back at Will. 'I mean I've got a working title …'

'Come on, spill,' he says, trying to coax it from me.

Part of me wants to swallow the idea but after everything I've been through, and especially now knowing my granddad's struggle, that's no longer an option. I straighten my shoulders and with a decisive nod I say, 'Tough Crowd.'

A mighty laugh erupts from Will. 'That is perfect.'

'Yeah, babes, I know,' I say as a calm descends and I smile to myself.

I know.

Acknowledgements

Though writing seems like a solitary pursuit, over the course of two novels, I've learned it's anything but. So many people have contributed directly and indirectly to getting this story into your hands and I'm forever grateful to every one of them. Starting with my amazing literary agent, Richard Scrivener, who has, aside from doing all the behind-the-scenes agenty things, been a cheerleader, confidante, coach and more; to Anja Stobbart who once again provided invaluable editorial support; Archie Maddocks who helped unearth more funnies; my three (yes, three) editors, Katie Seaman, Melanie Hayes and, finally, Clare Gordon, who've patiently shepherded me from a 200,000-word bloat fest down to the book you just read and I hope enjoyed; my copy editor Liz Hatherell and proofreader Michelle Bullock; the many folks involved in the technical aspects of creating physical, digital and audio versions of this novel such as cover designer, Emma Rogers, the sound team who produced the audio book, putting up with my stumbles and fumbles as I recorded it; and the sales, marketing and publicity legends including Kirsty Capes and Komal Patel in-house at HQ, and Robbie Wilson and

Anthony Hon at Epilogue, who've all been such an important part of this journey.

And as well as these dreamboats, I want to thank my friends and family who've supported me every step of the way. But also, you, my fantastic readers, some returning after reading my debut, *Asking For A Friend* and some coming to my books for the first time. Thank you!

And very, very, lastly, a massive thank you to the comedy circuit. I become a comedian in 2007. Acting work had dried up so I wanted a way to get stage time while I waited for auditions to come in. From my first gig, I loved it – the challenge of learning this amazing new craft, of being in front of an audience as myself rather than characters I could hide behind as an actor but also the sense of community. Having worked in a few creative fields, there really is nothing like the camaraderie of comedy. And though that world is, for the most part, in my rear-view mirror I want to acknowledge the many comics I've gigged with and who've been friends, supporters and colleagues even after I stepped away from the mic.

The UK comedy scene is one of a kind and if you take one thing from this book (aside from a peng new vocab) I hope it's a taste for live stand up, especially new material and open mic nights which are the life blood of the UK's brilliant and unique comedy scene.

ONE PLACE. MANY STORIES

Bold, innovative and
empowering publishing.

FOLLOW US ON:

@HQStories